THE LIGHT YEARS

THE LIGHT YEARS

Volume I of The Cazalet Chronicle

Elizabeth Jane Howard

MACMILLAN
LONDON

First published 1990 by
MACMILLAN LONDON LIMITED
4 Little Essex Street London WC2R 3LF
and Basingstoke

Associated companies in Auckland, Delhi, Dublin, Gaborone,
Hamburg, Harare, Hong Kong, Johannesburg, Kuala Lumpur,
Lagos, Manzini, Melbourne, Mexico City, Nairobi, New York,
Singapore and Tokyo

ISBN 0-333-53875-7

A CIP catalogue record for this book is available from the
British Library

Typeset by Macmillan Production Limited

Printed by Billings & Sons Limited, Worcester

For Jenner Roth

CONTENTS

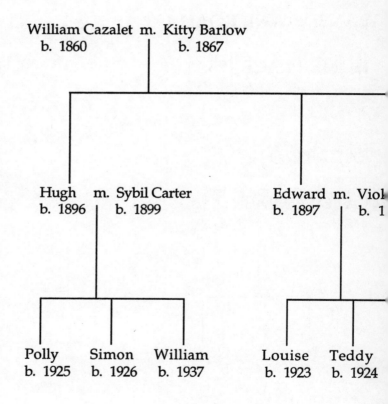

William Cazalet m. Kitty Barlow
b. 1860   b. 1867

Hugh m. Sybil Carter   Edward m. Viol
b. 1896   b. 1899   b. 1897   b. 1

Polly   Simon   William   Louise   Teddy
b. 1925   b. 1926 b. 1937   b. 1923   b. 1924

THE
CAZALET
FAMILY TREE

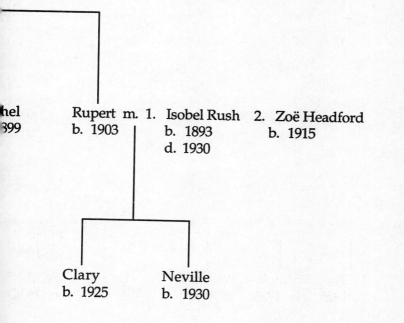

hel
399

Rupert m. 1. Isobel Rush   2. Zoë Headford
b. 1903   b. 1893   b. 1915
                 d. 1930

Clary   Neville
b. 1925   b. 1930

THE CAZALET FAMILIES AND THEIR HOUSEHOLDS

William Cazalet (the Brig)
Kitty (the Duchy), his wife
Rachel, their unmarried
   daughter

Mrs Cripps (cook)
Eileen (parlourmaid)
Peggy and Bertha
   (housemaids)
Dotty (kitchenmaid)
Tonbridge (chauffeur)
McAlpine (gardener)
Wren (groom)
Billy (gardener's boy)

Hugh Cazalet, eldest son
Sybil, his wife
Polly   ⎫
Simon   ⎬ their children
William (Wills) ⎭

Nanny
Inge (German maid)

Edward Cazalet, second son
Villy, his wife
Louise ⎫
Teddy ⎬ their children
Lydia ⎭

Emily (cook)
Phyllis (parlourmaid)
Edna (housemaid)
Nanny
Bracken (chauffeur)
Edie (daily help in the
   country)

Rupert Cazalet, third son
Zoë (second wife: Isobel died
   having Neville)
Clarissa (Clary) ⎫ Rupert's
Neville   ⎬ children
           ⎭ by Isobel

Ellen (nurse)

Jessica Castle (Villy's sister)
Raymond, her husband
Angela   ⎫
Christopher ⎬ their
Nora   ⎬ children
Judy   ⎭

PART ONE

LANSDOWNE ROAD
1937

The day began at five to seven when the alarm clock (given to Phyllis by her mother when she started service) went off and on and on and on until she quenched it. Edna, in the other creaking iron bed, groaned and heaved over, hunching herself against the wall; even in summer she hated getting up, and in the winter Phyllis sometimes had to haul the bedclothes off her. She sat up, unclipped her hairnet and began undoing her curlers: it was her half-day, and she'd washed her hair. She got out of bed, picked the eiderdown off the floor where it had fallen in the night and drew the curtains. Sunlight refurbished the room – making toffee of the linoleum, turning the chips on the white enamel washhand jug slate blue. She unbuttoned her winceyette nightdress and washed as her mother had taught her to do: face, hands and – circumspectly – under her arms with a flannel dipped in the cold water. 'Get a move on,' she said to Edna. She poured her slops into the pail and began to dress. In her underclothes, she removed her nightdress and slipped on her dark green cotton morning dress. She put her cap over her unbrushed-out sausage curls, and tied the apron round her waist. Edna, who washed much less in the mornings, managed to dress while still half in bed – a relic of the winter (there was no heat in the room and they never in their lives opened the window). By ten past seven they were both ready to descend quietly through the sleeping household. Phyllis stopped on the first floor and opened a bedroom door. She drew the curtains and heard the budgerigar shifting impatiently in his cage.

'Miss Louise! It's a quarter past seven.'

1

'Oh, Phyllis!'

'You asked me to call you.'

'Is it a nice day?'

'It's ever so sunny.'

'Take Ferdie's cloth off.'

'If I don't, you'll get up all the quicker.'

In the kitchen (the basement), Edna had already put on the kettle and was setting their cups on the scrubbed table. Two pots of tea were to be made: the dark brown one with stripes for the maids, and a cup taken up by Edna for Emily, the cook, and the white Minton now set out on a tray with its matching cups and saucers, milk jug and sugar bowl for upstairs. The early-morning tea for Mr and Mrs Cazalet was Phyllis's job. She would then collect all the coffee cups and glasses from the drawing room, which Edna would have started to air and clean. First, however, there was their own scalding cup of strong Indian. It was China for upstairs which Emily said she couldn't even abide the smell of, let alone drink. They drank it standing, before the sugar was even stirred to melting point.

'How's your spot?'

Phyllis felt the side of her nose cautiously.

'Seems to be going down a bit. Good thing I didn't squeeze it.'

'I told you.' Edna, who did not have them, was the authority on spots; her advice, copious, free and contrary, was, all the same comforting; it showed an interest, Phyllis felt.

'Well, this won't make us millionaires.'

Nothing would, Edna thought gloomily, and even though she had troubles with her complexion, Phyllis had all the luck. Edna thought Mr Cazalet was lovely really, and *she* never saw him in his pyjamas like Phyllis did every morning.

∞ ∞ ∞

The moment Phyllis had shut the door, Louise jumped out of bed and took the bird's cloth off his cage. He hopped about in mock alarm, but she knew that he was pleased. Her room, which faced the back garden, got a little of the morning sun, which she felt was good for him, and his cage was on the table in front of the window beside the goldfish tank. The room was small and crammed with her possessions:

her theatre programmes, the rosettes and two very small cups she had won at gymkhanas, her photograph albums, her little boxwood chest with shallow drawers in which she kept her shell collection, her china animals on the mantelpiece, her knitting, on the chest of drawers together with her precious tangee lipstick that looked bright orange but came out pink on the mouth, Pond's cold cream and a tin of Californian Poppy talc powder, her best tennis racquet and above all, her books that ranged from *Winnie the Pooh* to her newest and most prized acquisitions, two Phaidon Press volumes of reproductions of Holbein and Van Gogh, currently her two favourite painters. There was a chest of drawers filled with clothes that she mostly never wore, and a desk – given her by her father for her last birthday – made of English oak from a log that had proved to have a uniquely unusual grain, and contained her most secret treasures: a photograph of John Gielgud that had been *signed*, her jewellery, a very thin packet of letters from her brother Teddy written from school (of a sporting and facetious nature, but the only letters she possessed from a boy), and her collection of sealing wax – probably, she thought, the largest in the country. The room also contained a large old chest filled with dressing-up clothes – her mother's cast-off evening dresses, beaded tubes, chiffon and satin, stamped velvet jackets, gauzy, faintly Oriental scarves and shawls from some earlier time, dirty, teasing feather boas, a hand-embroidered Chinese robe, brought back by some relative from his travels, and sateen trousers and tunics – stuff made for family plays. When you opened it the chest smelled of very old scent and mothballs and excitement – this last a faintly metallic smell which came, Louise thought, from the quantity of tarnished gold and silver threadwork on some of the garments. Dressing up and acting was a winter thing; now it was July and very nearly the endless, wonderful summer holidays. She dressed in a linen tunic and an Aertex shirt – scarlet, her favourite – and went out to take Derry for his walk.

Derry was not her dog. She was not allowed to have one, and, partly as a way of keeping up her resentment about this, she took a neighbouring and very ancient bull terrier for a walk round the block each morning. The other part of taking him was that the house he lived in fascinated her. It was very large – you could see it from her back garden – but it was utterly unlike her house or, indeed, the house of any of her friends. There were no children in it. The manservant who let her in to collect Derry always went away to fetch him which gave her time to wander through the black and white marble hall to the open double doors of a gallery that looked down onto the drawing room. Every morning this room was in a state of luxurious after-a-party disorder: it smelled of Egyptian cigarettes – like the ones Aunt Rachel smoked – and it was always filled with flowers, smelly ones – hyacinths in spring, lilies now, carnations and roses in winter; it was littered with coloured silk cushions and there were dozens of glasses, open boxes of chocolates and sometimes card tables with packs of cards and scoring pads with tasselled pencils. It was always twilit, with creamy silk curtains half drawn. She felt that the owners – whom she never saw – were fantastically rich, probably foreign and possibly pretty decadent.

Derry, reputed to be thirteen which made him ninety-one according to the Dog Table of Ages that she had made, was quite boring to take for a walk as he was only up to a ramble with frequent and interminable stops at a succession of lamp posts, but she liked having a dog on a lead, could smile at people in a proprietary way that would make them think he was hers, and she lived in hope of finding that one of the occupants of the house or their decadent friends might actually have *passed out* in the drawing room so that she could examine them. It had to be a short walk because she was supposed to practise for an hour until breakfast at a quarter to nine, and before that she had to have a cold bath because Dad said it was so good for you. She was fourteen, and sometimes she felt quite young and ready for anything, but sometimes she felt languid with age – exhausted when it came to doing anything that was expected of her.

After she had returned Derry, she met the milkman, whose pony Peggy she knew well because she'd grown grass for her on a bit of flannel as Peggy never got to the country and anybody who'd read *Black Beauty* knew how awful it was for horses never being in fields.

'Glorious day,' Mr Pierce remarked, as she stroked Peggy's nose.

'Yes, isn't it.'

'Full many a glorious morning have I seen,' she muttered when she was past him. When she married, her husband would find her quite remarkable because she could think of a Shakespeare quotation for anything – anything at all that happened. On the other hand, she might not marry anybody because Polly said that sex was very boring and you couldn't really go in for marriage without it. Unless Polly was wrong, of course; she often was, and Louise had noticed that she said things were boring when she was against them. 'You don't know the first thing about it, George,' she added. Her father called everyone he didn't know George – all men, that is, and it was one of his favourite phrases. She rang the front-door bell three times so that Phyllis would know it was her. 'Let me not to the marriage of true minds admit impediment.' It sounded a bit grudging, but noble as well. If only she was Egyptian she could marry Teddy like the Pharaohs did and, after all, Cleopatra was the result of six generations of incest, whatever incest might be. The worst drawback about not going to a school was that you knew quite different things and she'd made the stupid mistake in the Christmas holidays of pretending to her cousin Nora, who did go to school, that sex was old hat which meant that she hadn't found anything out at all. Just as she was about to ring again, Phyllis opened the door.

∞ ∞ ∞

'Louise might come in.'

'Nonsense. She'll be out with the dog.' Before she could say anything else, he put his mouth, edged on its upper rim with his bristling moustache, upon hers. After a moment of this, she pulled up her nightdress and he was upon her. 'Darling Villy,' he said three times before he came. He'd never been able to cope with Viola. When he had finished he gave a deep sigh, took his hand from her left breast and kissed her throat.

'China tea. I don't know how you manage always to smell of violets and China tea. All right?' he added. He always asked that.

'Lovely.' She called it a white lie to herself, and over the years it had come to have an almost cosy ring. Of course she

5

loved him, so what else could she say? Sex was for men, after all. Women, nice women anyway, were not expected to care for it, but her own mother had intimated (the only time she had ever even remotely touched upon the subject) that it was the gravest possible mistake ever to refuse one's husband. So she had never refused him and if, eighteen years ago, she had suffered some shock accompanied by acute pain when she discovered what actually happened, practice had dissolved these feelings into those merely of a patient distaste, and at the same time it was a way of proving her love which she felt must be right.

'Run me a bath, darling,' she called as he left the room.

'I'll do that thing.'

She tried a second cup of tea, but it was cold so she got up and opened the large mahogany wardrobe to decide what to wear. She had to take Nanny and Lydia to Daniel Neal for summer clothes in the morning, and then she was lunching with Hermione Knebworth and going back to her shop afterwards to see if she could pick up an evening dress or two – at this time of year Hermione usually had things that she was selling off before everybody went away for the summer. Then she *must* go and see Mummy because she hadn't managed it yesterday, but she wouldn't have to stay long because she had to get back to change for the theatre and dinner with the Warings. But one could not go to Hermione's shop without at least trying to look smart. She decided on the oatmeal linen edged with Marina-blue corded ribbon that she'd bought there last year.

The life I lead, she thought (it was not a new idea, rather a reiteration), is the one that is expected for me: what the children expect, and Mummy always expected, and, of course, what Edward expects. It is what happens to people who marry and most people don't marry someone so handsome and so nice as Edward. But removing the idea of choice – or choice after a very early date – in her conduct added the desirable dimension of duty: she was a serious person condemned to a shallower way of life than her temperament could have dealt with (if things had been very different). She was not unhappy – it was just that she could have been much more.

As she crossed the landing to her husband's large dressing room that contained their bath, she heard Lydia on the top floor shouting at Nanny, which meant that her pigtails were being done. Below her, a C major exercise of von Bulow began on the piano. Louise was practising.

∞ ∞ ∞

The dining room had french windows that looked onto the garden. It was furnished with the essentials: a set of eight beautiful Chippendale chairs, given to them by Edward's father when they married, a large koko wood table at present covered with a white cloth, a sideboard with electric heaters on which were kidneys, scrambled eggs, tomatoes and bacon, cream-coloured walls, some pictures made of coloured wood veneers, and sconces (mock Adam) with little half-shell lampshades, a gas fire in the fireplace and a battered old leather chair in which Louise loved to curl up and read. The general effect was ugly in a subdued kind of way, but nobody noticed it at all, except Louise who thought it was dull.

Lydia sat with her knife and fork poised like Tower Bridge opening while Nan chopped up tomato and bacon. 'If you give me kidney, I'll spit it out,' she had remarked earlier. A good deal of early-morning conversation with Nan consisted of threats from either side, but since neither called one another's bluff it was difficult to know what the consequences might ever have been if either had gone through with them. As it was, Lydia knew perfectly well that Nan wouldn't dream of cancelling the visit to Daniel Neal, and Nan knew that Lydia would not dream of spitting out kidney or anything else in front of Daddy. He, Daddy, had bent over her to kiss the top of her head as he did every morning and she smelled his lovely woody smell mixed with lavender water. Now he sat at the head of the table with a large plate of everything in front of him and the *Telegraph* propped against the marmalade dish. Kidneys were nothing to him. He slashed them and the horrible awful blood ran out and he mopped it up with fried bread. She drank some of her milk very noisily to make him look up. In winter he ate poor dead birds he had shot: partridges and pheasants with little black scrunched-up claws. He didn't look up, but Nan seized her mug and put it out of reach. 'Eat your breakfast,' she said in the special quiet voice she used at mealtimes in the dining room.

Mummy came in. She smiled her lovely smile at Lydia, and

came round the table to kiss her. She smelled of hay and some kind of flower that made Lydia feel like sneezing but not quite. She had lovely curly hair but with bits of white in it that were worrying because Lydia wanted her never to be dead which people with white hair could easily be.

Mummy said, 'Where's Louise?', which was silly really, because you could still hear her practising.

Nan said, 'I'll tell her.'

'Thank you, Nan. Perhaps the drawing-room clock has stopped.'

Mummy had Grape Nuts and coffee and toast for breakfast with her own little tiny pot of cream. She was opening her post which was letters that came through the front door and skidded over the polished floor in the hall. Lydia had had post once: on her last birthday when she was six. She had also ridden on an elephant, had tea in her milk and worn her first pair of lace-up outdoor shoes. She thought it had been the best day in her life, which was saying a lot, because she'd already lived through so many days. The piano-playing had stopped and Louise came in followed by Nan. She loved Louise who was terrifically old and wore stockings in winter.

Now Lou was saying, 'You're going out to lunch, Mummy, I can tell from your clothes.'

'Yes, darling, but I'll be back to see you before Daddy and I go out.'

'Where are you going?'

'We're going to the theatre.'

'What are you going to?'

'A play called *The Apple Cart*. By George Bernard Shaw.'

'*Lucky* you!'

Edward looked up from his paper. 'Who are we going with?'

'The Warings. We're dining with them first; seven sharp. Black tie.'

'Tell Phyllis to put my things out for me.'

'I *never* go to the theatre.'

'Louise! That's not true. You always go at Christmas. And for your birthday treat.'

'Treats don't count. I mean I don't go as a normal thing. If it's going to be my career, I ought to go.'

Villy took no notice. She was looking at the front page

8

of *The Times*. 'Oh dear. Mollie Strangways's mother has died.'

Lydia said, 'How old was she?'

Villy looked up. 'I don't know, darling. I expect she was quite old.'

'Was her hair gone quite white?'

Louise said, 'How do they know which people who die to put in *The Times*? I bet far more people die in the world than would go on one page. How do they choose who to put?'

Her father said, 'They don't choose. People who want to put it in pay.'

'If you were the King, would you have to pay?'

'No – he's different.'

Lydia, who had stopped eating, asked, 'How old do people live?' But she said it very quietly and nobody seemed to have heard her.

Villy, who had got up to pour herself more coffee, noticed Edward's cup and refilled it now saying, 'It's Phyllis's day off, so I'll do your clothes. Try not to be back too late.'

'How old do *mothers* live?'

Seeing her daughter's face Villy said quickly, 'For *ages*. Think of my mother – and Daddy's. They're awfully old and they're both fine.'

'Of course, you could always get murdered – that can happen at any age. Think of Tybalt. And the Princes in the Tower.'

'What's murdered? Louise, what's murdered?'

'Or drowned at sea. Shipwrecked,' she added dreamily. She was *longing* to be shipwrecked.

'Louise, do shut up. Can't you see you're upsetting her?'

But it was too late. Lydia had burst into gasping sobs. Villy picked her up and hugged her. Louise felt hot and sulky with shame.

'There, my duck. You'll see I'll live to be terribly terribly old, and you'll be quite grown up and have great big children like you who wear lace-up shoes—'

'And riding jackets?' She was still sobbing but she wanted a riding jacket – tweed, with a divided back and pockets to wear when she was riding her horses – and this seemed a good moment to get it.

'We'll see.' She put Lydia back on the chair and Nan said, 'Finish your milk.' She was thirsty, so she did.

9

Edward, who had frowned at Louise, now said, 'What about me? Don't you want me to live for ever, too?'

'Not so much. I *do* want you to.'

Louise said, 'Well, *I* want you to. When you're over eighty, I'll wheel you about toothless and dribbling in a bath chair.'

This made her father roar with laughter as she had hoped and put her back into favour.

'I shall look forward to every moment.' He got to his feet and, carrying his paper, left the room.

Lydia said, 'He's gone to the lavatory. To do his big job.'

'That'll do,' said Nanny sharply. 'We don't talk about things like that at mealtimes.'

Lydia stared at Louise; her eyes were expressionless, but her mouth made silent turkey gobbling movements. Louise, as she was meant to, started laughing.

'Children, children,' said Villy weakly. Lydia was killing sometimes, but Nanny's *amour propre* must be considered.

'Go upstairs, darling. Now – we're going out soon.'

'What time do you want us, madam?'

'I should think about ten, Nanny.'

'See my horses.' Lydia had wriggled off her chair and rushed to the french windows, which Louise opened for her.

'You come.' She seized Louise's hand.

Her horses were tied to the railings in the back garden. They were long sticks of different colours: a piece of plane tree was the piebald; a silvery stick was the grey; a piece of beech collected from Sussex was the bay. They all had elaborate halters made of bits of string, grass mowings in flower pots beside each one and their names in coloured chalks on pieces of cardboard. Lydia untied the grey and started cantering about the garden. Every now and then she gave a clumsy little jump and admonished her mount. 'You mustn't buck so much.'

'Watch me riding,' she called. '*Lou!* Watch me!'

But Louise, who was afraid of Nan's displeasure and in any case had nearly an hour before Miss Milliment arrived and wanted to finish *Persuasion*, simply said, 'I have. I did watch you,' and went – as bad as a grown-up.

∞ ∞ ∞

10

Edward, having kissed Villy in the hall, been handed his grey Homburg by Phyllis – at other times of the year she always helped him into his overcoat – picked up his copy of the *Timber Trades Journal* and let himself out. In front of the house the Buick, black and gleaming, awaited him. There was the usual glimpse of Bracken filling the driver's seat, immobile as a waxwork, before, reacting to Edward's appearance as though he had been shot, he leapt from the car and was looming over the back door which he opened for Edward.

'Morning, Bracken.'

'Good morning, sir.'

'The wharf.'

'Very good, sir.'

After this exchange – the same every morning, unless Edward wanted to go anywhere else – no more was said. Edward settled himself comfortably and began idly turning the pages of his journal, but he was not reading it, he was reviewing his day. A couple of hours in the office, dealing with mail, then he'd have a look and see how the samples of veneer from the elm they had bought from the piles of the old Waterloo Bridge were getting on. The wood had been drying for a year now, but they had started cutting last week, and now, at last, they would discover whether the Old Man's hunch about it had been right or a disaster. It was exciting. Then he'd got a lunch at his club with a couple of blokes from the Great Western Railway which would, he was pretty sure, result in a substantial order for mahogany. A directors' meeting in the afternoon, the Old Man, and his brother – sign his letters – and then there might be time to have a cup of tea with Denise Ramsay, who had the twin advantages of a husband frequently abroad on business and no children. But like all advantages, this cut both ways; she was a little too free and was therefore a little too much in love with him; after all, it was never meant to be a serious Thing – as she called it. There might not turn out to be time to see her since he had to get back to change for the theatre.

If anyone had ever asked him if he was in love with his wife, Edward would have said of course he was. He would not have added that, in spite of eighteen years of relative happiness and comfort and three splendid children, Villy did not really like the bed side of life. This was quite common in wives – one poor fellow at the club, Martyn Slocombe-Jones, had once confided to him late at night after a game of billiards and rather a lot of excellent port that *his* wife hated it so much that she'd only let him do it when she wanted a baby. She was a damned attractive woman, too, and a wonderful wife, as Martyn had said. In other ways. They had five children, and Martyn didn't think she was going to wear a sixth. Rotten for him. When Edward had suggested that he find consolation elsewhere, Martyn had simply gazed at him with mournful brown eyes and said, 'But I'm in love with her, old boy, always have been. Never looked at anyone else. You know how it is.' And Edward, who didn't, said of course he did. That conversation had warned him off Marcia Slocombe-Jones anyhow. It didn't matter, because although he could have gone for her there were so many other girls to go for. How lucky he was! To have come back from France not only alive, but relatively unscathed! In winter, his chest played him up a bit due to living in trenches where the gas had hung about for weeks, but otherwise . . . Since then he'd come back, gone straight into the family firm, met Villy at a party, married her as soon as her contract with the ballet company she was with expired and as soon as she'd agreed to the Old Man's dictate that her career should stop from then on. 'Can't marry a gal whose head's full of something else. If marriage isn't the woman's career, it won't be a good marriage.'

His attitude was thoroughly Victorian, of course, but all the same, there was quite a lot to be said for it. Whenever Edward looked at his own mother, which he did infrequently but with great affection, he saw her as the perfect reflection of his father's attitude: a woman who had serenely fulfilled all her family responsibilities and at the same time retained her youthful enthusiasms – for her garden that she adored and for music. At over seventy, she was quite capable of playing double concertos with professionals. Unable to discriminate between the darker, more intricate veins of temperament that distinguish one person from another, he could not really see why Villy should not be as happy and fulfilled as the Duchy. (His mother's Victorian reputation for plain living – nothing rich in food and no frills or pretensions about her own appearance or her households had long ago earned her the nickname of Duchess – shortened by her own children to Duch, and lengthened by her grandchildren to Duchy.) Well, he had never prevented Villy from having interests: her charities, her riding and skiing, her crazes for learning the most various musical instruments, her handicrafts – spinning, weaving and so on – and when he thought of his brothers' wives – Sybil was too highbrow for him and Zoë too demanding – he felt that he had not done too badly . . .

∞ ∞ ∞

Louise's cousin, Polly Cazalet, arrived half an hour early for lessons because she and Louise had been making face cream out of white of egg, chopped parsley, witch hazel and a drop of cochineal to make it pinkish. It was called Wonder Cream and Polly had made beautiful labels which were to be stuck onto the various jars they had collected from their mothers. The cream was in a pudding basin in the garden shed. They were planning to sell it to the aunts and cousins and to Phyllis at a lower price because they knew she hadn't got much money. The jars had to be different prices anyway as they were mostly different sizes and shapes. They had been washed by Louise and were also in the garden shed. It was all kept there because Louise had stolen six eggs from the larder as well as the egg whisk when Emily was out shopping. They had given some of the yolks to Louise's tortoise, who had not liked them very much, even when mixed with dandelions (his favourite food) from Polly's garden.

'It's looks funny to me.'

They looked at it again – *willing* it to be nicer.

'I don't think the cochineal was a very good idea – it was a bit green.'

'Cochineal makes things *pink*, you fool.'

Polly blushed. 'I know,' she lied. 'The trouble is, it's gone all runny.'

'That won't stop it being good for the skin. Anyway, it'll go stiffer in time.' Polly put the spoon she had brought for potting into the mixture. 'The green isn't the parsley: it's got a sort of crust on it.'

'You get that.'

'Do you?'

'Of course. Think of Devonshire cream.'

'Do you think we should just try it on our faces before we sell it?'

'Stop *fussing*. You stick on the labels and I'll pot. The labels are awfully good,' she added and Polly blushed again. The labels said 'Wonder Cream' and underneath, 'Apply generously at night. You will be astonished at the change in your appearance.' Some of the jars were too small for them.

Miss Milliment arrived before they had finished. They pretended not to hear the bell, but Phyllis came out to tell them.

'No good selling *her* any,' Louise muttered.

'I thought you said—'

'I don't mean her. I mean Miss M.'

'Lord, no. Coals to Newcastle.' Polly often got things wrong.

'Coals to Newcastle would mean Miss M was as beautiful as the day.' This made them both double up laughing.

Miss Milliment, a kind and exceedingly intelligent woman, had a face, as Louise had once remarked, like a huge old toad. When her mother had reprimanded her for being unkind, Louise had retorted that she liked toads, but she had known that this was a dishonest reply because a face that was perfectly acceptable for a toad was not actually much good on a person. After that, Miss Milliment's – certainly astonishing – appearance was only discussed in private with Polly and between them they had invented a life of unrelieved tragedy, or rather lives, since they did not agree upon Miss Milliment's probable misfortunes. An undisputed fact about her was her antiquity: she had been Villy's governess who had admitted that she had seemed old then and, goodness knows, that was ages ago. She said 'chymist' and of course 'chymistry' and once told Louise that she had picked wild roses in the Cromwell Road when young. She smelled of stale hot old clothes especially noticeable when they kissed her, which Louise, as a kind of penance, had made herself do ever since the toad remark. She lived in Stoke Newington and came five mornings a week to teach them for three hours and on Fridays she stayed to lunch. Today she was wearing her bottle-green lock-knit jersey suit and a small, bottle-green straw hat with petersham ribbon, which sat just above her very tight, greasy bun of grey hair. They began the morning, as they always did, by reading Shakespeare aloud for an hour and a half.

Today was the last two acts of Othello and Louise was reading him. Polly, who preferred the women's parts – not seeming to realise that they weren't the best – was Desdemona, and Miss Milliment was Iago and Emilia and everybody else. Louise, who secretly read ahead of the lessons, had learned Othello's last speech by heart, which was just as well because the moment she got to

> ' . . . I pray you in your letters,
> When you shall these unlucky deeds relate,
> Speak of me as I am; nothing extenuate,
> Nor set down aught in malice.'

Tears rushed to her eyes and she would not have been able to read. At the end, Polly said, '*Are* people like that?'

'Like what, Polly?'

'Like Iago, Miss Milliment.'

'I don't suppose there are very many of them. Of course, there may be more than we know, because each Iago has to find an Othello for his wickedness.'

'Like Mrs Simpson and King Edward?'

'Of course not. Polly, you are stupid! The King was in love with Mrs Simpson – it's completely different. He gave everything up for her and he could have given her up for everything.'

Polly, blushing, muttered, 'Mr Baldwin could be Iago, he *could* be.'

Miss Milliment, in her oil-on-the-waters voice, said, 'We cannot really compare the two situations, although it was certainly an interesting idea of yours, Polly, to try. Now I think we had better do our geography. I am looking forward to your map you were going to draw for me. Will you fetch the atlas, Louise?'

∞ ∞ ∞

'I think that is rather *you*.'

'It is lovely. It's just that I've never worn this colour.'

Villy was arrayed in one of Hermione's bargains: a dress of

lime green chiffon, the bodice cut in a low V edged with gold beads and a little pleated cape that floated from the beaded shoulder straps. The skirt was simply cut in cunning gores that lay flat on her slim hips and flared out to a tremendous floating skirt.

'I think you look divine in it. Let's ask Miss MacDonald what she thinks.'

Miss MacDonald instantly materialised. She was a lady of indeterminate age – always dressed in a grey pin-striped flannel skirt and a tussore silk blouse. She was devoted to Hermione, and ran the shop for her during Hermione's frequent absences. Hermione led a mysterious life composed of parties, weekends, hunting in winter and doing up various amusing flats she bought in Mayfair and let at exorbitant rents to people she met at parties. Everybody was in love with her: her reputation rested upon the broad front of universal adulation. Whoever the current lover might be was lost in a crowd of apparently desperate, apparently hopeless suitors. She was not beautiful, but invariably glamorous and groomed and her drawl concealed a first-class brain and a reckless courage in the hunting field or indeed anywhere else that it was required of her. Edward's brother Hugh had been in love with her during the war – was reputed to have been one of the twenty-one men who had proposed to her during that period – but she had married Knebworth and shortly after the birth of her son, had divorced him. She was good with men's wives, but genuinely fond of Villy for whom she always made special knockdown prices.

Villy, standing in a kind of trance in the diaphanous frock that seemed to have turned her into some fragile exotic stranger, realised that Miss MacDonald was registering appreciation.

'Might have been made for you, Mrs Cazalet.'

'The midnight blue would be more *useful*.'

'Oh, Lady Knebworth! What about the *café-au-lait* lace?'

'That's brilliant of you, Miss MacDonald. Do fetch it.'

The moment that Villy saw the coffee lace she knew that she wanted it. She wanted all of them, and them included a wine-coloured moiré with huge puff sleeves made of ribbon rosettes that she had tried on earlier.

'It's utter agony, isn't it?' Hermione had already decided that Villy, who had come in for two frocks, should buy three of them, and knowing Villy, it was essential that she should forgo one. Stage whispers ensued.

'How *much* are they?'

'Miss MacDonald, how *much*?'

'The moiré is twenty, the chiffon is fifteen, the lace and the midnight blue crêpe could be sixteen each. Isn't that right, Lady Knebworth?'

There was a brief silence while Villy tried and failed to add things up. 'I can't have four, anyway. It's out of the question.'

'I think,' said Hermione consideredly, 'that the blue is a bit on the obvious side for you, but the others are all perfect. Supposing we made the moiré and the lace fifteen each, and threw in the chiffon for ten? How much does that come to, Miss MacDonald?' (She knew perfectly well, but she also knew that Villy was bad at sums.)

'That comes to forty, Lady Knebworth.'

And before she knew it, Villy had said, 'I'll take them. It's wicked of me, but I can't resist it. They're all so ravishing. Goodness, I don't know what Edward will say.'

'He'll adore you in them. Have them packed, Miss Mac-Donald, I'm sure Mrs Cazalet will want to take them with her.'

'I shall wear one tonight. Thank you so much, Hermione.'

In the taxi going to Mummy, she thought, I'm really ashamed of myself. I never used to buy a dress for more than five pounds. But they'll last for ever and I'm sick of wearing the same things. We do go out a lot, she added almost as though she was arguing with someone else, and I was fearfully good about the January sales. I only bought linen for the house. And I only bought Lydia things that she *needed* – except the riding jacket, and she wanted that so much. Shopping with Lydia had been a tearful business. She hated having her feet X-rayed in new shoes.

'I don't want nasty green feet!' and then she wept because Nan said she wasn't old enough for a riding jacket, and *then* she wept because Nan wouldn't let her wear it home on the bus. They had bought Chilprufe vests for next winter, two pairs of shoes, a pleated navy serge skirt on a liberty bodice and a dear little jacket made of velveteen to go with it. A linen hat for summer and four pairs of white cotton socks had completed their purchases. Lydia only really wanted the jacket. She wanted stockings like Lou instead of socks which were babyish, and she wanted a scarlet velvet jacket instead of the navy blue one. She did not like her indoor shoes because they had a strap and a button instead of laces. Villy felt that she deserved a treat after all that. There was still Louise to do, and Teddy when he got back from school, although he wouldn't need much. She looked at the three wonderful dress boxes that contained her booty and started trying to decide which she would wear for the theatre.

∞ ∞ ∞

As it was such a fine day, Miss Milliment walked to Notting Hill Gate to have her lunch in the ABC. She had a tomato sandwich and a cup of tea, and then, because she still felt hungry, a custard tart. So lunch cost nearly a shilling which was more than she knew she should spend. She read *The Times* during her lunch, saving the crossword for the long train journey home. Her landlady provided her with an adequate evening meal and toast and tea for breakfast. She sometimes wished that she could afford a wireless for the evenings, because her eyes did not stand up to all the reading she found herself having recourse to. Since her father – a retired clergyman – had died she had always lived in digs, as she put it. On the whole she did not mind very much, she had never been the domestic type. Years ago the man she had thought she was going to marry had died in the Boer War and her grief had eventually tempered into a humble acceptance that she would not have made a very comfortable home for him. Now, she taught; a godsend it had been when Viola had written and asked her to teach Louise and subsequently her cousin Polly. Until that happened she had begun to feel quite desperate: the money her father had left her just provided a roof over her head, but nothing else at all, and she had ended by not having the fare to get to the National Gallery, not to speak of those exhibitions that one had to pay to get into. Pictures were her passion – particularly the French Impressionists, and of them, Cézanne was her god. She sometimes reflected with a tinge of irony that it was odd that so many people had described her as 'no oil painting'. She was, in fact, one of the ugliest people she had ever seen in her life, but once she was sure of this she ignored her appearance. She clothed herself by covering her body with whatever came to hand cheapest and most easily; she bathed once a week (the landlady charged extra for baths) and she had taken over her father's steel-rimmed spectacle frames that served her very well. Laundry was either difficult or expensive so her clothes were not very clean. In the evenings she read philosophy and poetry and books about the history of art, and at weekends she looked at pictures. Looked! She stared, stayed, revisited a picture until it was absorbed into those secret parts of her bulky being that made memory, which then digested into spiritual nourishment. Truth – the beauty of it, the way that it could sometimes transcend the ordinary appearance of things – moved and excited her; inside, she was a paradise of appreciation. The five pounds a week that she earned from teaching the two girls enabled her to see all that she had time to see and save a little against the years when Louise and Polly would no longer require her. At seventy-three she would be unlikely to get another job. She was lonely, and entirely used to it. She left tuppence for the waitress and, trotting lightly, zigzagged her short-sighted way to the Tube.

∞ ∞ ∞

Phyllis began her half day by going to Ponting's. There was a summer sale on and she needed stockings. She also enjoyed a good look round although she knew this would mean that she would be sorely tempted to buy something – a blouse, or a summer dress that she did not need. She walked over Campden Hill to Kensington High Street to save the fare. She was a country girl and the walk was nothing to her. She wore her summer coat (pale grey slub) and skirt, the blouse Mrs Cazalet had given her for Christmas, and a straw hat that she had had for ages and retrimmed from time to time. She had grey cotton gloves and her handbag. Phyllis earned thirty-eight pounds a year and she sent her mother ten shillings a month. She had been engaged for four years now to the under-gardener on the

19

estate where her father had been gamekeeper until his arthritis forced his retirement. Being engaged to Ted had become part of the landscape of her life: it was no longer exciting – never had been, really, because they had known from the start that they would not be able to afford to marry for a very long time. Anyway, she had known him all her life. She had gone into service and come to London; they met about four times a year – on her fortnight's holiday when she went home, and on the few occasions when she could persuade Ted to come to London for the day. Ted hated London, but he was a good steady chap and he agreed to come sometimes – mostly in summer, because the rest of the year, what with the weather and everything, there was nowhere for them to go. They sat in tea shops and went to the cinema, and that was the best time because, if she encouraged him, he would put his arm round her, she could hear him breathing and he never knew what the film had been about. Once a year she brought him back to tea at Lansdowne Road and they sat in the kitchen with Emily and Edna plying him with food and although he cleared his throat a lot he became speechless and let his tea get cold. Anyway, she saved ten bob a month towards getting married and that left her with two pounds three and threepence for her days off and her clothes and everything she needed so she had to be careful. But she'd got the best part of thirty pounds in the Post Office. It was nice to have the future certain and she had always wanted to see a bit of life before she settled down. She would have a good look round Ponting's, and then she'd go for a walk in Kensington Gardens and find a nice bench to sit on in the sun. She liked watching the ducks and the toy boats on the Round Pond and then she'd have tea in Lyons and end up going to the Coronet or the Embassy in Notting Hill Gate, whichever one had the film with Norma Shearer in it. She liked Norma Shearer because Ted had once said she looked a bit like her.

Ponting's had the stockings on sale. Three pairs for four bob. It was ever so full of people. She looked longingly at the racks of summer dresses reduced to three bob. There was one with buttercups on it and a Peter Pan collar that would have been just right for her – she knew it – but she had the bright idea of popping into Barker's to see if she could pick up a remnant so she could make herself one. She was lucky. She found a pretty green voile with a trellis pattern of roses on it – three and a quarter yards for half a crown. A bargain! Edna, who was clever at dress-making, had patterns, so she needn't buy one of them. Sixpence saved, which was better than sixpence spent, as her mother would say. By the time she got to the Round Pond she felt very tired and it must have been the sun that made her sleepy because she dropped off and then she had to ask a gentleman the time and there was a whole crowd of dirty ragged children, some of them barefooted, with a baby in a battered old perambulator in front of her by the edge of the pond. They were fishing for sticklebacks which they put into a jam jar and after the gentleman had moved on one of them said, 'I wonder if I could trouble you for the toime?' and they shrieked with laughter and started chanting it, except the baby who had a dummy in its mouth. 'That's very rude,' she said as she felt herself going red. But they took no notice because they were common. *Her* mother would never have let her go out like that.

She had a bit of a headache and for a moment of panic thought she might have her monthly coming on. It would be four days early if she was, but *if* she was, she'd have to go straight home since she hadn't got anything with her. But walking back through the gardens to Bayswater Road, she reflected that no, she couldn't have, 'cos if she *was*, her spots would be much worse, and she still only had the one. Phyllis was nearly twenty-four: she'd been in service for just over ten years. When she'd started – in her first place, she'd gone crying to the head housemaid about the blood – Amy had simply shown her how to fold the strips of flannel and said everybody got it and it happened once a month. That was the only time anyone had ever mentioned it to her, except when Mrs Cazalet had shown her where the flannel was kept in the linen cupboard. But she didn't say anything, which, being a lady, Phyllis would have expected, and although she and Edna knew when each other had it, they never mentioned it either, because, being in service, they knew how ladies behaved. It seemed a funny thing to get, but if it happened to everyone, it must be all right. The flannel was put in a linen bag and sent to the laundry every week, 'sanitary napkins' they were called on the list. Naturally the servants had a separate bag. Anyway, she was all right, and she had two cups of tea and a fruit bun and by the time she got to the Coronet, she felt much better.

∞ ∞ ∞

Polly had stayed to lunch with Louise after lessons. There were Nan and Lydia as well. Lunch was dark brown mince and thick white spaghetti. Lydia called it worms and got smacked because their mother wasn't there, but she didn't cry much because she had spread her riding jacket out on Louise's leather reading chair to look at while she was eating. Louise talked about Othello nearly all the time, but Polly, who worried about other people's feelings and could see that Othello didn't interest Nan all that much, asked her what she was knitting and where she was going to spend her holiday. Nan was making a pink bedjacket for her mother and was off to Woburn Sands for her holiday in a fortnight's time. One of the worst features of even this amount of conversation with Nan was that Louise would accuse her afterwards of sucking up and it wasn't at all that: she could quite see why not everybody would be interested in Othello.

Lydia said, 'Nan's mother has bad legs. She has to keep them up all the time in case they drop off. They're *unusually* bad,' she added after thinking about it.

'That'll do, Lydia. We don't talk about people's legs at mealtimes.'

Which just makes us all think about them, Polly thought. For pudding there was gooseberry fool, which Polly didn't like but didn't dare to say so. Lydia had no such compunction.

'It smells of sick,' she said, 'greeny, hurried sick.' Nan picked her off her chair and carried her out of the room.

'Strewth!' said Louise, who was given to what she thought of as Shakespearean oaths. 'Poor old Lydia. She'll be for it now.' And indeed they could hear muffled wails from above.

'I don't want any.'

'I'm not surprised, I don't like it much, either. We'd better finish off the Wonder Cream. You did suck up to Nan.'

'I didn't, honestly.'

When they had finished potting and labelling the cream

they took it up to Louise's room. Then they lay on the lawn in the back garden until the Walls' man came round with his tricycle and cabinet of ices. They each had a lime Snofrute and lay on the lawn again and talked about the holidays and what they would do when they were grown up.

'Mummy wants me to be Presented.'

'What – be a deb?' Louise could hardly contain her contempt. 'Surely you want a proper career?'

'What could I be?'

'You're pretty good at painting. You could be a painter.'

'I could be Presented and *then* be a painter.'

'It doesn't work like that, Polly – honestly. You'd go to all those dances with stupid people proposing to you all the time and you'd agree to marry one of them out of sheer kindness. You know how bad you are at saying no.'

'I wouldn't marry anyone I didn't love.'

'Even that's not enough sometimes.' She was thinking darkly of John Gielgud and her endless dreams of saving his life in ways so spectacular and brave that he would have to marry her. They would live in a mansion flat (the height of sophistication – she only knew one family who lived in a *flat*) and play opposite one another in all the plays and have lobster and coffee ices for supper.

'Poor Lou! You'll get over it!'

Louise smiled her special sad, heroically vulnerable smile that she had practised in front of the bathroom mirror. 'I shan't. It isn't the kind of thing you *get* over.'

'I suppose not.'

'Actually,' Louise said, 'I sometimes rather enjoy it. You know – imagining what it would be like. And I don't think about it *all* the time.' This, she knew was partial honesty: sometimes she didn't think about it for days on end. I'm the kind of dishonest person who can't bear to be completely dishonest, she thought.

She looked at Polly, who was lying on her back with her eyes shut against the sun. Although Polly was twelvish, a year younger, she did not seem it. Polly was utterly direct, without guile. Tactless, it often got called: if you asked her what she thought, she told you – if she *knew* what she thought, but her honesty caused her much indecision and sometimes pain. She would look at you with her rather small dark blue eyes if you asked her things like could she bear to go in a submarine, or shoot their pony if its leg was broken, or die for her country without spilling any beans if she was a spy and got caught, and you would see her milky-white forehead furrowed by little glancing frowns as she went on staring at you while she struggled for truth – often failing. 'I don't *know*,' she would frequently say. 'I wish I did, but I'm not sure. I'm not *sure*, like you.' But Louise secretly knew perfectly well that she simply made decisions according to her mood, and that Polly's indecision was somehow more serious. This irritated her, but she respected Polly. Polly never acted, never played to the gallery as Nan said, and could not see the beach for the pebbles. And she was incapable of telling any kind of lie. Louise did not exactly tell *lies* – known to be a serious crime in the Cazalet family – but she spent a great deal of her time being other people who naturally thought and saw things differently from Louise so what she said at those times did not count. Being an actress *required* this kind of flexibility, and although Polly sometimes teased her about her variable reactions and she teased Polly back about being so serious and not knowing things, that was where the teasing stopped. Their worst, their most real, fears were sacrosanct: Louise suffered from appalling homesickness (could not stay anywhere except with the family – dreaded being sent to a boarding school) and Polly was terrified that there might be another war when they would all be gassed to death and particularly her cat Pompey who, being a cat, was not likely to be issued with a gas mask. Polly was an authority about this. Her father had a good many books about the war; he had been in it, had emerged with one hand gone, over a hundred pieces of shrapnel in his body that they couldn't get out and he got frightful headaches – the worst in the world, her mother said. And all the people in the photograph on his dressing-table – all soldiers in yellowy baggy uniform – were dead, except for him. Polly read all his books and asked him little casual trapping questions that simply proved to her that what she read – the slaughter, the miles of mud and barbed wire, the shells and tanks and, above all, the awful poison gas that Uncle Edward had somehow managed to live through – was all of it true, a true and continuing nightmare that had lasted over four years. If there was another war it could only be worse, because people kept saying how warships and aeroplanes and guns and everything that could make it worse had been improved by scientific development. The next war would be twice as frightful and go on for twice as long. Very secretly indeed, she envied Louise for only being afraid of boarding school; after all, she was already fourteen – in another two or three years she'd be too old to go to one. But nobody was too old or too young for war.

Louise said, 'How much pocket money have you got?'

'Don't know.'

'Look.'

Polly obediently unzipped her little leather wallet that she wore on a string round her neck. Several coins and some rather grey sugar lumps fell onto the grass.

'You shouldn't keep your horse sugar with your money.'

'I know.'

'Those lumps are probably poisonous by now.' She sat up. 'We could go to Church Street and I could come back and have tea with you.'

'All right.'

They both loved Church Street, particularly the top end, near Notting Hill Gate, for different reasons. Louise haunted the pet shop that had a never-ending supply of desirable creatures: grass snakes, newts, goldfish, tortoises, huge white rabbits, and then the things that she coveted but was not allowed – all kinds of birds, mice, guinea pigs, kittens and puppies. Polly was not always very good about waiting while Louise looked at everything and when she got too bored she went next door, which was a junk shop that sprawled onto the wide pavement and contained everything from second-hand books to pieces of china, soapstone, ivory, carved wood, beads and pieces of furniture, and sometimes objects whose use was utterly mysterious. The people in this shop were not forthcoming: two men – the father spent most of the time lying on a faded red velvet *chaise-longue* reading a paper and the son sat on a gilt chair with his feet up on a huge case of stuffed pike, eating coconut buns and drinking tea. 'It's for stretching gloves,' the father would say if asked; the son never knew anything. Today, Polly found a pair of very tall blue and white candlesticks, rather cracked and with a bit missing from the top of one, but extremely beautiful, she thought. There was also a plate – pottery, with blue and yellow flowers on it, dark delphinium blue, sun yellow and a few green leaves – about the most beautiful plate she had ever seen. The candlesticks were sixpence and the plate was fourpence: too much.

'There's a bit missing on that one,' she said pointing to it.

'That's Delft, that is.' He put down his paper. 'How much have you got, then?'

'Sevenpence halfpenny.'

'You'll have to choose. I can't let them go for that.'

'What would you let them go for?'

'I can't do you any better than ninepence. That plate's Portuguese.'

'I'll ask my friend.'

She rushed back to the pet shop where Louise was having an earnest conversation. 'I'm buying a catfish,' Louise announced. 'I've always wanted one and the man says this is a good time of year.'

'Can you lend me some money? Just till Saturday?'

'How much?'

'A penny halfpenny.'

'OK. I won't be able to have tea with you, though, because I want to get my catfish home.' The catfish was in a jam jar and the man had made a handle of string. 'Isn't he lovely? Look at his little lovely whiskers.'

'Lovely.' Polly didn't like them much, but knew that it took all sorts to make a world.

She went back to her shop and gave the man ninepence and he wrapped up the plate and the candlesticks very badly in old limp newspapers. 'Oh, Polly! You're always buying china. What are you going to do with it all?'

'For my house when I'm grown up. I haven't got nearly enough. I can buy tons more. The candlesticks are Delft,' she added.

'Gosh! Do you mean like Van Meer? Let's see. They'll look better when they're washed.'

'I know.' She could hardly wait to get home and wash them. They parted. 'See you tomorrow.'

'Hope your catfish is OK.'

∞ ∞ ∞

'And when are you off to Sussex?'

Villy, who had told her mother at least three times, answered a little too patiently, 'On Friday.'

'But that is the day after tomorrow!'

'Yes, Mummy, I did tell you.'

Making no attempt to conceal her disbelief Lady Rydal said, 'I must have forgotten.' She sighed, moved slightly in her craggy armchair and bit her lips from the pain. This was to show Villy that she was in pain, and to show that she suffered in silence, which was also, Villy felt, meant to open up vistas of what else she might be suffering in silence. She was a beautiful and rather dramatic old woman: due to a combination of arthritis and a kind of Victorian indolence (at the first twinge, she had taken to her chair, moving only up – and downstairs once a day, and to the dining room for luncheon and dinner accompanied by a stalwart, rubber-tipped stick), she had become not only shapeless, but chronically bored. Only her face retained its autocratic and arresting appearance: the noble brow, the huge eyes faded from their original forget-me-not, the little swags of porcelain complexion festooned and suspended by myriad tiny lines, the exquisitely chiselled Burne-Jones mouth, all proclaimed her to have once been a beauty. Her hair was now silver white, and she always wore heavy drop earrings – pearls and sapphires – that dragged on the lobes of her ears. Day after day she sat, cast upon her huge chair like a beautiful shipwreck, scorning the frail and petty efforts at salvage that her children attempted with visits of the kind that Villy was now making. She could do nothing, but knew how everything was to be done; her taste in the management of her house, her food, her flowers was both original and good, but she considered that there were no occasions left worthy of her rising to them, and the extravagance and gaiety that Villy could remember was now stagnant, mildewed with self-pity. She considered her life to have been a tragedy; her alliance to a musician was marrying beneath her, but when it occurred her widowhood was not to be trifled with – black garments and blinds were still half drawn in the drawing room although he had been dead two years. She considered that neither of her daughters had married well, and she did not

27

approve of her son's wife. She was too awe-inspiring for friendship, and even her two loyal servants were called by their
surnames. Villy thought that they stayed only out of respect and
affection for their dead master, but inertia was contagious and
the house was full of it: clocks ticked wearily; bluebottles at
the sash windows buzzed and sank into stupor. If she didn't say
or do something, Villy felt that she would drop off.

'Tell me your news.' This was one of Lady Rydal's familiar
gambits – difficult to answer since it carried with it studied
broad-mindedness together with a complete lack of curiosity.
Either Villy (or whoever was the target) would provide answers
that palpably bored her mother, or they would come up with
something that contained one of the formidable quantity of
things of which Lady Rydal disapproved. She disapproved of
any reference to religion made by anyone other than herself
(levity); she considered politics an unsuitable subject for a
lady (Margot Asquith and Lady Astor were not people she
would invite to her house); any discussion of the Royal Family's
private life was vulgar (she was probably the only person in
London who, from the outset of that affair, had ceased mention-
ing Edward VIII and who had never pronounced Mrs Simpson's
name); any reference to the body – its appearance, its requirements and, worst of all, its urges – was utterly taboo (even
health was tricky since only certain ailments were permissible
for women). Villy, as usual, fell back on telling her mother
about the children while Bluitt, the parlourmaid, cleared away
tea. This was a success; Lady Rydal wore her indulgent smile
throughout Lydia's antics in Daniel Neal, listened to Teddy's
latest letter from school and asked with affection after Louise,
of whom she was particularly fond. 'I must see her before she
disappears into the country. Tell her to ring me up and we may
arrange for her to pay me a visit.'

In the taxi going home, Villy reflected that this would
be difficult since there were only two full days left before
Sussex.

∞ ∞ ∞

Edward – he had dismissed Bracken after being driven back
to the office after lunch – collected the car keys from Miss

Seafang, his secretary, refilled his silver cigarette case from the ebony box that she always kept full on his enormous desk, and looked at his watch. Just after four – plenty of time for tea, if he felt inclined. The directors' meeting had been cancelled as the Old Man had wanted to get off to Sussex and Hugh had one of his headaches. If the Old Man hadn't wanted to get off, they would have had the meeting, and Hugh would have sat, screwing up his eyes, white and silent except when he hastily agreed to any proposition made. Hugh's headaches could never be mentioned; he became irritable and then furious at any concern so nothing could be said, which made Edward, anyway, feel worse. He loved his brother and he felt rotten about having survived the war unscathed when his brother had such bloody awful health because of it.

Miss Seafang put her neat head round the door. 'Mr Walters would be grateful if you could spare a moment, Mr Edward.'

Edward looked at his watch again, and registered anxiety and surprise. 'Good Lord! Ask him to wait until Monday, would you? I'm late for an appointment as it is. Tell him I'll see him first thing on Monday.'

'I'll tell him.'

'What would I do without you!' He gave her a dazzling smile, picked up his hat and went.

∞ ∞ ∞

All the way home in the Underground and then on the bus, Miss Seafang repeated that remark, savoured and enhanced the smile until it achieved the bloom of (gentlemanly, of course) romance. He understood her, realised her true worth, something nobody else had ever done – had indeed, distorted it so much that she would not have cared to acknowledge the dreary titbits: reliability, a light hand with pastry and being good with her nephews and nieces.

∞ ∞ ∞

It was not so much a question of whether he *wanted* to have tea with Denise, Edward reflected as he drove west from the city, it was a question of being decent. He hadn't told the poor little girl about his holiday because he knew it would upset her and he hated to see her upset. And next week, with Villy safely in Sussex when she would expect him to be freer, he wouldn't be at all because on those occasions the family closed in, and, except for one evening at his club, dinner parties had been arranged for him. So really, he *ought* to go and see her. Small and equal surges of responsibility and excitement beset him: he was one of those fortunate people who actually *enjoyed* doing the right thing.

∞ ∞ ∞

Denise was lying on the sofa in her green drawing room wearing a black afternoon dress with a wide red sash. She sprang gracefully to her feet when her maid announced him.

'Edward! How divine! You can't begin to imagine how bored I was!'

'You don't look bored.'

'Well – suddenly, I'm not.' She touched his cheek with her fingers: her nails were painted the same colour as her sash; a little breeze of Cuir de Russie reached him. 'Tea? Or whisky?'

'I don't think—'

'Darling, you must have something or Hildegarde will think it funny.'

'Whisky, then. Extraordinary name for a maid.'

'She's German, so it isn't. Say when.'

'I suppose I meant – extraordinary to have a German maid.'

'Oh – the agency was full of them. They don't cost any more and they work far harder. Lots of people are taking to them.'

There was a pause; Edward sipped his drink, and then, not because he wanted to know, but because he always found this part of things a bit tricky, he said, 'What were you reading?'

'The new Angela Thirkell. Quite amusing, but I bet you don't read novels, do you, darling?'

'I must honestly confess that I don't.' He didn't read at all, as a matter of fact, but luckily she didn't ask him, and so it became one more little grain in the molehill of her ignorance about him. The longer they knew each other, the more things there were like that.

She had arranged herself on the sofa again. From where he stood he could look down on the pretty nape of her neck accentuated by her bushy bobbed hair . . .

'Could we possibly go upstairs, do you think?'

'I thought you'd never ask.'

She was marvellous to make love to – seemingly passive but quite keen underneath. She had an unexpectedly voluptuous body; dressed, she gave an impression of girlishness, but naked she was quite another matter. He told her she looked her best without any clothes, but that didn't go down at all well. 'You make me sound like a tart!' and her large, pale grey eyes started to brim. But it might not have been what he said after all, because the next thing she said was, 'I gather you're going to Cornwall for your holiday.' Yes, he said, who told her? 'I ran into Villy at the hairdresser's. That was over a week ago, and you *still* haven't told me!' He explained how much he hated to upset her. 'Do you mean you would just have gone away and *not* told me?' and then she really started crying. He took her in his arms and rocked her and said of course of course not, did she really think he would do a rotten thing like that? Of *course* he wouldn't and it was only for a fortnight. 'I love you so dreadfully.' He knew she did. He made love to her again and it seemed to cheer her up. 'It's rather a Thing, isn't it?' she said, and having more or less agreed that it was, he reminded her that he wouldn't do anything to hurt Villy, whom he also loved. 'And she is your wife.' And after all, there was Nigel, a splendid chap really absolutely devoted to her as everybody knew, and he looked at his watch to make it easier to say that he had to go – good God, look at the time, he really *must* go. And he did, promising to be in touch next week, but it was a hell of a week – he'd do his best.

∞ ∞ ∞

Polly walked slowly home down Church Street with the limp newspaper flapping round her candlesticks. It was a lovely sunny evening; the sky was blue – a kind of *gentle* blue and people looked summery. The chandeliers in Mrs Crick's shop were gleaming magically with extraordinary unearthly blues and greens. Polly wondered who bought them: she never saw

anyone leaving the shop carrying a chandelier and she thought
that probably footmen came very early in the morning to get
them for palaces. Huge milk churns were standing outside
the dairy which was covered inside with beautiful green- and
white- and cream-coloured tiles. Polly had decided to have a
room in her house just like the dairy – not for being a dairy,
but a little room to sit and paint in. Louise had said why not
keep toads in it as it would be so nice and cool for them, but
Polly was only going to have cats in her house – a white one
and a black and white magician cat with very long whiskers.
Because, by then, Pompey would be dead: he was already old
– at least eight, the vet said – and he had been hit by cars, if not
actually run over, four times; his tail was broken at the end and
hung in a twisted way and he moved stiffly for a cat. She kept
planning not to think of him dying, but other thoughts led to it,
and she could feel her throat getting lumpy and hot. He could
live for another eight years, but she would not have her house
by then. She had saved twenty-three pounds fourteen shillings
and sixpence towards buying it, but they cost hundreds and
she was going to have to save someone's life or paint the most
amazing picture or dig up buried treasure in the summer to have
enough money. Or build it. In the garden would be Pompey's
grave. She had turned into Bedford Gardens now and was nearly
home. She wiped her eyes on a bit of the newspaper: it smelled
of fish and chips and she wished that she hadn't.

She had to put the candlesticks and the plate down
to let herself in. The front door opened straight into the
long drawing room. Mummy was playing Rachmaninov – a
prelude – very loudly and fast so Polly sat quietly until
she had finished. The piece was familiar because Mummy
practised and practised it. There was a tray of tea things
by the sofa, but they had not been touched: Gentleman's
Relish sandwiches and a coffee cake, but Polly knew that
eating them would constitute being unmusical, something
that her mother simply would not allow Polly to be, so she
waited. When it was over, she said, 'Oh, Mummy, you *are*
getting on!'

'Do you really think so? It is a little better, isn't it?'

Her mother got up from the piano and lumbered slowly
across the room to Polly and the tea. She was frighteningly fat

– not all of her, but her tummy – Polly was to have a brother
or sister in a few weeks.

'Shall I pour the tea for you?'

'Do, darling.' She cast herself upon the sofa. She wore
a linen dress – sage green – that made no concession to
pregnancy.

'Are you feeling all right?'

'I'm a little tired, but yes, darling, of course I'm all right.
Did you break up today?'

'No, it's tomorrow. But we finished *Othello* today. Are
you going out tonight?'

'I told you we were. The Queen's Hall. *Othello* seems
an extraordinary play for children of your age. I should
have thought *A Midsummer Night's Dream* would be far more
suitable.'

'We're reading all of him, so we're bound to get to the
extraordinary ones, Mummy. Louise chose to. We each choose
something, you see.'

It was funny how with grown-ups you had to say the
same things again and again. Perhaps that was why babies
were born with such big heads: the head stayed the same
and the person got larger, but it meant that there was the
same amount of room in your brain to remember things, so
the longer you lived, the more you forgot. Whatever she said,
Mummy was tired, anyway, she had bluey marks under her
eyes and the rest of her face was a kind of greeny white and
her stomach looked like a balloon under her dress. It would be
much better if babies were like eggs, but she supposed people
weren't the right shape for sitting on them. You could probably
do it with hot water bottles . . .

'Polly! I've asked you twice! *What* is in the dirty newspaper?'

'Oh! Just some stuff I got from the shop next to the
animal shop.'

'What *did* you get?'

Polly unwrapped the plate and showed it. Then she unwrapped the candlesticks and showed them. They weren't
a success as she knew they wouldn't be.

'I can't think why you keep buying all these odd things.
What are you going to do with them?'

Polly was incapable of lying, so she couldn't answer.

33

'I mean, darling, *I* don't mind, but your room is stuffed with junk. Why do you want them?'

'I think they're pretty, and I'll need some things of my own for when I'm grown up. Louise bought a catfish. What did you buy when you were my age, anyway?'

'Don't say "anyway" like that, Polly, it's rude.'

'Sorry.'

'I bought furniture for my dolls' house. The one you never play with.'

'I have played with it, Mummy, honestly.' She'd tried to like it but everything was made and done, there was nothing to do but arrange the same old bits of furniture and tea things; even the dolls already had names so they didn't feel hers at all.

'And I kept it all those years for when I had a daughter.'

She looked so sadly at Polly that Polly couldn't bear it.

'Perhaps the new baby will like it.'

'That reminds me, I wanted to have a little talk with you about that.'

Half an hour later, Polly trudged upstairs to her room with her china. Her room! She was being turned out of it for the blasted baby. *That* had been the little talk. It was the largest, sunniest room on the top floor and now some awful nanny and the baby were to have it, and she was to be turned out to the little one at the back: hardly room for anything. She wouldn't be able to see the lamplighter or the postman or the milkman or any of her friends. She'd be stuck in the back of the house with nothing but chimney pots. Simon had to keep the attic because he was a boy (why did that make any difference, for heaven's sake?). And it wasn't as though it was just her; it was Pompey as well, and he couldn't be expected to understand that. 'It's not *fair*,' she muttered. This seemed so true and so awful that tears began to run down her face. Simon was away nearly all the time at school so what did he want with a room with slanty ceilings and sweet little windows? She and Pompey might as well be living in the linen cupboard. No wonder Mummy had made a fuss about her china. There was no room for anything in the spare room which was all it was. She was a spare child too, she supposed. The thought made her sob. That was it. Not wanted in the family. She cast herself down on the floor beside Pompey who lay in a dress box on a blanket that it had taken her ages to

34

knit for him. He'd been asleep. When she woke him up to tell him, his eyes, which opened at once, went to slits of pleasure as he stretched luxuriously under her hand. But when she cried on him he sneezed and got up at once. She had noticed before that he did not seem to care for other people's feelings. If only they had a proper garden, there'd be a wheelbarrow and then she could load all her stuff up and go and live with Louise whose house was much larger, anyway. When her parents had gone to their concert, she would telephone Louise and see if she could borrow their wheelbarrow. She heard the front door downstairs which meant that Dad had come home.

∞ ∞ ∞

Hugh Cazalet usually drove himself. It hurt his eyes to read in a car and with nothing to take his mind off the way in which anybody else was driving him, he fretted, with various degrees of irritation and nerves, at the way in which they were doing it. Today, however, he got one of his 'heads' just before lunch, which he couldn't cancel as both Edward and the Old Man were already pledged and couldn't take his customer – a rising young architect employed (rather too much, Hugh thought) by the Board of Trade – out to lunch for him. So he had taken a taxi to the Savoy and picked at a meal with a total stranger whom he found early on he did not very much like. Boscomb contrived to be bumptious at the same time as calling him sir, which made Hugh feel an old fuddy-duddy although there could not have been more than six or seven years between them. He also wore a bow tie – something Hugh would never have dreamed of doing without a dinner jacket, and co-respondent's shoes in caramel and white: a bit of a bounder, really. But he was shopping for veneers for the lifts of a large office building he had designed – or at least was overseeing – and Cazalet's had an unrivalled stock of hardwoods which it was Hugh's business to sell. Food revived him, but the drink was a problem. Courtesy demanded that he drink with his guest: a dry sherry before lunch that he (as usual and mistakenly) thought might do him some good, some white burgundy with the fish and port with the cheese. He managed to avoid the port but by then his head was hammering. Arrangements were made for Boscomb to visit the wharf where he could view samples that were larger than four by four inches and finally Hugh was able to sign the bill and escape. Another cab and he was back at the office and could take some more of his dope. He told Mary, his secretary, to take his calls and leave him until the meeting – timed for three thirty – lay down on his chesterfield in the office and slept heavily.

His secretary woke him with a welcome cup of tea and the still more welcome news that the meeting was off. 'Mrs Cazalet rang to remind you about the concert tonight. Oh, and Mr Cazalet senior said that Carruthers will drive you home.'

He thanked her dismissively and she went. The whole damn office was like a bush telegraph, treating him as an old crock just because he had a bit of a headache. His rage and humiliation about his wretched body vented itself upon anyone who acknowledged it – his father for presuming to order him a chauffeur, his secretary for letting everyone know that he was having forty winks. Why couldn't the silly woman keep her mouth shut? He could have got a lift home with Edward, *if* he wanted one, and taken Sybil to the concert in a cab. He lit a Gold Flake to calm himself, and went to his desk to buzz Edward. But Edward had left, his secretary informed him, had left half an hour ago. There was a picture of Polly and Simon on his desk. Simon stared steadily at the camera with a look of sturdy bravado, smiling in his grey school-uniform shorts and shirt, a model yacht on his scarred, experienced knees. But Polly – his dear Polly – sat cross-legged in long grass looking away from her brother into some secret distance. She wore a sleeveless dress that had slipped a little over one bony shoulder and her expression was both stern and vulnerable. 'I was thinking,' he remembered her saying after he had taken the snap and asked her what was up. Polly! She was like a secret treasure to him. Whenever he thought of her he felt lucky. He never told anyone how much she meant to him – not even Sybil, who really, and sometimes he had to speak to her about it, made rather too much fuss of Simon. Well, a third child would balance things up. He stubbed out his cigarette, collected his hat and went in search of Carruthers.

∞ ∞ ∞

Louise had a rather dull tea with Lydia and Nanny, because Mummy was still out. She did show Lydia her catfish, but Lydia wasn't interested in him. 'Fish are dull,' she said, 'unless you could train him to be stroked.' She wore her riding jacket all through tea: it made her very hot and pink in the face and she got honey on one of the sleeves. That caused a rumpus because Nanny always cleaned up poor Lydia like a punishment. Louise escaped the nursery as soon as tea was over and pretended she had homework. The trouble with people of six was that they were actually rather boring to be with and although she was fond of Lydia, she was longing for her to be a more reasonable age. But perhaps she'll never catch me up: I'll always have read the books first, or by the time she comes down to dinner for a treat or can choose when she goes to bed I'll have been doing it for years and it won't seem at all treaty. Except, of course, that when they were grown up it wouldn't matter any more, as grown-ups were roughly the same whatever age they were.

She had wandered down to the hall where the *Evening Standard* had come through the letter box, and she took it to her perch on top of the boxed-in dining-room lift shaft – a good position, since it enabled her to collect Mummy the moment she got home and was out of Lydia's reach supposing she came in search of her. Papers usually turned out to be boring except for theatre reviews and a page by someone called Corisande, who seemed to go to a lot of grand parties and described people's dresses in a breathless admiring way. She looked for a picture of John Gielgud for her collection, but there wasn't one. The house seemed awfully quiet – just the grandfather clock ticking in the dining room. It would be no good unlocking the drawing-room bookcase to read a bit of one of the novels that Mummy said were not suitable for her age, because she, Mummy, might come back any minute. Otherwise, she could only think of things she *didn't* want to do: draw the map of the British Isles for homework, try and sell Edna a pot of the face cream before it went too runny, spend any more time with her catfish (Lydia's remark had slightly spoiled him for her), reread *Black Beauty* and have a good cry, or go on making Mummy's Christmas present – a needlecase in tiny cross-stitch and a rather dull pattern that she was sick of. It was her life and here she was wasting it, minutes ticking by, and all that was happening was that she was breathing and getting older. Supposing nothing at all happened for the whole of the rest of her life? She simply stayed here on the lift shaft getting older? They would have to hand her up larger clothes and sandwiches and how would she go to the lavatory? People did live on pillars, rather dirty saints had done it. She couldn't, because she'd have to feed Ferdie and the fish – except, if she could go away for holidays and leave them to Emily or Phyllis, she *could* be on a pillar. Anybody would be glad to feed the birds and fish that belonged to a saint. The trouble about being a saint was that it didn't seem to be very nice for them at the time, only afterwards, for other people, after they'd died. Working a miracle would be marvellous – being martyred would not. But supposing you could be a saint without being a martyr?

She heard a taxi. 'Let it be her. Please, God, let it be her.'

He did please and it was. She jumped down from the lift shaft just as Mummy opened the door. She was carrying three enormous cardboard boxes that looked as though they would have frocks in them. She rushed for a hug and knocked one of the boxes out of Mummy's hand.

'Darling! You're so clumsy!'

Louise's face burned. 'I know,' she said carelessly. 'I seem to have been born like it.'

'It's because you don't look what you're doing.' This remark seemed to Louise so meaningless (How could you *look* what you were doing? Either you were doing something or you were looking) that she stumped upstairs with the dress boxes without a word.

Villy was taking off her gloves and looking on the hall table for messages. 'Madam, Mrs Castle rang. No message.'

'Louise! Don't unpack those boxes until I come! Louise!'

'Yes. No, I mean, I won't.'

Villy went to the dark little study where she paid the household bills and where there was the telephone. Her sister never left messages when she rang, generally because what she had to say was too depressing and complicated to be put into a message. She gave the operator the number and while she waiting for Jessica to answer wondered with an apprehension that she felt to be selfish what would turn out to be the matter now. There wasn't much time before she should change, and there were Edward's things to be laid out . . .

'Jessica! Hallo. Got your message. What's up?'

'I can't tell you just now. But I wondered whether we could have lunch tomorrow?'

'Darling, it's Friday. Miss Milliment's day for staying to lunch and it's the last day of Louise's term and Teddy comes back from school . . . Of course, you could come to lunch but—'

'We wouldn't be able to talk. I do see. But if I came a bit early – do you think—'

'Yes. Do that. All is not well, I take it?'

'Not exactly. Raymond has had a new idea.'

'Oh, Lord!'

'I'll tell you about it tomorrow.'

Villy put the receiver back on its hook. Poor Jessica! The beauty in the family, a year younger, but married first at twenty-two, just before the battle of the Somme in which her husband had had one of his legs blown off and, worse, his nerves shattered. He came from an impoverished family; the Army was to have been his career. He had had – still had, in a way – enormous straightforward charm, everybody liked him. His blazing temper and his congenital inability to stick to anything did not emerge until you'd put your money into his chicken farm or, in Jessica's case, married him. They had four children and were extremely hard up. Although she never complained, Jessica clearly thought that Villy's life was carefree and perfect and the unspoken comparison frightened Villy. Because if it was true that she had everything, why wasn't it enough? She went slowly upstairs trying not to pursue this thought.

∞ ∞ ∞

When Polly had gone upstairs, clearly in a sulk, Sybil rang for Inge to take away the tea things. She felt exhausted. Having another baby after such a long gap did seem to upset everything horribly. The house was really not large enough for them, but Hugh was devoted to it. But when Simon was home – in the holidays, in fact, when Polly would be at home all day too – there was nowhere for them to *be* except in their bedrooms. Nanny Markby had made it clear that she did not expect the nursery to contain the older children. Of course, they would all be in Sussex this summer, but Christmas might be very difficult. She levered herself off the sofa and went to shut the piano. She did not remember her back being so bad with the other children.

Inge came in. She stood in the doorway waiting to be told what to do. An *English* maid would simply have done it, Sybil thought. 'Would you clear the tea things, please, ɪnge.'

She watched while the girl stacked the plates and loaded the tray. She was unprepossessing: large-boned with a pasty skin, greasy tow-coloured hair and rather prominent pale blue eyes, whose expression was alternately bland and shifty. Sybil felt uncomfortable about her instinctive dislike. If they were not going away, she would have got rid of Inge, but she did not want Hugh to have to cope with a new girl in her absence. When the tray was stacked, Inge said, 'Cook vill know what time dinner you haf.'

'Probably not until about ten o'clock – after the concert. Tell her to lay it in the dining room and then she may go to bed. And Miss Polly will have hers on a tray in her room at seven.'

Inge did not reply and Sybil said, 'Did you understand me, Inge?'

'*Ja.*' She said this with her eyes on Sybil's stomach and without moving.

'Thank you, Inge. That will be all.'

'You are very big for just one baby to have.'

'That will do, Inge.'

With a silence like the faintest shrug, she finally left with the tray.

She dislikes me too, Sybil thought. The way in which the maid had looked at her had been – she could not find the word – somehow horrible, cold and appraising. She climbed wearily up the stairs to her bedroom and wrenched off the green dress and put on her kimono. Then she ran a basinful of warm water and washed her face and hands. Thank goodness they had had a basin put in their room: the bathroom was on a landing half a flight up and she really found the stairs a trial. She took off her shoes and knee stockings. Her ankles were swollen. Her hair, that Hugh said was the colour of raw mahogany, was dressed in a small bun at the nape of her neck and cut short over her forehead – du Maurier hair, Hugh also said. She took out the pins and shook her hair loose; she really only felt better *déshabillée*. She took one look at their bed, and then found herself lying down on it. The baby was not kicking for once. It was wonderful to be lying down. She pulled a pillow out from under the counterpane, settled her head upon it and almost at once fell asleep.

∞ ∞ ∞

Edward, conscious of being rather late, slipped into the house, put his Homburg on the hall table and bounded up the stairs, two at a time, and went straight into the bedroom. Here he found Louise, in some sort of fancy dress, and Villy seated at her mirror combing her hair.

'Hallo, hallo,' he said.

'I'm Simpson,' Louise said.

'Hallo, darling,' Villy said, and turned her face towards his for a kiss. A little pot of rouge lay open on the rather bare dressing-table.

Edward turned to give Louise a hug, but she stiffened and withdrew. 'Daddy! I'm *Simpson*!'

Villy said, 'And I really can't have you kissing my lady's maid.'

He met her eye in the dressing-table mirror and winked. 'I'm most frightfully sorry,' he said. 'Can't think what came over me. Have I time for a bath?'

'Simpson, would you run Mr Cazalet's bath for him? And then you may put out my garnets.'

'Yes, madam.' She started to walk, as Simpson, out of the room and then remembered. 'Daddy! You haven't noticed!'

'Noticed what?'

Louise pointed to her mother, made a gesture clothing her own body and mouthed something that looked like 'you'. Then she stamped her foot and said, 'Daddy, you're so *stupid*!'

'That will do, Louise.'

'Mummy, I'm Simpson.'

41

'Then run Mr Cazalet's bath at once, or I shall get my own garnets.'

'Oh, all *right*, madam.'

'What was all that about?'

'I have a new dress.' She stood up to show him. 'Do you like it?'

'Lovely. Very nice indeed. Suits you.' Actually, he thought it rather dull. 'Hermione make it for you?'

'Oh, no, darling. It was just in her sale. Actually, I bought three. I feel rather guilty.'

'Nonsense.' He suddenly felt light-hearted. 'You know I like you to have nice clothes.'

When he had gone to his dressing room, Villy stood in front of her large looking-glass. He had not been very keen on the dress. But then men didn't really know: it was a useful dress – perfect for going to the theatre – and fitted well, the bertha round the scooped neckline concealing her rather small and sagging breasts. That dreadful fashion for binding them in the twenties, when everyone was mad about having a boyish figure, seemed to have destroyed her muscles. Unknown to Edward, she did exercises every morning in an attempt to restore them, but they did not seem to improve. The rest of her was in good shape. She sat down again at her dressing-table and carefully applied two little dabs of rouge: Mummy had always told her that make-up was vulgar and Edward professed not to like it, but she noticed that the women he seemed to find most entertaining wore a good deal. Hermione, for instance. Scarlet lipstick, painted nails and midnight blue mascara . . . She got her lipstick out of the drawer and applied the merest touch. As the colour was a dark carmine, this looked rather odd, and she rubbed her lips together to spread it. A touch of Coty's Ormande behind the ears and she was done.

Louise returned and the garnets were taken out of their flat and rather battered leather case; flat-cut eighteenth-century garnets, a necklace and drop earrings to match. She screwed on the earrings while Simpson struggled with the necklace clasp.

'You may put out my stamped velvet and the brown bead purse while I go and say good night to Miss Lydia.'

'All right, madam. Madam, Mummy, need I have supper with Nanny? Could I just have it in my room?'

'Why ever do you want to do that?'

'She's terrifically boring at meals. Well, all the time, really, but you notice it more at meals.'

'Don't you think it might hurt her feelings rather?'

'I could say I had a headache.'

'All right, then. Just for tonight.'

Lydia was already in bed in the night nursery. Her hair was still in pigtails with little damp tendrils escaping round her ears. She was wearing a blue flannel nightie. Her riding jacket was draped over a chair by her bed. The curtains were drawn, but the summer evening light seeped through chinks between the curtain rings and the stripe where they did not quite meet in the middle. She sat up at once when Villy came into the room, and cried, 'Oh, you elegant fowl!'

Villy was irresistibly touched. 'But I can't sing to you charmingly and sweetly like the Pussy-cat.'

'You *are* charming and sweet. Louise said you were going to the theatre. When can I go to one?'

'When you are older. At Christmas, perhaps.'

'Louise said if there were fires in theatres, people couldn't get out. You won't have a fire in your theatre, will you?'

'Of course not. And people can get out.'

'You might have a car accident.'

'Darling, I shan't. Why are you worrying?'

'I don't want *anything* – *ever* – to happen to you.'

'Darling, it won't,' and then she wondered why it made her sad to say that.

'I love my riding jacket. Would you undo my pigtails, please? They are much too tight for night. Nan always makes things all right for tomorrow, she never thinks about now. They *strain* me! They make all my hair straining to be longer.'

Villy undid the elastic bands and unthreaded the tight plaits. Lydia shook her head. 'Much better, Mummy. Do be careful to come back. You're quite old, and old people do have to be careful. You don't *look* old,' she added loyally, 'but I know you are. After all, I've known you all my life.'

Villy's mouth twitched, but she said, 'I do see. Now I must go, my duck.' She bent down. When Lydia hugged her, she held her breath with the fierce effort, so the hugs couldn't last very long. 'Please tell Nan *you* undid my pigtails.'

'Yes. Sleep tight. See you in the morning.'

By the time she had dealt with Nanny and come down from the top floor, Edward was emerging from his dressing room, smelling of lavender water and looking wonderfully handsome in his dinner jacket; Louise was kicking the skirting board by the open door to her bedroom.

'Did you tell her?' she immediately demanded.

'Nan? Yes, yes, I did. Where's my coat, Simpson?'

'On your bed. And I'm not Simpson any more: I've taken off my apron. You haven't seen my new catfish, Mummy,' she added, following her into the bedroom.

'I'll have to see him tomorrow.'

'Oh no, have a look at him now. He won't be new tomorrow.'

'Louise, we really have to go—'

Edward, who had gone down to the hall now called, 'Villy! Chop chop! We're going to be late.'

'Oh, Mummy! It's not fair! It wouldn't take you a *second*!'

'Don't be tiresome, Louise.' As she passed Louise's room on her way downstairs, she added, 'It looks a terrible mess in there. How many times have I told you that it's not fair on the maids if you keep it like that?'

Louise trailing sulkily down behind her muttered, 'I don't know.' At the bottom, Villy turned. 'Well, clear it up, darling, there's a good girl. Good night, now.' She bent to kiss her daughter, who held up her face in mute sacrifice.

'Good night, Lou,' called Edward. The front door slammed and they were gone. Three things on the floor! As if that was a terrible mess! If things were on the floor you could see them and that meant that you knew where they were. Grown-ups were the limit, sometimes. Children had a rotten time of it. At least Teddy would be home tomorrow and she would have someone decent to talk to. One of these days she would be *in* a play in London, and her parents – frightfully old by then – would come to see her, and beg her to go out to supper with them afterwards, but she and John Gielgud would be going to some terrifically glamorous party. 'I'm afraid you are too old,' she would have to tell them. 'You really ought to be in bed and just having Grape Nuts on a tray.' This made her feel better, and she wandered into the drawing room and got *The Painted Veil* by Somerset Maugham out of the locked bookcase and took it upstairs. She went into her parents' bedroom and tried on some of Mummy's rouge and in the middle of that Edna came in to turn the beds down.

'You didn't ought to do that, Miss Louise.'

'I know,' she said loftily. 'But I thought I ought to know what it felt like since eventually I shall be covered with the stuff. You won't tell, will you?'

'I may and I may not.' She was laying out Mr Edward's pyjamas – a lovely wine silk they were – enjoying doing Phyllis's job for once.

In the end, and to be on the safe side, Louise had to give her a pot – the smallest – of Wonder Cream in return for her silence.

∞ ∞ ∞

One of the things that Hugh most disliked about the maid was the way in which she always seemed to be lying in wait for his return in the evenings. This evening he hardly had time to take the key out of the front door before she was there. She tried to seize his hat as he was putting it on the hall table, with the result that it fell to the floor.

'I came your coat to take,' she said, as she retrieved the hat. It sounded like a kind of *sexy* accusation, he thought, telling himself for the millionth time not to be prejudiced about Germans.

'I haven't got a coat,' he said. 'Where is Mrs Cazalet?'

Inge shrugged. 'Up she went some time.' Still standing far too close to him, she added, 'You want a drink of whisky I make?'

'No, thank you.' He had actually to brush past her to get up the stairs. The movement made his head throb; he realised that he was dreading the Queen's Hall, but he hated disappointing Sybil so much that nothing would induce him to tell her.

She lay on her side, half wrapped in the green silk kimono that the Old Man had brought back from Singapore (each daughter-in-law had been given one, but the Duchy had chosen the colours – green for Sybil, blue for Viola and peach for Zoë), her narrow feet bare and touchingly white – one arm flung out with a cluster of delicate veins running from the inside of her wrist into the palm of her pretty hand. When he leant over her, a breast, hard as marble and white and veined, moved him: her extremities seemed too fragile to support the great bulk of her body.

'Hallo there.' She patted the bed. 'Tell me about your day.'

'Much as usual. Did you see the doc?'

She nodded, noticing the little tic above and to the side of his right eye. He'd had one of his heads, poor sweetie.

'What did he say?'

'Well – as a matter of fact he thinks – although he couldn't actually *hear* both hearts – we've probably got Tweedledee as well.'

'Good Lord!' He wanted to say, 'No wonder you've been done in,' but it wasn't what he meant, or only partly what he meant.

'It doesn't worry you?' It worried her: whether Nanny Markby would cope with two; whether Hugh would consent to move house; whether it would actually hurt twice as much . . .

'Of course not. It's very exciting.' He was wondering how on earth he would cope with the school fees if they turned out to be boys.

She heaved herself up so that she was sitting on the side of the bed. 'It does slightly make up for being the size of a house. I haven't told Polly, by the way.'

'Do you think, in view of this, that perhaps you'd better not go to Sussex?'

'Well, I won't go for so long. Just a week. Otherwise I shall see next to nothing of Simon.' Her back still ached – or perhaps it was aching from being in the same position.

'Do you really want to go out tonight?'

'Of course I do.' She was determined not to disappoint him. 'Unless, you don't?'

'Oh, no – I'm fine.' He knew how much store she set by concerts. He'd take some more dope; it usually got him through. 'Where's Polly?'

'Upstairs sulking, I'm afraid. I had to tell her about her move. She's making a fuss about it.'

'I'll pop up and say good night to her.'

∞ ∞ ∞

Polly lay on her stomach on the floor, tracing what looked like a map. Her straight silky hair – more golden and less red than her mother's – hung down each side of the black velvet snood hiding her face.

'It's me.'

'I know. I know your voice.'

'What's up, Poll?'

There was a pause, and then Polly said distantly, 'You shouldn't say "me", you should say "I". I should have thought you'd know.'

'It is I.'

'I know. I know your voice.'

'What's up, Poll?'

'Nothing. I hate geography homework.' She jabbed her pencil hard through the paper and made a hole. 'Now you've made me spoil my map!' She gave him an agonised frown and two tears shot out of her eyes.

He sat down on the floor and put his good arm round her.

'Nothing's fair! Simon has the best room! He gets a treat *every* time he comes back from school and I don't! He gets a treat the night before his term starts and I don't! You can't move cats about, they just go back to the old room and I hate that new nanny that's coming – she smells of peardrops and she doesn't like girls, she kept talking about my little brother. How does *she* know? If you aren't any of you careful I'll go and live with Louise only I don't think Pompey would go in a wheelbarrow otherwise I would have gone!' She took a gasping breath, but he could see that she felt better because she was watching for him to be shocked.

'I couldn't bear you to leave me and go and live with Louise,' he said.

'Would it really and truly horrify you?'

'It certainly would.'

'That's something.' She was trying to sound grudging, but he could see she was pleased.

He got to his feet. 'Let's go and look at your new room and see what we could do about it.'

'All right, Dad.' She felt for his hand, but it was the wrong arm; she gave the black silk sock that encased his stump a quick little stroke, then she said, 'It's nothing like as

47

bad as a trench in the war: I expect I'll get quite fond of it in the end.'

Her face was stern with the effort of concealing her concern for him.

∞ ∞ ∞

The moment that her parents had gone, Polly rushed to the telephone which was in the back bit of the drawing room near the piano. She lifted the receiver and held it to her ear. In a moment the operator was saying, 'Number, please.'

'Park one seven eight nine.' There was a click and then she heard the bell ringing and she started praying it wouldn't be Aunt Villy the other end.

'Hallo!'

'Hallo! Lou! It's me – Polly. Are you on your own?'

'Yes. They've gone to the theatre. What about yours?'

'A concert. What I'm ringing about is I'm having a new room. My father says I can have it painted whatever colour I like. What do you think about black? And he's going to have shelves put all round the walls for my things – all round and all over so there will be room for everything! Black would be good for china, wouldn't it?'

There was a silence the other end. Then Louise said, 'People don't have black walls, Polly, I should have thought you'd have known that.'

'Why don't they? People wear black clothes and there are black tulips.'

'La Tulipe noir was actually very dark red. I know – I've read the book. It's by a man called Dumas. It's actually a French book.'

'You can't read French.'

'It's so famous you can get it in English. I can *read* French,' she added, 'but not so that I can understand it properly. Of course I can *read* it.'

Louise seemed to be in a bate. So Polly asked about the catfish.

'He's all right, but he doesn't seem to like the other fish much.' Then while Polly was trying to think of another peace-making thing to say, she added, 'I'm stupendously bored. I've put on a lot of rouge and I'm reading a book called *The Painted*

48

Veil. It's got sex in it. It's nothing like as good as *Persuasion.'*

'Do you think dark red would be good?'

'You can get wallpaper like the sky and a sheet of different-sized seagulls that you can stick on. Why don't you have that?'

'There wouldn't be room for them with all the shelves.'

'Just don't have boring cream. Everything's cream here, as you know. It goes with everything, Mummy says, but in my view it just means you don't notice anything. Have dark red,' she added with a spurt of generosity. 'Have you done your map?'

'I did, but then I spoiled it. Have you?'

'No. Whenever I think about it I can't bear to begin. It's pointless to make a map of somewhere that there is a map of already. I wouldn't mind if it was an uncharted desert island. If you ask me, we are made to lead pointless lives – no wonder I'm bored to death.'

'*They* don't have to do it.' Polly was entering the game. 'I mean, *they* don't have to settle down after dinner and learn dates of the kings of England, or exports of Australia or do awful long division about sacks of flour.'

'I entirely agree with you. Of course they say they know it all but you can catch them out as easy as winking. The truth is they're just hell bent on pleasure.' Ganging up about their parents had made her friendly at last.

'They don't even let us break up in time to meet Teddy and Simon. *They* can go and we can't. That's not fair either.'

'Well, actually, Polly, that cuts both ways. Teddy and Simon don't *like* being met – except by Bracken.'

'Why don't they?'

'The other boys. They don't mind fathers, but mothers are an awful hazard – wearing silly clothes and showing their feelings.'

She didn't say anything about sisters, and Polly didn't want to ask. Simon's good opinion of her was so important that she did not choose to discuss it.

'This time tomorrow they'll be back. Having their treat dinners.'

'Well, we have them, too.'

'But we don't choose them. I say, Polly, that rouge. It won't come off.'

'Try licking your handkerchief and rubbing.'

'Of course I've tried that. It comes off on the handkerchief *and* it seems to go on staying on my face. I don't want it on all night.'

'Try some Wonder Cream.'

'I will. I gave Edna a jar. What's Simon's treat dinner?'

'Roast chicken and meringues. What's Teddy's?'

'Cold salmon and mayonnaise and hot chocolate soufflé. I *loathe* mayonnaise. I have my salmon dry.'

Their supper trays variously arrived, but they talked on and on, so in the end it was quite a nice evening.

∞ ∞ ∞

'Hey! I say! Are you awake?'

Simon didn't answer. He was fed up with Clarkson. He lay rigidly still because the dormitory wasn't really dark and Clarkson would be watching.

'Listen, Cazalet minor, I know you *are* awake. I only wanted to ask you something.'

It was jolly bad luck to be stuck in a dormitory of three, especially when Galbraith was the third. He was the senior, a sixth-form boy, but he was keen on owls and used to go off after Lights Out to watch them. Simon didn't actually mind because he'd given them quite a decent bribe, not only the Crunchies but some wizard swaps for cigarette cards – Galbraith only collected the natural history ones. Still, it left him stuck with Clarkson who went on and on about things that Simon simply didn't want to talk about.

'I mean, how do they know that pee won't come out – instead of the other stuff?'

'*I* don't know.'

'I mean – I've looked and there is only one place. Do you think Davenport got it wrong?'

'Why don't you ask him if you're so keen?'

'He wasn't talking to me, he was telling Travers. I can't ask him – he's a prefect. As if you didn't know,' he added.

'Well, it wasn't any of your business, then, was it? Why don't you just shut up?'

'Why don't you just boil your head? Why don't you just

50

tie two rocks round your feet and jump in the swimming pool? Why don't you . . .' He was on to a good vein now and would go on for hours, thinking of things that Simon might just do, if Simon didn't stop him.

'Psst!' he said. 'Someone's coming!'

They weren't, but it shut him up because what Galbraith had said he'd do to both of them if Matron came and found he wasn't there (cut off very small – unnoticeable to Matron – bits of them with his penknife to feed to his rat was the latest) had cowed them into perfect loyalty: Clarkson had bored (and frightened) Simon the whole term with his ruminations about what bits would hurt most and how long it would take them to die. So they both lay and waited a bit and Simon had just begun to have a lovely think about what he'd do the moment he got home – undo the crane he'd made with his Meccano last hols and start on the swing bridge like Dawson said he'd made (he'd let Polly help him undo the crane but not actually make the bridge), chocolate cake for tea with walnuts and crystallised violets on it and Mum would see to it that he got a walnut with his slice . . .

'You know the other thing Galbraith said?'

'What?'

'He said he's got an aunt who's a witch. And he could get her to cast a spell on us if we sneak on him. Do you think she could? I mean, could she actually turn us into something? I mean, look at *Macbeth* . . .' They were going to do *Macbeth* as the play next term so everyone had been reading it in English. There was a pause while they both contemplated this possibility – much more frightening, Simon thought, than cutting bits off them which would be bound to show in the end. Then Clarkson said nervously, 'What would you most like *not* to be turned into?'

'An owl,' said Simon promptly, 'because then I'd have Galbraith watching me every night.' Then as Clarkson let out a hoot of laughter, he added, 'Look out. You're beginning to sound like one!' This reduced Clarkson to helpless giggles and Simon had to get up and hit him quite a lot with his pillow to get him to shut up. After Clarkson had pleaded *pax* a good many times, Simon let him go on condition that he shut up for the night. He wouldn't have, but they heard Galbraith coming back up the drainpipe and at once both feigned sleep. Simon, however, lay awake for hours, wondering about Galbraith's aunt . . .

In a much larger dormitory at the other end of the house, Teddy Cazalet lay on his back praying, 'Please, God, let her *not* come to the station to meet me. But if she does come, at least let her not kiss me in front of everyone. At least let her not do that. And don't let her be wearing that awful silly hat she wore for Sports' Day. Please, God. Best of all – just let her not come.'

∞ ∞ ∞

'Comfy?'

'Mm.' She felt his moustache feeling for her face in the dark. He made no attempt to kiss her mouth, but to be on the safe side she added, 'Awfully sleepy. Delicious dinner Mary gave us, didn't she? Didn't she look lovely?'

'She looked all right. Play was a bit wordy, I thought.'

'Interesting, though.'

'Oh, yes. He's a clever chap, Shaw. Mark you, I don't agree with him. If he had his way, we'd probably all be murdered in our beds.'

She turned on her side. 'Darling, I warn you, I'm off.' But after a moment she said, 'You haven't forgotten about Bracken fetching Teddy? I mean, I'll go, of course, but it does help to have Bracken with the trunk.'

'Better if you don't. I told Hugh we'd pick up Simon as well and that means twice the clobber.'

'Teddy'll be frightfully disappointed if I don't meet him. I always do.'

'He'll be all right.' He put his arm round her, stroking the tender skin on her shoulder.

'Eddie – I *am* tired – truly.'

'Course you are.' He gave her shoulder a little pat and turned the other way. He shut his eyes and fell asleep almost at once, but relief, and guilt at her relief, kept Villy awake for some time.

∞ ∞ ∞

Miss Milliment sat in bed in her small back room in Stoke Newington. She wore a huge bolster-shaped nightdress of flannel and over it one of her father's pyjama jackets. She was sipping her usual glass of hot water, made by boiling a saucepan on the small gas ring her landlady had grudgingly allowed her to install for this purpose only, and reading Tennyson. The forty-watt bulb that hung from the ceiling was shadeless to afford her more light. Her hair hung in two oyster-shell coloured plaits each side of her soft meandering chins. Every now and then she had to remove her glasses to wipe the mist from them: Tennyson and the hot water combined to occlude. It was years since she had read the Laureate, as she still thought of him, but he had cropped up in her mind in the middle of supper. Why had stuffed sheep's heart, or, come to that, stewed apples and custard, made her think of Tennyson? Of course, it hadn't been the food, it had been the eating alone in Mrs Timpson's front room, a room so hushed and swathed against use that chewing and swallowing, even breathing the dead-cabbage air, seemed daringly disruptive. She ate there every evening, a relentless rota of menus that recurred every two weeks, but this evening, as she sought to cheer herself with thoughts of tomorrow's lunch at Lansdowne Road, the thought that next week there would be no Friday lunch, nor for six weeks after that, had assailed her. Panic – as sudden and painful as wind on the heart, from which she also suffered – occurred, and quickly, before it could take hold, she smothered it. Those summer holidays when she had been Polly's age – at Hastings, had it been? (Nostalgia was comforting, but slippery as an old eiderdown.) Or was it Broadstairs? What she remembered was a walled garden and going into a fruit cage with Jack and eating raspberries, only she had not eaten many because there was a bird trapped in the cage and she had spent most of the time trying to shoo it out . . . but what had the fruit cage to do with Tennyson? Oh, yes, she had left the door of the cage open for the bird and when this was discovered her brother – he was five years older and concise – had told them that it had been she. The punishment had been learning a hundred lines of *Idylls of the King* by heart. It had been the first time that she had realised the amazing gap between people and the results. Tennyson had been a revelation, the punishment had been

Jack's betrayal. Trying not to recall the miseries that Jack had caused her – he would remain a benignly neutral, even amiable, companion for weeks and then, without warning, abandon her – she wondered why betrayals seemed to stick more in the memory than revelations. Because, after all, she had Tennyson still – and Jack was dead. How she had adored him! It was for him that she had prayed to become prettier – 'Or pretty at all, God, as a matter of fact.' It was for him that she slowed down her wits, knowing somehow from the earliest moment that he could not bear to be second. But it was years before she had realised that he was actually ashamed of her, did not want her to be evident when his friends came to the vicarage and excluded her from any outside social arrangements that he made.

The first time that she heard herself described as no oil painting had been when she was twelve, trapped reading up an apple tree while her brother and his friend Rodney strolled beneath. She had started by thinking it would be a lark to hide from them, but almost at once it would have been unbearable not to stay hidden. They had not said much, but they had laughed – Jack had laughed, until Rodney made some remark about her face being shaped like a pear and Jack had said, 'She can't *help* it. She's quite a good sort, really, it just means that nobody will marry her.' Why was she going back over this painful wasteland? It was the sort of behaviour that she would advise any of the young people who had been in her charge against. It was, she supposed, because (when she was tired, of course) she could not help wondering (sometimes) whether there had been any other way for her – anything *she* could have done that might have changed her life. She had begged Papa to send her to university, for instance, but what money that was left after sending Jack had been kept for setting him up in some profession. So she had had to abandon any idea of a serious teaching career. Then, when Aunt May had died, naturally she had had to stay at home to look after Papa. This, of course, was years after she had lost Eustace, one of Papa's curates who had enlisted and died an army chaplain in the Transvaal. She had never understood how he had got accepted into the Army since he was even more short-sighted than herself. But he had, and Papa had refused to allow an engagement between them on the grounds that Eustace was to

54

be absent for an unknown amount of time. It would not make any difference, she had promised Eustace, but, of course, in the end it had: she was not sent his 'things', she had not even the dignity of having been engaged; no ring – just a few letters and a lock of his hair, sandy red . . . The letters had aged, the ink turning a rusty brown on the thin, yellowing paper, but the lock of hair had remained exactly the same sandy red colour, unnaturally bright. Papa had been actually *glad* that Eustace had died, remarking, as though conferring a great accolade, that he would not have liked to share her with anybody. Well, he had been spared that difficulty, had had her to himself well into his late eighties when he became hypochondriac, tyrannical and intermittently senile. Kind friends had described his death as a merciful release, but from her point of view, the mercy came rather late. His pension had died with him, and Eleanor Milliment had discovered freedom a good many years after it could have much practical value to her. Advised by her father's lawyer, she sold the contents of the cottage since many friends of Papa's – who were *most* kind – pointed out to her that she could not possibly afford to live in it. His collections of stamps and butterflies proved unexpectedly valuable, but some watercolours – of northern Italy by Edward Lear – fetched little more than the price of their frames.

Mr Snodgrass had been, he said, deeply disappointed that the sale had realised so little. However, by the time he and other kind advisors had been paid, the remaining capital was invested to bring her in an income of nearly sixty pounds a year which old Brigadier Harcourt-Skeynes had pointed out – unanswerably – was far better than a smack in the eye with a wet fish. So many things, she had thought, would be better than that, that it was hard to see it as a helpful remark, but the Brigadier was famous for his sense of humour. 'And you, Eleanor, are famous for rambling and going to bed too late,' she said aloud. She knew nobody now left who used her Christian name and so she used it whenever she needed admonishing. She must pay a visit along the passage, say her prayers and then it would be lights out.

∞ ∞ ∞

Sybil and Hugh sat in their candlelit dining room eating cold supper (slices of pork pie obtained from Bellamy's in the Earl's Court Road and a salad of lettuce, tomato and beetroot, with a bottle of hock – Sybil preferred white wine). The room, in the basement, was dark, and rather hot due to the kitchen range next door; it was also rather small for the quantity of furniture it contained – a two-pedestal oval table, eight Hepplewhite chairs and a long, narrow, serpentine sideboard. In spite of the french windows left ajar for air, the candle flames were motionless.

'Well, if he's right, I suppose we will have to.'

'He couldn't actually *hear* a second heart.'

'But we have to consider the possibility. The likelihood,' he corrected himself.

'Darling, you know I don't *want* to move – terrible upheaval – anyway, you know I love this house.' Now that he seemed to be accepting the idea of a move at last she was anxious that he should think she wanted it as little as he.

'I think it will be rather exciting.'

This duel of consideration for one another that they had conducted for the last sixteen years involved shifting the truth about between them or withholding it altogether and was called good manners or affection, supposed to smooth the humdrum or prickly path of everyday married life. Its tyranny was apparent to neither. Hugh pushed his plate away: he longed to smoke.

'Do smoke, darling.'

'Sure you don't mind?'

She shook her head. 'I'll have some gooseberries, though.'

When he had fetched them for her and lit his Gold Flake, she said, 'Of course, one solution would be to send Polly to boarding school.'

He turned sharply to look at her, and his head stabbed. 'No – I don't think that's a good idea,' he said at last, with exaggerated mildness and as though he had given a trivial point his courteous consideration. To forestall any argument he added, 'I've wanted a study for years. It will give me something interesting to do with my summer evenings while you're in the country.'

'I want to choose with you!'

'Of course. I'll only sound out the ground. Are we going to have coffee?'

'If you would like some?'

'Only if you would . . .'

In the end they decided against coffee in favour of bed. While Hugh locked the doors Sybil lumbered up the stairs carrying her shoes in one hand. Her feet had swollen so much that she was constantly taking off shoes and then being unable to put them on again.

'Will you have a look at Polly, darling? I really can't face more stairs.'

Polly lay on her side facing the door, which was ajar. Her bedside table had been moved so that without turning she would be able to see the tall candlesticks and pottery plate that was propped on it against her bedside lamp. There was a little smear of toothpaste at the side of her mouth. Pompey lay in the crook of her drawn-up knees. He heard Hugh (or noticed the extra light from the opened door), opened his eyes and then shut them at once, as though he'd never seen anyone so boring before in his life.

∞ ∞ ∞

Phyllis dreamed: she dreamed that she was standing, wearing ever such a lovely velvet gown and a ruby necklace, but she knew she wasn't going to the ball or anything because they were going to cut off her head, which wasn't fair, really, because all she'd done was say how nice he looked in his pyjamas, but His Majesty said it was adult something and she must die. She had never really liked Charles Laughton, he was nothing like such a gentleman as the Duke of Windsor and just because she was wearing Merle Oberon's clothes didn't mean she was her. It was all a terrible mistake, but when she tried to tell them, she found she couldn't speak at all – she was screaming inside and no words came out and someone was pushing her and if she didn't manage to scream they would do it and someone was pushing her on . . .

'Phyl! Wake *up*!'

'Oh! Oh, I *haven't half* had a nightmare!'

But Edna didn't want to hear about it. 'You woke me up. You always do that when you have cheese last thing,' and she got back into her bed and pulled the bedclothes over her.

Having said she was ever so sorry (even the sound of her own voice was reassuring), Phyllis lay with her eyes open, just glad to be her and not wanting to go to sleep in case she changed again into someone else. She knew she should have had the ham and tongue paste on her bread instead of the cheese. She thought about the green cotton with roses on it; it would be nice with a white piqué and white gloves to match; she turned over on her side and in no time she was lying back on one of those basket chairs they had for the garden, and Mr Cazalet was bending over her with a cocktail and saying, 'You look so pretty, Phyllis, in green. Has anyone ever told you that?' But they never had, because Ted never said anything like that . . . Mr Cazalet had a moustache exactly like Melvyn Douglas, which must feel funny when he kissed people but it was the kind of thing one could get used to – give her half a chance, and she *would* . . . get used . . .

∞ ∞ ∞

Zoë Cazalet adored the Gargoyle Club – *adored* it. She made Rupert take her on her birthday, at the end of every term, if Rupert sold a picture, on their wedding anniversary, and *always* before she was going to be stuck in the country for weeks with the children like now. She loved dressing up, she had two Gargoyle dresses, both backless, one black and one white, and with either she wore her bright green dancing shoes and long dangling white paste earrings that anyone might think were diamonds. She loved going to Soho at night, looking at all the tarts eyeing Rupert and the restaurants lit up with taxis arriving all the time, and then diving down the narrow side road off Dean Street and going up in the stern little lift and hearing the band the moment the doors opened – straight into the bar, with the Matisse drawings; she didn't think they were frightfully *good*, though, which shocked Rupert, who said they were. They would have a drink at the bar, Gin and It. There would always be one or two handsome, clever-looking men drinking alone and she enjoyed the experienced way in which they looked at her; they knew at a glance she was worth something. Then a waiter would tell them their table was ready, and they'd take a second drink with them into the large room whose walls were lined with little panes of mirror glass. The leader of the band always smiled at her and greeted her as though they went every night, which, of course, they didn't – couldn't – by a long chalk. They always chose their dinner and danced until the first course was served and the band played 'The Lady is a Tramp' because they knew she loved it. When she'd married him, Rupert hadn't been much of a dancer, but he'd got good enough – at a quickstep, anyway – for it to be fun.

Now the evening was nearly over; they were sitting with cups of black coffee and Rupert was asking her if she'd like some brandy. She shook her head. 'Two brandies.' He caught her eye. 'You'll change your mind.'

'How do you know?'

'You always do.'

There was a pause; then she said distantly, 'I don't like being known for always doing things.'

Damn! he thought. She was set to sulk: only two moves away from flying off the handle.

'Sweetie! You are full of surprises, but after three years, you must expect me to know some things about you. Zoë!' He took her hand: it lay passively in his. After a moment, he picked it up and kissed it. She pretended to ignore this, but he knew it pleased her.

'I tell you what it *is*,' she said, as though they were ending a long discussion on the subject. 'If you know everything about me, you won't love me any more.'

'What on earth makes you think that?'

'That's how men are.' She put her elbow on the table, propping her chin up with her hands, and gazed mournfully at him. 'I mean, one day I'll be old and fat and my hair will be grey and I'll have nothing new to say to you and you'll be completely bored.'

'Zoë – really—'

'Double chins, I'll probably have two or three of those.'

The waiter brought their brandies. Rupert picked his up and cupped it in his hands, swirling it gently so that the fumes reached him.

'I don't just love you for your appearance,' he said.

'Don't you?'

'Of course not.' He saw tears in her amazing eyes and his

heart lurched. 'Darling girl, of course not.' Saying it again, he believed it. 'Let's dance.'

Driving home – all the way to Brook Green – he saw that she had fallen asleep, and drove carefully, not to wake her. 'I'll carry her up to bed,' he thought, 'and then I'll be able to have a quick look at the children and she won't know.'

He left her in the car while he went to open the front door, could see lights on in the night nursery as he walked up the garden path and his heart sank. When he went back to the car to fetch her, she had woken.

'Help me, Rupert, I feel quite woozy.'

'I've got you.' He picked her up and carried her – into the house, and up the stairs to the first floor and their bedroom. As he tried to lay her on their bed, her arms tightened round his neck. 'I love you terribly.'

'I love you.' He disengaged her arms and stood up. 'See how fast you can get into bed. I'll be back in a minute.' And he escaped, shutting the door before she could reply.

He ran up the stairs, two at a time, and Ellen met him on the landing.

'What is it, Ellen? Is it Nev?'

'It didn't start with him. Clary had a bad dream and came in to me and that woke him and then he had one of his turns.'

He followed her into the room in which she slept with Neville. He was sitting bolt upright with his pyjama jacket unbuttoned trying to breathe and succeeding painfully each time at what seemed like the last possible moment. The room reeked of Friar's Balsam and menthol.

Rupert went and sat on his bed. 'Hallo, Nev.'

Neville inclined his head. His hair stood in tufts on his head like grass. He battled with another interminable wheezing gasp, and said, 'Air – won't go in.' There was another pause and he added in a dignified manner, ''Stremely difficult.' His eyes were bright with fear.

'I bet it is. Like a story?'

He nodded and was again racked; Rupert wanted to take him in his arms but that wouldn't help the poor little devil.

'Right, remember the rules? Every time I stop, you have to breathe. Once upon a time there was a wicked witch and the only person she loved in the world was a small, black and green – ' he stopped and somehow they both got through the hiatus ' – dinosaur called Staggerflanks. Staggerflanks slept in a dinosaur basket that was made of holly and thistles because he liked rubbing his back against the prickles. He had snails and porridge for breakfast, beetles and rice pudding for lunch and – ' It was, surely a little better? ' – grass snakes and jelly for supper.' He'd got him now; he was listening more than he was afraid. 'On his birthday, when he was a mere six feet long . . .'

Twenty minutes later he stopped. Neville, still wheezing a bit but breathing regularly, had dropped off. Rupert covered him, then bent to kiss his warm, sweaty forehead. Asleep, he looked startlingly like Isobel – the same bumpy forehead with fine blue veins at the sides, the same sharply defined mouth . . . He put his hand over his eyes as his last picture of her recurred: lying in their bed exhausted from her thirty-hour labour, trying to smile at him and bleeding to death. Afterwards he had tried to hold her, but she had become a thing – a dead weight in his arms, uncomforting and gone.

'You got him off nicely.' Ellen was warming some milk in a pan on the landing. She wore her bulky plaid dressing gown and her hair in a yellowish white pigtail down her back.

'I don't know what we'd do without you.'

'You don't have to do without me, Mr Rupert.'

'Is that for Clary?'

'I must settle her. She's a naughty girl. If I've told her once I've told her a dozen times she can come in to me quietly – there's no call to wake him up and frighten the poor little mite with her carry-on. You're not the only pebble on the beach, I told her, but she will work herself up. Still, that's life, isn't it?' she finished, pouring the milk into a mug with ducks on it. It was what she always said about anything difficult or bad.

'I'll take it in to her. You get to bed. Get your beauty sleep.'

'Right, then, I'll say good night.'

He took the mug and went into the children's room. A night light was burning by Clary's bed. Clary was sitting hunched with her arms round her knees.

'Ellen's made you some nice hot milk,' he said.

Without taking it, she said, 'You've been ages in there. What were you doing?'

'Telling him a story. Helping him to breathe.'

'He's stupid. Anyone can breathe.'

'People with asthma find it very difficult to breathe. You know that Clary, don't be unkind.'

'I'm not. It's not my fault I had a nightmare.'

'Of course it isn't. Drink your milk.'

'So that you can go downstairs and leave me. Anyway, I don't like hot milk – it gets horrible skin.'

'Drink it up to please Ellen.'

'I don't want to please Ellen, she doesn't like me.'

'Clary, don't be silly. Of course she does.'

'The person it is *knows* whether people like them or not. Nobody likes me enough. *You* don't like me.'

'That's nonsense. I love you.'

'You said I was unkind and you said I was silly.'

She was glaring at him; he saw the sticky marks of tears on her round, freckled face, and said more gently, 'I can still love you. Nobody is perfect.'

But instantly, and not looking at him, she muttered, 'You're perfect. I find you perfect.' Her voice trembled and the milk slopped.

He picked the skin off the milk and ate it. 'There. That shows you. I don't like milk skin either.'

'Daddy, I love you so much!' She took a deep breath and drank all the milk down. 'I love you as much as all the men in the world put together. I wish you were the King.'

'Why do you wish that?'

'Because then you'd be home all day. Kings are.'

'Well, the holidays start tomorrow so I will be. Now, I'm going to tuck you up.'

She lay back, he kissed her, and she smiled for the first time. She took his hand and laid it against her cheek. Then she said, 'But not the night times. I don't be with you then.'

'But every day,' he said, wanting to end on a lighter note. 'Good night, sleep tight.'

'Mind the bugs don't bite,' she finished. 'Daddy! could I have a cat?'

'We'll talk about that in the morning.'

As he shut the door, she said, 'Polly has one.'

'Good night,' he said with bracing firmness.

'Good night, darling Dad,' she answered in quite a chirpy voice.

So that, he thought, as he made his way downstairs, was that – for the moment, at least. But as he reached his own bedroom door – still shut – he suddenly felt incredibly tired. She couldn't have a cat because of Nev's asthma, and that would turn out to be just one more thing that she held against him. He opened the bedroom door praying that Zoë would be asleep.

She wasn't, of course. She was sitting up in bed, her bedjacket on her shoulders, doing nothing, waiting for him. He fumbled with his tie and had dropped it on top of his chest of drawers before she said, 'You've been a long time.' Her voice had the controlled quality that he had learned to dread.

'Clary had a nightmare and woke Nev up and he had a rather bad attack. I've been getting him to sleep.'

He put his jacket on the back of a chair and sat on it to take off his shoes.

'You know, I've been thinking,' she said, in a voice false with consideration. 'Don't you think Ellen is getting a bit past it?'

'Past what?'

'Coping with the children. I mean – I know they're not *easy* children, but she is supposed to be their nurse, after all.'

'She *is* their nurse, and a jolly good one. She does everything for them.'

'Not *everything*, darling. I mean, if she did everything you wouldn't have had to get Neville to sleep, would you? Be reasonable.'

'Zoë, I'm tired, I don't feel like wrangling about Ellen.'

'I'm not wrangling. I'm just pointing out that if you can't ever have a single evening to yourself – and whenever we go out something like this always seems mysteriously to happen – she can't be as marvellously competent as you seem to think!'

'I've told you, I really don't want to talk about this now – in the middle of the night. We're both tired—'

'Speak for yourself!'

'All right, then. I'm tired—'

But it was too late: she was hell bent on a scene. He tried silence, she simply repeated that perhaps he had never thought what it was like for *her* – never feeling she had him to herself, not for a single minute. He argued and she sulked. He shouted at her and she burst into tears, sobbing until he couldn't bear it and had to take her in his arms and soothe, and apologise, until, her green eyes swimming, she cried that he had no idea how much she loved him and held up her mouth – free now of the scarlet lipstick he never liked – to be kissed. 'Oh, darling Rupert! Oh!' and recognising her desire he felt his own, and kissed her and then couldn't stop. Even after three years of marriage to her he was in awe of her beauty and paid tribute by pushing aside what else she was. She was very young, he would think again and again at the many times like this one: she would grow up, and he would refuse to consider what that might mean. It was only after he had made love to her, when she was tender and affectionate and altogether adorable, that he could say, 'You're a selfish little thing, you know,' or, 'You're an irresponsible child. Life isn't all beer and skittles.' And she would look at him obediently and answer contritely, 'I know I am. I know it isn't.' It was four o'clock when she turned on her side and he was free to sleep.

HOME PLACE
1937

Rachel Cazalet always woke early, but in summer, in the country, she woke with the dawn chorus. Then, in the silence that followed, she drank a cup of tea from the Thermos by her bed, ate a Marie biscuit, read another chapter of *Sparkenbroke*, which was all rather intense, she thought, though well written, and then, as the bright grey light began to fill the room (she slept with her curtains undrawn to get the maximum fresh air) making the light from her bedside seem a dirty yellow – almost squalid – she switched it off, got out of bed, put on her woolly dressing gown and her shapeless slippers (extraordinary the way in which they ended up looking the shape of broad beans) and crept along the wide silent passages and down three steps to the bathroom. This room, facing north, had walls in tongue-and-groove pitch pine painted a dark green. It was always, even in summer, as cold as a larder, and it looked like a privileged horse's loose box. The bath standing on its cast-iron lion's feet had a viridian-coloured stain from water that dripped from ancient brass and china taps whose washers were never quite right. She ran a bath, placed the cork mat in position, and bolted the door. The mat had warped so that it wobbled when she stood on it; still, it was to be the children's bathroom and that wasn't the kind of thing they'd mind. The Duchy said it was still a perfectly good mat. The Duchy did not believe that baths were meant to be pleasant: the water should be tepid, 'Much better for you, darling,' the soap was Lifebuoy, just as the lavatory paper was Izal, 'More hygienic, darling.' At thirty-eight Rachel felt that she could have her bath unsuitably hot, and use a cake of Pears' transparent soap that she kept in her sponge bag. It was the grandchildren who bore the brunt of health and hygiene. It was lovely that they were all coming; it meant that there was masses to do. She adored her three brothers equally, but for different reasons – Hugh because he had been knocked up in the war and was so brave and uncomplaining about it, Edward because he was so wonderfully good-looking, like the Brig when he was young, she thought, and Rupert because he was a marvellous painter, and because he'd had such a tragic time when Isobel died, and because he was such a wonderful father, and sweet to Zoë who was . . . very *young* and chiefly because he made her laugh so much. But she loved them all equally, of course, just as – and also of course – she didn't have a favourite with the children who were growing up so fast. She had loved them most when they were babies, but they were nice as children, and often said the most killing things. And she got on well with her sisters-in-law, except, perhaps, she didn't feel she knew Zoë very well yet. It must be difficult for her coming late into such a large, close-knit family with all its customs and traditions and jokes that needed to be explained to her. She resolved to be particularly kind to Zoë – and also to Clary, who was turning into rather a dumpling, poor darling, although she had lovely eyes.

By now she had put on her suspenders, her camisole, her petticoat, her lock-knit knickers and coffee-coloured openwork worsted brown stockings and her brown brogues that Tonbridge polished until they were like treacle toffee. She decided on the blue jersey suit today (blue was far and away her favourite colour) with her new Macclesfield silk shirt – blue with a darker blue stripe. She brushed out her hair and wound it into a loose bun which she pinned to the back of her head without looking in the glass. She strapped on the gold watch the Brig had given her when she was twenty-one, and pinned the garnet brooch that S had given her for a birthday, soon after they had met. She wore it every day – used no other jewellery. Eventually, she took a reluctant peep into the mirror. She had fine skin, eyes that were sharp with intelligence and humour; in fact, her nice, but not remarkable, face – a little like a pallid chimpanzee, she sometimes said – was utterly unselfconscious and entirely without vanity. She tucked a small white handkerchief into the gold chain of her wrist-watch, picked up the lists she had accumulated throughout the previous day and went down to breakfast.

The house had originally been a small farmhouse, built towards the end of the seventeenth century in the typical Sussex manner, its front timber and plaster up to the first floor, which was faced with rose-coloured overlapping tiles. All that remained of it were two small rooms on the ground floor, between which was a steep little staircase that faced the front door that led to three bedrooms linked by two closets. At some time, its owner had been a Mr Home, and it was known simply as Home's Place. Somewhere in the 1800s this cottage had been transformed into a gentleman's house. Two large wings had been built on either side of it to form three parts of a square, and here honey-coloured stone had been used with large sash windows and roofed with smooth blue slate. One wing added large dining and drawing rooms, and a third room whose purposes had varied – it was currently used for billiards; the other comprised kitchen, servants' hall, scullery, pantry, larders, and wine cellar. This addition also provided eight more bedrooms on the first floor. The Victorians completed the north side of the square with a series of small dark rooms, which were used for servants' quarters, a boot room, a gun room, a room for the vast and noisy boiler, an extra bathroom and a WC below, and nurseries above with the bathroom already mentioned. The result of these various architectural aspirations was a rambling muddle built round a hall with a staircase that led to an open gallery from which the bedrooms could be reached. This open well, with its ceiling just short of the roof, was lit from two glass domes that leaked freakishly in bad weather causing buckets and dogs' bowls to be placed strategically. It was cold in summer and icy the rest of the year. The house was heated by log and coal fires in the ground-floor rooms: some of the bedrooms had fireplaces, but the Duchy regarded them as unnecessary except for an invalid. There were two bathrooms, one for the women and children on the first floor, one for the men (and servants once a week) on the ground. The servants had their own WC; the rest of the household shared the two that adjoined the bathrooms. Hot water for bedrooms was drawn from the housemaids' sink on the first floor and carried to rooms in steaming brass cans every morning.

Breakfast was in the small parlour in the cottage part of the house. The Duchy was Victorian about her drawing and dining rooms, using the latter only for dinner and the former not at all, unless there was company. Rachel's parents sat now at the gate-legged table on which the Duchy was making tea from the kettle that boiled over a spirit lamp. William Cazalet sat with a plate of eggs and bacon and the *Morning Post* propped up against the marmalade. He was dressed in riding clothes that included a lemon-coloured waistcoat and a wide dark silk tie with a pearl pin in it. He read his paper with a monocle screwing up the other eye so that his bushy white brow almost touched his ruddy cheekbone. The Duchy, dressed much as her daughter but with a mother-of-pearl and sapphire cross slung on a chain over her silk blouse, filled the silver teapot and received her daughter's kiss, emanating a little draught of violets.

'Good morning, darling. I'm afraid they are all going to have a very hot day for their journey.'

Rachel dropped a kiss on the top of her father's head and sat in her place, where she saw at once that there was a letter from S.

'Ring for some more toast, would you?'

'Iniquitous!' William growled. He did not say what was iniquitous, and neither his wife nor his daughter asked him, knowing very well that if they did, he would tell them not to worry their pretty little heads about *that*. He treated his newspaper as a recalcitrant colleague with whom he could always (fortunately) have the last word.

Rachel accepted her cup of tea, decided to enjoy her letter later, and put it in her pocket. When Eileen, their parlourmaid in London, arrived with the toast, the Duchy said, 'Eileen, would you tell Tonbridge that I'll want him at ten to go to Battle and that I'll see Mrs Cripps in half an hour?'

'Very good, m'm.'

'Duchy dear, wouldn't you like me to do Battle for you?'

The Duchy looked up from scraping a very little butter on her toast. 'No, thank you, darling. I want to speak to Crowhurst about his lamb. And I have to go to Till's: I need a new trug and secateurs. I'll leave the bedrooms to you. Did you make a plan?'

Rachel picked up her list. 'I thought Hugh and Sybil in the Blue Room, Edward and Villy in the Paeony Room. Zoë and Rupert in the Indian Room, Nanny and Lydia in the night nursery, the two boys in the old day nursery, Louise and Polly in the Pink Room, and Ellen and Neville in the back spare . . .'

The Duchy thought for a moment, and then said, 'Clarissa?'

'Oh, Lord! We'll have to put a camp bed in the Pink Room for her.'

'I think she'd like that. She'll want to be with the older girls. Will, shall I tell Tonbridge about the station?'

'You tell him, Kitty m'dear. I've got a meeting with Sampson.'

'I think we'll have lunch early today, so that the maids will have time to clear it and lay tea in the hall. Will that suit you?'

'Anything you say.' He got to his feet and tramped off to his study to light his pipe and finish his paper.

'What will he do when he's finished all the building here?'

The Duchy looked at her daughter and answered simply, 'He'll never finish. There'll always be something. If you've time, you might pick the raspberries, but don't overdo it.'

'Don't *you*.'

But with seventeen people coming to stay, there *was* a great deal to do. The Duchy spent a businesslike half hour with Mrs Cripps. She sat in the chair pulled out for her at the large, scrubbed kitchen table, while Mrs Cripps, arms folded, leant her bulk against the range. While the menus for the weekend were being arranged, Billy, the gardener's boy, arrived with two large trugs filled with peas, broad beans and Cos lettuces. He set them down on the scullery floor, and then stood speechless staring at Mrs Cripps and the Duchy.

'Excuse me, m'm. What do you want, then, Billy?'

'Mr McAlpine said to bring back the trugs for the potatoes.' He spoke in a whisper; his voice was breaking, which embarrassed him. He had also lately taken to staring at ladies.

'Dottie!' Mrs Cripps used her most refined shout. When Madam wasn't around, she screeched. 'Dottie! Where is that girl?'

'She's out the back.' This meant the lavatory, as Mrs Cripps well knew.

'Excuse me, m'm,' she said again, and made for the scullery.

When she had emptied the trugs and thrust them at Billy with instructions to bring back tomatoes with the potatoes, she returned to the business of meals. The Duchy inspected the remains of a boiling fowl that Mrs Cripps did not think could be stretched into rissoles for lunch, but Madam said that with an extra egg and more breadcrumbs it could be made to do. They fought their regular battle over a cheese soufflé. Mrs Cripps, who had got her place as a plain cook, had, none the less, recently mastered the art of making soufflés and liked to make them on any serious occasion. The Duchy disapproved of cooked cheese at night. In the end, they compromised on a chocolate soufflé for pudding as they would only be nine at night in the dining room. 'It will be eleven for luncheon tomorrow, as two of the children will be with us, and that will mean eight in the hall.'

And ten in the kitchen, thought Mrs Cripps.

'And the salmon for tonight? Is that standing up to this weather?' (William had been given a salmon by one of his friends at the Club.)

'It'll have to be cold, m'm. I'm poaching it this morning, to be on the safe side.'

'That will be very good.'

'And I've put cucumbers on the list, m'm. McAlpine says ours aren't ready.'

'How tiresome! Well, Mrs Cripps, I mustn't keep you: I know you have a great deal to do. I'm sure everything will be quite satisfactory.'

And she went, leaving Mrs Cripps to make four pounds of pastry, poach the salmon, get two huge rice puddings into the oven, mix a Madeira cake and a batch of flapjacks and strip and mince the chicken for the rissoles. Dottie, who emerged as soon as she heard the Duchy leave, was scolded and set to shelling peas, scraping ten pounds of potatoes and cleaning out the vast churn that would hold the eighteen pints of fresh milk to be delivered from the neighbouring farm. 'And mind you scald it when you've cleaned it out or we'll have the milk turning on us.'

Upstairs, the housemaids, Bertha and Peggy, were making up the beds – the two four-posters for Mr and Mrs Hugh and Edward, the smaller double for Mr and Mrs Rupert, the five little iron beds with thin, sinewy mattresses for the older children, the nurses' beds, the large cot for Neville, and the camp bed for Lydia. Rachel came upon them in the Pink Room and told them that another camp bed would be needed for Miss Clarissa. She then doled out the requisite number of bath and hand towels for these rooms, and settled the question of how many chamber pots would be required. 'I think two for each of the children's dormitories, and one for each of the other rooms. Have we enough?' she added with a smile.

'Only if we use the one that Madam doesn't like.'

'You can put that in Mr Rupert's room. Don't give it to the children, Bertha.'

The day nursery and the Pink Room had linoleum on the floor, and gingham curtains made by the Duchy on her ancient Singer on rainy afternoons. The furniture was white painted deal, the light was a single ceiling bulb with a white glass shade. They were children's rooms. Those of her brothers and sisters-in-law were better appointed. Here were squares of hair-cord carpet with a stained and polished wood surround, and in the Paeony Room, a Turkey carpet with the same. The furniture was mahogany; there were dressing-tables with wing mirrors and white crocheted cloths and marble washstand tables with china pitchers and bowls to match. The Blue Room had a *chaise-longue* – Rachel had put Hugh and Sybil there so that Sybil could put her feet up if she felt inclined. The thought of a new baby was tremendously exciting. Really, she adored babies, particularly when they were new. She loved the underwater movements of their hands: the fastidious pursing of their cherry pink mouths, their slaty eyes that tried to see you, and then became aloof. They were darlings, all of them. Rachel was Honorary Secretary of an institution called the Babies' Hotel that cared for temporarily or chronically unwanted babies up to the age of five. If parents, mainly musical or theatrical, went on tour, they could leave their baby there and the payment was modest. The babies who simply turned up, wrapped in blankets or sometimes newspaper in a cardboard box, were looked after free: the hotel was a charitable organisation with a full-time sister and matron. To provide staff and further augment their slender finances, they trained young girls to become children's nurses. She loved the work and felt it to be useful, the thing she wanted to do more than anything else in the world, and, as she would never have children of her own, it gave her access to a steady stream of babies, all in need of love and attention. Part of her work was to help the unwanted babies to be adopted, and it was awful to watch how, as they got older, their chances went down. It was sometimes very sad.

She was going through the grown-ups' rooms, looking to see that the drawers had clean lining paper, that the quilted biscuit boxes by the bedside table contained Marie biscuits, that the bottles of Malvern water were full, that the hanging cupboards had a fair number of coat-hangers – all things that, when she returned from Battle, she could tell the Duchy had been done and thus save her from fussing. The biscuits had become quite silent, crumbly and unappetising. She collected the boxes and took them down to the pantry to be refilled.

Mrs Cripps, balancing a large pie dish on the flat of her left hand, was slashing surplus pastry from the edges with a black knife. When Rachel gave her the message for Eileen, she said that the old biscuits would do for the girls' middle mornings. The kitchen was very hot. Mrs Cripps's remarkable complexion – a greenish yellow – was shiny with sweat, her straight greasy black hair was escaping in strands from outsize kirby-grips and the way in which she squinted at the pie down her long pointed nose made her look more like an overblown witch than usual. Pastry lay in moony slabs on the floured table, but her sausage-coloured fingers were not white beyond the knuckles: she had what was known as a very light hand. Seeing the pie reminded Rachel of the raspberries and she asked for a container to put them in.

'The fruit basket is in the larder, miss. I've sent Dottie out for some parsley.' She meant that she did not want to fetch the basket, but knew that Miss Rachel should not have to.

'I'll get it,' Rachel said at once, as Mrs Cripps knew she would.

The larder was cool and rather dark with a window covered with fine zinc mesh, in front of which hung two heavily infested fly papers. Food in every stage of its life lay on the long marble slab, the remains of a joint under a cage made of muslin, pieces of rice puddings and blancmange on kitchen plates, junket setting in a cut-glass bowl, old, crazed, discoloured jugs filled with gravy and stock, stewed prunes in a pudding basin and, in the coldest place beneath the window, the huge, silvery salmon, its eye torpid from recent poaching, lay like a grounded zeppelin. The fruit basket was on the slate floor, the paper that lined it red and magenta with juice.

As she opened the front door and stepped into what had been the old cottage garden she was assailed by the heat, by the sound of bees and the motor mower, by honeysuckle and lavender and the nameless old-fashioned climbing rose of ivory peach colour that was thickly wreathed round the porch. The Duchy's rockery, her latest pride and joy, was blazing with little mats and cushions and sparks of flowers. She turned right and followed the path round the house. On the west side was a steep bank that ended in the tennis court that McAlpine was mowing. He wore his straw hat with a black band, trousers as round as drainpipes, and, in spite of the heat, his jacket. This was because he was in view of the house; he took it off in the vegetable garden. He saw her and stopped, in case she wanted to say anything to him. 'Lovely day,' she called and he touched his forehead in acknowledgement. Lovely for some, he thought. He was fond of lawns, but a tennis court got messed up in no time with them all trampling about on it. He couldn't trust Billy with the mower, she seized up as soon as look at him, but was worrying about his leeks and grudged the time plodding up and down emptying grass clippings into his barrow. He approved of Miss Rachel, however, and did not mind her picking his raspberries as he saw from her basket she was about to do. She never left the cage open, like some he could mention. She is a nice, straight lady, although too thin; she ought to have married, unless it was just not in her nature. He looked at the sun. Nearly time to get a good cup of tea off Mrs Cripps; *she* was a sharp one, make no mistake, but she made a tidy cup of tea . . .

Billy, crouched on the path that ran between the main herbaceous borders, was clipping the grass edgings. He was awkward with the shears, opening them too wide and slashing with fierce ineptitude. He had to clip the same place several times to get it neat, but Mr McAlpine would be after him if he didn't. Sometimes he caught a piece of turf that came away with the shears, and then he had to jam it back and hope he wouldn't notice. He had a rubbed blister – the skin clean off on his right hand; every now and then he licked the salty dirt off it.

He'd suggested doing the mowing but it was no go after that time when the thing packed up on him – wasn't his fault, it needed servicing, but he got the blame. Sometimes this job was worse than school, and he'd thought that the minute he left school, his troubles would be over. Once a month he went home and Mum made a fuss of him, but his sisters had gone into service, and his brothers were much older, and Dad kept telling him how lucky he was to learn his trade under Mr McAlpine. After a few hours he didn't know what to do with himself and he missed his friends who were all working in different places. He had been used to doing things in a crowd; at school there'd been a gang of them who'd gone fishing, or picked hops in the season for cash. Here there wasn't anyone to do things with. There was Dottie, but she was a girl so he never knew where he was with her and she treated him like a boy when he was doing a man's job – sort of – earning his living, anyway, same as her. Sometimes he wondered about going to sea, or he might drive a bus; the bus would be better because ladies took buses; he wouldn't drive, he'd be a conductor, so's he could see all their legs . . .

'Working very hard, I see, Billy.'

'Yes, m'm.' He sucked his blister and at once she saw it.

'That looks horrid. Come and see me when you've had your dinner, and I'll put a plaster on it.' Then, seeing that he looked anxious as well as embarrassed, she added, 'Eileen will tell you where to find me,' and walked on. *She* was all right, although she did have very thin, knobbly legs, but then she was as old as Mum, a nice class of lady.

∞ ∞ ∞

William Cazalet spent his morning in the ways that he most enjoyed. He sat with the newspaper in his study, which was dark and crammed with heavy furniture (he made no concession to it having been the second parlour of the old cottage) worrying pleasurably about the country going to the dogs: that feller Chamberlain didn't seem to him to be much better than the other feller Baldwin; the Germans seemed to be the only people who knew how to organise things; it was a pity that George VI didn't have a son, and it looked as though he'd left it a bit late now; if they *did* have a state in Palestine he doubted whether enough Jews would go there to make a difference to the business – Jews were his chief competitors in the timber trade, and damnably good at it, but none had the hardwood stock that Cazalet's carried – neither the quality nor the variety. His huge desk was covered with veneer samples; with koko, Andeman padouk, pyinkado, ebony, walnut, maple, laurel and rosewood samples; these were not used for selling, he just liked to have them about. Often he had boxes made from the first cuttings of veneer from some particularly favoured log that had been maturing for years. The study contained a dozen or so, and there were more in London. The room was otherwise furnished with a brilliant red and blue Turkey rug, a glass-fronted bookcase that scraped the low ceiling, several glass cases with huge stuffed fish in them – he enormously enjoyed telling the stories about how he had caught them and regularly imported new guests for the purpose – and, increasing the gloom, large pots of scarlet geraniums on the window-sill in full unwinking flower. The walls were hung three deep with prints: hunting prints, prints of India, and prints of battles – all smoke and scarlet jackets and the whites of rearing horses' eyes. Newspapers that he had read were stacked upon chairs. Heavy decanters half full of whisky and port stood on an inlaid table with the appropriate glasses. A sandalwood statue of a Hindu god – a present from a rajah when he was in India, stood on top of a cabinet full of shallow drawers in which he kept his collection of beetles. His desk was chiefly covered with the plans for his new conversion of part of the stables: there were to be two garages below, and quarters for Tonbridge and his family – wife and small boy – above. Building was well under way, but he kept thinking of improvements and to that end had sent for the builder, Sampson, to meet him at the site. One of the four clocks struck the half hour. He got to his feet, collected his tweed cap from a hook on the back of the door, and walked slowly down to the stables. As he walked, he reflected that that nice feller he'd met in the train . . . what was his name? Began with a C, he thought – anyway he'd find out when they came to dinner; naturally he'd asked Mrs Whatshername as well. The only thing was he couldn't remember whether he had told Kitty they were coming; in fact, if he couldn't remember, it probably meant that he hadn't. He must get up some port; the Taylor '23 would be just the ticket.

The stables were built on two sides at right angles. To the left were the stalls where he kept his horses, to the right were the old loose boxes that were half converted. Wren was grooming his chestnut mare, Marigold; he could hear the steady soothing hiss before he got to the door. There was no sign of Sampson. The other horses shifted in their straw at his approach. William loved his horses, riding every morning of his life, and keeping one, a large grey of sixteen hands called Whistler, at livery in London. Whistler was in a stall now, and William frowned.

'Wren! I told you to turn him out. It's his holiday.'

'I've to catch that pony first. Never catch 'im once I've let t'other out.'

Fred Wren was a small man, wiry and hard. He looked as though all of him had been compressed; he'd been a stable lad turned jockey, but a bad fall had left him lame. He'd been with William for nearly twenty years. Once a week he got drunk so it was a mystery how he hauled himself up the ladder into the hayloft where he slept. This behaviour was known but tolerated because in every other way he was an excellent groom.

'Mrs Edward coming down, is she?'

'Today. They're all coming.'

'So I heard. Mrs Edward'll go nicely on the liver chestnut. Lovely seat on a horse, she has. You don't see many like 'er.'

'Quite right, Wren.' He gave Marigold a pat, and turned to go.

'One thing, sir. Could you tell those workmen to wash away their cement? They're blocking my drains.'

'I'll tell them.'

And you tell them to take their ladders down of an evening, and not leave my yard looking like a pigsty. Wood shavings, buckets and making free with my water – I've had enough of them and no mistake, the cheeky monkeys. Wren stood looking at the back of his employer as he thought this. But there was no stopping that old man: he'd have the stables down next, he shouldn't wonder. But the mere thought of that made him feel queer. When he'd first come to this place there had been no talk of motor cars and such. Now there were two of them, nasty smelly things. If Mr Cazalet took it into his head to collect any more of them, where would he put the contraptions? Not in my stables, he thought rather shakily. He was much older than he thought anybody knew and he didn't like modern times.

Wren fussing about the drains made William think. The new premises would need their own water. Perhaps he'd better sink another well. Then the garden and stables could share their water supply – instead of the garden using water from the house – and – yes! He'd do a spot of divining after lunch. He'd speak to Sampson about it, but Sampson didn't really know the first thing about wells – *he* couldn't find water to save his life. Cheered by the thought of yet another enterprise, he stumped over to the garages.

∞ ∞ ∞

Tonbridge held the car door open for Madam, and the Duchy climbed gratefully into the back of the old Daimler. It was cool after the heat of the high street and smelled faintly of prayer books. The boot was full of the large grocery order; her new trug and secateurs from Till's lay on the seat beside her, a case of Malvern water on the seat in front.

'We just have to collect my order from the butcher's, Tonbridge.'

'Very good, m'm.'

She eased a hat pin that seemed to be working its way through her hat into her head. It would be too hot now to pick the roses; she would have to wait until evening. She would have a short rest after luncheon, and then go out into the garden. In weather like this she begrudged every minute she could not spend there.

The butcher came out with her lamb in a parcel. He had been most apologetic about the last order having been unsatisfactory. He raised his boater to her as the car moved on.

Tonbridge got the sweets wrong. 'I want *mixed* fruits –

not just gooseberries. I'm afraid you must take them back.'

Tonbridge went slowly back into the shop. He didn't like having to buy sweets, and he hated taking them back because the woman who kept the shop was sharp with him and reminded him of Ethyl. But he did it, of course. It was all part of the job.

He drove the Duchy home at a lugubrious twenty miles an hour – the pace he usually reserved for Mrs Edward or Mrs Hugh when they were pregnant. The Duchy did not notice this; driving was for men, and they might go at what pace they pleased. The only driving she had ever done was in a pony cart when she was a great deal younger. But she sensed that the sweet business had upset him, so when they got home and he was helping her out of the car, she said, 'I expect you will be *most* relieved when the garages are finished, and you have a nice flat for your family.'

He looked at her, his mournful brown eyes with the bloodshot lower lids did not change and said, 'Yes, m'm. I expect I shall be,' and shut the car door after her. As he drove the car round to the back door to unload it, he reflected gloomily that his only chance of getting away from Ethyl was shortly to be lost. She'd be down here, nagging him, complaining about how quiet it was, with that kid of hers whining all the time and his life would be just as bad as it was when the family were in town. There must be a way out of it somehow, but he couldn't see what it was.

∞ ∞ ∞

Eileen had been behind herself all morning. It had started all right: she'd got her housework – the reception rooms – done before breakfast. But when she was washing the breakfast things, she discovered that all the china for the nursery meals hadn't been touched since Christmas: the whole lot needed washing, and of course Mrs Cripps hadn't been able to spare Dottie, and Peggy and Bertha had all the rooms upstairs to get ready. Eileen didn't like to say anything, but she did think that Mrs Cripps might have spoken to the girls about it and got it done earlier. It wasn't all done now, but there was an early dining room lunch, which meant that the kitchen wouldn't get theirs until nearly two. She was in the pantry, rolling water-beaded butter balls and setting them in glass dishes for lunch and dinner that evening.

The door was open and she could hear Mrs Cripps shouting at Dottie, who scuttled back and forth down the passage with the kitchen washing-up. Smells of new cake and flapjacks wafted from the kitchen, reminding her that she was *starving*, she never could fancy much breakfast and there'd only been a rock cake with middle mornings. In London, Mrs Norfolk provided a real sit-down meal for elevenses – tinned salmon or a nice piece of Cheddar – but, then, she wasn't having to cook for the numbers expected of Mrs Cripps. Eileen always came to the country with the family for Christmas and the summer holidays. At Easter she had her fortnight's holiday and Lillian, the housemaid at Chester Terrace, came down instead of her. Eileen had been with the family seven years; she was fond of them, but she adored Miss Rachel – one of the sweetest ladies she'd ever met. She couldn't think why Miss Rachel had never got married, but supposed she'd had a Disappointment in the war, like so many. But the summer was going to be hard work all the way, and that was a fact. Still, she liked to see the children enjoying themselves and Mrs Hugh would soon be having another and there'd be a baby again at Christmas. That was the butter done. She took the small tray of dishes to put in the larder and nearly ran into Dottie – that girl never looked where she was going. Poor girl, she had a summer cold and a very nasty cold sore on her lip in spite of all the vanishing cream that Eileen had kindly lent her. She was carrying a huge great tray piled with the kitchen china for laying up in the hall.

'You shouldn't put so much on a tray, Dottie. You might have a nasty accident.'

But it didn't matter how kindly you spoke to her, she still looked scared. Eileen guessed that she was homesick because she remembered how she'd felt when she first went into service: cried her eyes out every night, and spent all the afternoons writing letters home, but Mum had never answered them. She didn't like to think of those days. Still – we all have to go through them, she thought. It's all for the best in the end. She went to the kitchen to look at the time. Half past twelve – and she must get a move on.

Mrs Cripps was in a frenzy – stirring things, popping things in and out of ovens. The kitchen table was half covered with basins, saucepans, pastry-making apparatus and the mincer and empty jugs, all waiting to be washed up.

'Where is that girl? Dottie! Dottie!' There were huge dark patches under her arms, and her ankles bulged over the straps of her black shoes. She lifted a wooden spoon from a double saucepan, placed her forefinger flat upon it, tasted and seized the salt. 'See if you can find her, would you, Eileen, for me? There's all this to be cleared up, and the stove wants a good riddle – I don't know what they put in the coke nowadays, I really don't. Tell her to hurry, if she knows what the word means.'

Dottie was moonily laying a fork and then a knife, and then a spoon round the table. She paused between each of these gestures, snuffling and staring into space.

'Mrs Cripps wants you. I'll finish the table.' Dottie gave her a hunted look, wiped her nose on her sleeve and scuttled away.

Eileen could hear the girls laughing and talking with Mr Tonbridge, who was bringing in the shopping from Battle. *They* could lay the table and she would help Mr Tonbridge. She knew where things had to go, which was more than you could say for either Peggy or Bertha. But she had hardly got the butter and cream and the meat stowed in the larder and the Malvern water into her pantry before the word was passed that Mrs Cripps was dishing up. So she sped back through the kitchen, across the hall to the dining room to light the spirit lamps under the warmer on the sideboard, back to the hall where she rang the gong for luncheon, and back to the kitchen where dishes and plates were already piled upon the large wooden tray. She just had time to get across the hall with this and set plates and dishes in position when the family came in for lunch.

∞ ∞ ∞

Four hours later nearly all of them had arrived: the grown-ups were having tea in the garden, and the children in the hall with Nanny and Ellen. They had arrived in three cars: Edward

unloaded the suitcases and Louise carried hers – it was extremely heavy – into the hall. Aunt Rach had come with them to
tell them which rooms. She tried to help Louise with her case,
but Louise wouldn't let her: everybody knew Aunt Rach had a
bad back – whatever that might mean. She was delighted to be
in the Pink Room and bagged the bed by the window as she was
first. She saw the camp bed and realised that Clary would be
sleeping with her and Polly. This was a bore, because Clary,
although she was twelve (like Polly), seemed much younger,
and anyway, she was not much fun, and they had to be nice to
her because her mother was dead. Never mind, it was heavenly
to be here. She unpacked her case enough to get out her jodh-
purs so that she could ride immediately after tea. She'd better
unpack altogether or they would find her when she was in the
middle of something and make her stop and go and do it. She
hung up her three cotton frocks that Mummy had made her
bring, and bundled everything else into a drawer, except her
books, which she arranged carefully on the table by her bed.
Great Expectations, because Miss Milliment had set it for their
holiday book, *Sense and Sensibility*, because she hadn't read it
for at least a year, a funny old book called *The Wide Wide
World*, because Miss Milliment had said that she used to have
bets with a friend when *she* was a girl that whatever page they
opened it at the heroine would be crying, and, of course, her
Shakespeare. She heard a car arriving and prayed it would be
Polly. She needed someone to talk to: Teddy was aloof – he
didn't answer any questions about his school properly and he
wouldn't even play car numbers with her on the way down.
Let it be Polly. Please, *God*, let it be Polly!

∞ ∞ ∞

Polly was thankful to arrive. She always felt car-sick, although
she never actually was. They stopped for her twice, once on the
hill outside Sevenoaks and once the other side of Lamberhurst.
Each time she had stumbled out and stood retching, but nothing
happened. She had quarrelled with Simon on the way down as
well. It was about Pompey. Simon said that cats didn't notice
if people went away – which was an arrant lie. Pompey had
watched her packing and tried to get into the case. He simply

81

concealed his feelings in front of other people. He'd even tried to make *her* feel better about it, by going away and sitting in the kitchen – the furthest possible amount away from her that he could manage. Mummy had kept saying wasn't she excited about going to Home Place, and she was, but everybody knew you could feel two things at once – probably more than that. She didn't trust Inge to be kind to him although she'd given her a pot of Wonder Cream as a sort of bribe, but Daddy said that he would be back on Monday and she knew he was trustworthy. But then she'd miss Daddy. Life was nothing but swings and roundabouts. What with crying in London and feeling sick in the car, she had a headache. Never mind. As soon as they'd had tea, she and Louise would go off together to their best tree – an old apple that could be made into a kind of house with the branches being different rooms. It was her and Louise's tree; horrible Simon wouldn't be allowed up it. He had been told to carry her case up to her room, but as soon as they were out of sight of the grown-ups, he dropped it and said, 'Carry your own case.' 'Cad!' She picked it up and began on the stairs. 'Swine!' she added. They were the newest worst words she could think of: what Dad had said about a bus driver, and a man in a sports car on the way down. Oh dear! What with Pompey and Simon, things weren't too good. But there was darling Louise at the top of the stairs, down in a flash to help her with the case. *But* she was wearing her riding clothes which meant no tree after tea, so it was swings and roundabouts *again*.

∞ ∞ ∞

Zoë and Rupert had an awful journey; Zoë had suggested that Clary should go by train with Ellen and Neville, but Clary had made such a fuss that Rupert had given in, and said she'd better come with them. Their car, a small Morris, was not large enough for the whole family, and as it was, Clary had luggage crammed round her in the back. Quite soon she said she felt sick and wanted to be in front. Zoë said that Clary shouldn't have come in the car, if she was going to feel sick and she couldn't be in front. So Clary *was* sick – just to show her. They had to stop, and Dad tried to clean it up, but it smelled awful and everybody was cross with her. Then they had a puncture, and Dad had to change the wheel while Zoë sat smoking and not saying a word. Clary got out of the car and apologised to Dad, who was nice and said he supposed she couldn't help it. They were still in horrible awful old London when this happened. Dad had to unpack the boot to get at his tools and Clary tried to help him, but he said she couldn't really. He spoke in his patient voice that meant, she felt, he was awfully unhappy only he couldn't say. He must be – the most terrible thing had happened to him in the world and he had to go on living and pretending it hadn't and so, of course, she tried to copy his braveness about it because she knew it was so much worse for him. It didn't matter how much she loved him, it wouldn't make it up. The rest of the journey, they didn't talk, so she sang to cheer him up. She sang 'Early One Morning', and 'The Nine Days of Christmas', and an *area* it was called, by Mozart, she only knew the first three words and then it had to be la la la, but it was a lovely tune, one of his favourites, and the 'Raggle Taggle Gypsies O', but when she got to 'Ten Green Bottles', Zoë asked her to shut up for a bit – so, of course, she had to. But Dad thanked her for the lovely singing, so it was sucks to Zoë, and that was something. She spent the rest of the journey wanting to go to the lav, but not wanting to ask Dad to stop again.

∞ ∞ ∞

Lydia and Neville had a lovely time in the train. Neville liked trains more than anything, which was quite reasonable as he was going to be an engine driver. Lydia thought he was a very nice boy. They played noughts and crosses, but that wasn't much fun because they were too equal for anyone to win. Neville wanted to climb into the luggage rack above the seats: he said a boy he knew always travelled like that, but Nan and Ellen wouldn't let them. They did let them stand in the corridor, which was very exciting when they went through tunnels and they could see red sparks in the smoky dark and there was a lovely exciting smell. 'The only thing is,' Lydia said after thinking about it when they were told to come back into the carriage, 'that when you are an engine driver, where will you have your house?

Because wherever it is, you'll keep on going to somewhere else, won't you?'

'I'll take a tent with me. I'll put it up in places like Scotland or Cornwall – or Wales or Iceland. Anywhere,' he finished grandly.

'You can't drive a train to Iceland. Trains don't go over the sea.'

'They do. Dad and Zoë go to Paris in a train. They get into it at Victoria Station, and have dinner and go to sleep and when they wake up they're in France. So they do go across sea. So there.'

Lydia was silent. She didn't like arguments, so she decided not to have one. 'I'm sure you'll be a very good driver.'

'I'll take you free whenever you want to go. I'll go at two hundred miles an hour.'

There he went again. *Nothing* went at two hundred miles an hour.

'What are you looking forward to most when we get there?' She asked politely – she didn't particularly want to know.

'My bike. And strawberries. And the Walls' Ice Man.'

'Strawberries are over, Neville. It will be raspberries now.'

'I don't mind which they are. I can eat any old berry. I very-very-very-like ber-rys-ber-rys-ber-rys.' He began laughing, his face became bright pink and he nearly fell off his seat. This made Ellen say that he was getting silly; he was quenched by being told to put out his tongue and having the lower half of his face rubbed with a handkerchief and his spit. Lydia watched with distaste, but just as she was feeling rather superior Nan did exactly the same to her.

'Nasty smuts you got out in the corridor, I told you!' But it must mean they were nearly there and she was longing for that.

∞ ∞ ∞

The Cazalets were a kissing family. As the first lot (Edward and Villy) arrived, they kissed the Duchy and Rachel (the children kissed the Duchy and hugged Aunt Rach); when the second lot (Sybil and Hugh) arrived they did the same, and then the brothers and sisters-in-law kissed each other, 'How *are* you, darling?'; when Rupert and Zoë arrived he kissed everyone, and Zoë imprinted her brothers-in-law's faces with her light, scarlet lipstick and lent a creamy cheek to her sisters-in-law's mouths. The Duchy sat in an upright deck-chair on the front lawn under the monkey puzzle boiling the silver kettle for strong Indian tea. As each one kissed her she made her silent, lightning review of their health: Villy looked rather thin, Edward looked in the pink as he always seemed to; Louise was growing too fast, Teddy was reaching the awkward age; Sybil looked done up, and Hugh looked as though he was recovering from one of his heads; Polly was becoming a pretty child so nothing must ever be said about her appearance; Simon looked far too pale – some sea air would do him good; Rupert looked positively haggard and needed feeding up; and Zoë – but here her thoughts failed her. Incurably honest, she admitted to herself that she did not – like – Zoë and could not get past her appearance which, she felt, was a trifle *showy*, a little like an *actress*. The Duchy did not have anything against actresses in general, it was simply that one did not expect to have one in the family. None of the observations were apparent to anyone except Rachel, who quickly admired Zoë's tussore suit with white crocheted jumper and long string of corals. Clary had not come to kiss, and had rushed straight into the house.

'She was sick in the car,' Zoë explained in neutral tones.

'She's perfectly all right now,' Rupert said sharply.

Rachel got to her feet. 'I'll go and see.'

'Do, darling. I don't think she should have raspberries and cream, it would be too rich for her.'

Rachel pretended not to hear her mother. She found Clary coming out of the downstairs lavatory.

'Are you all right?'

'Why shouldn't I be?'

'Zoë said you were sick in the car coming down. I thought perhaps you—'

'That was ages ago. Which room am I in?'

'The Pink. With Polly and Louise.'

'Oh. Right.' Her suitcase stood in the passage outside the lavatory. She picked it up. 'Is there time to unpack before tea?'

'I expect so. Anyway, you needn't have tea if you don't feel like it.'

'There's nothing wrong with me, Aunt Rachel – honestly. I'm perfectly all right.'

'Good. I just wanted to be sure. Sometimes people feel awful after they've been sick.'

She took a hesitating step towards Rachel, put down the case, and then gave her a fierce and hurried hug. 'I'm tough as old wellingtons.' A look of doubt crossed her face. 'Dad says.' She picked up the case again. 'Thank you for worrying about me,' she finished formally.

Rachel watched her stump upstairs. She felt sad. Her back ached, and that reminded her to take out a cushion for Sybil.

When she returned to the tea party, Zoë was telling Villy about seeing the men's singles at Wimbledon, Sybil was telling the Duchy about the nanny she had found, Hugh and Edward were talking shop, and Rupert was a little apart, sitting on the lawn, hands round his knees, watching the scene. Everybody was smoking except for Sybil. The Duchy interrupted Sybil to say, 'Pour away your tea, darling, it will be cold. I'll give you another cup.'

Rachel proffered the cushion, and Sybil heaved herself up gratefully for it to be put in place.

Zoë, who observed this, gave Sybil a covert second glance and wondered how anybody *could* go about looking so monstrous. She could at least wear a smock, or something, instead of that awful green dress strained over her stomach. God! She hoped she'd never be pregnant.

Rachel took an Abdullah from the box on the tea table and looked about for a light. Villy waved her little shagreen lighter at her, and Rachel went over for it.

'The court is all ready for tennis,' she said, but before anybody could answer, they heard the car arrive. Doors slammed, and, seconds later, Lydia and Neville ran through the white gate. 'We went *over* sixty miles an hour.'

'Gracious!' exclaimed the Duchy kissing him. Over-excited she thought. It will end in tears.

'I betted Tonbridge he couldn't go fast, so he went!'

'He went how he would've went anyway,' Lydia said primly, bending down to her grandmother. 'Neville is rather young for his age,' she whispered very loudly indeed.

Neville turned on her. 'I'm not as young for my age as you

are! How can you be young for your age? You couldn't *be* your age if you were young for it!'

'That'll do, Neville,' Rupert said with his hand over the lower part of his face. 'Kiss your aunts and go and get ready for tea.'

'I'll kiss the nearest.' He planted a smacking kiss on Sybil's cheek.

'And the others,' ordered Rupert.

He sighed theatrically but did as he was told. Lydia, who had done her kissing, ended with Villy onto whom she flung herself.

'Tonbridge has a very red neck. It goes dark red if you talk about him in the car,' she said.

'You shouldn't talk about him. You should talk *to* him, or not at all.'

'Oh, *I* didn't. It was Neville. I simply noticed.'

'We don't want any tales,' said the Duchy. 'Run along now to Ellen and Nanny.' They looked at her, but went at once.

'Oh dear, aren't they priceless? They do make me laugh.' Rachel stubbed out her cigarette.

'Now – what about your tennis?' She wondered whether Villy minded her mother-in-law reprimanding Lydia, and she knew Villy loved to play.

'I'm game,' said Edward at once.

'Hugh, do play. I'll come and watch you.' Sybil longed to have a little rest in the cool of their bedroom, but she didn't want Hugh to be robbed of his tennis.

'I'm happy to play if I'm wanted,' but he didn't want to. He wanted to lie in a deck-chair and read – have a peaceful time.

For once, however, they were cheated of sacrificing themselves to each other's imagined requirements, as Zoë, leaping to her feet, proclaimed her interest in playing and said she'd pop up and change. Rupert immediately said, right, he'd play too, and there was the double. The Duchy was going to deadhead and pick her roses, and Rachel had just decided that as everybody seemed happy and occupied she could go to her room and read Sid's letter, when her father emerged from the house.

'Hallo, *hallo*, everybody. Kitty, it's quite all right, because

87

I've remembered now that the Whatsisnames couldn't dine with us, so they are just coming for a drink.'

'Who, dear?'

'Chap I met in the train. Can't for the life of me remember his name, but he was a very nice chap and, of course, I asked his wife as well. Pity I got up the port, but I expect we'll manage to drink it.'

'What time did you ask them, because dinner is at eight?'

'Oh, I didn't fuss about the time. They'll come about six, I should think. Ewhurst they're coming from – that's where the chap said he lived. Rachel, can you spare a minute? I want to read you the end of the British Honduras chapter before I start to compare their mahogany with the West African variety.'

'You read that bit to me, darling.'

'Did I? Well, never mind, I'll read it again,' and taking her by the arm he marched her firmly into the house.

'Why do you let him go in trains?' Hugh said to his mother as she went in search of her secateurs and trug. 'If he drove with Tonbridge, he wouldn't meet nearly so many people.'

'If he goes with Tonbridge, he insists on driving. And as nothing will stop him driving on the right-hand side of the road, Tonbridge is refusing to be driven by him. If he goes by train, then neither of them has to give way.'

'Don't the police have something to say about the right-hand side of the road?'

'They do, of course. But the last time he was stopped, he got very slowly out of the car, and explained that he'd always ridden that side of the road and he wasn't going to stop now just because he was motoring, and they ended up *apologising* to him. He'll have to stop soon: his eyesight is really quite bad. *You* have a word with him, dear, I expect he'll listen to you.'

'I doubt it.'

They parted, and Hugh went upstairs to be sure that Sybil was all right. He went up the cottage stairs, avoiding the children who were all having tea in the hall.

Tea was nearly over, and the older children were panting to be allowed to get down. They had all had the statutory piece of plain bread and butter, followed by as many pieces of bread and jam as they pleased (the Duchy did not approve of butter *and* jam – 'a bit rich', her uttermost condemnation) and then there were flapjacks and cake, and *then* there were raspberries and cream – all washed down by mugs of creamy milk that Mr York had delivered from the farm that morning. Ellen and Nanny presided, careful of each other's status, and more watchful and firm with their own charges than they were at home. Polly and Simon, unaccompanied, were no-man's land, which curiously subdued them. Manners seemed to make most people dull, Louise thought. She kicked Polly under the table, who, taking the cue, asked, '*Please*, may we get down?'

'When everyone has finished,' Nanny said.

Neville hadn't. They all looked at him. When he realised this he started shovelling in his raspberries very fast, until his cheeks bulged.

'Stop that!' said Ellen sharply, whereupon he choked, opened his mouth and a messy slide of raspberries dropped onto the table.

'You others may get down.' This they thankfully did, just as the scene was starting.

'Where are you going?' Clary called to Polly and Louise. She knew they were trying to leave her out.

'To see Joey,' they called, running to the north door. They did not want her, she thought. She decided to go for an explore by herself. At first, she did not notice where she was going, was too engaged in hating everyone; Louise and Polly always ganged up – like the girls at school. If she *had* gone with them to see Joey they wouldn't have let her ride him, or they would just have let her have one small turn on him at the end. Anyway, she was wearing her shorts and the stirrup leathers would have pinched her knees awfully. She could hear Neville's wails coming from an upstairs open window: serve him *right*, the silly fool. She kicked a stone with her foot and it hurt her toe—

'Look out!' It was horrible Teddy and Simon on their bicycles. What was horrible about *them* was that they simply wouldn't talk to her at all. They only talked to each other and grown-ups – but usually they got a bit nicer when the holidays had been going for a bit. She was at the corner of the house now, where to the left she could see the tennis court and hear them calling, 'Love fifteen,' and, 'Yours, partner!' She could offer to be a ball-boy, but she didn't want even to *see* Zoë, thank you very much. She heard Dad give his hooting laugh when he missed a ball. He didn't take games very seriously – unlike the others. To the right she could see the large part of the garden and in the distance, the beginnings of the kitchen garden. That's where she would go. She walked along the cinder path by the greenhouses, whose glass was painted a smeary white. She could see the Duchy in her large hat, snipping and bending over her roses, and decided to go through the greenhouses to avoid being seen. The first one smelled of nectarines that were fan-trained up the wall. Overhead was an enormous vine, the grapes like small, clouded, green glass beads. They wouldn't be at all ripe, but they looked very pretty, she thought. She felt one or two of the nectarines, and one fell off into her hand. It wasn't her fault, it simply toppled. She put it in her shorts pocket to eat somewhere secret. There were masses of pots of geraniums and chrysanthemums that were hardly in bud; the gardener showed them at the Flower Show. The last greenhouse was full of tomatoes, the yellow and the red; the smell of them was delicious and so overpowering it tickled her nose. She picked a tiny one to eat; it was as sweet as a sweet. She picked three more and stuffed them in her other pocket. She shut the last greenhouse door and stepped into the cooler, but still golden, air. The sky was pale blue with a drift of little clouds like feathers. By the kitchen-garden gate there was a huge bush with purplish flowers like lilac only pointed; it was littered with butterflies – white ones, orange ones with black and white on them, small blue ones and *one* lemon with tiny dark veins on it, the most beautiful of all, she thought. She watched them for a bit and wished she knew their names. Sometimes they were restless and went from flower to flower with hardly a pause. I suppose the honey gets used up out of each little flower, she thought. They have to go on until they find a full one.

She decided to come and see them often: in the end they might get to know her, but they seemed a bit unearthly for people – more like ghosts or fairies – they didn't *need* people, lucky things.

The kitchen garden, with walls all round it, was very hot and still. There was one long bed of flowers for picking, and the rest was vegetables. Plum and greengage trees were grown against the walls and a huge fig tree, whose leaves were quite rough to touch and smelled of slightly warm mackintosh. It had a lot of figs, and some had fallen to the ground, but they were still green and hard and shiny.

'Come and see what I've got!'

She hadn't noticed Lydia, who was squatting on the ground in the middle of two rows of cabbages.

'What have you got?' she said, copying a grown-up voice – not really wanting to know.

'Caterpillars. I'm collecting them for pets. This is my box for them. I'm going to make holes in the lid with Nan's smallest knitting needle 'cos they need some air, but they won't be able to escape. You can have some if you like.'

Lydia was nice. Clary didn't actually want any caterpillars, she was too old for them, but she felt pleased to be asked.

'I'll help you if you like,' she said.

'You can tell where they are because of the eaten bits of leaves. Only please pick them up carefully. As they haven't got any bones you can't tell what would hurt.'

'All right.'

'Do you want the very small ones?' Clary asked, after finding a whole lot on one leaf.

'Some, because they'll last longer. The big ones will go into cocoons and stop being pets.'

'Except for size they do look the same, though,' she said after a bit. 'Their little black faces are *just* the same, it's no good giving them names. I'll just have to call them them.'

'Like sheep. Only not awfully like sheep.'

This made Lydia laugh and she said, 'You don't have caterpillar shepherds. Shepherds know sheep quite well. Mr York told me. He knows his pigs and they all have names.'

When Clary thought they'd got too many, and Lydia said there were enough, they went to see if there were any strawberries left because Lydia said she was thirsty and if she went into the house for some water, Nan would find her and make her have a bath. But the only strawberries they found were all half eaten by things. Clary told Lydia about wanting a cat, and how her dad had said they'd have to think about it.

'What does your mother say?'

'She's not my mother.'

'Oh!' Then she said, 'I know she's not, really. Sorry.'

Clary said, 'It's all right,' but it wasn't.

'Do you like her? Aunt Zoë, I mean?'

'I don't have any feelings about her.'

'But even if you did, it couldn't be the same, could it? I mean, nobody could be like a real mother. Oh, Clary, I feel awfully sad for you! You're a tragic person, aren't you? I think you're terrifically brave!'

Clary felt extraordinary. Nobody had ever said anything like that to her before. It was funny; she felt lighter, someone *knowing* made it less of a hard secret, because Ellen always changed the subject in a brisk horrible way, and Dad never mentioned her – never once even said 'your mother', let alone telling her all the things she wanted to know. He couldn't help it, it was too awful for him to talk about, and she loved him far too much to want to make anything worse for him, and so there was nobody . . . Lydia was crying. She wasn't making any noise, but her lip was trembling and tears spurted out onto the strawberry straw.

'I'd hate my mother to die,' she said. 'I'd *hate* it – too much.'

'She's not going to die,' Clary said. 'She's the wellest person I've ever seen in my life!'

'Is she? Really the wellest?'

'Absolutely. You must believe me, Lyd – I'm far older than you and I know that sort of thing.' She felt in her pocket for a handkerchief for Lydia, and remembered the tomatoes. 'Look what I've got!'

Lydia ate the three tomatoes, and they cheered her up. Clary felt very old and kind. She offered Lydia the nectarine, and Lydia said, 'No, you have it,' and Clary said, 'No, you're to have it. You've got to.' She wanted Lydia to have everything. Then they took the caterpillars and went to the potting shed to see if Mr McAlpine still had his ferrets.

∞ ∞ ∞

Teddy and Simon rode their bicycles round the house and then round the stables, and finally down the road to Watlington and along the drive to the Mill House that their grandfather had bought and was rebuilding to be an extra holiday house for some of them. They did not talk much, both having to contend with the switch from Teddy being a prefect and Simon a junior at their school, to being ordinary holiday cousins who could rag each other. On the way back, Teddy said to Simon, 'Shall we let them play Monopoly with us?'

And Simon, secretly pleased to have his opinion asked, answered as casually as he could, 'We'd better, or they'll make no end of a fuss.'

∞ ∞ ∞

Sybil had a lovely peaceful time eating Marie biscuits – she kept feeling hungry in between meals – and reading *The Citadel* by A. J. Cronin, who had been a doctor, like Somerset Maugham.

Usually she read more seriously: she was somebody who read more to be enlightened and educated than for pleasure, but now she felt incapable of mental effort. She had brought T. S. Eliot's play *Murder in the Cathedral* with her, which she and Villy had seen at the Mercury, and Auden and Isherwood's *Ascent of F6*, but she didn't feel at all like reading them. It was lovely to be in the country. She really wished that Hugh could stay down for the week with her, but he and Edward had to take turns to be at the office, and Hugh wanted to be free when the baby was born. Or babies: she was practically sure there were two of them judging by the activity inside her. After this, they really must make sure that they didn't have any more. The trouble was that Hugh hated all forms of contraception; after seventeen years, she wouldn't actually have *minded* terribly if they stopped all that sort of thing altogether, but Hugh obviously didn't feel like that. She wondered idly what Villy did about it, because Edward wouldn't be a very easy person to say no to, not that one ought to do that, anyway. When Polly was born they had sort of decided that two was enough; they had been much poorer then and Hugh had worried about school fees if they had more sons, so they'd battled on with her Dutch cap, and douches, and Volpargels, and Hugh not coming inside her, until the whole business had seemed so worrying that she had completely stopped enjoying it although, of course, she never let him know *that*. But last year, early in December, they'd had a divine skiing holiday at St Moritz and after the first day when they were aching from exercise, Hugh had ordered a bottle of champagne for them to drink while they took turns to soak in a hot bath. She'd made him go first, because he'd hurt his ankle, and then he sat and watched her. When she was ready to come out, he'd held an enormous white bath towel out and wrapped it round her, and then held her, and then unpinned her hair and pulled her gently down onto the bathroom mat. She'd started to say something, but he'd put his hand over her mouth and shook his head and kissed her and it had been like it was when they first married. After that, they'd made love every night, and sometimes in the afternoons as well and Hugh did not have a single one of his heads. So her present state was hardly surprising and she was glad, because *he* was so pleased and always so sweet to her. I'm very lucky, she thought. Rupert's the funniest, and Edward the most handsome, but I wouldn't swap Hugh for either of them.

'I expected you to be fast asleep.' He came into the room with a glass of sherry in his hand. 'I've brought you this to buck you up.'

'Oh, *thank* you, darling. I mustn't drink too much or I'll pass out at dinner.'

'You drink what you want and I'll finish it.'

'But you don't like sherry!'

'I do sometimes. But I thought if you had this, you could skip the unknowns coming for a drink.'

'What have you been up to?'

'I read for a bit, and then the Old Man called me in for a chat. He wants to build a squash court behind the stables. Apparently it was Edward's idea, and he's started to choose the site.'

'It will be nice for Simon.'

'And Polly. All of us, really.'

'I can't imagine *ever* being able to play any game again.'

'You will, darling. It won't be built until the Christmas hols. You'll be as thin as a rake by then. Do you want a bath? Because if you do, you'd better get in quick before the tennis players and the children start.'

She shook her head. 'I'll have one in the morning.'

'You'll all have one, will you?' He stroked her belly and got up from the bed. 'I must get out of these shoes.' All male Cazalets had long bony feet and were constantly changing their shoes.

Sybil held out the sherry glass. 'I've had enough.'

He drained the glass – like medicine, she thought. 'By the way, what are we going to call them?'

'Or him or her, possibly.'

'Well?'

'Don't you think Sebastian's rather a nice name?'

'A bit fancy for a boy, isn't it? I thought it might be nice if we called him William after the Old Man.'

'If they were twins we could call them both names.'

'And girls? Or a girl?'

'I thought perhaps Jessica.'

'I don't like that. I like plain names. Jane or Anne. Or Susan.'

'Of course, there might be one of each. That would be best.'

They had had this conversation before, but before the possibility of twins had occurred. They did not agree about names, although they *had* agreed about Simon in the end, and Hugh had been allowed to choose Polly when she had wanted Antonia. Now, she said, 'Anne is a nice name.'

'I was thinking that Jess wouldn't be too bad. Where did you put my socks?'

'Top left-hand drawer.'

A car was heard in the drive.

'That will be the mystery guests.'

'I must say I'm jolly glad *you* don't keep inviting everyone you meet back for drinks and meals.'

'I don't go in enough trains. Do you want me to do anything about getting Polly and Simon towards bed?'

'It's their first night, let them rip. They'll come in when Louise and Teddy are made to.'

'Okey-doke.' He ran a comb through his hair, blew her a kiss and went.

Sybil got up from bed and went to the open window; the air smelled warmly of honeysuckle and roses, there were the metallic sounds of blackbirds settling down for the night and the sky was turning apricot streaked with little molten feathery clouds. 'Look thy last on all things lovely, every hour,' came into her mind. She leaned further out of the window and pulled a rose towards her to smell it. 'And since to look at things in bloom, fifty springs are little room,' – it was unlike Housman to allow anyone fifty springs, let alone three score years and ten. She was thirty-eight, and the thought that it might be a very hard labour and that she might die recurred now. The petals of the rose began to drop; and when she let go of it, it swung back with only the stamens left. She couldn't die, she was needed. Dr Ledingham was marvellous, and Nurse Lamb a brick. It was just one of those times when the pain and what it was for balanced each other. She had never told Hugh how frightened she had been – the first time – with Polly, nor how much more she had dreaded having Simon, because the notion that one did not remember one's labour was one of those sentimental old wives' tales.

∞ ∞ ∞

Polly and Louise had not ridden Joey in the end. He was still out, Mr Wren had said. He hadn't had the time to catch him but they could try if they liked, and he'd given them the halter. They could catch him and bring him in for the night, and then they could ride him in the morning. He looked rather cross, so they didn't argue with him. Louise pinched a handful of oats which she put into her pocket with the sugar lumps Polly had secreted at tea. Nan had seen her, but they had both known that she wouldn't like to say anything as Polly wasn't in her charge. They had walked along the damp, shady path in the field, and Polly had got stung by nettles and had held things up by needing dock leaves.

'Do hurry up,' Louise had said. 'Because if we catch him quickly, there will be time for a ride.'

But they hadn't caught him at all. He was standing in a corner of the field, looking very fat and glossy, eating the rich green grass. He raised his head when they called him and watched them approach. There was a small cloud of flies round his head and his tail swished regularly. Whistler stood head to tail beside him, also grazing. When he saw the girls he started to walk towards them in case they were bringing anything nice.

'We'll have to give Whistler some oats, to be fair.'

'All right – you get the halter ready and I'll do the feeding.'

But this was the wrong way round, Louise thought. She was sure Polly would muff the halter, and she did. Whistler plunged his soft nose into the handful of oats, spilling a lot of them. Joey saw this and came up for his share. She shut her hand and held it out to Joey who made an expert grab, but the moment Polly tried to put an arm around his neck, he tossed his head and cantered away – an insultingly short distance – where he stood daring them to try again. Whistler nearly knocked Louise over when he nudged her hand for more.

'Blast! You take the sugar, and I'll have the halter.'

'Sorry,' Polly said meekly. She knew she wasn't much good at this sort of thing. She was – only a bit – afraid of Joey.

They had another go with the sugar and the same thing happened, only this time Joey laid his ears back and looked quite wicked. When the sugar was gone, Joey wouldn't come near them, and even Whistler lost interest in the end.

'I bet Mr Wren *knew* he wouldn't let himself be caught,' Louise said crossly. 'He might have jolly well done it himself.'

'Let's go back and tell him.'

They climbed the gate in silence, and Polly felt Louise was on the verge of being cross. But then she suddenly said, 'It wasn't your fault about the halter. Let's not go and talk to Mr Wren. He's never nice to us when his face is so red.'

'Beetroot.'

'Doesn't it look awful with his stony blue eyes?'

'No one would put beetroot and blue together on purpose,' Polly agreed. 'What shall we do? Shall we go and see our tree?'

And to her joy, Louise agreed at once. The piece of rope, which they used to get up the first straight hard part, hung just where they had left it at Christmas. They collected bunches of daisies and Louise put them in her pocket for the climb, and when they were comfortably ensconced in the best branch that went up at one end so that they could sit facing each other, leaning their backs against the branch and the trunk respectively, Louise divided the daisies and they both made chains to decorate the branches.

Louise, who bit her nails, had to bite the holes in the stalks for threading, but Polly did hers with her longest nail. They discussed the holidays, and what they most wanted to do in them. Louise wanted the beach, and especially to swim in the St Leonards swimming pool. Polly wanted to have a picnic at Bodiam. Both she and Simon had birthdays in August, so they would be allowed to choose one day. 'But *he'll* choose the Romney, Hythe and Dymchurch Railway,' said Polly sadly. Then she said, 'Clary has a birthday, too – remember?'

'Oh, God! What will she choose?'

'We could bend her to our will.'

'Only by telling her how much we don't want to do something that we really want.'

'That's not bending. That's . . . ' she searched for the word, 'that's *conspiring*.'

'Why does she have to share a room with us? I don't actually *like* her much. But Mummy says I ought to because of her not having a mother. I do see that. It must be rotten for her.'

'She has Aunt Zoë' Polly said.

'She doesn't strike me as a particularly good mother. Awfully glam, but not a mother. Some people aren't cut out for that sort of thing, you know. I mean look at Lady Macbeth.'

'I don't think Aunt Zoë's terribly like Lady Macbeth. I know you think Shakespeare is wonderful but, honestly, people now aren't much like his people.'

'They jolly well are!'

They had a bit of an argument about that, which Louise won by saying nature imitated art and that that wasn't what *she* thought, but someone who really knew about that sort of thing. The sun sank, and the orchard, from being a gilded green, turned misty and sage with violet shadows, and it wasn't hot any more. They began to think about milk and biscuits and their mothers saying good night to them.

∞ ∞ ∞

'Why don't you and Rupert have the first bath? I'm quite happy to wait, and I've got to go and see that Nan is settling in, anyway. Coming, darling?'

And Edward, who had been winding down the net, joined her. Zoë watched them walk up the steps to the terrace. Edward put his arm round Villy's shoulders and said something to her that made her laugh. They had won quite easily – would have won all three sets if Edward, the best player, hadn't had a run of double faults and lost his service. She had to admit that Villy was good, too, not showy, but a steady player with a reliable backhand; she hardly missed a shot. Zoë, who minded losing, felt that it was because Rupert didn't take the game seriously enough; he was good at volleying, but sometimes, at the net, he had simply left balls for her that she was sure he should have taken, and so, of course, she had often missed them. At least they hadn't had Sybil playing; she served *underarm* and simply laughed when she missed things and asked people not to send such fast balls. The worst of playing with her was that everybody pretended she was just as good as everyone else. They were all so *nice* to one another. They were nice to her as well, but she knew that that was simply because she had become part of the family by marrying Rupert. She did not feel that they really *liked her*.

'I'm off for a bath,' she called to Rupert, who was collecting the tennis balls. 'I'll leave the water for you.' And she ran lightly up the steps before he could reply.

At least the water was hot. She had been wondering how she could decently go ahead and bag the first bath, and then Villy had, confoundingly, simply presented her with it. But it was a ghastly bathroom – freezing cold, and so *ugly*, with the pitch-pine walls and the window-sill always covered with dead bluebottles. She made the bath so hot she could hardly get into it and lay down for a good soak. These family holidays! You'd think if the Cazalets were so keen on their grandchildren that they'd look after Clarissa and Neville, and let her and Rupert go off and have a proper holiday alone together. But every year – except the first one when they'd been married and Rupert had taken her to Cassis – they had to come here for weeks and weeks and she hardly ever had Rupert to herself, except in bed. Otherwise all the days were spent in doing things with all these kids, everybody worrying about *them* having a good time, which they would, anyway, with the others to play with. She wasn't used to all this clannishness; it wasn't at all her idea of a holiday.

Zoë's father had died at the battle of the Somme when she was two. She couldn't remember him at all, although Mummy said that he'd played ride-a-cock-horse with her when she was eighteen months old. Mummy had had to take a job with Elizabeth Arden doing people's faces all day, so she had been sent to boarding school when she was five – a place called Elmhurst near Camberley. She'd been easily the youngest boarder and everybody had spoiled her. She had quite liked school; it was the holidays that she had hated in the peachy little flat in West Kensington, with her mother out all day and a succession of boring mother's helps to look after her. Buses and walks in Kensington Gardens, and tea in a tea shop was their idea of a treat. By the time she was ten she was determined to get away from home as soon as possible. As she grew older, she was given the heroine's parts in the school plays – not because she was any good at acting, but because of her looks. She decided that she would go on the stage as soon as she left school. She certainly wasn't going to end up like her mother, who had had, apart from her ghastly job, a succession of dreary old men, one of whom she even seemed to want to marry, but not after Zoë told her what he'd tried to do to her when Mother was out one day. There'd been a fearful scene and after that her mother had stopped dyeing her hair, and talked a lot about what a hard life she had.

The only subject upon which she and her mother were in animated agreement was Zoë's appearance. Zoë evolved from being a pretty baby to an unusually attractive child, and even managed to avoid the common eclipse of adolescence. She never lost her lithe figure, nor had spots or greasy hair, and her mother, who had made herself some authority on appearance, realised early on that her daughter was going to be a beauty, and gradually, all the hopes she had had for her own security and comfort – a nice man who would look after her and obviate the need to work so hard – were transferred to Zoë. Zoë was going to be such a stunner that she could marry anyone she liked, which meant, to Mrs Headford, someone who was so rich that providing for his mother-in-law would be nothing to him. So she taught Zoë to look after herself: to treat her fine thick hair with henna and yolk of egg, to brush her lashes nightly with Vaseline, to bathe her eyes with hot and cold water, to walk across rooms with books on her head, to sleep in cotton gloves with her hands soaked in almond oil – and much else. Although they had no help, Zoë was never expected to do housework, nor to cook; her mother bought a second-hand sewing machine and made her pretty frocks and knitted her jumpers, and when Zoë was sixteen and had passed her School Certificate and said she was sick of school and wanted to go on the stage, Mrs Headford, who was by now a little afraid of her, at once agreed. Dukes had been known to marry people from the theatre, and as she was in no position to bring her daughter out, with a Season and all that, this seemed a viable alternative. She told Zoë that on no account should she marry an actor, made her a simple but exquisitely fitting green dress that matched her eyes for auditions and waited for her daughter's fame and fortune. But Zoë's lack of acting ability was masked by her lack of experience, and after two managers had advised her to go to an acting school, Mrs Headford realised that she was back to paying school fees. For two years Zoë attended Elsie Fogerty's Academy and learned to enunciate, learned mime, learned to walk and some dancing and even a little singing. Nothing availed. She looked so ravishing, and tried so hard, that her teachers went on attempting to turn her into an actress far longer than they might have done had she been plainer. She remained wooden, self-conscious and altogether unable to make any lines that she spoke seem her own. Her only talent seemed to lie in movement; she liked dancing and in the end it was mutually agreed that perhaps she had better concentrate upon that. She left the school and took lessons in tap and modern dance. The only thing to be said for the acting school was that although a number of students had fallen in love with her, Zoë had remained aloof. Disregarding the obvious reason for this, Mrs Headford rashly assumed that Zoë was 'sensible' and knew what she was to achieve.

Zoë had kept up with one friend from Elmhurst – a girl called Margaret O'Connor. Margaret lived in London and when she became engaged to a doctor, 'quite old, but frightfully nice', she invited Zoë to go dancing with them. 'Ian will bring a friend,' she said. The friend was Rupert. 'He's had an awful time. Needs cheering up,' Margaret told her in the Ladies at the Gargoyle Club. Rupert thought Zoë the most beautiful girl he'd ever seen in his life. Zoë fell instantly and madly in love with Rupert. Six months later they were married.

'. . . Are you there?'

Zoë got out of the bath, wrapped herself in a towel and unlocked the door.

'This place is like a Turkish bath!'

'Better than an igloo. I suppose the dining room will be freezing, as usual?'

The closed look on his face made her regret that remark. He loathed her criticising his parents. He got into the bath and began washing his face vigorously. She bent over and kissed his streaming forehead.

'Sorry!'

'What about?'

'Nothing. I'll wear my frock with the daisies on it. Shall I?'

'Fine.'

She left him.

I'll take her to the flicks in Hastings next week, Rupert thought. She's never had a proper family life, that's why she finds it so strange. The thought that having been without it she might now be grateful occurred and went without his pursuing it.

∞ ∞ ∞

Neville and Lydia sat each end of the bath. He was sulking with Lydia because she'd gone off without him. When she said don't splash, and he hardly had, he smacked his heels on the water hard and really splashed her. Ellen and Nan had gone to get their suppers, so he would do what he liked. He picked up the sponge and held it threateningly, eyeing her. Then he put it on top of his head, and she laughed admiringly. 'I can't do that. I don't like bath water getting in my eyes.'

'I like bath water getting everywhere. I drink it.' He held the sponge up to his mouth and began to suck noisily.

'It's all soapy – you'll be sick.'

'I shan't because I'm used to it.' He drank some more of the stuff to show her. It got less nice and he stopped. 'I could drink the whole bath if I wanted to.'

'I suppose you could. I saw a ferret eating a bit of a rabbit with its fur on.'

'If it was only a bit of a rabbit, it must have been dead.'

'It might have been a whole rabbit and that was the last bit that it was eating.'

'I'd wish I'd seen it. Where was it?'

'In the potting shed. In a cage – it belongs to Mr McAlpine. It had little red eyes. I think it was mad.'

'How many ferrets have you seen in your life?'

102

'Not many. Only a few.'

'All ferrets eat things, you know.' He was trying to imagine what a ferret looked like; he'd never seen an animal with red eyes.

'I'll come and see it with you tomorrow,' he offered. 'I'm used to that kind of thing.'

'All right.'

'What will we get for supper? I'm 'stremely hungry.'

'You wasted your raspberries,' Lydia reminded him.

'Only about the last fourteen. I ate some of them up. Mind your own business,' he added. 'Shut up, blast you.'

Villy came into the bathroom before Lydia could say anything back. 'Hurry up, children. Lots of people want baths.' She held out a towel and Lydia climbed out and into her arms. 'What about you, Neville?'

'Ellen will get me,' he answered, but Villy got another towel and helped him out.

'He swore, Mummy! Do you know what he just said?'

'No, and I don't want to hear. You must stop telling tales, Lydia – it's not nice at all.'

'No, it isn't,' Lydia agreed. 'In spite of the awful things he said I won't tell you what they are. Will you read to me, Mummy? While I'm having my boring old supper?'

'Not tonight, darling. People are coming for drinks and I haven't changed. Tomorrow. I'll come and say good night to you, though.'

'I should jolly well hope you will.'

'She jolly well hopes you will,' said Neville, mimicking her. 'She thinks it's the least you can do.' He grinned at Villy showing the pink gaps where the tips of much larger teeth were just showing.

∞ ∞ ∞

Edward decided to go and have a whisky and soda with the Old Man while he was waiting for his bath. There was a problem at one of the wharfs that he particularly wanted to discuss without Hugh being there. And this seemed a good chance as he'd seen Hugh being taken around the garden by the Duchy. Accordingly, he put his head round the door of the study and his father, who was sitting at his desk cutting a cigar, welcomed him.

'Help yourself to a whisky, old boy, and give me one.'

Edward did as he was told, and settled himself in one of the large chairs opposite his father. William pushed the cigar box across to his son and then handed him the cutter. 'So. What's on your mind?'

Wondering at the way he always knew, Edward said, 'Well, actually, sir, Richards is rather on my mind.'

'He's on *all* of our minds. He's going to have to go, you know.'

'That's what I wanted to talk about. I don't think we should be too hasty.'

'Can't have a wharf manager who's practically never *there*! Never there when you want him, at any rate.'

'Richards had a rotten war, you know. Got a chest wound he's never got over.'

'That's why we employed him in the first place. Wanted to give him a fair chance. But you can't run a business by looking after crocks.'

'I absolutely agree. But after all, Hugh—' He had been going to say that Hugh's health wasn't too good and they wouldn't dream of sacking *him*, when the Old Man interrupted.

'Hugh agrees with me. He thinks that perhaps we needn't get rid of him altogether but could give him some easier job – less responsibility and all that.'

'And less pay?'

'Well, might have to adjust his salary. Depends what we can find for him.'

There was a silence. Edward knew that if the Old Man dug his toes in nothing would move him. He felt momentarily angry with Hugh for discussing this with their father behind his, Edward's, back, but then he reflected that that was exactly what he was doing himself. He tried again.

'Richards is a good chap, you know. He's intensely loyal; he cares about the firm.'

'I should damn well hope so! I should damn well hope that everybody we employ is loyal – poor look-out if they weren't.' Then he relented a bit, and said, 'We could find him something. Put him on to managing the lorries. I've never thought much of Lawson. Or give him a job in the office.'

'We can't pay him six hundred a year for a job in the office!'

'Well – send him out to sell. Put him on commission. Then it's up to him.'

Edward thought of Richards with his weedy frame and his apologetic brown eyes. 'That wouldn't do. It wouldn't do at all.'

'What do you suggest?'

'I'd like to think it over.'

William drained his whisky. 'Married, isn't he? With children?'

'Three, and one on the way.'

'We'll find something. What you and Hugh should do is concentrate on who is to take his place. It's vital that we get a good man.' He looked at Edward with his piercing blue eyes. 'You should know that by now.'

'Yes, sir.'

'Are you off?'

'I'm going to have a bath.'

When he had gone, William thought that he had never tried to say that Richards was any *good* at his job, so Hugh had been quite right.

∞ ∞ ∞

Rachel, in her bedroom, could see that the mystery guests had arrived. They came through the white gate from the drive in that uncertain wandering way that people employ when they approach a strange house whose front door is not immediately visible. She put Sid's letter back into her cardigan pocket; no good to read it now, she would waste it by hurrying. All day, she had been trying to find a quiet, uninterrupted time for it, and been defeated, by her senses of kindness and duty, and by the sheer number of people everywhere. She must now go and help the Duchy find out what on earth the newcomers were called. This difficulty was overcome by her hearing her father emerge from his study, shouting his greeting, 'Hallo, hallo, hallo. Delighted you've come. Clean forgotten your name, I'm afraid, but it happens to all of us sooner or later. Pickthorne! Of course! Kitty! The Pickthornes are here! Now what can I get you to drink, Mrs Pickthorne? A spot of gin? All my daughters-in-law drink gin, filthy drink, but the ladies seem to like it.'

Rachel heard the chink of the drinks trolley being wheeled

out of the house, by Hugh, she saw. Perhaps she *could* just read her letter before she went down? At that moment there was a knock on her door – a timid, rather inexperienced knock.

'Come in!'

It was Clary; she stood with one hand clutching the other, round which was tied a whitish bandage.

'What is it, Clary?'

'Nothing much. Only I think I might have rabies.'

'What on earth makes you think that, my duck?'

'I took Lydia to see Mr McAlpine's ferret in the potting shed. And then Nan came out for her and she went, and then I went back to look at the ferret, and he'd stopped eating the rabbit because it was nearly all finished and he looked so lonely in his cage so I let him out and then he bit me – a bit – not much but he drew blood and you have to take a hot iron or something and *burn* the place, and I'm not brave enough and I don't know where the irons are in this house, anyway. That's what they say in a Louisa Alcott book and Dad's in the bath and he didn't hear me, so I thought you could take me to the vet or something—' She gulped and added, 'Mr McAlpine will be furious and cross so could *you* tell him?'

'Let's look at your hand.'

Rachel unwrapped what turned out to be one of Clary's socks from her hot grey little hand. The bite was on her forefinger and did not look deep. While she washed it with water from her ewer, and got iodine and plaster from her medicine chest, Rachel explained that rabies had been stamped out in England so burning was not in order. Clary was brave about the iodine, but something was still worrying her.

'Aunt Rach! Could you come with me to help get him back into his cage? So that Mr McAlpine won't know?'

'I don't think either of us would be much good at that. Now you must go and see Mr McAlpine and apologise to him. He'll get it back.'

'Oh, *no*, Aunt Rach! He'll be so awfully angry.'

'I'll come with you, but you must do the apologising. And promise never to do anything like that again. It was a very naughty thing to do.'

'I didn't mean it to be. And I'm sorry.'

'Yes, well you must tell *him* that. Off we go.'
So her letter was postponed again.

∞ ∞ ∞

The Pickthornes stayed until twenty past eight, by which time
some chance remark made by their host finally convinced Mrs
Pickthorne that they had not, after all, been asked to dinner. 'We
really must be going,' she said twice – tentatively, and then with
desperation. Her husband, who had heard her the first time, had
pretended not to – staving off until the last possible moment the
confrontation with her in the car. But it was no use. William got
heartily to his feet and, grasping her forearm quite painfully,
escorted Mrs Pickthorne to the gate, so that her farewells had
to be strewn over her shoulder *en route*. Mr Pickthorne had to
follow: he managed to forget his hat – a Panama – but the child
who had been handing round little biscuits fetched it for him as
Uncle Edward told her to. 'You must come again *soon*,' William
shouted when they were safely in the car. Mr Pickthorne gave
a glassy smile, and clashed his gears before rumbling off down
the drive. Mrs Pickthorne pretended not to hear.

'Thought they'd never go!' William exclaimed as he stumped
back through the gate.

'They thought you'd asked them to dinner,' Rachel said.

'Oh, I don't think so. They can't have. Did I?'

'Of course you did,' said the Duchy calmly. 'It's very
tiresome of you, William. Most unfair on them.'

'They'll go sulking back to a quarrelsome tin of sardines,'
said Rupert. 'I wouldn't like to be Mr Pickthorne much. It'll
be all his fault.'

Eileen, who had been hovering for a good half-hour, now
came out to say that dinner was served.

∞ ∞ ∞

'What he *said* was,' this was his fourth attempt, ' "You must
come over and dine." And *later*, just when we were getting
out of the train, he said, "Come about six and have a
drink." '

'Exactly!'

'Well, it's all my fault as usual,' he said, to break some minutes of uncompanionable silence.

'Oh, that makes it all right, does it? It's all your fault so we needn't say any more?'

'Mildred, you know I can't stop you saying anything you like.'

'I've no wish to continue the subject.'

'There's nothing to eat at home,' she said very soon afterwards.

'We could open a tin of sardines.'

'Sardines! *Sardines!*' she repeated, as though they were tinned mice, as though nobody would think of putting them in a tin unless they were mad. 'You can have sardines if you're so keen on them. You know perfectly well what they do to me.'

I know what *I'd* like to do to you, he thought. I'd like to throttle you quite slowly, and then chuck you down the well. The viciousness of this thought, and the ease and speed with which it occurred, appalled him. I'm as bad as Crippen, he thought. Evil beyond belief. He put a hand on her knee. 'Sorry I spoilt your evening. It isn't as though you get a great deal of fun, is it? I don't mind what I have. Whatever you knock up will be very nice, like it always is.' He glanced at her and saw he was on the right lines.

'If only you'd *listen* to people,' she said. 'I expect we've got some eggs.'

∞ ∞ ∞

Dinner seemed to take ages, Zoë thought. They had cold salmon and new potatoes and peas, and there was a rather delicious hock to drink (although William, who considered white wine to be a ladies' drink, had a bottle of claret) and then chocolate soufflé and finally Stilton and port, but it took a long time because they were all talking so hard that they forgot to take vegetables when they were handed them, and the men had second helpings of salmon, and then, of course, all the vegetables – Rupert got up to hand them round and during all this they were talking about several things at once – the theatre – well, she was interested in *that* but not *French* plays and Shakespeare and plays in verse. But then Edward had turned to her and asked her what plays she liked and when she said she hadn't seen any lately, he told her about a play called *French Without Tears*, and just as she was thinking that the title sounded pretty boring, he laughed and said, 'Do you remember, Villy, that wonderful girl, Kay something-or-other, and one of the men said, "She gave me the old green light," and the other one said he thought she'd be pretty stingy with her yellows and reds?' And then when Villy had nodded and smiled as though she was humouring him, he'd turned again to Zoë, 'I think you ought to see that some day, it would make you laugh.' She liked Edward, and she felt he was attracted to her. Earlier, as they'd been going into the dining room, he'd said what a pretty dress she was wearing. It was a navy voile with large white yellow-centred daisies on it and rather a low V neck, and once she felt sure that Edward was looking down her dress and turned her head to look at him and he had been. He gave her a small smile and winked. She tried to frown but, actually, it was the best moment at dinner and she wondered whether he was falling in love with her. Of course, that would be terrible, but it wouldn't be her fault. She'd be distant, but very understanding; she'd probably let him kiss her once, because once wouldn't count; she would be taken by surprise, or he would think she had been. But she'd explain to him how it would all be no good because it would break Rupert's heart, and, anyway, she loved Rupert. Which was true. They would be having lunch at the Ivy – this would be after the kiss; the lunch would be to explain everything. Now she was married she hardly ever got invited out to lunch, and as an art master Rupert was far too poor for her to take people. He would be pleading with her just to let him see her occasionally – she began to wonder whether perhaps he might not be allowed to do that . . .

'Darling! Wasn't he the man who kept staring at you at the Gargoyle?'

'Which man?'

'You know who I mean. The small man with rather bulging eyes. The poet.'

'*I* don't know. I don't say "What's your name?" to people who stare at me!'

She felt she had scored, but there was a moment's silence,

and then Sybil said, 'Dylan Thomas at a nightclub? How interesting!'

Rupert said, 'That's it.'

The Duchy said, 'Poets used to be seen everywhere. It's only nowadays that they seem to have gone underground. They were quite *persona grata* in my youth. One met them at luncheon and perfectly ordinary occasions like that.'

'Darling Duchy, the Gargoyle is four floors up.'

'Really? I thought all nightclubs were underground, I don't know why. I've never been to one.'

William said, 'Too late now.'

And she replied serenely, 'Far too late,' and rang for Eileen to clear the plates.

Edward further endeared himself to her by saying, 'Never seen the point of poetry, can't understand what the fellers are getting at.'

And Villy, who heard him, said, 'But, darling, you never read *anything*. No use pretending it's just *poetry* you don't read.'

While Edward was saying good-humouredly that one high-brow member in the family was quite enough, Zoë eyed Villy appraisingly. She didn't seem right for Edward, somehow. She was sort of – well, you couldn't say she wasn't attractive, but she wasn't glamorous. She had a bony nose that was too big, a bony face but heavy eyebrows that were quite dark, not grey like her hair, and a boyish figure that was, none the less, lacking in allure. Her eyes were brown, and not bad, but her lips were too thin. Altogether, she was a surprising person for handsome Edward to have married. Of course, she was terribly good at things – not just riding and tennis, but she played the piano, and some sort of pipe instrument, and read French books, and made real lace on a pillow and bound books in floppy soft leather, and wove table-mats and then embroidered them. There seemed to be nothing that she couldn't do, and no particular reason why she should do any of it – Edward was far richer than Rupert. And she was also what Zoë's mother (and consequently Zoë) called well connected, although Zoë now never actually said that sort of thing aloud. Villy's father had been a baronet; Villy had a picture of him in a silver frame in their drawing room; he looked fearfully old-fashioned, with a drooping white walrus moustache, a wing collar with a tight tie, and large melancholy eyes. He'd been a composer – and quite well known, something she wished Rupert would become; there was a lot of money in portrait painting if you got to paint the right people. Lady Rydal, though, was a real battleaxe. Zoë had only met her once, here, soon after she was married. The Duchy had asked her to stay because they'd all been very fond of Sir Hubert and were sorry for her when he died. She'd made it clear that she disapproved of painted nails, and the girls wearing shorts and the cinema and women drinking spirits – a real kill-joy.

'. . . What do you think, silent Zoë?'

'Rupert says I'm no good at thinking about anything,' she replied. She hadn't been listening and hadn't the faintest idea of what they had been talking about – not the *faintest*.

'I never said that, darling. I said you operated on your intuition.'

The Duchy said, 'Women are perfectly capable of thought. They simply have different things to think about.'

Edward said, 'I really don't see why Zoë should think about Mussolini.'

'Of course not! The less she thinks about that sort of thing the better! Don't you worry your pretty little head about that wop dictator,' the Brig added kindly to his daughter-in-law. 'Although I have to say that he's made a good job of planting eucalyptus and draining all those swamps. I have to give him that.'

'Brig, darling! You talk as though he planted them himself.' Rachel's face crumpled with amusement. 'Imagine him! Every button doing overtime on his uniform when he bent down—'

Sybil, who up until then had been listening affectionately to the Brig's extremely long story about the second time he went to Burma, said, 'But he's also built some pretty good roads, hasn't he? Had them built, I mean?'

'Of course he has,' said Edward. 'Generated employment, got people to work. And, my God, I bet they work harder than they do here! I sometimes think that this country could do with a dictator. Look at Germany! Look at Hitler! Look what he's done for his people!'

Hugh was shocked. 'We don't want a dictator, Ed! You can't think that!'

'Of course we don't! What we need is a decent socialist government. Someone who understands the working classes. They'd work if they had a decent incentive.' Rupert looked defiantly round the room at his Tory family. 'This lot think of nothing but preserving the *status quo*.'

The chocolate soufflé arrived and deflected them from this well-worn jungle path, although Zoë could hear Edward mutter that there was nothing much wrong with the *status quo* that *he* could see.

After the soufflé, Sybil and Villy said they were going to bottle the children up for the night, and Zoë, who did not want them to see how little Clary liked her, sat tight. Rachel, who had observed this, said she was going to fetch her cigarettes. The Duchy suggested that they leave the men to their cheese and port.

∞ ∞ ∞

Louise and Polly had had their bath together and left the water for Clary as they had been told to do, but she didn't seem to be about, and they didn't see why they should find her. They brushed their hair and plaited Louise's, which was difficult because it wasn't long enough yet for a good plait. She had decided to grow it, so that when she was an actress she wouldn't have to wear wigs. 'Although if you act someone very old, you'll have to have a white one,' Polly said, but Louise said the only old person she wanted to play, and it was *play* not act, was Lear and they weren't yet fair about letting women play the decent Shakespeare parts.

'I'll probably have to start with Hamlet,' she said.

'I can't see why you couldn't just be Rosalind – or Viola. They both wear men's clothes.'

'But underneath they're women. That's the point. I'll put the elastic band on – other people always tweak.'

'You know, Polly, you really ought to think what *you're* going to do – you're getting a bit old not to know.'

'I know I am. I think I'd quite like to marry someone,' she said some minutes later.

'That's *feeble*! All kinds of people get married! That's neither here nor there!'

'I knew you'd say that.' Any minute now Louise would start making awful suggestions. She'd done it so often that Polly thought she must have run out of ideas by now, but she never had.

'A fishmonger? You could wear a long apron and nice little straw hat.'

'I'd hate it. It's so surprising and awful when blood comes out of fish.'

'You'd be good at arranging them on the slab.'

'If only they weren't fish, I would.'

'It's not good being squeamish, Polly. There's hardly anything you can be if you're that. *I* shall have to stab people, and strangle them, and faint down flights of stairs.'

'If you're going to be like that, I shall read.'

'All right, I won't. Let's go and find Teddy and Simon and play Monopoly.'

But in the schoolroom they found Teddy and Simon in the middle of a game which looked like going on for ages.

'We'll play the next one with you,' one of them said, but it was an idle promise because the chances were that they'd be made to go to bed long before it finished.

'You can stay here if you shut up,' the other one said, so, of course, they took their supper trays and went back to their room. Louise tried to slam the door and spilt a lot of her milk.

'If only Pompey was here! He loves spilt milk, much more than in a saucer.' They got a face towel and mopped it up, and Polly kindly offered to go and ask for some more.

'Please ask for it in a mug. I simply loathe milk in a glass – it makes the milk seem all watery.'

After supper they got into their beds and Polly did her knitting that she'd been making since the Christmas holidays, a thick, very pale pink jumper, and Louise started *The Wide Wide World* and was soon snuffling and wiping her eyes on the sheet. 'Everything to do with God seems very sad,' she said. Polly stopped her knitting – at least she'd done nearly an inch – and read *The Brown Fairy Book* because it was not much fun not reading when the other person was. She put on a light and moths came in, little flittery ones and fat ones that thudded against the lampshade.

When Villy and Sybil came, they at once asked where Clary was.

Polly said, 'Don't know.'

Louise said, 'We'd clean forgotten her,' but they both knew there would be trouble. After some questioning they went in search of her. Then Aunt Rachel came in and asked the same thing.

'We don't know, Aunt Rach, honestly. She didn't come to the schoolroom for supper. We left the bath for her.' Louise tried to make that sound kind, but it didn't because it wasn't. Aunt Rachel went out of the room at once, and they could hear her talking to their mothers. They looked at each other.

'It's not our fault.'

'Yes, it is,' said Polly. 'We didn't want her to come with us after tea.'

'Blast! The trouble is she makes me feel so awful and that makes me not like her. Much.'

After a pause, Polly said, 'She doesn't make you feel awful – it's how we are to her that does. We'll have to—' but then Aunt Villy came in and she shut up.

'Now listen, you two. You must not gang up on Clary. How would you like it if she and the other one of you did it to either of you?'

'We honestly didn't gang up,' Louise began, but Polly said, 'We promise we won't any more.'

But Aunt Villy took no notice of this and said, 'I blame you, Louise, most, because you are the oldest.' She was turning down Clary's bed, and then opening her rather battered suitcase. 'You could at least have helped her unpack.'

'Polly is the same age as Clary, and I don't help *her* unpack.'

Aunt Sybil came in now, and said, 'She's nowhere to be found. Rachel is asking in the kitchen, but I think we ought to get Rupert.'

'Shall we go and look for her, Aunt Syb?'

But her mother said at once, 'You will do no such thing. You will unpack her suitcase really nicely, and one of you may fetch her supper from the schoolroom. I am very displeased with you, Louise.'

'I'm sorry. I'm *truly* sorry.' Louise rushed to the suitcase and began taking Clary's clothes out.

Polly got out of bed to go and fetch the tray. She sensed that her mother was not so cross as Aunt Villy was with Louise, whom she knew was by now really upset. Then she realised that her mother realised this too. Their eyes met before Sybil said, 'Have you any idea where she might be?'

Polly thought as hard as she could, but she wasn't Clary, so how could she think? She shook her head. The mothers went away and Louise cried.

In the end, after Rupert had been told, and the uncles joined in the search, and even Zoë had walked about the tennis court, calling for her, and people had been to the stables, and the gardener's cottage, and the greenhouses and even into the wood, it was Rachel who found her. She had slipped up to her room to get a coat and join the outside search and there was Clary asleep on the floor. She had made herself a little bed of armchair cushions, and Rachel's coat was over her. She was fast asleep with her sandshoes beside her. On Rachel's pillow was a note. 'Dear Aunt Rach, I'd rather sleep in your room. I hope you don't mind. I only didn't undress because of getting cold. Love from Clary.' Rupert said he'd wake her up and talk to her and then take her to her room, but Rachel said much better to leave her where she was and got her a blanket and a proper pillow.

So coffee was drunk very late that first evening, and then the Duchy and Villy played duets for a bit, which Zoë found awfully boring because it meant that you couldn't talk. Sybil went to bed first, and Hugh said he'd go with her.

'What was that all about, do you think?'

'Well, Louise and Polly are great friends. They see each other nearly every day in London. I expect Clary felt left out.'

'Here – I'll do that for you.' He took her hairpins out and laid them one by one on the palm of the hand she held out to him. 'You're too tired,' he accused, so tenderly that her eyes pricked.

'Too tired to hold my arms above my head. Thank you, my darling.'

'I'll undress you.'

She stood up and pulled the smock dress over her head.

'Villy made too much of it with Louise. She always does.'

'Well, that's not our business.' He unhooked her brassière

and eased the shoulder straps down her arms. She stepped out of her knickers and kicked off her sandals standing before him, naked, grotesque and beautiful. 'Where's your nightie?'

'On the bed, I think. Darling. You must be sick of me looking like this.'

'I marvel at it.' Then he added more lightly, 'I feel privileged to behold you. Go to bed.'

'It can't be that easy for Rupert.'

'Don't you worry about him.'

She heaved herself into bed.

'I wish you weren't going back on Monday.'

'I'm sure I could swap with Edward if you wanted me to.'

'No – no, I don't. I'd rather have you in London when it's born.'

He went to the curtains and drew them apart. The light woke him in the morning, but he knew – or thought he knew – that she liked them open.

'You don't have to draw them. I really don't mind.'

'I *like* them open,' he lied. 'You know I do.'

'Of course.' It was no good her wanting them shut when she knew he liked air. The light did wake her in the mornings, but it was a small price to pay for someone she loved so much.

∞ ∞ ∞

' . . . and I honestly think that if only Zoë made the slightest attempt to pull her weight as a stepmother, poor little Clary would be a much easier child.'

'She's awfully young, you know. I expect she finds the family *en masse* a bit overwhelming. I like her,' he added.

'I know you do.' Villy unscrewed her earrings and put them back into their battered little box.

'Well, it's good that *someone* likes her – apart from Rupert, of course.'

'I don't think he *likes* her. He's mad about her, but that's not the same thing at all.'

'That's all too subtle for me, I'm afraid.' He spoke indistinctly, because he'd taken out his plate to clean it.

'Darling, you know perfectly well what I mean. She's full

116

of SA.' Villy mentioned this in a facetious tone that did not conceal her disgust.

Edward, who was very well aware of Zoë's sex appeal but sensed that this was dangerous ground, changed the subject to Teddy and listened amiably while Villy said how worried she was about his eyes, and did Edward think he was leaving his prep school too young, and hadn't he grown in the last term *unbelievably*? In fact, she went on chattering after they were in bed and he wanted her to stop.

'First night of the holidays,' he said, kissing her, and feeling with one hand for the short soft curly hair at the back of her neck.

Villy strained away from him for a moment, but she was only turning off the light.

∞ ∞ ∞

' . . . I *do* try but she simply doesn't like me!'

'I think she feels that you don't like her.'

'Anyway, it's Ellen's job to know where she is. I mean – surely she's not meant to *just* look after Neville? She's meant to be the children's nurse, isn't she?'

'Clary is twelve, a bit too old for a nanny. Still, I agree with you, she should have seen that Clary went to bed.'

Zoë didn't reply. She felt she had shifted the balance of blame, felt consequently less guilty – able to be softer.

Rupert was cleaning his teeth and spitting into the slop pail. He said, 'I'll have a talk with Ellen tomorrow. And Clary, too, of course.'

'All right, darling.' It sounded, irritatingly, like a concession (about what?). I don't want to row about it, he reminded himself. He glanced at her to see how she was getting on with the interminable business of cleaning her face. She was using the transparent stuff from a bottle; it was nearly over. She caught his eye in the dressing-table glass and began one of her slow confiding smiles; he watched the beguiling dimple below her right cheekbone appear, and went over to her, pulling the kimono off her shoulders. Her skin was cool as alabaster, as lustrous as pearls, the warm white of a rose. He thought, but did not say these things; his deepest adoration of her could not

117

be shared; somewhere he knew that her image and herself were not the same, and he could only cling to the image through secrecy.

'It's high time I took you to bed,' he said.

'All right, darling.'

When he had made love to her, and she had turned, with a sigh of content, onto her side, she said, 'I will try harder with Clary, I truly promise you I will.'

He remembered, irresistibly, the last time she had said that and answered as he had before, 'I know that you will.'

∞ ∞ ∞

My darling, I wonder if you will ever know how much you are that? I don't know how long this will be, because I am writing this in the common room, where, as you know, everybody resting between bouts of teaching comes for a fag and a cup of coffee, and, unfortunately, a chat. So I get interrupted, and in twelve minutes' time Jenkins minor will loom to murder a perfectly harmless little piece of Bach. Last Wednesday was lovely, wasn't it? I sometimes think, or perhaps I *have* to think, that we get more out of our precious times together than people who do not have our difficulties, who can meet and be affectionate openly and when they please. But oh! How I miss you! You are the most rare, miraculous creature – a much better person than I in every imaginable way. Sometimes I wish you were not so entirely *good* – so unselfish, so generous and untiring in your attention and kindness to all. I am greedy; I want you to myself. It's all right; I know that this isn't possible; I shall never repeat my unspeakable behaviour of the night we went to the Prom – I shall never hear any Elgar again in my life without shame. I know that you are right; my sister depends upon me in all sorts of ways, the blasted finances as you call them, and you have your parents, who have both come to depend on you. But sometimes I dream of us both becoming free to be alone together. You are all I want. I would live in a wigwam with you or a seaside hotel – the kind with paper carnations on the dinner tables and people with half-bottles of wine with their initials on

118

the label. Or a Tudor bijou gem on the Great West Road, with a pink cherry and a laburnum tree and a crazy-paving path – anywhere, my dearest Ahry, would be transformed by you. If wishes were horses . . . I thought perhaps that I might—

Oh, Jenkins minor! The dandruff rained down upon his fiddle from which came the most dreadful sounds – like some small animal caught in a trap. I sound cruel, but he lied to me about his practising – he is not a winning child. What I had been going to say was that *if* I rang early next week, perhaps the dear Duchy would have me for a night? Or failing that, to luncheon? Or – most bold of all – perhaps you could meet me at the station, and we could lunch somewhere in Battle and go for a walk? These are only wild suggestions; you need only say when I ring that it wouldn't do for it not to do. Just to hear your voice will be wonderful. Write to me, my dear heart, write to me I beg—

'Aunt Rach?'

Instinctively, she folded the letter and put it out of sight. 'Yes, my duck. I'm here.'

'Is it all right? You aren't cross?'

Rachel got out of her bed and knelt on the floor beside her niece. 'I was most honoured to be chosen.' She stroked Clary's fringe back from her forehead. 'We'll have a lovely talk tomorrow. Go to sleep now. Are you warm enough?'

Clary looked surprised. '*I* don't know. How do I feel?'

'Warm enough.' Rachel leaned down and kissed her.

'If I'd really got rabies, you wouldn't be able to kiss me 'cos I'd bite, wouldn't I?'

'What *have* you been reading?'

'Nothing. Someone told me about it at school. A horrible girl from South America. You wouldn't like her, she's *so* horrible.'

'Good night, Clary. Off you go.'

'Are you going to sleep now?'

'Yes.'

So then, of course, she had to put the letter away and turn out the light.

∞ ∞ ∞

On Saturday, Villy went riding with her father-in-law, Edward and Hugh played tennis with Simon and Teddy, Rupert took Zoë out to lunch in Rye, Polly and Louise took turns to have riding lessons on Joey, who, caught by Wren and doomed to an hour's trotting and cantering pointlessly round the same old field, got his own back by puffing himself up when he was saddled so that the girths would hardly go round his huge grass-fed belly and then deflating so that the saddle slipped sideways and decanted Polly onto the ground. With Louise, he only managed to switch his tail so sharply that he stung her eyes when she was trying to mount him.

Clary took Lydia to see butterflies and then they found a heap of sand left by the builders and Clary had an idea. 'It's quite a long idea,' she said, sternly, because Neville was tagging along and she wanted to put him off, but it didn't work. 'I want to be *in* the idea,' he said, so in the end she let him. Under her direction, they set about moving nearly all the sand to a secret place behind the potting shed.

Rachel picked more raspberries, and black and red currants for Mrs Cripps to make summer puddings, typed excerpts from John Evelyn's *Diaries* for her father's book, and finally joined Sybil under the monkey puzzle to tack yards of rufflette onto dark green chintz for the Duchy to machine after luncheon.

The Duchy had her morning interview with Mrs Cripps. The wreck of the salmon was inspected; it would not stretch to being served cold again with salad – was to be turned into croquettes for dinner to be followed by a Charlotte Russe (this was a compromise between them; Mrs Cripps did not like making croquettes, and the Duchy thought that Charlotte Russe was too rich in the evening). For Sunday lunch they would have the roast lamb and summer pudding. That settled, she was free to spend the morning in her garden; dead-heading, clipping the four pyramids of box that were stationed at the end of the herbaceous borders guarding the sundial with Billy to sweep up and clear away the clippings.

By noon, everybody was too hot to go on doing all these things. The fathers felt that they had worked long enough on Teddy's serve and Simon's backhand and the boys were both frantic for lunch – still an hour away – and went on their traditional and lightning raid upon the tins of biscuits by their parents' beds. Today, it was easy; they swiped the lot from Uncle Rupert's room, knowing he was out, and ate them in the downstairs lavatory.

Villy, after the ride, had to be taken by William round the new buildings. She was longing to change out of her riding clothes, but her father-in-law, fully dressed in flannel shirt, lemon gaberdine waistcoat and tweed jacket with gaberdine breeches and leather boots, seemed impervious to the heat, and spent a good hour explaining not only what they had done but the alternative plans that had been rejected.

Louise and Polly, abandoned by Wren who said he had to get back and see the other horses, had one more turn each on Joey, who was sweating a lot and less and less inclined to co-operate; he had taken to ambling and stopping to snatch mouthfuls of grass. 'He smells lovely, but he's not very faithful,' Polly said, as she dismounted. 'Want another turn?'

Louise shook her head. 'If only there were two of him we could go for a proper ride. Hold him while I take the saddle off.' Polly, who secretly did not like riding nearly as much as Louise, agreed. What she was thinking was that now they could have the rest of the day doing much nicer things. She stroked Joey's tender nose, but he nudged her impatiently – it was sugar not sentiment he was after. When Louise had heaved the saddle off his back, she unstrapped his bridle and slipped it over his face. He stood for a moment, and then, tossing his head with a theatrical gesture, cantered a few paces until he was out of reach. 'I'm afraid he really doesn't like us much,' Louise said. She felt that she had the reputation for being marvellous with animals and Joey did not behave at all as though he agreed with this.

'He likes you better than me,' said loyal Polly; although it had never been mentioned, she knew how Louise felt. They trudged on down the cart track from the field to the stables taking turns with the saddle.

Clary had had a good morning. The sand had all been heaped into an old cold frame in the kitchen garden. The glass lid had long since gone and the bottom made an ideal boundary for her idea. First of all the sand had to be patted completely smooth: they tried with bare feet, but hands turned out to be better. Clary was best at this, and in order to have the peace and quiet to do it properly she sent the others to fetch things.

'What sort of things?' Neville was getting fractious: 'What are we trying to do? Why don't we get some water and make mud?' he complained.

'Shut up. If you don't want to play with us, you can just go away. Or you can do what Clary says. She's the oldest.'

'I don't want to go away. I do want to play. I want to know what we're supposed to be doing. I don't want to waste my time,' he added rather grandly.

'Your time!' Lydia scoffed, trying to think of the smallest thing she knew. 'It's not worth a hundred or a thousand.'

Clary said, 'We're making a garden. We need hedges, and gravel for paths, and – yes – and a lake! And trees, and flowers – we need everything! One of you collect the gravel, only the tiniest gravel. You do that, Neville. Get a seed box out of the greenhouse for it.'

'What shall I do?'

'I want you to guard the sand. And scrape moss off the wall at the bottom there,' she added, as Lydia began to look disappointed.

'Where are you going?'

'I'll be back soon.'

On her way back from her successful and unnoticed raid in the house – Zoë's nail scissors out of her manicure set and the small round mirror out of the maids' lavatory – she came upon a trug full of box clippings (Billy had been called to his dinner). Her mind was a riot of possibilities: with the scissors, she could plant grass and cut it short so that it would be a lawn, and the box would make a tiny hedge to edge the gravel path – or it could be in a pattern for flower beds. There was no end to what she might do to make the most beautiful garden in the world. For once, she was glad that Polly and Louise weren't about; they might have had ideas, and she wanted it to be entirely her own.

When she got back, she found that Lydia had tired of collecting moss, had picked some daisies, was sticking them just anywhere into the sand. 'I'm putting in the flowers for you,' she said. Clary let her do it at one end of the sand. Lydia was small and you couldn't expect too much and she knew that if you were too small you didn't like being made to feel it.

Just as Neville came back with hardly any gravel, but a whole lot of other things that wouldn't have been the slightest use, they heard Ellen calling them to come in to get ready for lunch.

'It's a deadly secret,' Clary warned. 'You mustn't say a word to them. Say we've been playing in the orchard. We'll come out after lunch and do all the proper making.'

'*We* have to have blasted rests,' Neville reminded her. 'For a whole blasted hour.'

'It isn't fair!'

'*I* used to have to,' Clary said quickly before Lydia could work herself up. 'When you're twelve, you won't have to.'

'Supposing I don't get to twelve?' It seemed to her very unlikely.

'I'll get to it first,' Neville said. 'There'll be one holiday when you'll be the *only one* having a rest.'

'Don't quarrel. If you go in all smeary with tears, they'll ask what we've been doing.'

They composed their faces to uniform conspiratorial blandness and went up to the house.

∞ ∞ ∞

At one o'clock Eileen sounded the gong for lunch.

'Gracious! I haven't done the bag!' Rachel sprang to her feet, felt the familiar twinge in her back that seemed always to be there when she made an unconsidered movement, and went quickly into the house. 'Don't worry about the curtains,' she called, in case Sybil should tire herself trying to fold and carry them. The bag, kept in a drawer of the card table in the drawing room, was a small linen affair with R.C. embroidered in blue cotton chain stitch. It had been Rachel's school brush and comb bag, but now it contained eight cardboard squares, six of them blank and two marked D.R. As the children came downstairs from washing for lunch, they each pulled a square out of the bag. This ritual was because the Duchy had decreed that two children should be allowed into the dining room for lunch in order that they should learn how to behave at meals with the grown-ups; the method of choosing had been evolved to stop squabbling and the perennial allegations of injustice. Today, Simon got one of the tickets, and then Clary.

'I don't want it,' she said, put it back like lightning, and drew a blank. 'My father's out, you see,' she said quickly to Rachel. Really, she was afraid that Lydia and Neville might spill some beans about the garden if she was not there to stop them.

Rachel let this pass. 'But next time you must stick to the rules,' she said mildly.

Neville was late for lunch. He came down with Ellen holding his hand (a sure sign of humiliation and wrong-doing).

'I'm sorry we're late. Neville had lost his sandshoes.'

'I only lost *one* of them.' The fuss that people could make about one miserable shoe was beyond him. In the end, Teddy got the other ticket for which he was profoundly grateful. He was not ready yet to make the difficult change from an all-male society at school – except for Matron and the French mistress, both objects of continual, covert derision – to eating and talking with all these women and babies.

He decided to sit next to Dad and Uncle Hugh and then they could talk either about cricket, or possibly, about submarines, in which he had lately become interested. Lunch was hot boiled gammon and parsley sauce (the Duchy had a Victorian disregard for weather when planning menus), with new potatoes and broad beans followed by treacle tart. Simon loathed broad beans, but Sybil ate them for him. She's a pretty broad bean herself, he thought and then choked trying not to laugh at such a marvellous joke; he didn't want to hurt his mother's feelings, and nobody would like being called broad except a bean. This set him off again; Dad hit him on the back, and his plate fell out onto the table cloth – a jolly embarrassing meal.

Teddy ate an enormous lunch – two helpings of everything and then biscuits and cheese. He had decided to make Simon play tennis immediately after lunch because later on the grown-ups would probably hog the court. Dad had said that he could practise his serve on his own, but that wasn't much fun if there was nobody to return the balls and, worse, nobody to tell him whether they were in or not. If he worked at it, he could end up playing for England. The thought of the board at Wimbledon Cazalet *v.* Budge made the back of his neck prickle. 'Brilliant New Player Annihilates Budge!' would be the headline. Of course, it might not be Budge by then, but whoever it was – Hell's bells and buckets of blood, it would be a pretty exciting week. The thing would be to get Fred Perry to coach him; there couldn't be anyone better in the world than Fred. It was rotten that one couldn't play tennis in winter at school, but he'd be able to play squash or racquets to keep his eye in. He decided to write to Fred Perry to see what he would advise. Dad and Uncle Hugh had been no good to talk to: they'd been arguing about whether to get something called a Dictaphone in their office or not. Dad wanted one because he said it would be more efficient, but Uncle Hugh said it took the same amount of time to dictate to a secretary as it did to a machine, and he believed in the personal touch. The women were talking about babies and rotten things like that. God! He was glad he wasn't a woman. Having to wear skirts and being much weaker – hardly ever doing anything really interesting like going to the South Pole or being a racing driver, and Carstairs said that blood poured out of them in streams from between their legs whenever there was a full moon, an unlikely tale because there was a full moon every month and obviously they'd die from loss of blood, and, anyway, he'd never *seen* any of them doing it, but Carstairs had a gory nature, he was always on about vampire bats and the Charge of the Light Brigade and the Black Death. He was going to be a detective when he grew up – on murder cases; Teddy was glad he wouldn't be seeing any more of Carstairs. His new school loomed up in his mind like an iceberg: what he could see of it was frightening enough and that was only a fifth (or was it a sixth?), as frightening as he knew it would be when he actually had to *go* to it. Ages away – the holidays had hardly started. He caught Simon's eye across the table and made a batting movement with his right arm which knocked over his glass of water.

∞ ∞ ∞

Lunch in the hall was difficult for Clary in ways she hadn't thought of. Neville and Lydia behaved beautifully, didn't say a word about their garden, and Clary offered to look for and find Neville's missing shoe, which went down well with Ellen. But Polly, who felt guilty that she and Louise had again left Clary out by going off and riding together and not even asking her whether she wanted to come, was now suggesting all kinds of things that she and Louise would do in the afternoon with Clary, like go to the stream in the far wood and make a dam, and when Clary didn't seem very keen on that, a tennis tournament, or making a log house in the wood. 'Well, what *would* you like to do?' she said at last.

Clary felt Lydia's and Neville's eyes fixed on her. 'Go to the beach,' she said. The beach meant cars and grown-ups, so she knew that Polly and Louise couldn't do anything about *that*. They gave up; it was common knowledge, Louise said, that they were going to the beach on Monday and not before.

∞ ∞ ∞

After lunch, Villy drove Sybil to Battle to buy flannel and white wool. They had made this plan at breakfast, but had a tacit agreement to keep quiet about their trip in order that no children should clamour to join them. Now they drove in a peaceful silence, easing comfortably into their customary summer relationship. They saw each other in London, naturally, but this was more because of their husbands' affection for one another than from their own choice. But, since they both became life members of the Cazalet family at about the same time, they had had years of natural proximity to develop an undemanding intimacy of a kind they did not either of them have with anyone else. They had married the brothers two years after the war: Sybil in January, Edward and Villy the following May. The brothers had suggested a double wedding, had even mooted a double honeymoon, but this had been averted by Villy having to finish her contract with the Russian ballet, and Sybil wanting to marry before her father's leave was up and he went back to India. Sybil's godmother had provided the necessary background (her mother had died in India the previous year), Edward had been best man and they had gone to Rome for their honeymoon – Hugh said France was too full of things that he wanted to forget. Edward had taken them to see

Villy dance with the ballet at the Alhambra and Sybil had been deeply impressed by Villy actually being a professional dancer. They had seen Petroushka (Villy had been one of the Russian peasant women) and Sybil, whose first visit to the ballet it was, had been overwhelmed by Massine in the title role. Afterwards they had waited for Villy to come out of the stage door wearing a coat with a white fur collar, and her hair – long in those days – done in a bun and a little silver arrow sticking in the side of it. They had all gone to the Savoy for supper, and Villy seemed the most sophisticated and glamorous person Sybil had ever met. Under the coat, she wore a black chiffon dress embroidered with brilliant green and blue crystal beads that showed her elegant narrow knees, with green satin shoes to match that made Sybil's beige stamped velvet trimmed with Irish lace seem dull. She had been bubbling with energy and, egged on by Edward, chattered all evening about the Russian company and touring; about Paris, and rehearsing with Matisse dropping paint pots onto their heads, and not being paid for weeks, living on a pint of milk a day and lying in the beds between rehearsals and performances; of Monte Carlo and the glittering audiences; of how Massine and Diaghilev quarrelled, and how some of the company gambled away their salaries in a single night.

It had seemed to her then incredible and heroic of Villy to give up such a life for marriage, but Villy, who seemed as much in love with Edward as he was with her, made light of it. They were married from Villy's home in Albert Place, and her father composed an organ suite for the service which was noticed in *The Times*. Villy had cut off her hair and was fashionably shingled for the wedding, which Sybil had attended feeling terribly queasy with her first pregnancy – the one that had ended with a stillborn son. Apart from being married to brothers, they had little in common to begin with but with the Cazalets, being married to brothers meant steady, continuous meetings: evenings when the brothers played chess, winter holidays when they went skiing – Sybil was hopeless at that, invariably twisted an ankle, once broke her leg, while Villy whirled down most daring runs with a verve and skill that earned her much local admiration. They played bridge and tennis. They went to theatres and to restaurants where they dined and danced. One evening, at the Hungaria, Villy said something in Russian to the leader of the orchestra, and he played some Delibes and Villy danced by herself on the cleared floor and everyone applauded. When she returned to their table and Edward said perfunctorily, 'Well done, darling.' Sybil had noticed tears in her eyes, and wondered whether giving up her career had turned out to be so easy for Villy after all. Villy never mentioned her dancing days again, continued in her role of wife and, subsequently, mother of Louise and then Teddy and Lydia as though it had never happened. But Sybil had observed her restless energy, which, like water, streamed out in any direction it could find. She got a loom and wove linen and silk. She learned to play the zither and the flute. She learned to ride, and was soon exercising horses for the Life Guards – one of the two women in London allowed to do so. She worked for the Red Cross, took blind children to the seaside. She sailed a dinghy in small boat races. She taught herself Russian: for a short time she joined a Gjieff sect (Sybil only found out about this because Villy tried to make her join it too). Some of the crazes – like the sect – did not last long. Resisting a sudden urge to say, 'Are you happy?' she said, 'I suppose the shops in Battle may be shut.'

'Good Lord! Of course, they will be. How stupid! We could go on to Hastings.'

'The shop at Watlington'll be open.'

'Will it?' Villy had slowed and was looking for somewhere to turn.

'It somehow always is. They'll have white wool. And almost certainly flannel.'

'Right.' Villy stopped at someone's drive and then backed into it.

'It seems so inefficient. If only I'd kept Simon's things. But I never thought I'd need them again.'

'I chucked everything out, too. One can't keep everything,' Villy said. 'I'll help you, if you like.'

'It would be angelic. I'll never forget that christening robe you made for Teddy.' It had been the finest white lawn, embroidered in white thread with wild flowers, and all the seams joined by drawn threadwork. The sort of work usually done by nuns.

'You can borrow it, if you like. There won't be time to make another of those.'

'I didn't mean that. I'm just aiming at four flannel nighties and a shawl.'

They were passing the white gates of the house on their way up the hill to the shop at Watlington. Villy said, 'I'm sure the Duchy would help.'

'She's making one of her lovely tussore smocks for Clary's birthday.'

'Goodness! I'd forgotten that. What are you giving her?'

'I can't think. I don't know really what she likes. She's not a very happy little girl, is she? Rupert says she's not doing well at school either. A bad report, order marks, and she doesn't seem to have made any friends.'

'I shouldn't think Zoë would be very nice to them if she did.'

Neither of them liked Zoë, and both knew that they were about to embark upon a Zoë talk, which happened every holidays and always ended by them saying that they really must stop. This time they stopped because they had reached their destination – an old white-painted clapboard farmhouse the ground floor of which had been rather casually converted into a shop. It sold a little of everything: groceries, vegetables, packets of seeds, chocolates, cigarettes, elastic and buttons, knitting wool, eggs, bread, Panama hats, trugs, willow-pattern mugs and brown teapots, flowered Tootal cottons, fly papers, bird seed and dog biscuits, door mats and kettles. Mrs Cramp produced a roll of white flannel and cut the five yards required. Mr Cramp, at the other counter, was cutting bacon in the machine. A heavily encrusted fly paper hung above it, and banged against his bald head every time he collected a slice and put it on the scales, and sometimes a long-dead fly fell like a dried currant onto the counter. His customer, in the middle of narrating some indeterminate misfortune, fell silent when Sybil and Villy entered the shop, and only the weather – not a drop of rain for two weeks and looking as though it would hold up for the harvest – was discussed while the ladies were in the shop.

'And white wool, Mrs Hugh. Paton's two-ply; would that be what you were after? Or we do have the fleecy Shetland.'

'I'll make the shawl,' said Villy. They chose the Shetland, and Sybil bought a reel of white cotton.

'Mrs Cazalet Senior keeping well, is she? That's right.'

The flannel was wrapped in a piece of soft brown paper and tied with string. The wool was put into a paper bag. Mrs Cramp avoided Sybil's stomach like the plague.

But as soon as Villy had left the shop, she said, 'She's near her time, or I'm a Dutchman.'

And Mrs Miles, who had been buying the bacon, said, 'It wouldn't surprise me if it was twins.'

Mrs Cramp was shocked. It was her prerogative to remark on her customers. 'They don't have twins,' she said. 'Not ladies.'

In the car, Villy said, 'Do you think it would be a good idea if Clary left school and joined our two with Miss Milliment?'

'Very good for Clary. But do you think Rupert could afford it?'

'Two pounds ten a week! It *must* be cheaper than her school.'

'He probably gets a special rate for being a schoolmaster. He may not pay at all, except for the extras.'

'Our two have extras.'

'Rachel might help with those. Or the Duchy might speak to the Brig. Or you could – on one of your rides. He'd probably listen to you – you get on so well with him.'

'Let's talk to Rupert first.' Villy ignored this compliment as she did all the others these days. 'There would be fares, of course. She'd have to walk to Shepherd's Bush and take the Underground. But I do feel it would be a family atmosphere for her, and that's what she needs. I don't think she gets much of that at home.'

Sybil said, 'Of course, Zoë will start having a family one of these days.'

'God forbid! I'm sure she doesn't want babies.'

Sybil said, 'As we all know, it isn't always a question of wanting them.'

Villy glanced at her, startled. 'Darling! Did you – not—'

'Not really. Of course I'm pleased about it now.'

'Of course you are.' They were both treading water: not exactly out of their depths, but not wanting to feel their ground.

∞ ∞ ∞

Most of Rupert's and Zoë's day was very good. They drove
to Rye, quite slowly because Rupert was enjoying the first
morning of his holidays and being in the country and the
beautiful day. They drove past fields of wheat with poppies
and fields of hops that were nearly ripe, through woods of oak
and Spanish chestnut and lanes whose high banks were thick
with wild strawberries and stitchwort and ferns, and hedges
decorated by the last of the dog-roses bleached nearly white by
the sun, through villages with white clinker-built cottages with
their gardens blazing with hollyhocks and phlox and roses and
sometimes a pond with white ducks, small grey churches with
yew and lichen-covered tombstones, past fields of early hay,
and farms with steaming manure and brown and white chickens
finding things to eat. Sometimes they stopped, because Rupert
wanted to look properly at things, and Zoë, although she didn't
really know *why* he wanted to, sat contentedly watching him.
She loved his throat with the large Adam's apple, and the way
his dark blue eyes narrowed when he was staring at things and
the small half-apologetic smile he gave her when he had looked
enough, let in the clutch and resumed driving.

'Oh, this country!' he said once. 'To me, it is the best
in England.'

'Have you been everywhere else?'

He laughed. 'Of course not. I'm just indulging in a spot
of prejudice!'

On the last of these stops he got out of the car: she
followed him, and they went and leaned on a gate. They
were on a crest of land, where they could look down and
away for miles with all the things that they had seen separately
on the drive spread out before them in a vast expanse, green
and golden and gilded, varnished by sunlight. Rupert took her
hand.

'Darling. Don't you think that's a ripping view?'

'Yes. And the sky is such a lovely blue.' She thought for
a moment, and then added, 'It's the kind of blue that nothing
else actually *is*, isn't it?'

'You're perfectly right . . . *what* a good remark!' He squeezed
her hand, delighted with her. 'It's the kind of thing that is so
obvious that nobody says it. Notices it, I mean,' he added, seeing
her face. 'No, really, Zoë darling, I mean that.' And he did: he

so much wanted her to be an appreciator – of something other than themselves.

In Rye he bought her presents. They were walking down one of the steep roads to the harbour and there was a very small shop window crammed with jewellery, small pieces of silver and, in front, there was a tray of antique rings. Rupert decided that he wanted to buy her one so they went inside. He chose a rose diamond one with black and white enamel round the hoop, but she didn't like it. She wanted an emerald with rose diamonds round it, but it was twenty-five pounds – too much. So she settled for a fire opal surrounded by seed pearls and that was ten pounds, but Rupert got it for eight. They didn't know it was a fire opal until the man told them, just thought it was a marvellous dazzling orange colour, but Zoë was much keener on it once she knew. 'It's really unusual!' she exclaimed, holding out her white hand for them to see.

'Wouldn't suit everyone, madam, but it's perfect on you.'

'There, madam,' said Rupert when they were outside. 'And what would madam like to do next?'

She wanted a book to read in the evening when everyone was sewing and playing the piano and things. So they went to a bookshop, and she chose *Gone With The Wind*, which she knew everyone was reading and was said to have good passionate scenes in it. Then they had lunch in a pub – or rather in the garden outside it: ham and salad and Heinz's mayonnaise and half a pint of bitter for Rupert and a shandy for Zoë. They didn't talk about the children at lunch, or afterwards, when they went to Winchelsea because Rupert wanted to see the Strachan glass there, but as they were driving back to Home Place, Zoë said, 'Oh, darling, we've had such a lovely time, and I do love my ring.'

Rupert said, 'Haven't we just? Now we must go back to the bosom of the family. The madding crowd.'

'Madding?'

'It's a book by Thomas Hardy.'

'Oh.' What a lot he knew.

'And we must think of something splendid to do with the children tomorrow.'

'I should think they are quite happy with their cousins, and everything.'

'Yes. But I meant with all of them. Must do our bit.'

She was silent. He added gently, 'You know, darling, I think you'd feel quite differently about family life if you had a baby. If we had one,' he added.

'Not yet. I don't feel old enough.'

'Well, one day you will be.' She was twenty-two: a *young* twenty-two, he told himself.

'Anyway,' she said, 'I don't think we could afford it. Not unless you get another job. Or become famous, or something. We aren't rich – like Hugh and Edward. They have a proper staff to do things. Sybil and Villy don't have to *cook*.'

It was his turn for silence. Ellen did most of the cooking, and he and Clary were out to lunch every day, but poor little Zoë did hate cooking, he knew that, had not got much beyond the frying pan or tins in three years.

'Well,' he said at last, he couldn't bear to disrupt their day out, 'it was just a thought. Think about it.'

Just a thought! If he had had any idea of how she felt about having a baby, he wouldn't even mention it. Her fear, which amounted to panic, meant that she never got beyond her imagination of pregnancy – getting larger and larger, her ankles swelling, waddling about, feeling sick – and the labour, frightful pain that might go on for hours and hours, might indeed kill her as it did some people she had read about in novels. And not only *read* about: look at Rupert's first wife! She'd died that way. But even if she didn't die, her figure would be ruined: she would have flabby breasts with the nipples too large, like Villy and Sybil whom she had seen in their bathing suits, her waist would be thick and she would have those fearful stripes on her stomach and thighs – Sybil again, Villy seemed to have escaped that – and varicose veins – Villy, but not Sybil – and, of course, Rupert would no longer love her. He'd pretend to for a bit, she supposed, but she would *know*. Because the one thing she knew for certain was that her appearance was what people were interested in or cared about: she hadn't anything else, really, to attract or keep anyone *with*. She had used it all her life to get what she wanted, and she had never wanted anything so much as Rupert. So now she must use it to *keep* him. She knew, without thinking about it too much, that she wasn't clever, either at doing things or at thinking about them;

her mother had always said that this wasn't important if you had the looks, and she had learned that very well. Why didn't Rupert understand all this? He'd got two children anyway, and they cost a lot and were a constant source of anxiety. Sometimes she wished that he was thirty years older, too old for anyone but herself to care about – too old, anyway, to want to be a father, content with just being with her. In the three years of their marriage, he had only talked about having a baby twice before: once at the beginning, when he had assumed that she would want to get pregnant, and then about six months later when she had stupidly complained about what a nuisance Dutch caps were. He had said, 'I couldn't agree with you more. Why don't you just stop using one, and let nature take its course?' She had got out of that somehow – said that she wanted to get used to being married first or something, anything to stop him talking about it – and after that she had put the cap in long before he came from the school and never said any more about it at all. She had thought that perhaps he had given up the idea; now it was horribly clear that he hadn't. The rest of the drive home was silent.

∞ ∞ ∞

Clary worked hard all afternoon. To begin with, she worked feverishly against time, because she knew that when Lydia and Nev had finished their rest they would rush out and want to do things and get in the way and do things wrong. But they didn't come out; in fact, the nurses had taken them for a hot sulky walk up to the shop at Watlington, but as the time went by and they didn't come, she felt able to take things more slowly, to stop and consider the next thing to do. The mirror was in place, sunk in the sand, it looked like water, and she edged it with moss which made it even better. She made a lovely hedge of tiny pieces of box stuck close together in the sand, had to do that twice, because she hadn't made the sand firm enough to start with. Then she made a gravel path that ran beside the hedge to the lake, and then it seemed to need another hedge on its bare side, so she did that. Poor old Lydia's daisies were drooping by now, so she pulled them out; it was no good putting flowers in, she needed plants. Also, she thought they ought to be planted in earth, very tiny fine earth, or they would die. She got some potting compost out of the potting shed and made a bed that started square and ended rather egg-shaped. She collected some scarlet pimpernel, and some speedwell – straggly, but it filled up the space – and some stone crop off the kitchen-garden wall and a very small fern. That helped, but there was still a lot of room, so she collected some heads of lavender and stuck them at the back in bunches. They looked like a plant if you put them like that, and they were dry things who wouldn't mind just being stalks. They looked very good. It'll take weeks to make the whole garden, she thought. It was one of the lovely things about it. She needed trees, and bushes, and perhaps a little seat for people to sit by the lake which she had constantly to polish with some spit, her finger and one of her socks, because it got sandy at the least little thing. There was the lawn to make, which would be tufts of grass planted close together and trimmed with Zoë's nail scissors. The bell went for tea, and she didn't want to go, but they'd be sure to come and find her if she didn't. So she went, taking Neville's shoe with her to please Ellen. Walking back to the house, she thought that perhaps she would like someone to see her garden: Dad, or Aunt Rach? Both of them, she decided.

∞ ∞ ∞

After tea, all the children played the Seeing Game – one of the traditional holiday games devised by themselves. Teddy half felt that he had outgrown it, and Simon pretended to feel the same, but this was not true. It had been invented by Louise and was a kind of hide and seek, only you didn't catch people; it counted if you saw them and could identify who they were, and involved constant mobility on the part of the hunted, who, when caught, were locked in an old dog kennel until rescued by a friend. The hunter won only if he succeeded in catching everybody and incarcerating them. Lydia and Neville, who spent most of the time in the kennel as they were easy to catch, enjoyed it most, because they were playing with the others, although they wailed that it was unfair to be caught so much, when Polly, for instance, was hardly caught at all. Hugh and Edward played tennis.

Villy and the Duchy played two pianos – Bach concerti – and Sybil and Rachel cut out the nightdresses on the table in the morning room. Nanny read bits of *Nursery World* aloud to Ellen while she did the ironing. The Brig sat in his study writing a chapter about Burma and its teak forests for his book. The day, which had been hot and golden with a sky of unbroken blue, was settling to longer shadows with midges and gnats and young rabbits coming out into the orchard.

Flossy, who allowed Mrs Cripps to own her because of Mrs Cripps's connections with food, got up from her basket chair in the servants' hall, stretched her totally rested body, and slipped out of the casement window for her evening's hunting. She was a tortoiseshell, with hard-wearing fur and, as Rachel had once observed, like most well-fed English people she hunted merely for the sport and was very unsporting in her methods. She knew exactly when the rabbits went into the orchard, and one of them, at least, would not stand a chance against her formidable experience.

∞ ∞ ∞

When Rupert and Zoë returned from their outing, she had said that she was going to get her bath in before all the children and tennis players used the hot water. Rupert, alone in their bedroom, wandered to the window from which he could see his sister and Sybil sewing under the monkey puzzle. They sat in basket chairs on the smooth green lawn backed by the green-black yew hedge against which their summer dresses – Rachel's blue and Sybil's green – had a kind of aqueous delicacy. A wicker table was set between them, littered with a sewing basket, a tea tray with willow-patterned cups; a pile of creamy material completed the scene. He did not need even the corner of the herbaceous border on one side, nor the corner of the white gate to the drive at the other. He wanted to paint, but by the time he got his materials prepared, they might be gone: he wanted to draw them from the window where he stood, but Zoë would be back and that would not do. He rummaged in his canvas bag for his largest drawing block and packet of oil pastels and slipped down the smaller staircase to the front door.

∞ ∞ ∞

'It's not fair! You never said you'd stopped playing!'

Louise opened the kennel door.

'We're telling you now.'

'We didn't *know* till now. It's not *fair!*'

'Look, we've only just stopped,' Polly said. 'We couldn't tell you before because we hadn't.'

Lydia and Neville stumped out of the kennel. They had not wanted the game to stop and they hated it not being fair. Neither of them had had the chance to be the See-er.

'Teddy and Simon are bored of it. They've gone on a hunt. There aren't enough of us for a proper game.' Clary joined them.

'Anyway, it's time for your baths. They'll be coming for you any minute.'

'God blast!'

'Take no notice of him,' Louise said in her most irritating voice.

'Honestly, Louise, you are sickening! Too, *too* sickening!'

When Lydia said that she sounded exactly like Mummy's friend, Hermione; Louise could not help admiring the mimicry, but she wasn't going to say so. She didn't want two actresses in the family, thank you very much. She gave Polly their secret signal and they ran – suddenly, and very fast – away from Lydia and Neville, who started to follow them, but were quickly out of sight. The wails of rage only drew Ellen's and Nanny's attention to their whereabouts and they got carried off for their baths.

∞ ∞ ∞

When Clary went to find Dad and Aunt Rachel to show them her garden, she found she couldn't have either of them. Dad was sitting on the large wooden table used for outdoor tea drawing Aunt Rach and Aunt Syb, alternatively staring at them, then making sudden irritable marks on his pad. She stood watching him for a bit: he was sort of frowning, and every now and then he drew a deep sighing breath. Sometimes he rubbed the marks he had made with his finger. In his left hand he held a small bunch of chalks, and sometimes he stuffed the one he had been using back and took another one. Clary thought that *she* could hold the bunch of chalks for him, but as she moved nearer to say this, Aunt Rach put her finger to her lips so she didn't say anything. And she couldn't go and ask Aunt Rach to come because then she would be in the picture, so she just sat down on the grass and watched her father. A lock of his hair kept falling forward across his bony forehead and he kept pushing or shaking it back. I could hold his hair back for him, she thought. Why can't there be something like that I could do for him, so that he couldn't do without me? 'Clary is indispensable,' he would say to people who came to admire his painting. By now, she was grown up, with her hair in a bun and skirts down her legs like the aunts, and her face was thin and interesting, like Dad's, and people – in taxi cabs and orangeries like Kensington Gardens – proposed to her, but she would give them all up for Dad. She would never marry because of being so terrifically indispensable, and since Zoë had died from eating potted meat in a heatwave – known to kill you according to the Duchy – she was all that Dad had in the world. Dad would be famous, and she would be . . .

'Rupert! Where did you put my book? Rupert!'

Clary looked up, and there was Zoë in her kimono shouting through the open bedroom window.

There was a pause as she watched his face change, and then change again into patient good humour.

'You must have left it in the car.'

'I thought you brought it in.'

'I didn't, darling.' Turning to look at her, he spied Clary. 'Clary'll fetch it for you.'

'What book?' She got to her feet reluctantly. If Dad asked her she'd have to get it.

'*Gone With The Wind*,' called Zoë. 'Bring it up to me, would you, Clary darling, there's an angel.'

Clary trotted off. She'd never felt less like an angel in her life. Zoë had only said that to make it sound as though she was fond of her, and she jolly well wasn't. And I'm not fond of her, she thought, not remotely, the tiniest bit fond. I hate her! One of the reasons she hated Zoë was feeling like that. She didn't hate anyone else, which showed she wasn't a hating person, but Zoë made her feel horrible, and sometimes wicked: things like potted meat would never occur to her about anyone else. But she'd thought of dozens of ways in which Zoë might die, and if Zoë died from any of them it would be her fault. She hoped there would be another way that she hadn't thought of – must be – people could die from nearly anything. A snake bite or a ghost frightening her to death, or something Ellen called a hernia that sounded pretty bad. There she went, making it more likely to be her fault. She shut her eyes and held her breath to stop her thoughts. Then she opened the car door, and found the book on the back seat.

∞ ∞ ∞

The evening settled into a hot still night. Delirious moths rammed the parchment lampshades again and again and silvery powder from their collisions fell from time to time onto Sybil's sewing. She had been given the whole sofa so that she could put her feet up. The Brig and Edward were playing chess and smoking Havana cigars. They played very slowly, with occasional admiring grunts at the other's skill. The Duchy was setting in the puff sleeves of the tussore frock for Clary. It was richly smocked in cherry silk: the Duchy was famous for her smocking. Zoë was curled in a battered armchair reading *Gone With The Wind*. Hugh, in charge of the gramophone, had chosen Schubert's posthumous B flat sonata – known to be one of the Duchy's favourites – and was listening with his eyes closed. Villy was embroidering one of her enormous set of table mats in fine black cross stitch on heavy linen. Rupert lay in a chair at the end of the room, legs stretched straight out, arms hanging over the chair arms, half listening to the music, half watching the others. How like Edward was to their father, he began. The same forehead, with the hair growing from a centre peak and receding – in Edward's case far more than their father's – each side of it. The same bushy eyebrows, the same blue-grey eyes (although Edward's way of looking you straight in the eye came from the Duchy, one of whose chief charms it was. 'I don't agree with you at all,' she would say, and you liked her for it), high cheekbones, military moustache. The Brig's, apart from being white, was longer and more luxuriant; Edward kept his to a military bristle. Their hands were the same shape with long fingers and rather concave nails, the Brig's speckled with liver spots, Edward's with hair growing on the backs. The curious thing about moustaches was how you lost the mouth; it became an unconsidered feature, much as he supposed a chin would that sported a beard. Edward, though, had a glamour that seemed to come from neither parent; although undoubtedly he was the best looking of the three of them: the glamour came from his apparent unconsciousness of either his appearance or his effect upon other people. Clothes, for instance, became glamorous simply because he was wearing them – tonight a white silk shirt with a bottle green foulard silk scarf knotted round his throat and linen trousers of the same colour, but when you came to think about it, he must have *thought* about his outfit, *chosen* those things – so perhaps he wasn't so unconscious, after all? He certainly knew that women found him attractive. Even those who did not were always immediately aware of him: Zoë, for instance, said that although he wasn't her type, she could see that he might be very attractive to some. Part of it was the way in which Edward always seemed to be enjoying himself, to be living in the present – to be *engrossed* in it, never appearing to consider anything either side of it.

Rupert, being six and seven years younger than his brothers, had escaped the war – had been a schoolboy while his brothers were in France. Hugh had been the first to go – joined the Coldstream Guards – and Edward, unable to join him because of his age, got himself into the Machine Gun Corps a few months later. Edward soon had his first MC and was recommended for a Victoria Cross. But when Rupert had tried to question him about it, for the vicarious glory of being able to impress other boys at school, Edward had said, 'For peeing on a machine gun, old boy – to cool it down a bit. It got too hot and jammed,' and looked embarrassed. 'Under fire?' Yes, Edward had admitted that there had been quite a bit of firing. Then he changed the subject. By the time he was twenty-one he was a major with a bar to his MC, and Hugh was a captain and had won his cross and been wounded. When they had finally come home from the war neither of them talked about it; with Hugh, Rupert had felt that it was because he couldn't bear to, whereas with Edward, it seemed more that he'd done with all that and was only interested in what was going to happen to him next – joining the firm and marrying Villy. But Hugh had never been the same. His head wound had left him with bad headaches, he'd lost a hand, his digestion wasn't good and he sometimes had rotten dreams. But it wasn't only that: Rupert had noticed, and he still noticed, that there was something about his expression, about his eyes, a haunted look of outrage, anguish, even. If you called his name and he looked at you straight – like Edward, like his mother – you caught this expression before it dissolved to the mildness of anxiety and thence to his habitual affectionate sweetness. He loved his family, never sought company outside it, never looked at another woman, and had particular affection for all children, particularly babies. It was when he looked at, or thought about, Hugh that Rupert felt irrational pangs of guilt that he had not shared the unknown hell.

The Schubert came to an end and Sybil, without raising her eyes from her sewing, said, 'Bed, darling?'

'If you're ready.' He put the record away, walked over to his mother and kissed her. She patted his cheek.

'Sleep well, darling.'

'I'll sleep like a log. Always do, here.' As he walked over to his wife, he gave Rupert a little smile and then, as though to snap any sentiment, winked. Rupert winked back: it was one of their old habits.

There was a general folding up of work and movement for bed. Rupert looked at Zoë, completely engrossed; he had never known her so caught by a book before.

'Can I interest you in bed?'

She looked up. 'Is it that late?'

'Getting on. It must be a marvellous book.'

'It's quite good. All about the civil war in America,' she added, as she marked her place. Villy's lip curled and she met Sybil's eye fleetingly. She had discussed the book with Sybil when it came out earlier in the year, having borrowed it from Hermione; she had glanced at it, she said, and it seemed to her that the heroine had a mind as shallow as a soup bowl, thinking of nothing but men, frocks and money. Sybil had suggested that the bits about the civil war were supposed to be rather good, and Villy, who had not glanced at those bits, said that they seemed to her to play a very minor part. Sybil had said that it didn't sound her kind of book. Sybil had handed her sewing to Hugh to hold, had swung her legs over the side of the sofa, but could not rise unaided, and Rupert went to help her. Villy decided to go to bed also, and to be asleep before Edward had finished his game.

'Where's Rachel?' someone asked, and the Duchy, putting her steel-rimmed spectacles into their needleworked case, answered, 'She went to bed early, had rather a head.'

In fact, Rachel had gone to the Brig's study after dinner to telephone Sid with whom she had a delightful – and extravagant – conversation lasting six minutes, about the arrangements for Sid to come down to lunch. Monday had been fixed as a good day, as most of the family would be going to the beach. 'Won't they want all the cars, then?' S had said. But Rachel didn't think so, and if they did, she would bicycle to Battle to meet the train. Sid had been enchanted by the idea of Rachel on a bicycle, and had been difficult to cut short, but, after all, it was her parents' telephone, though when she said this, Sid simply replied, 'Yes, my angel,' and went on talking. That was why it had been six minutes instead of the statutory three that was thought proper in the family for a long-distance call. After it, and, of course, unable to share her excitement and joy with the family, Rachel had decided to read in bed and have an early night, and meeting Eileen with the coffee tray in the hall, had asked her to tell Mrs Cazalet that she had a headache and would not be down again. But on her way up she thought she would look in on the girls and be sure that Clary was settling in. Louise and Polly were in their beds – Louise was reading, Polly was knitting – and Clary lay on her stomach on the floor writing in an exercise book. They were all flatteringly pleased to see her. 'Sit on *my* bed, Aunt Rach. I'm reading a frightfully sad book – it's full of God and people bursting into tears. It's in Canada with a nasty aunt in it. Not at all like you,' she added. Rachel sat on Louise's bed. 'And what's Polly making?'

'A jersey. For Mum. For Christmas. It was for her birthday but it's a secret so it's very hard to knit it for long. Don't tell her.'

'It looks very difficult.' It did: some lacy pale pink stitch with bobbles on it. 'It's a good thing that it's called dirty pink,' said Polly. 'It's got far less pink than when I started.'

'Dirty pink was in last year,' said Louise. 'By the time you've finished it, it'll be terrifically out. But as your mother's not very fashionable, she probably won't mind.'

'People wear colours that suit them any time,' said Polly.

'People with auburn hair are supposed to wear green all the time. And blue.'

'What an authority you are upon fashion, Louise.' She needed a mild snub. She turned to Clary, who had been writing steadily. 'And what are you up to?'

'Nothing much.'

'What are you writing? A journal?'

'Just a book.'

'How exciting! What's it about?'

'Nothing much. It's the life story of a cat who can understand everything in English. He was born in Australia but he's come to England for some adventures.'

'Quarantine,' said Louise. 'He couldn't.'

'How do you mean he couldn't? He just has.'

'He'd have to spend six months in quarantine.'

'I expect you could put that in, and then have him in England,' said Polly kindly.

Clary shut her book and got into her bed without another word.

'She's sulking now.'

Rachel was distressed.

'You're being very unpleasant, Louise.'

'I didn't mean it.'

'That's not good enough. You can't say unpleasant things and then pretend you didn't mean them.'

'No, you can't,' said Polly. 'It just makes your character worse in the long run. What it *is* is that you wish *you*'d thought of writing a book.'

This shaft went home, Rachel noticed. Louise blushed and then she told Clary she was sorry, and Clary said all right.

Rachel kissed them all in turn: they all smelled sweetly of damp hair, toothpaste and Vinolia soap. Clary hugged her and whispered that she had a surprise to show in the morning. Louise apologised again in a whisper; Polly just giggled and said she had nothing worth whispering.

'Be nice to one another and lights out in ten minutes.'

'How *arbitrary!*' she heard Louise exclaim after she had left. 'How too, too arbitrary! If she'd said half past nine – or *ten*, I could understand it, but just ten minutes after whenever she leaves . . . ' The small grudge would unite them, anyway.

∞ ∞ ∞

On Monday, Hugh left Sybil in bed, ate a hurried breakfast with the Duchy, who had risen early for the purpose, and left the house by seven thirty for London. He didn't think that Sybil should go to the beach and begged his mother to dissuade her. The Duchy agreed; the day promised to be a scorcher, there were plenty of uncles and aunts to look after Polly and Simon, and sitting on hot pebbles in blazing sun when you were unable to bathe (which, of course, was out of the question for Sybil in her condition) was agreed to be unsuitable. Hugh, who resisted an impulse to say goodbye to his wife after breakfast – not wishing to wake her again – felt relief. Sybil, lying in bed and longing for him to come up, listened to his car starting, got out of bed in time to see it disappearing down the drive. She was thoroughly awake by now, and decided to have a long, luxurious bath before anybody else wanted the bathroom.

∞ ∞ ∞

It was after ten before they were ready to go. They went in three cars, crammed with towels, bathing suits, picnic baskets, rugs and whatever personal equipment each one thought necessary for their pleasure. The younger children had buckets and spades and a shrimping net, 'Which is very silly, Neville, because there's not a single shrimp there.' The nurses took knitting and *Nursery World*, Edward his camera. Zoë took *Gone With The Wind*, her new halter-necked bathing costume – navy blue with white piqué bows at neck and back of waist – and some dark glasses; Rupert took a sketch pad and some charcoal; Clary took a biscuit tin for collecting shells or anything; Simon and Teddy took two packs of cards – they had recently learned bezique; Louise took *The Wide Wide World* and a jar of Wonder Cream (it wasn't lasting well – had gone all watery at the bottom with a kind of greenish scum on top, but she felt

it had to be used up), and Polly took her Brownie box camera
– her best present from her last birthday.

Villy took a book about Nijinsky and his wife in a beach
bag that also contained a jar of Pomade Divine and Elastoplast
and a spare bathing costume – she hated sitting about in a wet
one. Edward, Villy, and Rupert were to drive the cars, which
were slowly crammed with occupants, who, by the time they
got moving, were already sticky and, in some cases, tearful
from the heat and the conviction that they had been put in
the wrong car.

Mrs Cripps watched them go from her kitchen window.
Apart from all the cooked breakfasts, she had been hard at
it since seven o'clock, making sandwiches with hard-boiled
eggs, sardines, cheese and her own potted ham, with seed cake
and flapjacks and bananas for pudding. There was now time for
a nice cup of tea before Madam came with her orders.

For reasons she did not wish to define, Rachel found
it difficult to inform the Duchy of her arrangements. She
decided against asking for the car; the bicycle – in spite
of the heat – would leave her much freer. However, when
the Duchy came upon her at breakfast and asked her, she
felt bound to divulge them, saying that she and Sid would
enjoy lunch at the Gateway Tearooms, but the Duchy, who
regarded meals in hotels or restaurants, or even tearooms as
an absurd waste of money as well as being an unbecoming
practice, insisted that she bring Sid back for lunch and had
rung the bell for Eileen to tell Tonbridge to have the car round
in half an hour before Rachel could protest at all. We can go for
a walk after lunch, she thought. It will be just as good, really.
Nearly as good. She had been deflected from any argument by
Sybil, who limped into the morning room, apologising for being
late, and sank into a chair with evident relief. She had lost her
balance getting out of the bath, she explained, she seemed to
have twisted her ankle. Rachel, who had been a VAD in the last
years of the war, insisted on seeing it. It was badly swollen and
was clearly extremely painful. The Duchy fetched witch hazel
and Rachel procured a crêpe bandage and some lint, and the
ankle was bound up.

'You really ought to keep it up,' Rachel said, and moved a
second chair in front of Sybil, carefully putting the bruised foot

on a cushion. This meant Sybil was sitting at an angle that was not at all comfortable and, almost at once, her back started to ache. It had taken her ages to dress because of her ankle and she felt tired already – at the beginning of the day. Rachel left to go to Battle, and the Duchy, having poured some tea and ordered Sybil some fresh toast, repaired to the kitchen to see Mrs Cripps. When Eileen appeared with the toast, Sybil asked her for a cushion for her back, and while this was being fetched she looked at the morning paper that had been left open at the foreign news page. Someone called Pastor Niemoller had been arrested after a large service in a place called Dahlem – she had never heard of it. She decided that she didn't want to read the paper, and actually she didn't want to eat anything either. She leant forward for Eileen to put the cushion behind her and, as she did so, felt as though a hand was slowly gripping her spine in the small of her back. She scarcely had time to notice this before the grip loosened and was completely gone. How odd, she began to think, and then without warning she was sucked into a whirlpool of paralysing, mindless panic. That, too, receded and little fragments of coherent fear reached the surface of her mind. Polly and Simon had been *late* – Polly eleven days and Simon three. She was between three and four weeks before her time, the fall couldn't have hurt it – or them – Hugh would be in London by now, the fall had been a shock, that's all it was . . . Ridiculous! She began to assess her body for reassurance. She was sweating, it was pricking under her arms, and when she touched her forehead it was damp. Her back – *that* was all right now, nothing except the mild ache that came when she was in the wrong position or stayed in one for too long.

She moved her foot, and was almost relieved by the sudden twinge of pain. Ankles could be agony, but that was all it was. Her mouth was dry, and she drank some tea. It was simply bad luck, when she'd planned to go for a little walk in the garden that she hadn't seen properly this year. She imagined herself walking barefoot on the well-kept lawn, cool still from dew, and soft and springy: she really wanted to walk about *now*. The frustration made her feel irritably restless – What was Eileen doing hanging about—

'Are you all right, Mrs Hugh?'

'Quite all right. I twisted my ankle, that's all.'

'Oh, that's what it is.' Eileen seemed reassured. 'Ever so painful, that can be.' She picked up her tray. 'You'll ring if you want anything, won't you, madam?' She leant over the table and moved the little brass bell within Sybil's reach. Then she went.

Perhaps I ought to be in London, not to be so far away, thought Sybil. I could have gone back with Hugh – got a taxi from the office. She really couldn't go on sitting like this, it was too uncomfortable. She would like to ring up Hugh and see what he thought, but it would only worry him so she wouldn't do that. If she got up and got one of the walking sticks out of Brig's study – only across the passage – she could then go into the garden. It might be quite possible to walk if she had a stick. She turned and heaved her leg off the chair; her ankle responded with such a stab of agony that her eyes filled with tears. Perhaps she had better ring for Eileen to get it . . . but then she became aware of the hand on her spine again, not painful, but menacing, with the promise of pain. She remembered it now. It was the mere beginning – the grip would become a vice, and then a knife that would slowly surge downwards cleaving her spine and stopping seconds after it became intolerable, then apparently vanish but, in reality, lie in wait for another, more murderous assault . . . She must get up – get to – Supporting herself by the table, she rose to her feet, then remembered the bell – now out of reach – and as she leant over the table to get it, felt the warm flood of her waters breaking, It's gone all *wrong*! she thought, as tears began to stream down her face, but she reached the bell and rang it and rang it for ever for someone to come.

Which they did, of course, much sooner than it felt to Sybil. They sat her back in the chair, and the Duchy sent Eileen for either Wren or McAlpine, whoever could be found first, while she telephoned Dr Carr. He was out on his rounds, but could be reached, they said, and would come at once. She did not tell her daughter-in-law that he was out, said calmly that he was on his way, and that Eileen and one of the men would carry her up to her room, and that she, the Duchy, would not leave her until the doctor came. 'And everything will be all right,' she said, with all the reassurance she could muster, but she was afraid, and wished that Rachel was there. Rachel was always wonderful when things were difficult. It was not good that the waters had broken so soon; she could see no sign of blood, and did not want to alarm Sybil by asking about it. If *only* Rachel was here, she thought almost angrily, she who is always here *would* be away at a time like this. Sybil was biting her lips trying neither to scream nor to cry. The Duchy took one of her hands in both of hers and held it hard; she remembered that it was good to be grasped so and she upheld the conspiracy of silence in childbirth that was naturally proper for women like themselves. Pain was to be endured and forgotten, but it was never really forgotten, and looking at Sybil's mute distress she could remember it too well. 'There there, my duck,' she said. 'It'll be a lovely baby – you'll see.'

∞ ∞ ∞

Rachel would have liked more time to get ready to meet Sid. She would also have liked them to be able to have lunch at the White Hart alone together, but she would not have dreamed of going against the Duchy's wishes in that matter, or, indeed, any other – a state of affairs that had applied all her life. There had, twenty years ago, been the excuse that she was too young – eighteen, in fact – the young man in question had urged her to greater freedom, but really, of course, she had not wanted to be in the least bit free with *him*. As she grew older, the reason for her obedience became her parents' age rather than her own, and the notion that at thirty-eight she could still not order her own time to suit herself, or in this case, her and Sid, did not seriously impinge. It was a pity, but to dwell upon one's own wishes would be morbid, a Cazalet term that implied the uttermost condemnation.

So she sat in the back of the car and looked on the bright side. It was a beautiful hot shimmering day, and she and Sid would have a perfectly lovely walk after luncheon together – might even take some Osborne biscuits and a Thermos with them and thus legitimately skip family tea.

Tonbridge drove at his usual twenty-eight miles an hour, and she longed to ask him to go faster, but he had never been known to be late for a train and asking him to hurry would look ridiculous.

In fact, they were early as she had already known they would be. She would wait on the platform, she told Tonbridge, who then mentioned that he had something to collect from Till's for McAlpine.

'Do that now, and we'll meet you outside Till's,' Rachel ordered, pleased to have recognised the opportunity in time.

The station was very quiet. The one porter was watering the station flower beds, scarlet geraniums, dark blue lobelia and white alyssum, remnants of the decorative fervour inspired by the Coronation. There was one passenger with a child on the far side waiting to go to Hastings for a day at the sea, judging by the bucket and wooden spade and picnic bulging from a carrier bag. Rachel walked over the bridge to where they sat, then decided that she didn't want to get involved with anyone – wanted to meet Sid in silence – but she was glad when the train puffed slowly towards them as she felt she was being unfriendly. Then it stopped and doors flapped open and there were people and then there was Sid walking towards her smiling, wearing her brown tussore suit with the belted jacket, bareheaded, cropped hair and a nut-brown face.

'What ho!' said Sid, and they embraced.

'I'll carry it.'

'You will not.' Sid picked up the businesslike little case which she had relinquished to greet Rachel, and tucked Rachel's arm in her own.

'I imagined you bicycling to meet me, but I suppose the bridge defeated you. You look tired, darling. Are you?'

'No. And I didn't bicycle. I'm afraid we've got Tonbridge and lunch at home.'

'Ah!'

'But a lovely walk afterwards, and I thought we'd take tea with us so we wouldn't have to come back for it.'

'That sounds a splendid idea.' It was resolutely said, and Rachel glanced at her in search of irony, but there was none. Sid met her eye, winked and said, 'Bless you, my angel, for always wanting everybody to be happy. I meant it. It *is* a splendid idea.'

They walked out of the station in a silence that for Rachel

was blissfully companionable, for Sid so full of wild happiness that she was unable to speak. But, eventually, as they passed the Abbey gates, she said, 'If we take a picnic, won't the children want to come too?'

'They're all at the beach. They won't be back until tea-time.'

'Ah! The plot thins, in the most admirable manner.'

'And I thought you might stay the night. There's a camp bed we could put in my room.'

'Is there really, darling? I must wait for the Duchy to ask me, though.'

'She will. She's very fond of you. It's a pity you haven't brought your fiddle. But you could borrow Edward's. You know she loves playing sonatas with you. How's Evie?'

'I can tell you about that in the car.' Evie was Sid's sister, renowned for minor and often wilful ill health. She did part-time secretarial work for a well-known musician and relied upon Sid, with whom she lived, to manage their slender resources and to look after her whenever she needed or felt like it.

And so, in the car, with Sid holding her hand, Rachel asked about Evie, and was told about her hay fever, the possibility of an ulcer, although the doctor didn't think it was that, and her plan that Sid should take her away for a seaside holiday some time in August, and preserving the proprieties in the presence of Tonbridge had a certain charm, making them both want to laugh because in a way it was so silly – they didn't really want to talk about Evie in the least. They looked at each other or, rather, Sid would glance at Rachel and be unable to look away, and Rachel would find herself transfixed by those small, brownish, eloquent, wide-apart eyes, and would feel herself beginning to blush when Sid would chuckle and produce some idiotic cliché such as 'every silver lining has a cloud', in the voice she would use for reading a motto from a cracker, adding 'or so they say,' which broke the tension until the next time. Tonbridge, driving slightly faster – he was looking forward to his dinner – couldn't make head or tail of what they were on about.

They no sooner drew up beside the gate that led to the front door when Eileen, who had been watching for them, ran out and said that Madam said that Miss Rachel was to go up to

Mrs Hugh's room immediately as the baby had started and the doctor hadn't yet arrived. Rachel sprang out of the car without a backward glance and ran into the house. Oh, Lord! thought Sid. Poor darling! She meant Rachel.

Sybil sat in bed, propped up by pillows; she refused to lie properly, which the Duchy felt was wrong but she was far too anxious and alarmed to try to insist. Rachel would do it, and here at last was Rachel. 'The doctor *is* coming,' said the Duchy quickly and gave Rachel a little frown meaning don't ask when. 'If you will stay with her, I'll see to towels. The maids are boiling water,' and she went, glad to do something she could accomplish. She had been beginning to find Sybil's pains more than she could bear. Rachel drew up a chair and sat beside Sybil.

'Darling. What can I do to help?' Sybil gasped and threw herself forward with clenched hands, pressing on the bed each side of her thighs. 'Nothing. I don't know.' A bit later, she said, 'Help me – undress. Quick – before the next one.' So in between the pains Rachel helped her out of her smock, her slip and her knickers, and finally into a nightdress. This took a long time as with each pain they had to stop, and Sybil gripped Rachel's hand until she thought her bones would break.

'Supposing it's born before he comes?' Sybil said, and Rachel knew that she was terrified by the thought.

'We'll manage. It's going to be all right,' she soothed, but she hadn't the faintest idea what to do. 'You mustn't worry,' she said, stroking Sybil's hair back from her forehead. 'I used to be a VAD. Remember?'

And Sybil seemed comforted by that, gave Rachel a small trusting smile and said, 'I'd forgotten. Of course you were.' She lay back for a moment and shut her eyes. 'Could you tie my hair back? Out of the way?' But by the time Rachel had found the strip of chiffon indicated upon the dressing-table Sybil was again racked, her hand searching blindly for Rachel's hand.

'Oh, *God* – let the doctor come,' Rachel prayed as Sybil uttered a moan.

'Sorry about that. It's all a bit Mary Webbish, isn't it? Straining at bedposts and all that?' And as Rachel smiled at the gallant small joke, she added, 'It does *hurt* rather.'

'I know it does, darling. You're tremendously brave.'

Then they both heard a car, which surely must be the doctor, and Rachel went to the window. 'He's come!' she said. 'Isn't that good?' But Sybil had crammed her fist into her mouth and was biting her knuckles not to scream and seemed not to hear her.

He was an old man, an elderly Scot with gingery brindled hair and moustache. He came into the room taking off his jacket and putting down his case and was rolling up his shirt-sleeves as he talked.

'Well, well, Mrs Cazalet, so I hear you had a wee fall in the bath this morning and your baby's decided to make its way out.' He looked around the room, saw the jug and basin and proceeded to wash his hands. 'No, I can manage quite well with cold, but we'll be needing some hot water. Perhaps you would arrange that, Miss Cazalet, while I examine the patient?'

'But I'll need you back in five minutes,' he called, as Rachel left the room.

On the landing, she found the housemaids with covered pails of hot water, and a pile of towels laid on the linen chest. Downstairs she found the Duchy with Sid. Her mother was deeply agitated. 'Rachel! I feel I must ring Hugh.'

'Of course you must.'

'But Sybil begged me not to. She doesn't want him worried. It seems wrong to do exactly what she doesn't want.'

Rachel looked at Sid, who was looking at the Duchy with a kind of protective kindness that made Rachel love her. Now, Sid said, 'I don't think that's the point. I think Hugh would mind very much if he hadn't been told what was going on.'

The Duchy said gratefully, 'Of course you are right. Sensible Sid! I'm so glad you are here. I'll do it at once.'

When she had gone, Sid held out her battered silver case and said, 'Have a gasper. You look as though you need one.'

And Rachel, who usually smoked Egyptian cigarettes, finding Gold Flake too strong, took one, and found her hand was shaking as Sid lit it for her. 'It is ghastly,' she said. 'The most ghastly pain. I didn't realise. Has the doctor got a nurse coming?'

'Apparently not at once, anyway. He tried his usual midwife and she was out on a case, and the district nurse said she couldn't come until some time in the afternoon. He's told me what to do. I'm sorry about our day.'

'It can't be helped.'

'Have you been asked to stay?'

'I have. The plan is that Mrs Cripps should make a picnic tea and I should deflect the beach party – keep the children out of the way until it's over. It's curious, isn't it?' She added after a pause, 'How for the most important events in people's lives everybody has to keep out of the way, know nothing about it.'

'Oh, but, they might hear her. Not that Sybil would make a sound if she could possibly help it.'

'Exactly.'

Sensing Sid's faintly ironical expression, Rachel was conscious of the fleeting but familiar sensation of Sid's foreignness – at least, that was how she put it to herself. Sid's mother had been a Portuguese Jewess whom her father had met on tour with the orchestra in which he played. He had married and fathered two daughters, Margot and Evie, and then abandoned them, gone to Australia; he was always referred to – rather bitterly – as Mr Sidney of that ilk. They had had a hard impoverished life, their mother eventually dying of TB and homesickness (her family cut her off at her marriage). It was difficult, Sid said, to know which had been worse. But all this, and the fact of her coming from a family of musicians, made her seem foreign and this in turn seemed to make her keener on confronting things than Rachel's family had ever been. 'I've seen nothing but spades since I was a baby,' Sid once said. 'How can I call them anything else?' As soon as her mother was dead, Margot had abandoned the name she had always loathed and called herself Sid. Like many couples whose cultural backgrounds are very different, they both had ambivalent attitudes in their behaviour to one another: Sid, who recognised that Rachel had all her life been overprotected from either financial or emotional reality, wished to be the person who protected her most, and at the same time could not resist the occasional dig at the middle-class Englishness of it all; Rachel, who knew Sid had not only had to fend for herself, but really for her mother and sister as well, respected her independence and authority but wanted Sid to understand that the understatements, discretion, and withholding were an integral part of the Cazalet family life, existing only to uphold affection and good manners. 'I can *understand,'* Sid had once said during an early confrontation, 'but I can do that perfectly well without *agreeing*. Don't you see?' But Rachel did not see at all; for her, understanding meant tacit agreement.

To each of them some of these thoughts had recurred, but there was no time for any of that now. Rachel stubbed out her cigarette and said, 'I must go back. Would you ask the Duchy to get one of the maids to bring me an apron?'

'Of course I will. God bless. Tell me if there's anything I can do.'

'I will.'

I have only to do exactly what he tells me, she thought, as she went upstairs, and it's utterly ridiculous to mind about blood so much. I must simply think of something else.

∞ ∞ ∞

Coodden really wasn't the best beach for the children, Villy thought, as she shifted her bottom on the boulderish pebbles and tried to find a more comfortable bit of breakwater for her back. Even on such a calm and blazing day, the sea was surprisingly cold – a steely blue far out, but near them an aquamarine swell that heaved endlessly in and broke upon the steeply shelving shore in a creamy fringe that swooned and melted to green again and was sucked out beneath the next wave. The boys were all right, they were good at swimming from school, but the girls were afraid of going out of their depth, hobbled over the pebbles, waded a few steps, swam two or three strokes again and again, until she made them come in, teeth chattering, cold and slippery as fishes, to have their backs rubbed, to be given pieces of Terry's bitter chocolate or hot Bovril. There were no rock pools for Lydia and Neville, and almost no sand; Lydia got swept off her feet by the undertow and wept bitterly for ages in spite of Villy's soothing. Neville, who had watched it all with horror, announced that he was not going to use the sea today at all, 'Except for water for my bucket.' 'Then you won't get any chocolate,' Clary had said and was at once told to mind her own business by Ellen, who was pinning a handkerchief with safety pins to Neville's Panama hat so that a square of white covered his already pink bony shoulders.

Ellen and Nanny sat in their hats, grey cardigans and sensible belted cotton dresses, their legs stretched out in front of them in thick pale cotton stockings with black double-strap shoes, their knitting on their laps. A day at the beach must be purgatory for them, Villy thought. Neither would have dreamed of bathing, their authority with the children was shaky, undermined by the presence of parents, but at the same time they were responsible – for Lydia and Neville not catching cold or getting a touch of the sun, or going off with strange children from whom they might catch something.

Now Nanny, who had begun to dress Lydia, was forestalled by Edward, who said he would take her out on his shoulders as Rupert was going to do with Neville (neither liked the idea of their offspring being afraid of the water). 'Tell the boys to come in when you do,' Villy called; it would be a point of honour with them not to come in until they were made to. She looked across at Zoë, who had curled herself up against the breakwater on a car rug and was rubbing some cream on her legs – which was the only part of her in the sun – rather a common thing to do in public, Villy thought, then felt ashamed. Whatever the poor girl does, I'm horrid about it. Rupert had tried to make her bathe, but she wouldn't, said she knew it would be too cold. She had never let any of the Cazalets know that she couldn't swim.

Villy watched as Edward and Rupert picked their way out into the sea with Lydia and Neville clinging to their backs like nervous little crabs. When they began to swim, Lydia screamed with excitement and Neville with fear, their screams mingling with the sea cries of other children, afraid of waves, not wanting to come in, shocked by the cold, afraid of being splashed by the swimmers. The fathers went on swimming until Rupert was in danger of being strangled by Neville and had to come in. Neville's hat had blown off and Villy watched as Simon and Teddy raced to retrieve it, like little otters.

The girls, clad now in their shorts and Aertex shirts, were starting to ask about lunch. Polly and Clary were collecting smooth flat pebbles and putting them into Clary's biscuit tin, and Louise lay flat on her stomach, apparently untroubled by the stony beach, reading and wiping her eyes with a bath towel.

'How soon?' one of them said.

'As soon as the others come in and get changed.' He

waved to Edward who was carrying Lydia now and shouting to the boys.

Lydia returned triumphant and very cold; Edward dumped her beside Villy, against whom she leant, pigtails dripping, teeth rattling.

'I swam much further than you did,' she called to Neville.

'You're freezing, darling.' Villy wrapped her in a towel.

'I'm not. I'm boiling really. I'm *making* my teeth chatter. This is how Nan dresses in the morning. Look!' She held the towel around her, turned her back and made humping movements of someone wriggling into stays, a fine imitation of clumsy decorum. Edward caught Villy's eye and they both managed not to laugh.

Teddy and Simon came in quickly enough the moment that Edward shouted, 'Lunch!' They came rushing in from the sea, running easily over the pebbles, their hair plastered to their heads, the straps of their bathing dresses dropping over their shoulders. A super bathe, they said; they hadn't wanted to come in; there was no point in changing as they were going back immediately after lunch. Oh, no, they weren't, said Edward. They had to digest their lunch first. People got cramp and drowned if they bathed immediately after a meal.

'Have you known anyone who actually drowned, Dad?' Teddy asked.

'Dozens. You get changed. Chop chop.'

'What does chop mean?' asked Lydia nervously.

'It's Chinese for quick,' said Louise. 'Mummy, can we start unpacking lunch? Just to see what there is?'

Zoë helped unpack the picnic, and the nannies stopped combing hair and clicking over tar on Lydia's bathing dress and spread a rug for the children to sit on. Zoë was pleased because Rupert had knelt beside her and ruffled her hair and asked how was his little bookworm, which made her feel interesting in a different way. The children ate ravenously, except Lydia refused her hard-boiled egg, which she described as dead. 'I never eat dead eggs,' she said, so Teddy ate it for her. Neville spilled his orange squash on the car rug and Clary got stung by a bee and cried until Rupert sucked out the sting and explained how much worse it was for the bee who, he said, would be dead as a doornail by now. After lunch, Lydia and Neville were made to have rests in the shade of the breakwater by the nannies, the grown-ups smoked and the older children played a rather shaky game of Pelmanism on the pebbles with the cards they had brought. Clary was the best at that by far, never seeming to forget a card, although, as Simon pointed out, some of them got tilted by the pebbles and continued to be visible if you cheated, which he seemed to feel might be the case with Clary. Then the boys wanted to bathe again, claimed that they had been promised a second go. The tide was going out, and the others decided to paddle – not possible when they had arrived. Goodness! thought Zoë. It goes on and on. She had got to the bit in *Gone With The Wind* where Melanie was starting to have her baby and Scarlett couldn't get the doctor to come, and decided she didn't want to read that now. Rupert was walking with Clary along the beach hand in hand, Clary looking up at him and swinging his arm. Perhaps if I got better with his children, he wouldn't want any more, she thought. This seemed a good, but difficult, idea. She imagined herself nursing Neville with pneumonia or something fatal of that kind; sitting up with him night after night, stroking his forehead and refusing to leave his side for an instant, until he was pronounced out of danger. 'He owes his life to you, darling,' Rupert would say, 'and I owe you more than I can ever repay.' She felt she was rather like Scarlett: beautiful, brave and quite straightforward about things. She would make Rupert read the book and he would see.

By four o'clock everybody was ready to go home – although the children would not admit it. '*Must* we? We've hardly been here a minute.' Banana skins, egg shells, the crusts of sandwiches, the Bakelite mugs were packed away, personal belongings lost and found and established with their owner, keys mislaid and discovered. They began the tramp back up the beach and along the dirt track to the cars that, parked in the sun, were now like furnaces. Villy and Rupert and Edward wound down the windows but the seats were burning and Neville said he could not sit on them and had to be placed on Ellen's lap. Edward drove their Buick, and Villy the Brig's old Vauxhall, which had a villainous gearbox having been driven by countless non-owners and, in any case, being pretty old. Rupert took Zoë and Ellen in his Ford with Neville and Lydia who clamoured to go with Neville as they had begun to play I Spy. Clary was glad to go with Villy and the girls, Nan went in Edward's car in front, which she relished, and the boys at the back. They drove in tandem with Villy leading in case her car broke down. The girls quarrelled about who should sit in front, Louise saying she was the oldest and Clary saying she was sick in the back. Villy settled for Clary. She had a headache from the sun and began to look forward to a tepid bath and sitting on the lawn sewing with Sybil. 'But it is good for them to get some bathing and sea air,' she told herself.

∞ ∞ ∞

Rachel returned to the bedroom to find that Dr Carr had mysteriously converted it from a scene of amateur emergency into a place where something serious was happening with a predictable outcome. Sybil now lay on her side, with her knees drawn up, and he was putting a cold compress on her ankle.

'Mrs Cazalet is doing very well indeed,' he announced, 'over half-way dilated, and the baby is the right way round. We'll need some towels to put under her, and you might send for the kitchen scales, and then you can rub her back – here – low, down each side of the spine when the pains come and tell her to breathe. The more you have the pain, Mrs Cazalet, the deeper you breathe. Is there a wee table I can have for my paraphernalia, Miss Cazalet? Is there a bell in this room? Ah! well, then, we can make our demands. Breathe, Mrs Cazalet, try to relax and breathe.'

'Yes,' Sybil said. She did not look nearly so frightened now, Rachel saw, kept her eyes on the doctor with a look of trustful obedience that amounted almost to adoration.

The towels were spread, a table was covered with a clean cloth and forceps, scissors, and a bottle with gauze pads beside it were duly arranged. Peggy brought up the scales, announcing with awe that Mrs Cripps had cleaned them herself, and was told to change the pails of hot water every twenty minutes to ensure that they would be hot enough when required. All this induced a sense of order and purpose, but when everything was arranged there was order, but the purpose seemed to recede. Rachel, who knew she knew nothing, began to wonder how long it was to take. Surely, if one had had babies before, it was supposed to be quicker? But quicker than what? After an unknown but very long amount of time, Dr Carr examined Sybil again, 'No need to leave the room, Miss Cazalet,' and when he had finished, straightened up with a little grunt and said that it would be some time yet and that he needed to telephone his wife to tell her to tell his partner to be ready to take evening surgery. Rachel told him where the telephone was and then resumed her seat beside Sybil who lay still upon her back. Her eyes were closed, and this, with her hair – dark at the roots from sweat – scraped back from her forehead, gave her a graven appearance. She opened her eyes, smiled at Rachel and said, 'Polly took ages, but Simon was quite quick. He won't be long, will he?'

'The baby?'

'The doctor. Oh, here it comes.' But it was not the baby, simply another pain. She heaved herself onto her side so that Rachel could rub her back.

The Duchy had done everything that she could think of. She had rung Hugh as calmly as possible and suggested that he go home and collect the baby's clothes to bring down with him. Yes, they had got a doctor. Dr Carr was well known for his delivery of babies. And Rachel was helping, everything was fine. She had visited the kitchen again to find that Mrs Cripps had put everybody to work. The maids were making sandwiches and laying a small tray of cold meat and salad for lunch; Dottie was staggering to and fro with large enamel jugs to fill the huge pan and kettle on the range and Mrs Cripps herself, her greenish face luminous with energy and sweat, was rubbing furiously at the weighing cradle of the kitchen scales, while Billy had been told to bring in fresh hods of coal with which to stoke the range. A state of grim excitement prevailed. Mrs Cripps had earlier announced that ladies were chancy in confinement and she shouldn't be surprised whatever became of Mrs Hugh, whereupon Dottie burst into theatrical tears and had to be slapped by one of the maids to give her, as Mrs Cripps observed, something to cry for. When the Duchy came in, everybody stopped what they were doing and looked at her as the bearer of tidings of whatever sort.

'Mrs Hugh is doing well, and the doctor is here. Mr

Hugh will be coming down this evening. Miss Sidney and I will lunch in the morning room, but we shan't want very much. I see you are all very busy so I won't disturb you. I don't think the beach party will be back much before four, Mrs Cripps, but we should have the hampers ready for them when they come.'

'Yes, m'm. And would you like lunch served now, m'm?'

The Duchy looked at her watch strapped to her wrist in which a thin lace handkerchief was tucked.

'One thirty, thank you, Mrs Cripps.'

Leaving the kitchen, she paused in the hall, wondering whether she should go and see whether Rachel was managing, whether she wanted anything. Then she remembered that Sid was stranded with nothing to entertain her, so she provided Sid with *The Times* and a glass of sherry, said that luncheon was on its way, and that she would be back in a tick. She had become desperately worried about what the poor baby was to wear when it was born. Hugh was very unlikely to arrive with its clothes in time, and meanwhile it needed warmth. In her bedroom, which was all white muslin and pale blue washed walls, she searched for and found the white cashmere shawl that Will had brought back for her from one of his trips to India. It had become cream-coloured with age and washing, but it was still as soft and light as feathers. It would do. She hung it on the banister rail outside Sybil's room. Then she went downstairs for luncheon.

∞ ∞ ∞

In spite of being told several times by his mother that everything was fine, and that he was not to worry, Hugh was, of course, worried. It's the possibility of twins, he thought as he drove back to Bedford Gardens. Twins might mean complications and he did not like to think of Sybil without her own doctor and midwife. If only it had happened yesterday, he thought, or, better still, in three weeks' time when it was supposed to happen. Poor pet! She must have been overdoing it; we shouldn't have gone to that concert, but she'd seemed so keen on it. When he'd gone into the Old Man's room to tell him, his father had smiled and said, 'Well, I'm damned!' but

160

he'd seemed quite cool about it, and when Hugh said that he was going down at once, after calling briefly at home, the Old Man grunted and said, 'Women's business. Much better keep out of the way till it's over, my boy.'

Then he shot a keen glance at this eldest son – unpredictably nervous now since that bloody war – and said that of course Hugh must go if he thought it right. He'd be down in the evening, he added, by his usual train.

Bedford Gardens was delightfully quiet: most people were away with their children. He parked his car, walked up the path and let himself into the house. As he slammed the door, he heard a sound upstairs, of someone running across the room – their bedroom. He put his hat on the hall table and was about to go upstairs, when Inge appeared at the top of them. She was heavily made up and wearing what he recognised at once as the pink silk dress that Sybil had bought last year for a wedding. She stared at him as though he was an intruder until he was constrained to say, 'It's me, Inge.'

'I not thought you back till night-time.'

'Well, Mrs Cazalet's started the baby, and I've come back for its clothes.'

'They are in nursery,' she said, and vanished up the stairs. When he reached the bedroom floor the door was shut, and he guessed she was in their room feverishly tidying up. He had immediately decided to pretend he didn't recognise the dress, he couldn't sack her now or he'd have to stay until she left, and that would hold him up. He went on up to the nursery, seething in rage, saw the clothes all laid in a basket; he found a suitcase and tipped them in and shut the case again. The bedroom door was still closed. He went on down to the drawing room and remembered that he wanted his camera to take pictures of Sybil and the child. His desk, at one end of the room, was in total disarray as though it had been plundered: drawer open, paper all over the place. What the hell! He'd *have* to sack her.

It was bad enough that she should dress up in Sybil's clothes and use her make-up, although he didn't think Sybil *had* that much make-up, but rifling his *desk* – was she after money or something? She was behaving like a common thief or burglar, or, the thought struck him unpleasantly, a spy of some sort, although God knew there was nothing worth spying on. This was ridiculous. No, it wasn't entirely – she was German, wasn't she? He'd never liked her and couldn't leave her alone in the house now; she might do something – decamp with everything of value she could carry, set fire to the place – anything. He put the camera beside the suitcase, and went back upstairs.

It took him precisely an hour. She had all Sybil's clothes strewn about the room, her shoes, her jewellery – everything. He told her to get dressed in her own things, pack and leave. She must be out of the house in half an hour and, first of all, she was to give him the keys. She stuck out her bottom lip and swore under her breath in German, but she didn't argue. He waited outside the room until she had changed into her own cotton frock and then waited in the bedroom while she was upstairs packing. It reeked of Sybil's scent, Tweed, that he always gave her on her birthday. He attempted to tidy the room, hang a few things back in the wardrobe, but it was all such a mess he despaired. His heart was pounding with anger, and a headache was starting – all he needed for the long drive. 'Hurry up!' he shouted up the stairs. She seemed to be a long time, but eventually appeared carrying two obviously immensely heavy cases. 'The keys,' he said. She looked at him with pure hatred and thrust them painfully into his hand.

Then quite slowly, and with horrible accuracy, she spat on him. '*Schweinhund!*' she said.

He stared back at her pale protracted eyes that were full of cold malice. He wiped his face with the back of his hand. The hatred he felt for her frightened him. 'Get out,' he said. 'Get out before I call the police.' He followed her down, watched her open the door and slam it with ferocity behind her.

He went into the bathroom and washed his face and hand, laving them again and again in cold water. Then he took a couple of his pills, and then he thought he'd better be sure that the house was properly locked up. It wasn't. The back door from the kitchen was ajar. After that he went round the basement and ground floor making sure that every window was secure. Then he remembered Pompey, but when he eventually found the poor cat he was on Polly's bed and he was dead – strangled with Polly's winter dressing-gown cord. Polly's beloved cat, the creature she loved most in the world. It was too much. He sat on his daughter's bed and put his face in his hand. For a few seconds he sobbed until some early upbringing message told him that this would not do, so he stopped and blew his nose. He looked at Pompey, who lay rigidly stretched out the cord still strained round his neck. His half-open eyes were still bright; his fur was warm. When he undid the cord, he saw that it had been expertly knotted. It struck him then that strangling a cat without a sound was not an easy thing to do, unless you had practice – the thought caused a shiver of revulsion. But he had to get on. He wrapped Pompey in a bath towel and carried him downstairs, with the notion that he would bury him in the back garden, but one look at the baking soil covered with iris roots changed his mind. He would take Pompey to Sussex, find the right time to tell Polly and help her to bury him – the Duchy would provide a good spot for a grave. He must, in any case, *tell* Polly that Pompey had died, but not how. She must never know how cruelly malevolent people could be – let her have the pure grief. I'll get her another cat, he thought, as he packed the car, putting Pompey in the back of the boot. I'll get her *twenty* cats – any cat she wants in the world.

∞ ∞ ∞

'I always thought that Adila's sister was so much better than Adila. She was quieter – less flamboyant.'

Sid, although she did not agree with the remark – that is to say that she had not the distaste for flamboyance that was so evident in the Duchy – was none the less pleased that the subject of violinists was proving to be the right distraction for her. They had progressed from a profound and mutual admiration for Szigeti and Hubermann to the D'Aranyi sisters. Now, she said that they were wonderful together, set each other off, were perfect with Bach, for instance. The Duchy's eyes glowed with interest.

'Did you hear that? They must have been marvellous.'

'Not at the concert. At a friend's house one evening. They suddenly decided to do it. It was unforgettable.'

'But I don't think *Jelly* should ever have performed that Schumann. He clearly did not want it performed, and it seems wrong to have gone against his wishes.'

'Hard to resist though, if you had uncovered the manuscript.'

Sensing dangerous ground – the Duchy would never have considered that something hard to resist was a reason for resisting it – she added, 'Of course, Somervell wrote his concerto for Adila which is one reason why she has been heard far more often in public than her sister. Those Brahms Hungarian dances for encores! Marvellous, don't you think? Number five, for instance.'

Sid agreed – nobody could play a Hungarian dance like a Hungarian.

The Duchy patted her mouth with her napkin and rolled it into its silver holder. 'Have you heard this new young boy – Menuhin?'

'I went to his first concert at the Albert Hall. He played the Elgar. An amazing performance.'

'I never felt it was right that there should be these child prodigies. It must be awfully hard on them – no real childhood and all the travelling.'

Sid thought of Mozart, and remained silent. Then the Duchy added, 'But I have heard him and he is wonderful – such a grasp of the music and, of course, he is not a child any more. But isn't it interesting? All the people we have mentioned, not to speak of Kreisler and Jourchim, are Jews! One has to hand it to them. They really are remarkable fiddlers!' Then she looked at Sid and went slightly pink. 'Dear Sid, I hope you don't . . . '

And Sid, wearily used to the blanket anti-Semitism that seemed to envelop the English, answered with the practised good humour that she had needed to cultivate since she was a child, 'Dear Duchy, they *are*! I wish I could say "we", but I have no false notions about my talent – perhaps it is my gentile blood that has prevented me from getting to the top.'

'I do not think that is important. The great thing is to enjoy it.'

And make some sort of living from it, thought Sid, but she did not say this.

The Duchy was still feeling unhappy about what she described to herself as her slip. 'Dear Sid! We are so fond of you. Rachel is devoted to you, you know. You must stay a few days so that you can see more of each other. I do hope that you will have time for that.'

She put out her hand to Sid, who took it as though it was full of a handful of rich crumbs that she could not resist. 'You are very kind, Duchy dear. I should love to stay a day or two.'

The Duchy's frank and troubled eyes cleared and she gave Sid's hand a little pat. 'And perhaps we might play together – the amateur and the professional? Edward's Gagliano is here.'

'That would be lovely.' Edward's Gagliano was a darn sight better than her own fiddle. He never played it now: it lay in its case, still marked Cazalet Minor from his school days, and it was kept in the country.

The Duchy rang for Eileen to clear lunch and got up from the table.

'I think perhaps I will see whether they want anything upstairs. Will you keep an ear out for the beach party returning?'

'I will.'

When the Duchy had gone, she lit another cigarette and wandered outside to the basket chairs on the lawn. She could see the drive and the gate from there. The usual welter of ambivalent feelings was churning away inside her: offence rising at this frightful lumping of people into a category for reasons of race; a creeping, but irresistible gratitude for being classed as an exception to the rule – the mongrel's view, she supposed, but she had other reasons for craving approval, if not affection, which neither the Duchy nor any of her family nor the people she worked with nor anyone at all, in fact, excepting possibly Evie would ever know anything about if she could help it – because of Rachel, her dear most precious and secret love. It had to be secret if she was to keep Rachel, and life without Rachel was not something she could bear to contemplate. Evie did not actually *know*, but she had some inkling and had already started to use her damnable intuition for manipulative purposes – like this deadly fortnight by the sea she said they must have. Evie always sensed the moment attention was not primarily on herself and depending on the occasion became more ingeniously demanding. And this occasion, the great occasion of her life, was dynamite. If only I were a man, she thought, none of this need be. But she did not want to be a man. Nothing is simple, she thought. Yes, one thing was: she loved Rachel with all her heart and nothing could be simpler than that.

∞ ∞ ∞

Sybil lay with her legs apart and her knees up, the mound of her belly obscuring all but the top of Dr Carr's head, pale pink and shiny, as he bent to see how things were going. For a long time they hadn't been at all: the pains had gone on, but the cervix had not continued to dilate; she seemed stuck. Dr Carr was wonderfully reassuring, but she was so tired and sick of the pain that she wanted it to stop more than anything else, and for the past hour – hours – whatever it had been – there seemed to be no reason why it ever should. In the middle of this examination, another splitting surge of pain began – enormous, like a freak wave, and she tried to writhe away from it, but could not because Dr Carr was holding her legs.

'Push, Mrs Cazalet – bear down – push now.' Sybil pushed, but this increased the agony. She shook her head weakly and stopped, felt the pain ebbing, taking all her strength away with it. Sweat stung her eyes and then tears. She whimpered – it wasn't fair to hold her down to make things worse when she was too tired to bear any more. She looked weakly for Rachel, but Dr Carr was talking to Rachel who was too far away. She felt stranded, abandoned by both of them.

'You're doing very well now, Mrs Cazalet. When the next pain starts, take a deep breath, and really push.'

She started to ask him if something was happening at last. 'Yes, yes, your baby's on its way, but you must help. Don't fight the pains, ride them. Go with them, you're nearly there.' She did it twice more, and then, just before the third time, she felt the baby's head, like a heavy round rock crammed in her, beginning to move again and she gave a cry not simply of pain but of excitement at her child coming to life out of her. And after that, the last two or three waves – although they seemed to be breaking her open with a new shriller agony – did not engulf her as before: her body's attention was all focused upon the amazing sensation of the head moving down and out. She saw Rachel standing over her with a small white pad and shook her head – she did not want to lose track of this baby's journey as had happened twice before with the others, and so she raised herself so that she could see its arrival. The doctor shook his head at Rachel, who put the pad away. Sybil let out a long sighing breath, and then the head was out – eyes tightly shut, wispy hair dark wet – the crumpled shoulders and then the rest of the tadpole body was lying on the bed. Dr Carr tied and cut the cord, picked up the baby by its ankles and slapped it gently on its slippery bloodstained back. The baby's face screwed up as though in grief at leaving its watery element, and then its mouth opened and it expelled its first breath in a thin, wavering cry. 'A beautiful boy,' said Dr Carr. He was smiling. Sybil's eyes were fixed upon his face with some mute appeal. He looked at her with tender kindness, almost as though they were lovers, and laid the baby in her arms. Rachel, watching Sybil's face as she received this little bloodied creature – now crying fiercely – found herself in tears. The room was full of excitement and love.

Then Dr Carr became briskly practical. Rachel was told to put warm water in a basin to bathe the baby while he attended to the afterbirth. Rachel tied a towel round her waist and gingerly took the baby from Sybil. She was terrified of hurting him. Dr Carr saw this and said brusquely, 'He's not made of glass, he won't break,' took the baby from her and laid him on his back in the basin. 'You support his head and sponge him down. Like so,' and went back to Sybil.

The baby, who had stopped crying, lolled in the bath, his slaty eyes, now open, roving about the room, his fingers opening and closing into a fist, his knees turned out, his feet at right angles to his legs, a bubble of mucus coming out of one nostril. Dr Carr, who seemed to miss nothing, looked at him, then cleaned his nostrils with a twist of cotton wool. The baby frowned, arched his back so that all his tiny ribs showed, and cried again. His skin, the colour of the smallest pink shells, was as soft as a rose. He made slow random movements with an arm or a leg, and sometimes he seemed to look at Rachel, but his gaze was inscrutable. She sponged him carefully, even humbly: he looked at once so vulnerable and majestic.

'You can take him out now and dry him, and then we'll put him on the scales. Just over seven pounds, or I'm a Dutchman, but we need to be sure. There we go, Mrs Cazalet.' The room was suddenly full of the smell of warm blood. It was a quarter to five.

∞ ∞ ∞

Hugh did not reach Home Place until twenty minutes after his son was born. He had had a puncture and had had trouble getting the tyre off the car. He arrived to find the Duchy feeding Rachel with ham sandwiches and tea, Mrs Pearson, the midwife, had arrived and Dr Carr, after a quick cup, was back with his patient for the delivery of the second baby – there were twins, after all – but he did not expect that to take long. Rachel came with him to fetch the baby clothes from the car.

'I should like to see Sybil. Do you think it would be all right if I went up?' he said as they walked back into the house.

'Darling Hugh, I don't know. What do you usually do?'

'Well, Sybil doesn't like me to until everything's all ship-shape, but it hasn't been like this before.'

'Well, we've got to take the clothes up, anyway. Your son is making do with a cashmere shawl.'

'Is he fine?'

'He's *wonderful!*' she said so fervently, that he looked at her with a little smile, and said, 'I didn't know that aunts could be so *épris.*'

'Well, I was there, as a matter of fact. Mrs Pearson couldn't come at once so I sort of helped.'

'Did she have a bad time?'

'I don't think it's ever exactly a picnic. She was marvellous, very brave and good. Dr Carr said that the second one would be quite quick, he thought,' she added hurriedly, in case she had said too much of the other thing.

'Oh, good, you're a brick, Rach. I wonder if they'd let me see her – just for a second.'

But when they got up to the room, Mrs Pearson came to the door, said something to Sybil, and then turned back to say that Mrs Cazalet sent her love but would rather see him later, and Hugh, sure that Mrs Pearson was needed by his wife, did not dare ask her to show him his son.

∞ ∞ ∞

Sybil, in the throes again of excruciating labour, longed for
Hugh, but it was out of the question to submit him to even
a brief sight of her like this. She was stuck, and the first baby
had torn her, and in spite of Dr Carr's assurances, she felt as
though this would go on for ever, or until her strength gave
out. In fact, it all went on for another hour and a half, at the
end of which time it was clear that this baby was not coming
out by the head – would be a breech. Dr Carr had to use forceps to hold the baby's legs together and by then, Sybil was
glad to have the chloroform, and so this time she did not see
the bruised and battered little creature that came out with the
cord round its neck and could not be got to breathe. They kept
her under for the afterbirth, washed and stitched her and then
Dr Carr sat by her until she was conscious enough to be told
that the baby was dead. She asked to see it and was shown. She
looked at the tiny limp white body, and then reached out and
touched its head. 'A girl. Hugh will be so sad.' A tear slipped
down her face: she was too exhausted to cry.

There was a silence: then he said gently, 'You have a
beautiful son. Would you like your husband to come and see
you both?'

Half an hour later, Dr Carr climbed wearily into his old Ford.
He had been called out the previous night, had taken morning
surgery and done five calls before delivering Mrs Cazalet, and
he was not as young as he used to be. In spite of forty years'
experience, the birth of a baby still moved him and he had a
rapport with women in labour that he never felt about them at
any other time. It was rotten luck that the second baby had
been stillborn, but at least she had the other one. My God he
had tried with that second baby, though – she would never
know how much. He'd pressed and released that wee chest
minutes after he'd known it was hopeless. Mrs Pearson had
wanted to wrap it up, put it away out of sight, but he'd known
the mother would want to see it. When he'd gone downstairs,
they'd given him a fine drop of whisky, and he'd warned Mr
Cazalet that his wife was very tired and not to stay with her long;
all she needed was a nice cup of tea and a sleep, no emotional
scenes, he had wanted to add, but looking at the father's face,

he thought there wouldn't be any of that. He looked a decent, understanding man – not like some of them who became breezy and facetious and often drunk. Now he must get back to Margaret. In the old days, he used to come home full of tales about deliveries, excited, even exalted by having witnessed the same old miracle. But after they lost both their sons in the war, she couldn't stand to hear about any of that and he kept it to himself. She had become a shadow, acquiescent, passive, full of humdrum little remarks about the house and the weather and how hard he was on his clothes, and then he'd bought her a puppy, and she talked endlessly about that. It had become a fat spoiled dog, and still she talked about it as though it were a puppy. It was all he could think to do for her, as his grief had never been allowed to be on par with hers. He kept that to himself as well. But when he was alone in the car like this, and with a drop of whisky inside him, he thought about Ian and Donald who were never spoken of at home, who would, he felt, be entirely forgotten except for his own memory and their names on the village monument.

∞ ∞ ∞

'I *did* ask her, and she just said, never you mind.' Louise looked across the glade resentfully at her mother who was smoking and laughing and talking with Uncle Rupert and someone called Margot Sidney. She and Polly and Clary had withdrawn from the main picnic – over in any case for some time now – in order to have a serious discussion about exactly how people had babies but they weren't getting anywhere. Clary had pulled up her shirt, fingered her navel doubtfully and suggested that it might be the place, but Polly, secretly horrified, had immediately said that it wasn't big enough. 'Babies are quite large, you know, about like a medium doll.'

'It's got all sorts of wrinkles in it. It might stretch.'

'It would be much better if they just laid eggs.'

'People are too heavy for eggs. They'd break them sitting, and it would be scrambled baby all over the place.'

'You're revolting, Clary. No. I'm afraid it must be – ' she leant over Polly and mouthed, 'between the legs.'

'No!'

'It's the only place left.'

'Who's revolting now?'

'It's not me. *I* didn't plan it. It's common sense,' she added loftily, trying to get used to the ghastly idea.

'It's certainly common,' said Clary.

'*I* think,' Polly said dreamily, 'that really all they have is a sort of pip, quite large compared to a grapefruit, and the doctor puts it in a basin of warm water and it sort of explodes – like a Japanese flower in those shells – into a baby.'

'You're an absolute *idiot*. Why do you think they get so fat if all they have is a pip? Look at Aunt Syb. Can you honestly believe that all she has inside her is a *pip*?'

'Also, it's known to be dangerous,' Clary said. She looked frightened.

'It can't be all that dangerous – look at all the people there are,' Louise began, and then remembered Clary's mother and said, 'You might be right about the pip, Polly, I expect you are,' and winked very largely at Polly to make her realise.

Soon after that, Aunt Rachel came and found them and told them that Aunt Sybil had had a baby boy, and a little girl who had died, and was terribly tired so would they all go home quietly and not make a noise? Simon, who was up a tree at the time, said, 'Good show,' and went on hanging from a branch by his knees and asking people to look, but Polly rushed to Aunt Rachel and said she wanted to go and see her mother and the baby at once. Everybody was glad to be going home.

Rachel and Sid slipped out at about six for a walk. They walked fast – almost furtively – round the drive to the gate into the wood in case any of the family saw them and suggested coming too. Once in the wood, they began to stroll along the narrow path through it that led to the fields beyond. Rachel was very tired; her back ached from leaning over Sybil's bed, and the news of the stillborn baby had upset her very much. When they reached the stile into the meadow that slipped gently uphill before them, Sid proposed that they go only as far as the large single oak that stood by itself a few yards from the wood and sit for a bit, and Rachel gratefully agreed. Although, if I had suggested a five-mile walk, Sid thought, she would have agreed to that even though she is

171

dead beat. The thought filled her with tender exasperation; Rachel's unselfishness was formidable to her, and often made decisions a matter of strenuous perception.

Rachel arranged her back against the oak, accepted a gasper from Sid, who lit it for her with the little silver lighter that had been an early present on her first birthday after they had met, nearly two years ago. They smoked for a while in silence. Rachel's eyes seemed fixed upon the green and golden meadow starred with poppies and ox-eye daisies and buttercups, but not as though she saw these things, and Sid watched Rachel's face. Her fine complexion was pale and drawn, her blue eyes clouded, smudged above her high cheekbones with fatigue, her mouth trembling, making small movements of compression and resolution as though she was afraid of crying. Sid reached out and took one of her hands. 'Easier if you tell,' she said.

'It seems so *cruel*! All that agony and effort and then that poor little thing born dead! Such ghastly, frightful bad luck!'

'There is one baby, though. That's a great deal better than if there had only been one in the first place.'

'Of course it is. But do you think it will always miss its twin? Aren't they specially devoted?'

'Only if they're identical, I believe.'

'Yes, that's right, I'd forgotten. The awful thing is that I can't help being glad I wasn't there for the second part. I should have blubbed.'

'Darling, you weren't, and if you had been you probably wouldn't have blubbed out of consideration for Sybil, but if you had it wouldn't have been the end of the world, you know. Crying isn't a crime.'

'No, but it's unsuitable when you get to be my age.'

'Is it?'

Looking at Sid's tender, ironical expression, Rachel said slowly, 'Well, *we* were brought up to think that part of growing up was learning not to cry at things. Except music and being patriotic and things like that.'

'Elgar would be a hole-in-one, you mean?'

This made Rachel laugh. 'Dead right. I wonder what the Cazalets did for tears before Elgar!'

'We don't have to consider the Dark Ages of the Cazalets.'

'We do not.' She took the little white handkerchief from her wrist and wiped her eyes. 'How absurd one is!'

Then they began to talk about themselves. Rachel asked about the seaside holiday that Evie wanted to go on, and Sid said how much she did not want to go, leaving out only the fact that it was going to be very difficult to afford – Rachel's affluence and Sid's lack of it embarrassed them both – and Rachel said did she feel she had to go because Evie really *needed* it, in which case, why not go to Hastings, and then they could both come to Home Place for lunch, etc. But Sid said that she was afraid of Evie finding out about them – her and Rachel.

'But, darling, there's nothing really for her to find out!'

This was both true and untrue, Sid knew. She said. 'Well, she's a very jealous person. Possessive.'

'You are all she has in the world. I think that's understandable.'

She *makes* me all she has in the world, Sid thought, but did not say so. Like many people who criticised and urged others to be more open, she preserved thickets of secrecy for herself. In this case, she called it loyalty to Evie; Rachel, incapable of manipulative practices, would not in the least understand them in anyone else. Then Rachel sighed with contentment, and said, 'It is so lovely that you're here now,' with such heartfelt affection, that Sid was able to put her arms round her and kiss her for the first time that day, an exquisite but different pleasure for each of them.

∞ ∞ ∞

Hugh, although he hoped he had concealed it, had been shocked by the sight of Sybil. She lay under a clean sheet flat on her back with her hair loose on the square white pillow and beside all this white her face had a grey, waxy appearance and her eyes were closed. He thought she looked as though she was dying but Mrs Pearson, who had answered the door, said cheerfully, 'Here's your husband to see you, Mrs Cazalet,' as though nothing very much was the matter. 'I'll just pop down and see to some tea for her,' she added and rustled out.

Hugh sought a chair, and drew it up to the bed.

Her eyes had opened when she heard Mrs Pearson, and now she looked at him without expression. He took her hand and kissed it; she frowned slightly, shut her eyes again, and two tears rolled slowly out. 'Sorry. It was twins. I slipped. Sorry.' She made some small movement in the bed and flinched.

'Darling girl, it's all right.'

'No! He tried to make her breathe. She never breathed. All that and she never lived.'

'I know, darling. But what about the lovely boy? May I see him?'

'He's over there.'

As Hugh gazed at the profile of his son, lying on his side and sternly asleep, she said, '*He*'s all right. There's nothing wrong with *him*!' Then she added, 'But I know you wanted a daughter.'

He came back to her. 'He looks marvellous. And I *have* a very nice daughter.'

'She was so much smaller! So tiny – pitiful. When I touched her, her head was still warm. No one will ever have known her – but me. Do you know what I wanted?'

'No.' He found it difficult to speak.

'I wanted her back inside me – to keep her safe.' She looked at him with streaming eyes. 'I really wanted that.'

'I want to take you in my arms,' he said, 'but it's difficult when you're flat on your back.' Then, unable to stop himself, he gave one dry sob, and held her hand to his face.

At once, she raised herself and was holding him. 'It's all right. I wanted you to know, but not to – don't be sad! It isn't as though – when he wakes, you'll see how beautiful he is – you mustn't be sad – remember Polly – darling . . . ' And as she held him, comforting him about her own grief, he began to recognise the extent of it and his pity for her was dissolved by her love. He took her in his arms and laid her carefully back on the pillow, smoothing her hair, softly kissing her mouth, telling her that she was right, that they had Polly, and that he loved her and his new son. When Mrs Pearson came back with the tea they were holding hands.

∞ ∞ ∞

Hearing that Polly and Simon were going to see their new brother, who had been put in his basket in Hugh's dressing room for the purpose, the other children clamoured to be allowed to go, too. Afterwards, when Villy went to say good night to Lydia she overheard her and Neville discussing the baby.

'I simply didn't like him,' Neville was saying. 'I can't see why *anyone* would like him.'

'He did look a bit – red and wrinkly – like a tiny old person.'

'If he starts like that, what do you think he'll turn into?'

'I tremble to think.'

'You tremble to think,' he scoffed. 'I don't *tremble*. I just think he's horrible. I'd rather have a Labrador than him—'

'Neville! After all, he is a human *bean*.'

'He may be. He may not.'

At this point, Villy, straightening her face, interrupted them.

∞ ∞ ∞

After Polly had seen her new brother, Hugh said that he wanted to talk to her.

'Now?' She had planned to play Monopoly with Louise and Clary.

'Yes.'

'Here?'

'I thought we'd take a turn in the garden.'

'All right, Dad. I must just tell the others. I'll meet you in the hall in five secs.'

He took her to the seat by the tennis court and they both sat on it. There was a short silence, and Polly began to feel anxious.

'What is it, Dad?' His face was looking very craggy which it did when he was tired. 'Nothing bad?'

'Well, it is, rather.'

She caught the sleeve of his coat. 'It's nothing about Mummy, is it? You wouldn't let me see her! She's – perfectly – all right, isn't she?'

'No, no,' he said, stricken by her face. 'No. Mummy is simply very, very tired. She went to sleep and I didn't want us to wake her. You'll see her in the morning. No, it's—' and then he told his carefully prepared tale. How he had had to go home to collect the baby's things, and how, coming down from the nursery floor, he had seen Pompey lying on the bed and had gone to give him a stroke, and found that he was dead – had obviously just quietly died in his sleep, which was terribly sad, but from his point of view was the best way for a cat to die. 'He wouldn't have known anything, Poll – just gone to sleep and not woken up. Which is,' he said, looking at her earnestly, 'of course, much worse for you than for him.'

'Which is, of course, the best way round,' she said. She had gone white, and her mouth was trembling. 'How simply awful for *you*! To just go in and find him like that! Poor Dad!' She threw her arms around him, weeping bitterly. 'Oh, poor Pompey to be dead! He wasn't awfully old – Why would he die like that? Do you think he thought I wasn't coming back, and—'

'I'm sure it wasn't that. And we don't know how old he was. He was probably much older than he looked.' He had been acquired in a carrier bag from Selfridge's – a present from her godmother, Rachel, for her ninth birthday. 'He was grown up when you got him.'

'Yes. It must have been a frightful horrible shock for you.'

'It was. Want a hanky?'

She took it, and blew her nose twice. 'He must have used up his nine lives. Dad! You didn't – just throw him away, did you?'

'Good Lord, no! As a matter of fact, I brought him down here. I thought you might like to give him a proper funeral.'

She shot him a look of such radiant gratitude, that his heart lurched. 'Yes,' she said. 'I might quite like to do that.'

On their way back to the house, they discussed Pompey's remarkable life – or lives: run over three times, marooned at the top of a tree for two days until the Fire Brigade got him down, shut in the wine cellar for nobody knew how long . . . 'But that's only five of them,' Polly said sadly.

'He probably used some of them up before you knew him.'

'That must be it.'

As they neared the house, she said, 'Dad! I've been thinking. It might not mean that he had nine lives as the *same cat*: it might mean that he's simply going to be nine different cats. Well, eight more.'

'It might. Well,' he finished, 'if you come across a kitten who looks as though he might be Pompey having another life, let me know, and I'll get him for you.'

'Oh, Dad, would you? I'll keep a strict look out.'

∞ ∞ ∞

That was the beginning of that summer, which merged in many of their minds with other summers, but was remembered chiefly as the summer that young William was born, and there was that sad matter of the other baby; but remembered by Polly as the summer that Pompey died and his splendid funeral; remembered by old William Cazalet as the summer he clinched the deal over buying the Mill Farm down the road; remembered by Edward as the summer when, offering to stand in for Hugh at the office, he met Diana for the first time; remembered by Louise as the summer she got the Curse; remembered by Teddy as the summer when he shot his first rabbit and his voice started going funny; remembered by Lydia as the summer she got locked in the fruit cage by the boys who forgot her, went off to play bicycle hockey and then to lunch and nobody found her until half-way through lunch (it was Nan's day off) and she'd worked out that when gooseberries were over, she'd die of nothing to eat; remembered by Sid as the summer when she finally understood that Rachel would never leave her parents, but that she, Sid, could never leave Rachel; remembered by Neville as the time his loose tooth came out when he was on his fairy cycle which he could only dismount by running into something so he swallowed the tooth and didn't dare tell anyone, but waited in terror for it to bite him inside; remembered by Rupert as the summer when he realised that in marrying Zoë he had lost the chance of being a serious painter, would have to stick to schoolmastering to provide her even with what she thought of as the bare necessities; remembered by Villy as the summer when she got so bored that she started to teach herself to play the violin and made a scale model of the Cutty Sark which was too large to put into a bottle, something she had done with a smaller ship the previous summer; remembered by Simon as the holidays Dad taught him to drive, up and down the drive in the Buick; remembered by Zoë as the frightful summer when she was three weeks late and thought that she was pregnant; remembered by the Duchy as the summer that the tree paeony first flowered; remembered by Clary as the summer she broke her arm falling off Joey when Louise was giving her a riding lesson and when she sleepwalked into the dining room when they were all having dinner and she thought it was a dream and Dad picked her up and carried her to bed; remembered by Rachel as the summer she actually saw a baby being born, but also the summer when her back really started to go wrong, was only intermittently right for the rest of her life. And remembered by Will, whose first summer it was, not at all.

PART TWO

LATE SUMMER 1938

'I wonder *why*,' Jessica asked herself yet again, 'he's so particularly awful before we go away?' It wasn't that *he* hadn't been asked. Edward and Villy were always charming to him, but he wouldn't come with them. Worse, he didn't altogether stay away either: usually, as now, he said he would probably turn up for the last weekend of the fortnight, which somehow seemed like a threat, and at the same time didn't stop him from making her feel that she was wilfully abandoning him. But a free country holiday for the children was not to be rejected and, if she was honest with herself (which of course she thought she invariably was) she could do with some country air, not having to cook, to worry about stretching the housekeeping money with all four children at home needing quantities of food that it made her exhausted even to think about – let alone the washing and ironing. Oh, the bliss of sitting on a lawn sipping a gin and lime while somebody else cooked dinner!

He was back again, standing in the bedroom doorway, waiting with exaggerated patience for her to shut her suitcase. He always insisted upon loading the car for her, which was a sort of coals-of-fire kindness. As a matter of fact, even with the roof rack it took a bit of doing for five of them, but he made a regimented meal of it – insisting upon everybody's luggage being stacked on the pavement beside the car before he would begin.

'Sorry, darling,' she said as brightly as she could.

He picked up the case and raised his eyebrows. 'Anybody would think you were going away for six months,' but he said it every time she ever went away, and she'd long ago stopped explaining that one needed as much for two weeks as for six

months. Watching him limp heavily down the stairs with the
case she felt familiar urges of guilt and pity. Poor Raymond!
He hated his job – bursar at a large local school – he was a
man who needed physical action to feel good-humoured and
his leg precluded that entirely. He had been brought up with
money and now had none, excepting for uncertain expectations
from a fractious aunt, who at regular intervals implied that she
might have changed her mind and would leave him her art
collection – one Watts, a Landseer and over five hundred
queasy watercolours painted by her late husband – instead of
her money. But if he *had* the money it wouldn't last: he'd use
it up on some hopeless, mad idea. He was not much good at
working with people – things got on his nerves and he flew off
the handle at unexpected moments – but on the other hand
he had no business sense whatsoever and therefore needed a
partner. Any minute now he would give up his present job, she
knew, in favour of some new scheme, but any money for that
would have to come out of selling this house to go somewhere
even less congenial and cheaper. Not that she liked the house
(a semi-detached Tudor bijou gem, as she described it when
she had wanted to make Edward laugh), erected soon after
the war by speculative builders as part of the growing ribbon
development along a main road to East Finchley. It had mean
little rooms, passages so narrow that it was difficult to walk
along them carrying a tray without barking your knuckles,
and already there were long slanting cracks in the walls, the
casement windows had warped and let in the rain, and the
kitchen always smelled of damp. It had a long narrow back
garden at the end of which was a shed that Raymond had built
when he had his mushroom-growing venture. It was now used
by Judy as a house in which she could have her friends – a
mercy, really, because being the youngest she had the smallest
room, which was so small that there was no room for anything
else besides her bed and her chest of drawers.

　'Jessica! Jessica!'

'Daddy wants you, Mummy!'

'It's the milkman, Mummy. He wants to be paid.'

She paid the milkman, sent Christopher to hurry the older
girls, went into the drawing room to make sure she had shut
the piano and covered it with the paisley shawl against the

sun, told Judy to go to the lavatory and finally, when she could think of nothing else to do, went out of the front door, down the crazy-paving path to join the jigsaw front gate – now open, with Nora sitting upon it – to watch the final packing arrangements.

'The object of the enterprise, Christopher, in case you hadn't realised, is to stop the cases slipping.'

'I know, Dad.'

'You know, you *know*? How absolutely extraordinary that it didn't occur to you to put some rope through the handles, then! I suppose I have to conclude that you simply aren't very bright.'

Christopher went scarlet, climbed onto the running board and began to thread the rope through the handles. Watching his thin paper-white arms below his rolled-up sleeves and his shirt tail hanging out from his trousers as he stretched up, Jessica felt love and hatred converge in her at the spectacle of her son and her husband doing respectively their best and worst. She looked up at the sky: the earlier blue had faded to a milky pale grey, there was not a breath of wind, and she wondered whether they'd reach Sussex before a thunderstorm.

'That looks marvellous,' she said. 'Where's Angie?'

'Waiting upstairs. She didn't want to hang about in the heat,' said Nora.

'Well, get her. I thought you were supposed to tell both girls to come down.'

'I'm sure he did, darling, but you know Angie. Call her, Nora.'

Judy, the youngest, emerged from the house. She went up to Jessica and indicated that she wanted to whisper. Jessica bent down.

'I tried, Mummy, but not a drop came out.'

'Never mind.'

Angela, wearing a blue Moygashel suit that she had made herself, came slowly down the path. She wore her white shoes and carried a pair of white cotton gloves; she looked as though she was going to a wedding. Jessica, who knew that this was to impress her Aunt Villy, said nothing. Angela was just nineteen, and had recently become both dreamy and demanding. '*Why* don't we have more money?' she would wail, when she wanted more pocket money – she called it dress allowance – and Jessica had to refuse her. 'Money isn't everything,' she had once said in Nora's hearing, who had immediately shot back at her, 'No, but it's something, isn't it? I mean, it's not *nothing*.'

Raymond was now saying goodbye to them. He kissed Angela's pale and passive cheek – Dad was sweating, and she simply loathed sweat – and Nora, who hugged him so fiercely that he was pleased. 'Steady *on*,' he said. He clapped Christopher painfully on the shoulder, and Christopher muttered something and got quickly into the back of the car.

'Goodbye, Dad,' Judy said. 'I expect you'll have a spiffing time with Aunt Lena. Give Trottie my love.' Trottie was Aunt Lena's pug; a rotten name, as Nora had remarked, as he was so fat he could never have trotted in his life.

Angela got carefully into the passenger seat in front.

'You might have asked,' said Nora.

'I'm the oldest. I don't have to ask.'

'Oh, so you *are*, I can't think how I can have forgotten that.' This was a painfully accurate imitation of her father when he was doing his schoolmaster sarcastic act, Jessica thought. She kissed his hot damp face and gave him the little mechanically intimate smile that secretly so enraged him.

'Well, I hope you all enjoy yourselves more than I shall,' he said.

'There are more of us so we ought to,' Nora replied cheerfully. She had a gift for the amiable last word.

Then they were off.

∞ ∞ ∞

These days, it seemed to Louise that whatever she was doing her mother stopped her and made her do something else that she would never want to do, anyway, and particularly not if she was already doing something. This morning she was stopped from going to the beach with Uncle Rupert, Clary and Polly because Mother told her that her cousins were coming and it would be rude not to be there to greet them.

'*They* wouldn't think it in the least rude.'

'I'm not interested in what you think they'd think,' said Villy sharply. 'In any case, I'm sure you haven't tidied your bedroom.'

'It doesn't *need* tidying.'

Villy's answer to this was to take her daughter by the arm and march her upstairs to the large back attic that Louise was being made to share with Nora and Angela.

'I thought so,' she said. 'The proverbial pigsty.' She twitched open a drawer that was bulging with Louise's half-worn clothes and other things.

'How many times have I told you that it is disgusting to keep your knickers in with your other clothes?' She managed to make it sound disgusting, Louise thought. She's always managing to make me sound like that, as though she sort of hates me. For answer, she pulled the drawer right out and tipped its contents onto her bed.

'And books as well! Really, Louise! What *is* this book?'

'It's called *Chin Ping Mei*. It's about sixteenth-century China,' she said sulkily, but she was alarmed.

'Oh.' Villy knew that the girls were doing China with Miss Milliment and that they had all become passionate about anything Chinese – Sybil had told her about Polly's growing collection of soapstones and Louise's room at home was full of little shattered pieces of embroidery. 'Well, put all your books on the mantelpiece. Get everything looking nice, there's a good girl, and you might pick some roses to put on the dressing-table which, incidentally you will also have to clear to make room for Angela's things. Do it quickly, because Phyllis will be wanting to make up their beds.' And she went, leaving Louise considerably relieved. She decided to tidy everything perfectly, and then go and read in the hammock by the duck pond. Although she did not understand the Chinese book much, she knew that it contained a good deal of stuff of which her mother would deeply disapprove. It was nearly all about sex, but of such mysterious kinds that Louise, who began reading it for information, felt more at sea than ever. But the food and clothes and other things that happened fascinated her, and it was jolly long, which was the chief criterion by which she bought second-hand books, because she still only got sixpence a week pocket money and was constantly short of reading matter.

It was their first holiday at Mill Farm, bought and given by the Brig to his sons for their families. This time, because of Aunt Jessica and her cousins, it was their own family, plus Neville and Ellen as company for Lydia. The others were all up the road at Home Place, but they met every day. Mill Farm was white clinker-built weatherboarding with a tiled roof. It was approached by a drive edged with chestnuts and ending in a formal sweep before the front door. To the side of the drive and in front of the house was a paddock that had probably once been an orchard since it still contained a few very old cherry and pear trees, and in a little hollow near the road end of the paddock was the duck pond – out of bounds to the younger children as Neville had fallen into it on their first evening. He had come out all green with duckweed, like the Dragon King, Lydia remarked, from *Where The Rainbow Ends*, a play she had seen for her Christmas treat that had frightened her very much. The house had been a farm until shortly before the Brig bought it. It had only contained four bedrooms and a pair of attics above, a large kitchen and sitting room below and so he had had a heady six months planning and building a wing on the back – four more bedrooms, and two bathrooms above, a large sitting room and dining room and a small, extremely dark study that looked onto the walls of the old cow shed. He had wired the house for electricity, but water was obtained from two wells, one of which had already run dry and rabbit's fur was reputed to have come out of the kitchen cold tap. The Duchy had had a hand in the interior, so it was all white walls and coconut matting, indeterminate floral chintzes and large plain parchment lampshades. There were fireplaces in the sitting room and dining room, and a new range in the kitchen, and a small grate in the best (old) bedroom, but otherwise it was without heating. Not a house for winter, Villy had thought when she first saw it. It was furnished with whatever any of the families had to spare – iron bedsteads, one or two nice pieces that Edward had picked up from Mr Cracknell in Hastings, some of Rupert's pictures and an extremely ancient gramophone in a laurelwood cabinet, with a horn and at the bottom a place for records, which the children played incessantly on rainy days, 'The Teddy Bears' Picnic', 'The Grasshoppers' Dance', 'The Gold and Silver Waltz', and, Louise's favourite, Noel Coward singing 'Don't Put Your Daughter On The Stage, Mrs Worthington'. This last they sang whenever the grown-ups made them do things they disliked: it had become, Villy remarked, a kind of 'Marseillaise'. There were still a number of old farm buildings at the back, beyond which the hop fields stretched with luxuriant geometry.

Villy had brought down their cook, Emily, and Phyllis, who was helped out by a local woman called Edie who arrived on her bicycle each day and did most of the housework. Nanny had left in the spring when Lydia had begun going to Miss Puttick's school in the mornings, and since it had been decided that Neville should stay at the farm to play with Lydia, Ellen had come with him, and was in charge of both of them. Which left Villy comparatively free, she supposed, to ride, to play tennis, to practise the violin which she had worked hard at all year, to read Ouspensky and ponder on things like negative emotion – something to which she felt herself peculiarly prone – to do a little gardening, and the shopping in Battle for the endless meals. Today, Edward, who was taking a long weekend, had gone to Rye with Hugh to play golf. When he returned to London, she and Jessica were going to have their mother to stay for a week. That was an event, of a kind; at least, it was something which she felt she should do and it would enable Lady Rydal to see all of her grandchildren at once, but Villy, knowing how tired Jessica would be, had arranged that she should have a clear week before their mother arrived. She had worried about leaving Edward in London with only Edna to do for him, but he had said that he would use his club, and certainly he seemed to go out a good deal. She was looking forward to having Jessica to herself; although Raymond was supposed to be joining them at some point, there still would be plenty of time to talk about things. By things, she meant Jessica's husband – and Louise, who had become quite trying lately. Villy was seriously beginning to wonder whether she should not have sent her to a boarding school – look at Teddy! After three terms he seemed to her much improved, was quiet, polite, rather silent, but that was better than being noisy, and nothing like as selfish and moody and wrapped up in himself as Louise. A year ago, Louise would have been so excited at the prospect of her cousins coming to stay that she would not have *dreamed* of wanting to go to the beach, and she was too old now to keep her things in such a squalid mess. If she was asked to do the least little thing, she sulked. Edward always took her

part, treated her as though she was already grown up: he had
bought her the most unsuitable nightgown for her last birthday
and took her to the theatre and out to supper – just the two of
them – and kept her out far too late so that she was like a bear
with a sore head the next day. He introduced her to people as
his eldest unmarried daughter, which irritated Villy profoundly
although she did not quite know why. Well, perhaps fifteen was
just a difficult age; she was still a child, really. If only Edward
would treat her as one.

∞ ∞ ∞

'I think we're in for another war.' Hugh was not looking at
him, and spoke in the quiet casual way that meant he was
serious.

'My dear old boy! What makes you say that?'

'Well, look at it! The Germans have occupied Austria.
That feller Hitler making speeches about the might and power
of the Third Reich all over the place. That stuff about all those
German girls sent over as servants having been on propaganda
courses. All those military displays. You don't go on and on
increasing your army if you don't mean to fight. All these Jews
coming here, most of them with nothing.'

'Why do you think they're doing that?'

'I suppose they know he doesn't want them.'

'Exactly.'

'I don't hold *that* against him. We could do with a few
less of them in our business.' Edward maintained some
fixed notion that any success in the business was due to
him and the Old Man, and any failure was due to the
nefarious business virtuosity of the Jews. It was a notion,
rather than a thought, one of those maxims that gain veracity
from repetition by their owner. Hugh did not agree with this or,
rather, he thought that their Jewish counterparts were better at it
without seeing any reason why they shouldn't be. He remained
silent.

'Anyway, all Jews are perfectly capable of looking after
themselves,' Edward concluded. 'We really don't have to bother
about them. I like some Jews, anyway – Sid, for instance, she's
a bloody good sort.'

'And when you said that, she said she supposed it was because she was only half Jewish.'

'Exactly! She's got a sense of humour about it.'

'Would you have one about people getting at you because you were English?'

'Of course I would. The best thing about the English is the way they can laugh at themselves.'

They choose what to laugh at, though, Hugh thought. They choose things like their understatements and lack of emotion in an emergency (courage) and—

'Listen, old boy. I know you're really worried. But the Boche won't dare *fight* us. Not again – not after the last time. And a feller at the club told me that the stuff they're producing, tanks and armoured cars and so forth, is as shoddy as hell. It's all show.'

They were sitting in the clubhouse at Rye after their round. Hugh, although he loved the game, would not play often as due to his being one-handed, his form was not up to much. But Edward insisted on them playing together, and made careful efforts, missing putts and so on, not to win too easily. Now, he said, 'Anyway, me dear old boy, you've done more than your share in the last show,' and instantly realised that he couldn't have said anything worse.

There was a pause, and then Hugh said, 'You don't seriously think I'm worrying about my own skin?' He had gone white around the mouth, a sign that he was very angry.

'I didn't mean it like that. What I meant was that I don't think there's a ghost of a chance that we shall have a war, but if I'm wrong, then it's the young blokes' turn. You won't catch *me* volunteering.'

'Liar,' said Hugh, but he gave a faint smile. 'Let's have a spot of lunch.'

They ate large plates of the excellent scrambled eggs for which the club was famous, followed by cheese and celery with a pint of beer. They talked about the business, and whether the Old Man's idea of inviting Rupert into the firm was a good one. Hugh thought it might be, Edward thought not; their father, with his inexhaustible energy – he was writing a paper on the technique of classifying hardwoods by photographing the grain, and having finished the building of a squash court at

Home Place for family use – was now contemplating a swimming pool, as well as travelling up to town every day to the office, although his sight was failing and Tonbridge refused to let him drive himself any more which was just as well, Edward said, since he drove, as he rode a horse, on the right-hand side of the road, 'Although people hereabouts are pretty used to him doing that.'

'All the same, if his sight gets much worse, he oughtn't to do that train journey alone.'

Hugh stopped lighting his cigarette and said, 'But he could never retire, it'd kill him.'

'I agree. But between us we can see that he never has to retire.'

On the way home, Hugh asked, 'How's Mill Farm?'

'It seems fine to me. Villy says it will be freezing in winter but the children love it. Of course she has more to do than at Home Place. Housekeeping and so forth.'

'I suppose so.'

'She's got Jessica and her brood coming today. And the old battleaxe some time next week. I think I shall absent myself for that.'

'Do you want to stay with me? I'll be on my own.'

'Thanks, old boy, but I think I'll stay put. Friday night's Amami night, if you know what I mean. Not *on* Friday, of course.'

This – to some – mysterious reference to a well-known advertisement for shampoo meant that Edward was having an affair, never mentioned overtly between them, but known by Hugh as surely as if it was. Edward had always had affairs: when he married, Hugh had thought that that would be the end of them (he would not have dreamed of looking at another woman after he married Sybil) but not very long afterwards – perhaps a couple of years – he had noticed little things that had made him wonder. Edward would sometimes leave the office rather early, or Hugh would come into his room and find him telephoning and he would cut the call short in a clipped and businesslike voice, and once he had blown his nose on a handkerchief that had a large cyclamen smudge on it, and when Edward had seen him staring at it and noticed the smudge himself, he'd rolled the handkerchief into a small ball and dropped it into the wastepaper basket and made a self-consciously wry face.

'Dear me, how careless,' he had said. And Hugh, moving from anger on Villy's behalf, felt sorry for both of them.

Now, he said, 'Well, I'll come up with you on Monday, if I may, then I can leave the car for Sybil.'

'Of course, old boy. I can give you a lift into the office in the mornings, anyway.'

Sybil and Hugh had moved, in the spring, to a larger house in Ladbroke Grove which was just around the corner from Edward and Villy. The new house had been rather an expense, cost nearly two thousand pounds and, of course, being larger, had required more furniture, so Hugh had not bought the little car for Sybil that they had once contemplated.

'Do you remember when the Brig used to take us to Anglesey for our summer hols in that first motor he bought? And we used to sit in the back mending punctures the whole way?'

Edward laughed. 'And we only just managed to keep up with them. Lucky there were two of us.'

'And the Duchy always wore a green motoring veil.'

'I love veils on women. Neat little hats with a veil tilted over their noses. Hermione used to wear them. It made her look so dazzling – and desirable. No wonder we all wanted to marry her. Did *you* ask her?'

Hugh smiled. 'Of course I did. Did you?'

'You bet. She said she married the twenty-first man who proposed. I've often wondered who the others were.'

'I expect a good many of them are dead.'

Edward, who did not want the war to come back into their conversation making Hugh, as he described it, morbid, said quickly, 'I shouldn't think being married stopped people making propositions.'

'Speak for yourself!'

'Actually, I was, old boy. After she was divorced, of course.' Hugh glanced at him ironically. 'Of course.'

∞ ∞ ∞

'She could have come if she'd really wanted to.'

'Do you think?'

'I know so. Louise usually manages to do what she really

wants. I'm afraid she's just not . . . *serious* enough about the museum.'

Clary tried to look sorry about this but she wasn't, really. Best of all she liked to have Polly to herself. Since she had been doing lessons with Miss Milliment, she spent nearly all her time with the other two, who had always been best friends, and she wanted Polly for her best friend, which meant, naturally, that Louise would have to stop being that. Now, she said, 'She's aged rapidly in the last year – getting all lumpy.' She smoothed her own flat chest with pride.

'She can't help that!' Polly was shocked.

'I know. But it isn't the lumps. It's her attitude. She treats me like a child.'

'She does me a bit, too,' Polly admitted. 'Well, I told her we'd have the museum meeting after tea. Her cousins are coming today, but they'll probably play tennis and then we can go to the museum and have it.'

'I still think you ought to be president. After all, you thought of it.'

'Louise is the oldest.'

'I can't see that makes the slightest difference. It was your idea. I vote we vote. If I vote for you and you vote for you, she'll have to resign!'

'Mm, I'm not sure if that's fair.'

They were at Camber, lying on the flat sand very near the shallow sea, so that when they dug their toes in, the water seeped out, faintly cool and delicious. It was after lunch: Rupert, in charge of the party (Zoë had a headache and had not come), had built a large and most elaborate castle with moat round it – ostensibly to amuse Neville and Lydia but they were quickly bored.

'There's not much we can do with it,' Lydia explained to him.

'No – it's not a castle that's much use to us,' Neville echoed. 'We really prefer to build our own.'

So they did. They built it too near the sea, so that it wouldn't stay firm and kept subsiding and they quarrelled gently about it and then built one too far up the beach so although Neville kept getting pails of water for the moat it emptied faster than he could replenish it.

Rupert, who had immediately realised that in fact he

had been building for his own pleasure, continued to cut crenellations with his pallet knife on the four corner towers. He looked entirely involved and he wanted to be that, wanted to recapture that marvellous single-minded absorption in the present matter so often to be seen in the children. 'When I paint,' he began, and was at once lost. He hadn't produced a single picture. He was lazy, got too tired after a day at school, the children needed a good deal of his free time. And there was Zoë, of course. The fact was that Zoë resented him painting: she somehow managed to want to be married to a painter who didn't actually *paint*. The first time he had discovered this had been last Christmas when he had wanted to spend ten days with a chap he had been at the Slade with – Colin had a decent studio and they were going to share a model and work – but Zoë had wanted to join Edward and Villy skiing at St Moritz, had wept and sulked about it so much that he had given in. There hadn't been time or money for both. 'I can't see why you couldn't paint in Switzerland if you really wanted to,' she said, after she had got her own way.

It had been a curious holiday, good in unexpected ways. It was really far too expensive for him, and it was only afterwards he had realised how much, and how unobtrusively, Edward had paid for all of them: the drinks, dining out, buying the girls and all the children presents; ski lifts, hiring skates for Zoë who preferred skating, all kinds of things like that. And he had been very kind to Zoë as well, often staying at the rink with her while Rupert and Villy had gone skiing. Villy was a marvellous skier: brave and graceful and very fast. He could not really keep up with her, but he liked her company. Skiing clothes suited her boyish shape and she wore a scarlet woolly hat that made her look very young and dashing in spite of her brindled hair. Once, when they went up in the ski lifts, and he was gazing at the dazzling white and violet-shadowed slopes the cloudless blue azure sky and the ink-black trees in the valley below them, he turned to exclaim how beautiful it was but, seeing her face, he said nothing. She sat, with her elbow on the railing of the lift, one gloved hand against her face, her heavy eyebrows – so much darker than her hair – slightly drawn together, her eyelids half lowered over her eyes so that he could not tell their expression, her mouth – that he had always rather admired as an aesthetic, rather than a sensual, feature – compressed, the whole giving him the impression of trouble. 'Villy?' he said uncertainly. She turned to him.

'I've got to have all my teeth out,' she said. 'The dentist wrote to me last week.' But before he could even take her hand, she gave an awful little artificial smile and said, 'Oh, well! It will all be the same a hundred years hence!'

Pity shrank in him. 'I'm so sorry,' he said.

'Don't let's talk about it any more.'

He made one last effort. 'No, but that's awful for you!'

'I shall get used to it.'

'Have you – have you told Edward?'

'Not yet. I don't suppose he'll mind. After all, he's had most of his out.'

'It's different for women,' Rupert began. He was trying to imagine how Zoë would respond to such a letter. God! She'd think it was the end of the world!

'Everything's different for women,' Villy said. 'I wonder why?'

They had reached the top. No more was said and she never referred to it again.

In the evenings they had dined and danced. Both the girls loved dancing and never wanted to stop, although he was so full of fresh air and exercise that he wondered how they – Edward, particularly – kept it up. By midnight, he was dropping, but Zoë always wanted to stay until the band stopped. In the end, they would all four trail upstairs to their adjoining rooms on the first floor of the hotel and would stand outside them: Edward would kiss Zoë, Rupert would kiss Villy; the sisters-in-law would unite their cheeks for the glancing second that family protocol required, and then finally separate for the night. Zoë, who was enjoying everything so much that her pleasure had begun to feel like a reproach (if this was what made her happy, why couldn't he give her more of it?), would kick off her shoes, unzip her new scarlet dress and drift about in her pale green cami-knickers and the new paste drop earrings he had given her for Christmas, sitting on the end of the bed for a moment to take off her stockings, wandering to the dressing-table to tie back her hair with a large tortoiseshell clasp preparatory to creaming her face, chatting, reminiscing happily about the day, while he, in bed by now, watched her, glad that she was so merry and content.

'Aren't you glad I made you come?' she said one evening.

'Yes,' he said, but he scented danger.

'Edward suggested this morning that we might all go to the South of France next summer. He and Villy went for their honeymoon and I've never been. What do you think?'

'It might be lovely.'

'You sound as though we shan't go.'

'Darling, I don't think we can afford two holidays abroad. Anyway, we can't leave the children again.'

'They're perfectly happy with your family.'

'You can't expect Hugh and Sybil to do all the work.'

'I should have thought the South of France would be a wonderful place for you to paint.'

'Yes, it would be. But not affordable this year. Anyway, if I have a painting holiday, it has to be just that. Not what you would call a holiday at all.'

'What do you *mean*, Rupert?'

'I mean,' he said, already weary with his own resentment, 'that I'd want to *paint* all the time. Not take you to the beach, go for picnics, dance all night. I'd want to *work*.'

'Oh, Lord!' she said. 'Trust you to be so *earnest* about it.'

'That's exactly what I'm not. If I was earnest, as you put it, I'd do it anyway. I wouldn't be deflected by you or anyone else.'

She swung round on the dressing-table stool, 'What do you mean "anyone else"?'

'You don't like me painting, Zoë.'

'What do you mean "anyone else"?'

There had been a short silence: her stupidity was beginning to frighten him. Then, as he could see that she was about to reiterate her idiotic question, he said, 'I mean that nothing would deflect me. Neither you nor any*thing* else. But it's all right. I'm not earnest, I'm hardly earnest at all.'

'Oh, darling!' She came swiftly over and sat on the bed. 'Oh, darling! You sound so sad, and I love you so much!' She put her arms round his neck and her scented, silky hair fell each side of his face. 'I don't mind us being poor – honestly!

I don't mind anything as long as I'm with you! I could get a part-time job, if you like – if it would help! And I think you're a marvellous painter: I do – really!' She lifted her head to gaze at him, adoring and sincerely contrite.

As he put his arms round her and drew her into bed, he discovered, with a sad, but grateful amazement, that loving her did not depend – as he'd been afraid it did – upon his admiration. Later, lying awake while she slept, I married her, he thought, and she has always given me all of herself. It was I who invented some other part of her that she would not give. But I was wrong: there was nothing to withhold. The discovery was painful and astonishing; then it occurred to him that if he loved her enough, she might change. He was not yet able or willing to accept that this was unlikely, or even impossible: he clung to the more welcome idea that though a person might be transformed by love they could not be transformed without it.

Since that night, he had discovered that insights do not, in themselves, alter either attitudes or behaviour: that it was more a matter of small – sometimes very small – constant effort, but sometimes, in the last months, when she bored or irritated him, facts of their relationship that he had hitherto been unable to accept, he could also feel some tenderness for her, and he had become very protective towards her with other people. Sometimes, often, like that evening, he had reverted to resentment of her for her limitations, and anger with himself for not having recognised them sooner.

'Dad! Jolly good sandcastle, Dad. Dad, would you possibly be a sea-lion to show Polly? I don't mean now,' Clary added quickly. 'I know you need a sofa to dive off and we haven't any socks to make fish. But after tea?'

At Christmas, when they gave the grown-ups marks out of ten for funniness, generosity and being non-spoilsports, Rupert had come top for funny, a fact of which Clary was immensely proud; his sea-lion and his gorilla, which had graduated to King Kong, were deeply admired, and repetition, as Villy had remarked, was the soul of wit so far as the children were concerned.

'Polly has seen my sea-lion.'

'Not for ages, Uncle Rupe. Honestly, I've almost forgotten.'

'OK. After tea. *Once*. Time to go home now, I think.'

'Oh, good. And can we stop for ices on the way home?'

'I should think there's a distinct possibility that we might. Who'll pack up the picnic things?'

'We will,' they both said. Rupert sat by the sand dune and smoked a cigarette and watched them do it. He was glad that Clary had become such friends with Polly, and the lessons with Miss Milliment seemed to have worked out very well. Now that she had Polly as a friend, she was much easier at home, less jealous of Neville, less prickly with Zoë, and far less possessive of himself. She was growing up. Although she was the same age as Polly one would not think so to look at them. They had both grown in the last year but whereas Polly seemed uniformly a larger size and was now something of a beauty, with Sybil's coppery hair, a milk and roses complexion, rather small, brilliantly dark blue eyes and long, thin, elegant legs, Clary had simply shot upwards, was thin as a rake. Her dark brown hair, still with a fringe, was dead straight, her face sallow, often with dark smudges under her eyes – which were startlingly like her mother's, sea-grey, candid, searching eyes – her best feature. She had rather a pug nose and when she smiled there was a gap where she had had one of her top teeth out; the dentist had said she had too many, and now she wore a painful brace that was to eliminate the gap. Her arms were like sticks, and she had the long bony Cazalet feet. In the last year she had become clumsy: tripped up, knocked things over, as though she was not used to her size. 'Clary! Come here a moment. Just want to give you a hug,' he said.

'Oh, Dad! I'm boiling already!' But she returned the hug and planted a kiss on his forehead so firmly that he could feel the metal of the brace.

'Boiling!' he jeered. 'You're always boiling, or freezing, or starving or dropping from fatigue. Don't you ever feel ordinary, like the rest of us?'

'About one in a million times,' she said carelessly. 'Oh, don't let Neville bring that jellyfish back! It will only stink and die, or slop over in the car and hurt itself.'

'And, anyway,' Polly said, 'it's not a *pet*! You couldn't, by the wildest stretch of imagination, turn a jellyfish into a *pet*!'

'I could,' Neville said. 'I shall be the first person in the world to do that. I shall call him Bexhill and *live* with him.'

∞ ∞ ∞

By midday at Mill Farm the sun had gone, it was breathlessly still and very hot; the sky was like lead and the birds were quiet. Edie, bringing in a basket of washing off the line, said there would be thunder she shouldn't wonder, and Emily, who was cross from the heat of the range and the fishmonger not calling, which meant no ice so the butter was oily and the milk was on the turn, said, 'What could you expect?' She hated the country and regarded thunder as yet another rural disadvantage. The kitchen had been painted a dull pale green, a colour that Villy had insisted was soothing to a cook's temper, but it didn't seem to have done much good. The kitchen had had their dinner, but Phyllis had one of her headaches and hadn't fancied it – a nice Irish stew and treacle tart – and one thing Emily could not stand was people picking at her food. A nice drop of rain would clear the air, Edie said, and the cows were lying down in Garnet's field out back so it was likely, and should she change the fly papers in the larder? Madam had forgotten to order more papers, Emily replied – they would have to stay as they were; but Phyllis said, oh, no, they couldn't *really* – they turned her stomach every time she went in there to fetch anything, and she clapped her hand to her mouth as though worse might follow. So Emily followed Edie into the larder to inspect the papers. They hung, motionless, like Victorian bell-pulls heavily encrusted with jet and, as Edie remarked, were no longer any use to man nor beast. 'This has always been a terrible place for flies,' she said. 'There's papers up at the shop. I'll pick up a packet on my way in the morning, shall I?'

'You might as well have that lot down, then,' Emily replied. Edie's good nature staggered her (she seemed prepared to do all kinds of things that weren't her place) and she could only respond grudgingly. 'Them flies!' she muttered to Phyllis. 'You never get flies like that in London!'

∞ ∞ ∞

Having spent half the morning organising her household, Villy found herself at a loose end – not exactly with nothing to do, but with nothing that mattered very much. Like my life, she thought. She indulged in self-pity like a secret drinker, could not do without it and clung to the belief that, provided she confined it to times when she was alone, nobody would ever know. Indeed, like those drinkers who positively refuse a drink when it is offered to them by somebody else, she brushed aside the concern for her that her implicit behaviour would, from time to time, excite in other people. She did not want her griefs contracted to frustrations, her sense of tragedy reduced to misfortune – or, worse, bad luck or bad management. Virtue, in her eyes, must be sacrificial, and she had given up everything to marry Edward. 'Everything' was her career as a dancer. At the time, this had seemed not only reasonable, but right. She had fallen in love with a man whom she could see was universally attractive (she remembered how, soon after she met him, she had thanked God that Jessica was already married or she wouldn't have stood a chance) and when it became clear – which it did very soon – that he was serious, she found herself volunteering to his parents at luncheon the second time he had taken her to see them, that dancing and looking after Edward did not go together. That this decision was the most momentous of her life had not struck her at the time; then, when she thought about it, it seemed that she was giving up not very much for everything.

But over the years, of pain and distaste for what her mother had once called 'the horrid side of married life', of lonely days filled with aimless pursuits or downright boredom, of pregnancies, nurses, servants and the ordering of endless meals, it had come to seem as though she had given up everything for not very much. She had journeyed towards this conclusion by stages hardly perceptible to herself, disguising discontent with some new activity which, as she was a perfectionist, would quickly absorb her. But when she had mastered the art, or the craft, or the technique involved in whatever it was, she realised that her boredom was intact and was simply waiting for her to stop playing with a loom, a musical instrument, a philosophy, a language, a charity or a sport and return to recognising the essential futility of her life. Then, bereft of distraction, she would relapse into a kind of despair as each pursuit betrayed her, failing to provide the *raison d'être* that had been her reason for taking it up in the first place. Despair was what she called it to herself; her sensibilities – never aired – had become a hot-house full of exotic species labelled tragedy, self-abnegation, a broken heart and other various heroic ingredients that were being forced to constitute her secret martyrdom. As she saw herself as one thing and all other people as another, she could have no friends close enough to explode this unhappy state of affairs. But, well beyond common misfortune herself, she could acknowledge its existence for other people, and be full of real active and useful kindness towards them. She was like someone with a broken back who would gladly do the washing up for someone with a headache. Accident, illness or poverty released her generosity: she had sat up all night with Neville during an asthma attack so that Ellen might get some sleep, it was she who drove Edie's brother, an epileptic, to Tunbridge Wells to a specialist, who every year contrived to buy a suit or dress that would become Jessica who could never afford anything new for herself. For the rest, she wondered, uneasily sometimes, why she could not be like the Duchy, content with her garden and her music, or like Sybil, revelling in her baby and her new home, or even like Rachel, who seemed fulfilled by her charitable work and by being the perfect daughter. But the utter impossibility of being a perfect daughter to *her* mother now occurred. Lady Rydal was famous for standards of behaviour that no one living had ever been able to achieve, least of all a daughter. Jessica, who had looked like breaking that record, had, of course, spoiled it all by marrying an impoverished nobody – albeit good-looking and gallant, but given her beauty and her compliant disposition, Lady Rydal had set her sights far higher than a commoner with charm and medals. She had regarded the marriage as yet another of the personal tragedies encompassing her life – 'Poor darling Jessica has thrown herself away' – and nobody but Lady Rydal would ever understand the anguish this cost her as she frequently said to Villy and anyone else who got trapped into having tea with her. No, it was all very well for *Rachel* – after all, she didn't have anything much else to do.

By now, she had checked up on the girls' room. Except for

getting flowers, Louise had at last – at least – done what she had been told. The room was as tidy as a small dormitory in a school, the beds made up and clean towels on the towel-horse, the dressing-table now bare and Louise's books stacked along the mantelpiece. She looked out of the window just at the moment her sister's car turned into the drive and went down to meet them.

∞ ∞ ∞

After she had tidied the room, Louise had taken her book to the hammock, but could not settle down to reading it. This was yet another new, odd and uncomfortable feature of her life: last summer her only worries would have been sharing something like a hammock fairly with Polly, but when it came to her turn for whatever it was, she would, at once plunge into it as though she had not any other existence. Now, her existence seemed always to be intruding upon any activity; she seemed to herself a larger, more disparate person, who was never wholeheartedly engaged – whatever she did, some bit of her sat on the sideline, jeering, making insidious alternative suggestions: 'You're far too old for that book – anyway, you've read it before.' Age came into it a great deal; she seemed to be too young or too old for most things.

Last summer it hadn't felt at all like that. Then, she had *believed* in the Wonder Cream she and Polly had made. Then, she had been seriously involved in Pompey's funeral, had organised the whole thing – even the Duchy playing the Funeral March with the drawing-room windows wide open. She had made a wreath of deadly nightshade; Pompey had been wrapped in an old black velvet jacket belonging to Aunt Rachel and the funeral tea had consisted of blackberries and Marmite sandwiches which, Polly had agreed, showed more respect than strawberry jam. Then, she and Polly had spent hours in their apple tree and lying on their beds dying with laughter over their 'Knock, knock, who's there?' jokes, and playing bicycle polo with the boys, and Ogres and the Seeing Game with all the others. *Now*, when these ploys were suggested – by Lydia and Neville, and often Polly and Clary – she never really wanted to play them. She did sometimes, because she *had* wanted to, but then she often left in the middle because she wasn't honestly enjoying it. She still liked going to the beach and playing tennis, but she wanted to play with the grown-ups and *they* usually expected her to play with the children.

She'd thought at first that the trouble was being at Mill Farm instead of Home Place. She didn't like Mill Farm. It seemed poky and rather dark after the other house. But it wasn't just that. It wasn't just the summer holidays, either. It might have begun last autumn term when Clary had started having lessons with her and Polly. She had quickly realised that Miss Milliment especially liked Clary. Clary worked hard, and was surprisingly good at writing things. She'd written a long poem and nearly a whole play, which was very funny and a good idea – about grown-ups having to spend a whole day as children whether they liked it or not. Louise had pointed out that it wasn't an original idea – look at *Vice Versa* – but Miss Milliment had said that originality did not depend upon an idea so much as it depended upon treatment, and Louise, not for the first time, had felt snubbed. She also quickly recognised that Polly and Clary were becoming best friends and had half minded this and half felt relieved by it. Polly didn't seem to be getting older at the same speed she was. This was partly because of her getting the Curse, which had been a horrible shock because nobody had said one word about it until one day when she had an unusual pain and gone to the lavatory and thought she might be bleeding to death. Mummy had been having tea with a Red Cross person in the drawing room, and Louise had had to find Phyllis to go and ask her to come. And then although, of course, it was a great relief when Mummy said that she wasn't going to die, it somehow wasn't all right in any other way. Mummy said it was a horrid thing that happened to girls once a month for years and years; it was a disgusting, but quite ordinary, thing to do with having babies, but when Louise tried to find out some more about it (how could a quite ordinary thing be disgusting?) her mother, who certainly looked disgusted, said that she did not wish to discuss it now and would Louise please take her knickers off the floor and go and wash them? And put on a clean pair, she had added, as though Louise was so disgusting she wouldn't do that unless she was told. Thereafter, when she had a headache and stomach cramps, her mother would ask, in a particular way that she came to hate, whether she was unwell. Which is what it came to be called. She had discovered that it was called the Curse at Christmas when she had suddenly got it and had to ask Aunt Zoë for a napkin and Aunt Zoë had given her an extraordinarily neat thing out of a box which, it turned out, you could throw away instead of having to keep in an awful bag for the laundry. 'You mean to say you have those ghastly bits of cloth you have to fold up with cotton wool like one had at school? That's positively Victorian! It's not so awful – you poor old thing! It's just the Curse! We all get it,' she said in a friendly, light-hearted way that made Louise feel much better. 'I get spots,' Louise had said, longing to talk about it. 'That's bad luck, but you probably won't go on getting them. Just leave them alone, don't do anything to them,' and she had given Louise some marvellous expensive cream out of a little pot for a Christmas present and Louise felt tremendously grateful to her – not so much for the cream as for talking about it. It seemed very strange that nobody ever did. The only thing her mother *had* said was that one never, never talked about it – particularly not to the boys, or even Polly. But the next time she asked whether Louise was unwell, Louise said, 'I'm not unwell, I've simply got the Curse. Aunt Zoë calls it that, and I'm going to.' Watching her mother, she knew she was annoyed but couldn't say anything back. But when she told Polly about it, because she didn't see why Polly should be as frightened as she had been, Polly simply said, 'I know. Mummy told me. I just hope I won't get it for ages and ages.' This had made her mother not warning her about it worse – very nearly, Louise thought, as though she had *meant* her to be frightened. From then on, she watched her mother for signs of affection and the opposite, wrote them down in her secret diary and added them up each month. So far the opposite was winning easily, except in March, when she had come home from Polly's house and found her mother on the sofa in the drawing room, crying, something that she had never seen before in her life. She had rushed to the sofa, knelt by it, asked her again and again what was the matter. Her mother took her hands away from her face, and Louise saw that it was all puffy and bruised and she had wet, frightened eyes. 'They've taken out all my teeth,' she said.

She touched the sides of her face and began to cry again.

'Oh, *darling* Mummy—' She felt overwhelmed with pity – and love. Tears rushed to *her* eyes, and she wanted to hold her mother, to take the pain away, have it herself instead, only she was afraid that hugging her might make it hurt more, but her mother was treating her as an equal, something that she recognised as never having happened before, and she wanted passionately to be the right friend.

Her mother was searching in her pocket for a handkerchief and trying to smile. 'Darling, I don't want to worry you—' she seemed to have teeth, after all. Her mother saw Louise seeing this, and said, 'He made me put them in at once. But oh, Louise! They do hurt! Rather.'

'Would it be better if you took them out. Just for a little while?'

'He said to keep them in.'

'Shall I get you some aspirin?'

'I've taken some, but it doesn't seem to have done much good.' After a moment she added, 'Do you think it would be all right if I took some more?' Again, it was the appeal to an equal.

'Yes, I do. And I think it would be better if I put you to bed with a hot water bottle.' She sprang to her feet to ring the bell. 'I'll tell Phyllis to bring up *two* bottles.'

'I don't want the servants to see me like this.'

'No, of course not, darling. I'll look after you. I'll see to everything.'

And she had. She had helped Villy upstairs, helped her to undress, found bedsocks and her lacy jacket: her mother was very cold. She had lit the gas fire, drawn the curtains, rushed to the door when Phyllis knocked and taken the hot water bottles blocking her view of the invalid. She had administered the aspirin and arranged the pillows, drawn up the eiderdown and throughout her mother had seemed acquiescent and grateful.

'You're a good little nurse,' she said; she was obviously in pain.

'Would you like me to stay with you?'

'No, darling. I'll try and sleep. Tell Daddy, will you? When he gets back?'

'Of course I will.' She stooped, and kissed Villy's soft

clammy forehead. 'I'll leave your door ajar, and then you can call if you want anything.'

She sat on the stairs for ages, on the curve so that she could hear if her mother called and see when her father returned, wondering whether perhaps she ought not to sacrifice her career to become a nurse. She was gliding about darkened wards at night with a lamp, relieving the agonised sufferings of wounded soldiers with a touch of her delicate but experienced hands, soothing their last moments with her gentle voice . . . 'Given up everything – wanted in Hollywood – the Duke of Hungary mad for her . . . '

'Lou? What on earth are you doing sitting there?' She had rushed downstairs and told him. 'Lord! Of course!' It almost sounded as though he had forgotten. 'Where is she?' Louise explained what she had done, and her father had said jolly good, what a sensible girl she was, but he said it so admiringly that being sensible sounded almost glamorous. She followed him upstairs, warning him to be quiet.

'I won't wake her, just pop my head around the door.'

She was asleep. He put a finger on his lips and went into his dressing room. Then he beckoned her.

'I wonder whether you would care to dine with me tonight, Miss Cazalet? If you have no previous engagement?'

'I do happen to be free.'

'Run along and change, then. I'll meet you in the drawing room in twenty minutes.'

So she changed, into the dress that Hermione had suddenly given her for Christmas, that her mother disapproved of on the grounds that it was far too grown-up. It was a heavenly pale blue chiffon, and you couldn't wear a bra or a vest or anything but a pair of knickers under it as it was backless, with tiny shoulder straps and a deep V neck – a totally grown-up dress. She had put up her hair with a lot of combs – it didn't feel awfully safe, but as long as she didn't shake her head or laugh too much it would probably stay up – and with it she wore her Christmas present jewellery, an opal and seed pearl necklace given to her by Uncle Hugh, her godfather. She had her Tangee lipstick and some whitish face powder and a tiny little bottle of scent called Evening in Paris that Aunt Zoë had given her. She put a good dab behind each ear, and then she longed to look at herself, but the only full-length mirror was in her mother's bedroom. 'Oh, poor Mummy!' she thought, but she couldn't help rather hoping that her mother was asleep, because she somehow knew that her mother would not approve of this kind of changing. When she was ready, she listened outside the bedroom door and then peeped in; her mother was still asleep. So then she gathered up her skirts and sailed downstairs.

Phyllis had brought in the drinks, and her father was making himself a cocktail.

'I say! You do look smart!'

'Do I?' She felt smart wasn't quite the right word but, after all, he was only her father. And then he made it all right by offering her a sherry, so he was taking her seriously, she felt.

They had a lovely evening: a fish soufflé and roast pheasant and then angels on horseback, and her father gave her a glass of both wines – a hock and a claret – and afterwards he played the gramophone – Tchaikovsky, who was his favourite, and he told Louise about how he used to bicycle up to London from Hertfordshire to go to the Proms, which was when he had first heard that symphony, twenty miles of bicycling each way, but worth it. He played the gramophone rather quietly, because of the invalid, and when Phyllis brought the coffee, he ordered some consommé for her. 'Bring it here and Miss Louise will take it up.'

But she got him to take it, because she was afraid of what her mother would say about the dress. Then that seemed frivolous and hard-hearted, and she planned to go and say good night when she'd got into her dressing gown. When her father came down, he said, 'She's feeling better, and she says it's time you went to bed, and she'd like to say good night to you.'

'Oh, Dad! I'm not in the least bit tired!'

'Of course not. But all the same.'

She went to kiss him, and he put his arms round her and gave her one kiss on her cheek and then one, surprisingly, on her mouth, which he'd never done before. His moustache was bristly and for a second she felt something soft and wet and realised it was his tongue. It was horrible: she supposed it had somehow slipped out by mistake and felt embarrassed for him and wriggled out of his arms. 'Good night, then,' she said, not looking at his face, and ran out of the room. Upstairs she thought, poor old Dad; he had false teeth like Mummy did now, and it probably made kissing people quite difficult.

Mummy was lying propped up with all the pillows. She'd had some soup, she said, it had been just what she wanted.

'Did you have a nice evening with Daddy?'

'Oh, yes. We played the gramophone.'

'Good, darling. And thank you so much for being so sweet to me.'

'Is it better? Is it hurting much less?'

'I think it is.' It clearly wasn't. 'I'm going to take some more aspirin and Daddy's going to sleep in the dressing room tonight. Off you go, darling.'

'Yes, I will.' She realised that she wanted to get to her room and shut the door before he came up. This was funny – she'd never felt like that before. She'd not written about the evening with her dad in her diary.

She heard her cousins' car in the drive, and decided that she was pleased about them coming. Angela was probably already too old to be much fun, but she had always liked Nora who, though plain – a bit ugly, in fact – was nowhere as bad as Miss Milliment and Christopher was a far more interesting boy than Teddy or Simon: last year he had been mad about butterflies and they had gone off hunting with nets and a killing bottle, and then they had lain in a cornfield and eaten corn kernels, and he had told her how much he hated his school, and how being at home was pretty awful too because his father was always getting at him. Louise, who had been brought up on the family notion that Aunt Jessica's husband was somehow not the sort of person she should have married, sympathised hotly – even invented things about her own father to make Christopher feel better. Only now I wouldn't have to invent, she thought. But of course I couldn't possibly tell him anything about that. For the first time since it had happened she thought about it. Because after the night when he had taken her out for her birthday treat, which had been completely lovely until they had got home, after supper at the Ivy restaurant, and he had driven them home, had let them quietly into the house ('Mustn't wake Mummy') and she had thrown her arms round his neck to hug and thank him for her lovely treat – it had happened again, only worse. He'd kissed her in just the same horrible way, only this time he'd put his hand under her frock and hurt her breast, and his other arm was so tightly round her that she couldn't stop it, although she did in the end because he took his mouth away and started to say something about her growing up, and she wrenched herself free. 'I'm *not!*' she began to say, thought she was going to be sick, and ran a few steps up the stairs, but she'd forgotten her long dress and caught her heel in her skirt and had to stop to free it, and as she straightened up she saw him standing there looking up at her – he had become an enemy – smiling.

She had stood in the dark behind the closed door of her room, possessed by some nameless terror, like a terrible dream, only it wasn't a dream. He would come up the stairs – any minute – he might come into her room – no key – how could she stop him? This thought occurred, recurred, recurred, recurred, but she could not respond – she could not move at all. She heard his steps coming up and could only stand with her hands pressed over her mouth to keep everything from coming out. Only now she knew that the terror had consumed her voice, that her scream would be simply a louder silence.

His steps – the only thing in the world – came nearer – reached the landing outside her door – a pause – then they went on to his dressing room, and there was an unknown amount of time before she heard him walk across the landing to the bedroom where her mother slept and shut the door. And then she heard a horrible sound, like a retching sob, and when she turned on the light it must have been her, because there was no one else in the room.

She couldn't remember much after that: could just recall hanging over her basin trying to be sick. Then she thought, why hadn't she run upstairs and gone straight to Mother's room and woken her and told her? But at once she knew that her mother would be very angry, would blame her for being dirty and disgusting, and *he* – the enemy – would agree and it would be far worse, and perhaps it *was* her fault because she now felt so ashamed. So she swallowed everything down and was not sick. And the next day, at breakfast, he had been exactly as he used to be, as though nothing had happened, as though the whole thing belonged to *her* and had had nothing to do with *him* at all. And her mother waited until he had gone to the office to say that if she was going to be so ungrateful and sulky after a treat, people would not want to give her any more of them. She found a key to one of the other bedrooms that fitted her door, and after that, she tried never to be alone with him. But there was no one she could tell. That was the worst thing.

The feeling of extreme discomfort that came over her whenever she encountered her father now descended, a huge grey blanket that engulfed her and made her feel both betrayed and somehow guilty, and also, if she *tried* to think about it, frightened, and just remembering her birthday evening was worse than that: she felt shaky and sick; her mouth was dry and she kept swallowing – nothing. She might have to leave home, but being more frightened of something else hadn't made her less frightened of that.

'Oh, God! Why can't it be last summer when nothing was wrong?' But it couldn't be. 'It will all be the same a hundred years hence,' her mother was fond of saying about practically anything, a completely annoying remark since it involved not caring what was happening during the hundred years and that rendered life utterly pointless. Perhaps it was. Perhaps it was a gigantic terrible secret that grown-ups kept from children – like there being no Father Christmas, or getting the Curse; perhaps being grown-up, something she had always looked forward to, meant just that. That must be nonsense. They couldn't all be as cheerful as they were if they knew that. And there was God, who was supposed to be pretty kind to people and who had presumably made the rules about whether life was pointless or not. She decided to have a jolly serious conversation with Nora, who was a year older, about life to see whether she knew anything useful. Cheered by this, she went into the house.

∞ ∞ ∞

'Well, darling? How goes it?'

Villy had ensconced Jessica on the wicker *chaise-longue* in the drawing room. Lunch was over, and the children had all dispersed. Villy had tucked herself up in the huge, shapeless armchair opposite, had lit a Gold Flake and settled down for a good chat. A table with a coffee tray on it lay between them; Villy had drawn the blinds on the south window, and the room was suffused with aqueous light that was restfully cool and conducive to intimacy.

Jessica sighed, and smiled, and crossed her elegant ankles and stretched her long white arms clasping her head before she said, 'It's sheer *heaven* to be here. I can tell you that. It was a nightmare drive. Poor Christopher was sick, and Judy kept wanting to go to the lav, and Nora quarrelled with Angela about sitting in front and the car overheated on that hill – you know, coming out of Lamberhurst, I think—'

'Well, you're here now. And Mama doesn't come until next week. And Edward goes to London tomorrow. We'll be on our own, except for the riff-raff. We're dining at Home Place tonight, but there's plenty of time for a rest.'

'Heavenly!' She shut her heavy-lidded eyes and for a moment there was silence in the room except for the distant ticking of the grandfather clock in the hall.

Then Villy, in a voice charged with neutrality, asked, 'How is Raymond?'

'Very cross, poor darling, about my leaving him. He's off to Aunt Lena tomorrow. I don't think he was much looking forward to it.'

There was another little silence, then Jessica added, 'She's ninety-one, but except for not hearing a word one says, she's really in splendid health, but I suppose if you do absolutely nothing from morning till night except eat four regular meals a day and bully your servants there's no reason why you should feel worn out.'

'She is devoted to Raymond, though, isn't she?'

'She adores him. But there is this other rather awful nephew – the one who emigrated to Canada whom she rather *holds* over Raymond's head.'

'I suppose,' Villy said delicately, 'that when she . . . I mean, it would make all the difference?'

'Oh, darling! I'm not sure that it would any more. The moment Raymond gets his hands on any money at all, he thinks of some frightful scheme that needs far more than whatever it is he's got and then, of course, it all goes wrong because there wasn't enough money in the first place. I mean, the idea he had about boarding people's dogs when they go away. He completely left out that most of the year people don't, and then in August they all do, and, of course, it cost a fortune to build separate kennels and even then we had a dog in every room, and in winter the kennels all got wet rot and weren't fit for canine habitation. So really I actually dread Aunt Lena dying. Raymond simply hates his present job; he'd do anything to get out of it.' She gave her charming, defeated smile and said, 'But I dread to think what might be the alternative.'

'He's impossible!'

'Yes, he's impossible, but he's the children's father. He can be a perfect lamb, sometimes.'

Villy equated this with charm, which she had been brought up to distrust; charm in their mother's eyes had been synonymous with worthlessness. Lady Rydal had distrusted Edward for his charm, and the fact that he was richer than Raymond was marred by his money having come from Trade – a situation that had required her to be as broad-minded as she had always said she was. Edward, however, without even trying, had succeeded in charming her in a way that Raymond had totally failed to do. As Lady Rydal, in any case, had had lower expectations of Villy than she had had of Jessica, Edward turned into a satisfactory son-in-law. It was poor Jessica who bore the full brunt of her disappointment. Looking at her sister, of whom, when they were younger, she had been so jealous, Villy felt a rush of affection, pity and sentiment. Jessica was so *thin*; her white, pre-Raphaelite face, coloured faintly by the sunlight filtered through the green drawing-room blinds, was gaunt with fatigue: there were mothy shadows under her eyes and in the hollows below her high cheekbones, fine declining lines each side of her pale, chiselled mouth, and her poor, once beautiful hands were now roughened, thickened by washing clothes and cooking—

' . . . although he can be awfully difficult with Christopher.'

'What?'

'Raymond. He keeps wanting Christopher to be tough and athletic – all the things *he* used to be – and Christopher's the dreamy type, and much clumsier than usual because he's growing so fast. It's all being a bit tricky. I keep apologising to each of them for the other.'

'I think Christopher's a dear.'

'He's not an all-rounder, like your Teddy.'

209

'I'm sure he's far brainier.'

Jessica took this, not as a compliment to her son's brains, but as a criticism of his outdoor capacities and replied a little coldly, 'I don't think he's particularly brainy.'

Meaning, Villy thought, that darling Teddy was an absolute nit-wit, which of course he wasn't. She lit another cigarette. Jessica wondered when there would be tea.

'Angela is looking quite beautiful. Just like you, of course, an absolute knock-out.' Daughters were safer ground, and it was a handsome peace-offering. Jessica responded at once. 'Villy, I just don't know what to do with her. She only just scraped through her matric. She isn't interested in anything except clothes and her appearance about which she is completely *obsessive*. I'm sure we weren't so aware of ourselves at her age. Or were we?'

'I don't think we were allowed to be. I mean, everybody knew you were beautiful, but it wasn't *mentioned*. Mama would have had a fit if it had been.'

'Well, of course, I don't keep telling her how pretty she is. But other people do. And she seems to think it entitles her to a far more exciting life than we can provide, and what's more, that she ought not to have to do anything to get it. I think sending her to France was a mistake. It's since she's come back from there that she's been so sulky and passive.'

'It's probably just a phase. What are you going to do with her next?'

'I want her to do a shorthand and typing course because I'm afraid she is going to have to get a job of some sort. But, of course, she thinks that is far too dull. I mean, she wouldn't think of nursing, and she couldn't possibly teach, so what else is there?'

Villy agreed that there was absolutely nothing. 'Of course, she'll get married,' she said eventually.

'Yes, but, darling, *who to*? We really aren't in a position to entertain and her doing a Season is out of the question. But that simply means she doesn't meet anyone suitable. What are you going to do about Louise?' she added.

'Well, when she finishes with Miss Milliment, we'll send her to France, of course. After that, I haven't thought. She still says she wants to be an actress.'

'At least she wants to *do* something. She's grown up a lot this last year, hasn't she?'

It was Villy's turn to sigh. 'She sulks too, and can be most tiresome at times. I think Clary has put her nose out of joint. She and Polly have become great friends since Clary started with Miss Milliment – three isn't always a good number. And, of course, Edward spoils her and is always encouraging her to put on grown-up airs, which is absurd at fifteen. Did you have trouble with Nora? But no, you wouldn't have, would you? Nora has always been an angelic child.' She said this with emphasis. Nora had always been the plain one and needed compensatory virtues.

'She's always been an easy child, although she's not getting on very well with Angela at present.'

'She's probably jealous of her.'

Jessica shot a shrewd glance at her sister, thinking, How funny it is, that people always think everyone else will feel the same as they do, as she answered, 'Oh, no! Nora's never been jealous of anybody.' Then, unable to resist having remembered, she added, 'Do you remember that time when you cut off my hair and put it in a biscuit tin and buried it in the back garden?'

'I didn't cut it all off!'

Just enough to make me look like an idiot at the school prize-giving, Jessica thought, but she said, 'Mama was always very hard on you, I thought. All that fuss about you wanting to be a dancer. And you were so good at it!'

'Daddy was the one who supported me.'

'You were *his* favourite.'

'They were shocking about that, weren't they? Quite barefaced!'

'Well, it taught us not to be.'

They both thought of their amazing sons, and then told themselves that, anyway, they didn't show it. Then Judy interrupted them, sick of her rest, she said, and what could she do, when was Lydia coming back, and would it be tea soon? She wore shorts and a yellowing Chilprufe vest. 'Angela's locked herself in the bathroom for ever, so I had to use the pot,' she added.

'Judy, I've told you not to walk about the house in your vest. You don't need it in this weather, anyway.'

'I do.' She stroked her chest. 'I love it.'

There were sounds in the drive of a car arriving.

'That will be Lydia and Neville back,' said Villy. 'You can have tea with them.'

'Go and put on your blue Aertex shirt first, darling. You don't want them to see you like that.'

'I don't mind at all how they see me.' But seeing her mother's face, she went.

Rupert, carrying a bundle of damp towels and a picnic basket, took her place in the doorway. He looked extremely hot.

'Two children returned more or less intact. Where shall I put these? Oh, Jessica, how nice. I didn't see you!' He went over to the sofa and exchanged kisses with her.

'Rupe, you look exhausted. It was sweet of you to take them all. Stay and have a cup of tea.' Villy rang the bell, and Phyllis, who had been cutting bread and butter in the pantry with a pounding headache, looked at the kitchen clock and noticed that it was just after four and tea was supposed to be at four thirty. Still, they were out to dinner, so when she'd done the nursery tea and washed everything up she could go to bed with some aspirin.

'Phyllis, we just want a pot of tea for the three of us now, and the children can have theirs at the usual time.'

'Yes, m'm.' She picked up the coffee tray.

'I'm afraid Neville's brought a jellyfish back.'

'Didn't you tell him it would die?'

'Of course I did. But he wants it for a pet.' He turned to Jessica. 'It's his asthma. He's always wanting a cat or a dog, and they're lethal for him. So we get goldfish, earthworms and tortoises – and now the wretched old jellyfish.'

He collapsed on the sofa and closed his eyes. 'God! Aren't the young *exhausting*? Even if you tire them out, a mere ice-cream will stoke them up again. They spent most of the journey back having a competition about what would be the worst way to die. They thought of the most ghastly ways. Better warn Ellen that Neville will probably have nightmares tonight.' He opened his eyes. 'How's Raymond?'

'Fine. He's gone to visit his aunt. Coming next week, probably.'

'Oh, good.' Rupert liked Raymond, with whom he felt,

212

without being able to define exactly how, he had something in common.

There was a short, peaceful silence, and then Angela entered the room. Entered, was the way to put it, Villy thought. She stood for a second in the doorway before moving, with studied grace, into the room. She was wearing a sleeveless piqué dress of the palest lemon yellow and sandals and a silver bracelet on one white wrist. She had spent the entire afternoon washing and setting her hair that hung in a long page boy bob at the back with little flat curls round her face like ram's horns, which reminded Villy of Hermione's hair. Rupert got to his feet.

'I say! Is this really Angela?'

'The same old me.' She presented her perfectly powdered face for him to kiss.

'No,' he said. 'Not the same – not at all.'

'Shut the door, darling,' her mother said. 'Oh, no – don't. Phyllis is coming in with the tea. Where are the others?'

'What others?'

'Louise and Nora. And Neville and Lydia. You know perfectly well who I mean.'

'Oh – the *children*! I haven't the faintest.' She disposed herself gracefully on the arm of the sofa.

Phyllis came in with the tea, and Villy said, 'We shall want another cup for Miss Angela.'

'Angela can fetch it,' Jessica said somewhat sharply.

'Don't you move. I'll get it for you.' Rupert followed Phyllis out of the room. When he returned with the cup, Angela said, 'Oh, *thank* you, Uncle Rupert. Although you aren't really my uncle, are you?'

'I think you could drop the uncle, in any case.'

'Oh, thanks.' She gave him a demure and – if only he knew it – much practised smile. Villy, pouring out the tea, exchanged glances with Jessica. She's a bit of a minx, thought Rupert, but bloody attractive, and briefly wondered whether Zoë practised her early charms on any *old older* man who had come her way. Probably. Jessica was asking him about Zoë, and he said she was fine, she was learning to drive, whereupon Angela said she was dying to learn and would he teach her? Rupert, looking rather harassed, said he would see, and took out his case for a cigarette.

'Oh, please! Could I have one? I'm dying for a smoke.' She selected one from the proffered case, put it between her immaculately painted lips and leant towards him for a light.

We can't afford cigarettes, Jessica thought, with some desperation, for how could she be stopped? Raymond had forbidden it until she was eighteen, and she had been promised a gold watch if she did not smoke until she was twenty-one, but this was another habit she had formed in France.

'You know Daddy doesn't like you to smoke,' she said now.

But Angela simply answered, 'I know he doesn't. But I can't help that. If one didn't do any of the things one's parents didn't want one to do, one would hardly be able to *move!*' she explained to Rupert.

There was the distant rumble of thunder, and Rupert said he'd better go or he'd get soaked putting the car away. He called to Neville to say he was off and instantly the door burst open and the three younger children surged in.

'Mummy! He's got a jellyfish and he says it's cruel to stroke it and stroking *anything* can't be cruel, can it?'

'Oh, yes, it can. If you touch him I'll cut you up into tiny pieces and fry you in boiling oil,' said Neville. 'He's my jellyfish, and he doesn't like girls. He'd sting you to death if I gave him the chance.'

'He likes *me*,' Lydia said. 'You said he did.'

'He likes you *so far*.'

'Where have you put him, Neville?'

'In the bath.'

'How revolting!'

'Don't take any notice of Angela. She says everything's revolting or else that she hasn't the faintest,' said Judy whose accurate mimicry of her sister in no way obscured her scorn.

'And, Mummy,' said Lydia caressing her mother, 'we've used up all the dining-room salt and the water still doesn't taste at all seaish, so I'm afraid we had to use all the big jars in the kitchen, but we can do without salt, can't we, and for him it was an emergency.'

'Yes, I see, but you might have asked.'

'We might have asked,' Neville conceded, 'and you might have said no. And then where would we be?'

'Well, I warned you, Nev, old chap, that jellyfish don't take kindly to being removed from the sea. And the sort of salt we use isn't the same. Goodbye, all. See you later. Thanks for the tea.' Rupert kissed his son, ruffled his hair, and left.

'Oh dear,' said Villy, getting up. 'I think I had better sort this out.'

Jessica and her eldest daughter were left among the tea-cups. Angela examined her nails, which were painted pale pink with the half-moons left carefully white. Jessica watched her for a moment, wondering what on earth went on in that shining and seemingly empty head.

Angela was repeating her dialogue with Rupert. 'The same old me.' He had kissed her cheek and said, 'No. Not the same at all.' *He*, at any rate, noticed her. His admiration, which naturally he had had to conceal to some extent since they had not been alone, was none the less apparent. He's really sweet, she thought, and went over it all again. Nothing could come of it, of course; he was married, but it was well known that married people fell in love with other people. She would have to be very strong, explain to him that she could not possibly do anything to hurt Aunt Zoë, and then he would love her more than ever. She expected it to be quite tragic and mark her for life, and was looking forward to it.

∞ ∞ ∞

Simon had spent a wizard day with Teddy, who was not only two years older but in Simon's view pretty marvellous in every way. In the morning they had played seventeen games of squash, until they were both so *boiling* they had to stop. They were fairly evenly matched: Teddy, being taller, had the longer reach, but Simon was very good at placing balls, in fact, potentially the better player. They played American scoring because the games, though sometimes longer, came to a predictable end, and part of the fun was to tell the grown-ups how many games they had played. 'In *this* heat?' their uncles and aunts and parents would say, and they would grin: they were impervious to heat. They had played in just their shorts and their tennis shoes until their hair was soaked and their faces were the colour of beetroot. Teddy won by two games

– a respectable conclusion. They stopped, not because they were too hot, of course, but because they were starving, and it was half an hour till lunch, so they had a quick snack of motoring chocolate and tomatoes from the greenhouse. Teddy told Simon, who had good and awful reasons for wanting him to know, more about his new school at which Simon was to join him in the autumn. Everything that he said filled Simon with terror, which he concealed beneath a breezy interest. This morning the subject had been what happened to new boys and Simon had been told about them being strapped in a bath and the cold tap turned on very slowly and everybody going away and leaving them to drown. 'And do they – often?' he had asked with a thudding heart. 'Oh, I don't think *much*,' Teddy had replied. 'Someone usually comes back and turns off the taps and unties them.' *Usually!* The more he heard about it, the less Simon felt that he could possibly stand it, but in twenty-three days he would be there – in about fifty days, he might even be actually dead. Sometimes, he went to the really ghastly lengths of wishing he was a girl so that he wouldn't have to face this frightful place that seemed to be full of awful rules that nobody told you till after you'd broken them and were in trouble, and trouble was a pretty mild word for it. Teddy, he felt, was unbelievably brave and probably could stand anything, whereas, *he*, who had felt homesick at Pinewood although it got better towards the end, *he knew* that it would start all over again in a new place: the feeling sick, and having nightmares, and forgetting things and having to rationalise how much he thought about home because it made him blub, and blubbing meant you got bullied, and then he got tummy aches and couldn't stop going to the bog, and masters made sarcastic remarks and everybody laughed. Teddy would be senior to him and naturally couldn't be his friend. Making friends with senior boys was completely out; they would call each other Cazalet and simply say hallo when they met, just as they had at Pinewood. Every night he prayed that something would happen so that he needn't go, but he couldn't think of anything much that that could be except scarlet fever or a war – and neither of them were in the least likely. The worst of it was that there was nobody to talk to about it: he knew exactly what Dad would say – that everybody went to public school, it was just one of those things, old man – and Mummy would say that she would miss him too, but he'd soon settle down, people did, and he had the holidays to look forward to, hadn't he? Polly would be nice about it, but she didn't know how awful it was as she was only a girl. And Teddy – how could he tell Teddy whose friendship he prized too deeply to incur scorn, which he was pretty sure Teddy would feel. In spite of this, he still managed to enjoy his holidays and even sometimes forgot next term, but it would suddenly come back without the slightest warning, like the lights fusing, and he would be sick with fear and wish that he could be dead before the end of September. However, he hadn't felt bad all the morning playing squash, and when Teddy praised his corner shots he felt a little rush of happiness.

Lunch was in the dining room because so many of them were at the beach, which meant washing properly, a great fag, but on the other hand meant second helpings were hotter – good. They had rabbit pie and castle puddings, which fortified them nicely for the immense bicycle ride Teddy had planned for them. They were going up past Watlington to Cripps Corner, then Staplecross, out on the Ewhurst Road, then right down a narrow lane and right again onto the Brede Road and back to Cripps Corner where they stopped for Snofrutes and choc bars – they were pretty hungry by then, but it was mostly downhill on the way back, and Teddy made them go past Home Place to Mill Farm to see if his father was back because he'd been promised a rabbit shoot before dinner. Simon was not considered old enough to shoot, but Teddy had said that he might come with them if he liked. Aunt Villy annoyingly suggested that he might like to play with Christopher instead, but although Christopher was older he was no good at games because his glasses steamed up and he couldn't see the ball. Anyway, they couldn't find him. So Simon said he had promised to get home for tea and went back to Home Place by himself. But it had been a wizard day, and there was Monopoly to look forward to with Teddy after dinner. When he got back, Mum was playing with Wills on the lawn, putting him on his tummy with a toy just out of reach to get him to crawl. Wills was wearing his nappy: his back was a pinky biscuit colour.

'Should he have all that white fur down his spine?'

217

'It's not fur, darling, it's tiny golden hairs. They've got bleached by the sun.'

Considering he was rather fat – he just had creases where his wrists and ankles ought to have been – only had one tooth and couldn't say a single word, Wills was rather a nice baby, he thought. He picked up the teddy bear and moved it gently up to Wills's face. Wills looked up at him and smiled as he grasped the bear's ear and brought it to his mouth.

'He'll never learn to crawl if you do that.' Sybil took the bear and put it just out of Wills's reach. Simon thought he was going to cry as his face went a dark pink and he started to make heavy breathing noises. But then he suddenly stopped, and looked as though he was thinking hard about something. Then he looked very pleased and there was a ghastly smell. Simon withdrew in disgust. 'I think he's *done* something.'

'I'm sure he has. Clever boy!' She picked him up. 'I'll take him in and change him. Oh, darling, you've torn your shorts *again!*'

Simon glanced down. They'd been torn since before lunch – on a nail on the greenhouse door. He was surprised she hadn't noticed sooner, but Wills seemed to take up all her attention these days. How she could cuddle somebody who was stinking like that he didn't know.

'Go and change them before tea. And put them in my room and I'll mend them.'

Simon groaned. It was a point of honour with all the cousins to object to having to change, on the grounds that if they didn't they would be made to change more than ever. 'Oh, Mum, I could change when I have my bath. I can't possibly be expected to change *twice* in one day, *three* times if you count putting on my clothes in the mornings.'

'Simon, go and change.' So he went. Outside his grandfather's study he heard his father's voice, and stopped. Perhaps Dad would give him some tennis practice after tea. But his father's voice went on and on; he was reading something – the boring old *Times*, probably. Grown-ups seemed devoted to newspapers, read them and talked about what was in them every day at meals. The poor old Brig could hardly see, so people had to read to him an awful lot. He shut his eyes to see whether he could find his own room if he was blind, and it took ages, even with him cheating a bit at the top of the stairs. When he reached his bedroom door, he bumped into Polly coming out. 'I've just put a notice on your bed,' she said. 'Why are your eyes shut?'

He opened them. 'Nothing. I was just experimenting.'

'Oh. Well, the notice is about the museum meeting. It's at five o'clock in the old hen-house. You are cordially invited to attend. You can read the notice. It's on your bed.'

'So you said. Anyway, you've told me so I don't need to.'

'Are you coming?'

'I might. I might not. I'm going to have tea now.'

She followed him into his room.

'Simon, it's no good having a museum if people aren't interested.'

'It's more of a Christmas holidays thing to me.'

'You can't shut a museum for nearly a whole year every year. All the exhibits will get in a terrible state.'

He thought of the pieces of slipware from the kitchen garden, the rusty nail and bit of stone picked up at Bodiam and the Georgian penny donated by the Brig and said, 'I don't see why they would. If they've lasted till now, they can last a few more years without people looking at them. Anyway, I know them by heart.' He undid his snake belt so that his shorts fell to his ankles and shuffled over to his drawer for the other pair. 'Why don't you ask Christopher? He could be Curator of Natural History.'

'Good idea! I'll ring up Mill Farm and get him.'

But she got Aunt Villy who had no idea where Christopher was.

∞ ∞ ∞

Christopher had sat through a lunch he had not in the least wanted as he still felt sick. Car journeys were always bad: if he took off his specs he got a crashing headache, if he kept them on he was sick. At least it had been Mum driving. When it was Dad it was far worse, because Dad made him feel such a mutt and always made a fuss about stopping, so Christopher got frightened of being sick *in* the car, which would make a fearful row. Sometimes he actually hated Dad so much he imagined him falling down dead or just struck by lightning so that although he might not be actually dead, he couldn't speak another word. This, of course, made him feel wicked and ashamed of himself. But most of the time, he imagined himself doing amazing things – or perhaps quite ordinary things to most people, but things he was hopeless at – frightfully well, so that his father would say, 'I say, Chris, old boy, that was superb. I've never met *anyone* who could do that – let alone you!' He would bask in the glow of admiration, and sometimes his father would even throw a careless arm around him which, as they were men, implied deep affection – possibly, although it would never be mentioned, love. Sometimes, he would imagine his father making sarcastic, funny remarks not about him but somebody else, and inviting him to laugh at them with him. This was a kind of disgusting luxury: he was instantly ashamed of it, and then felt really awful. How could he agree to be an audience or party to something that he knew was so painful just because he wasn't the victim? And he would go back to hating his father, and hating himself for wanting approval from such a foul person. He must be loathsome too, which, in turn, made it quite reasonable for Dad to go on getting at him. And it was true that he was rotten at all the things Dad thought important, sports, games, even things like making model aeroplanes and maths. And he couldn't tell stories or make jokes and he was always knocking things over – namby-pamby bull in a cheap china shop, his father had said last week when he'd broken the sugar basin. In the last three years he'd developed a stutter which was always worse when people asked him questions, so nowadays he'd just go on trying to do whatever his father wanted, like packing the car this morning and not say anything at *all*. He was used to being a complete failure and only wished they'd leave him alone, but Mum was always trying to make him feel better by asking him about things she knew he was interested in, and that made him want to cry so he'd taken to not saying much to her either. He knew she must love him a lot to bother and despised her for it: it was stupid to love someone hopeless just because they were your son when there was nothing else to be said for them. But now, in spite of feeling queasy and having a bit of a headache, he was completely conscious of a kind of lightness, of feeling both free and safe – a funny mixture. Getting away from London from Dad and from school was enough to make anyone happy, he thought. After lunch, he had put on his sandals and sneaked off, and nobody saw him go.

He went down the farm drive, and up the hill towards Home Place, where they had always stayed before. He found his usual way through a hedge above Home Place drive and skirted the little copse that ran above a bank along the kitchen side of the house. He reached the bridle path that led to the field in which they usually kept horses. There were two of them under the clump of Spanish chestnuts, nose to tail, brushing the flies from each other. He walked slowly up to them to see if they wanted to talk to him, and they did. They had their wonderful warm horse smell and he buried his face in the pony's neck to take great breaths of it. The old grey whickered softly and looked at him with large eyes that had a bloom like black grapes. He had sunken bits in his forehead above his eyes and yellow teeth: he was quite old. When he left them, they began to follow him but soon gave up. He went across two fields, walking more slowly now because he felt well away from everyone. It was amazingly hot and still, the only sound was the high grasses brushing against his knees, and if he stopped, tiny insects' noises – minute spurts of zooming or ticking sounds. The sky was a kind of bleached blue, hardly blue at all, and the trees in the wood he was heading for were motionless. In the place where he'd found them last year, he found two enormous mushrooms, which he picked. He took off his shirt and wrapped the mushrooms in it; he might need food if he got hungry. The last field before the wood ended in a sloping bank with a hedge at one end of which was the gate into his wood. He walked slowly down the hedgerow that was crowded with bryony, blackberries, hawthorn and wild rosehips. A few of the blackberries nearest the ground were ripe, and he picked what he could find. The tiny bright green crab apples were not ripe, nor the sloes, nor the hazelnuts, although they were delicious – small juicy kernels that tasted pale green. He collected a few of them for his store. I might never go back, he thought. I might just live here.

A jay announced his entrance to the wood. He had noticed that it was always a blackbird or a jay – usually a jay – that made a sudden flight with noisy warning cries. Knowing this and it happening made him smile.

His little brook was just the same. Never more than a yard wide, it ran crystal clear over pebbles and round small sandy shoals, between banks that were almost flush with the water, and lined with brilliantly green moss, or steeper with wild garlic and ferns. The place where he had made a dam still had a much wider pool, although the dam was broken down and rotting. He sat on a bank, kicked off his sandals and sank his feet into the deliciously cool water. When his feet began to ache with cold, he got up and began to walk upstream till he got to the island. It was too small to live on, or even really to *be* on, but the banks on one side of the stream sloped gently upwards to a sunlit glade. Here, last year, he had tried to build a house by hammering in some old chestnut fencing stakes in pairs, and filling the gap with branches he had cut from the hazel and elder. He had only achieved one wall, and this was now silvery and brittle and, with the dead leaves fallen from the branches, full of holes. He did not feel like building any more of it today; instead he made a little bonfire which he lit with his magnifying glass. When it was going nicely, he got a forked stick and toasted his mushrooms one by one. He peeled them first, licking the rich brown from the spores off his fingers. He was ravenously hungry. The mushrooms did not toast very well, they simply got rather smoky, but at least they had not become all slippery with grease and frying. He chewed them very slowly – they tasted quite magical and might easily effect some great change in him. Then he ate the blackberries, which had become rather squashed in his shirt that was now stained with blue patches from the juice. What was interesting was how different blackberries could taste from each other: some quite nutty, some acid, some reminding him perfectly of bramble jelly. His fire was now a heap of bright grey ash. He got a great wedge of moss which he soaked in the stream and put on the ashes. There was a gentle hissing and the blue smoke changed to white. He was ready for the pond.

The pond lay in a deep hollow at the far end of the wood. It was overhung by branches of enormous trees, some of which were slowly falling into it. The water was black and still: there were bulrushes and two dragonflies. He took off his shorts and waded in the thick oozing mud, which made iridescent bubbles come up onto the water. Just as he was about to throw himself in for a swim, he saw a small adder, its elegant head erect above the water, its body undulating as it swam silently across the middle. He knew it was an adder because of the V on its head; it was funny that it also made a V ripple each side of its neck. He waited till it reached the opposite bank and instantly disappeared. He'd been lucky to see it. Then he threw himself forward onto the soft black water, which was warmish compared to the stream. It was rather a small pond for swimming, and getting out was always awful, because of the mud; he knew he'd have to go back to the stream to wash because of the fuss they'd make at home about a small amount of dirt, which would, anyway, have dried on him by the time he got back. There was a delightful marshy smell – like concentrated bulrushes. He hadn't seen the heron, which was often there, but the adder was a tremendous bonus. After he had washed off most of the mud, he lay in his glade beside the wall of his house, and went to sleep.

When he woke, the sun had gone and the birds were making evening noises. He put on his shirt, and started home. The first field was full of rabbits; the older ones feeding, the young ones playing. He would have liked to watch them for a bit, but he could come back early in the morning and do that. He was hungry again. He could tell by the state of the sun that he would have missed tea, but there might be something he could coax out of the maids to last him until suppertime. He broke into a steady trot. Three mallard were flying from the small river that bounded the field towards his wood: going to his pond, he expected, they might be the same three he had seen there last year. Why can't I live here? he thought. Never go back to London again in my life, be a farmer or do people's gardens or something. Or look after animals, or someone's estate. He had been looking down, because of rabbit holes, but the sound of a single shot made him look up and he stopped. Rabbits were running towards him, away from the gate into the horse field. There was a second shot, and a rabbit keeled over a few yards away, tried to get up, made an awful soft screaming sound and fell back again, twitching. He ran up to it and touched its fur: it was warm – and dead.

'We didn't see you – had no idea you were there.' It was
Uncle Edward with Teddy, who emerged from the shadows
of a large tree.

'I got him!' Teddy was exultant. He picked up the rabbit by
its hind legs: there was scarlet blood on its white stomach. He
swung it round in the air. 'My first this hols!'

Christopher looked from father to son. Uncle Edward was
smiling indulgently, Teddy was beaming. Neither of them
thought it in the least horrible, which he knew it was.

'A good clean shot,' Uncle Edward was saying.

'He screamed,' Christopher blurted, and felt tears scorching
his eyes. 'It can't have been *that* clean.'

'He won't have felt anything, old boy. It was too sudden.'

'Oh, well, he's dead now, isn't he?' his voice sounded
artificial, even to him. 'Got to go,' he muttered turning away
just as the tears spurted out of his eyes, and broke into a run.
He scrambled over the gate and momentarily looked back. They
were walking away from him, towards the bank by his wood:
they were going to try and kill more. A fox might have got it,
but it would have needed it. They were doing it for some damn
stupid idea of fun; the rabbit meant nothing to them. If he was
living in his wood, he would have bows and arrows and he
would kill rabbits from time to time, but it would be for food,
like the fox. Not that that made it any better for the rabbit.
He was walking now that he'd got well away from them in
the smaller field where there was not a rabbit to be seen.
No wonder it was difficult to watch any wild animals unless
you waited for ages; they knew people were awful and quite
sensibly ran or flew away from them. He tried to think about
death – it happened to everything, of course, in the end, but
making it happen was probably wicked, well, it was murder,
which people got hung for if they just killed one other person,
but got medals for in wars. He would be a pacifist like a boy's
father at school and he'd rather be a vet than a doctor any
old day because it seemed that animals didn't have enough
people on their side. Then, because he saw a Painted Lady,
he remembered how he'd killed butterflies last year just to
collect them and he had honestly to admit to being a bit
of a murderer himself. The fact that he didn't want to do
it any more was only because he'd got all the kinds that

were in this part of the country, so there was nothing very marvellous about stopping. He was no better than his cousin, who was, after all, a year younger – only fourteen. But if he was serious about not murdering things, he ought to give away his collection. This was a horrible thought: Mum had given him a collector's chest with twelve shallow drawers, and he'd only just got everything properly arranged, with each specimen set on pale blue blotting paper and a little white ticket to say what each one was. Perhaps he needn't give the chest away as well and he could use it for collecting something else. The point was, he loved the butterflies and wanted to keep them, but he could also see, rather uncomfortably, that that wasn't the point. It was no good *saying* you were against something if you went and did the opposite. He wondered whether being a pacifist would turn out to be like this, only worse; he didn't know much about what it entailed, except that Jenkins got ragged about having a father who was one. He supposed he'd be bullied about it, but he was used to that: they already bullied him about his father being the school bursar. Perhaps he could put off being a pacifist until he left school, and just begin by being against people killing animals for any reason except when they needed to eat them? That certainly meant giving away the butterfly collection. Giving the chest away with it would hurt his mother's feelings. There he went again; it might, but the point was, he wanted to keep the chest. 'Admit it!' he said furiously aloud.

'Admit what? Hallo, Christopher! Are you coming to the museum meeting? It's happening now in the old hen-house. You are cordially invited to attend.'

It was Polly. He'd gone into the stable yard of Home Place without thinking because he'd always stayed there before. Polly was sitting on the wall that led to the kitchen garden. She wore a bright blue dress and was eating a Crunchie. His mouth watered.

'Want some?' She held the bar waveringly down to his mouth. 'That was a pretty large bit.'

He nodded. When his mouth was less full, he said, 'I missed tea.'

'Oh, poor you!' She gave him the rest of the bar. So then he felt he had to go to the museum meeting.

225

∞ ∞ ∞

When Rupert got back to Home Place to put the car away, he could hear Mrs Tonbridge making a scene in the flat above the garage that the Brig had so misguidedly built for them. He could hear her yelling even before he switched off the engine. Then there was the sound of a piece of china being smashed and, after a moment, Tonbridge emerged in his shirt-sleeves looking more pinched and gloomy than usual. He stopped and stood in the doorway at the foot of the stairs, then took a cigarette from behind his ear and lit it. His hands were shaking. Rupert, who had been collecting bathing towels from out of the boot, pretending not to have heard anything, straightened up and greeted him.

Tonbridge, with one expert movement, pinched out the cigarette and put it back behind his ear. 'Good evening, Mr Rupert.' The boot was still open. 'I'll take the lunch in, sir.' He hadn't been able to eat any of the awful tea Ethyl had provided him with, with her blinding on about the country being too quiet and, anyway, everything fried kicked up his ulcer something wicked, which well she knew and much she cared. Mrs Cripps would give him a nice cup of tea and a fairy cake before he went off to fetch Miss Rachel from the station. Rupert, who guessed that he would do anything to get away from Mrs Tonbridge, took one end of the handle of the heavy wicker picnic basket and they marched with it to the kitchen back door. Rupert walked around to the front. The door of his father's study was open and he began calling as soon as he heard Rupert's steps.

'Hugh? Edward? Which one of you is it?'

'It's me, Dad.'

'Oh, Rupert. The very feller I wanted to see. Come in, my boy. Have a whisky. Shut the door. I wanted to have a word with you.'

∞ ∞ ∞

'Darling, eat your cake.'

'I suppose if I can't *have* it, I'd better.' Then she saw Rachel's eyes cloud with comprehension and pain and added

226

quickly, 'Don't mind me. I always feel blue when you go.' She broke off a piece of the walnut cake with her fork and ate it. 'I meant it would be quite nice to be able to take it to eat on the bus on the way home.'

Rachel's face cleared. 'Why don't you? Better still, have another piece for the bus. Have mine. I don't want it a bit.'

They were sitting in Fuller's in the Strand, having tea before Rachel caught her train to Battle. She had been up for the day, attending a meeting that was called to raise funds for her Babies' Hotel. That had been in the morning, and she had met Sid for lunch – a picnic of ham and rolls and apples consumed amid the dust sheets at Chester Terrace. The house was shut for the summer, with only old Mary caretaking in its vast and cavernous basement. Afterwards, they had walked in the Park, arm in arm, discussing, as they nearly always did, the problems of the holidays and Evie's health and state of mind, and the consequent difficulties of Sid coming down to stay. It had been finally determined that Rachel should sound out the Duchy about the possibility of Evie coming too, if the conductor for whom she worked as a secretary went on tour and did not need her.

'Walnut cake reminds me of going back to school,' Rachel now said. 'The Duchy used to take me out to tea, but I always felt homesick and I couldn't eat anything. So do have it,' she added.

'Righty-ho.' Sid picked up the piece, wrapped it in the paper napkin, and put it in her battered bag. Rachel had been eating or rather not eating a piece of buttered toast.

'You know I'd stay up if I possibly could.'

You possibly could, thought Sid, if you weren't so damnably unselfish.

'My darling, I've come to accept that you live for others. It's just that – sometimes – I wish that I could be one of them.'

Rachel put down her cup. 'But you couldn't ever be!' There was a silence, her face flooded with colour that slowly ebbed away as Sid watched. Then, in a voice that was both casual and unsteady and not looking at Sid, she said, 'I'd always rather be with you than anyone in the world!'

Sid found she was unable to speak. She put her hand over Rachel's, then, meeting those troubled innocent eyes, she winked and said, 'Oy, oy! We must catch your blasted train.'

They paid for their tea and walked without speaking to Charing Cross to the platform barrier.

'Want me to see you off?'

Rachel shook her head. 'It's been such a lovely day,' she said, and tried to smile.

'Hasn't it just? Goodbye, my darling. Mind you ring.' She put two fingers on Rachel's face, stopped for a moment when she reached her mouth to receive the minute trembling kiss. Then she turned clumsily away and walked out of the station without looking back.

∞ ∞ ∞

'The fact is, my dear, that it's jolly unfair. We're the *only* ones who aren't allowed grown-up supper.'

'Wills isn't.'

'*Wills!* He hardly exists! He's not even a *child*.'

'Well, we don't have to have supper with him. And I quite like him, anyway. He is my brother,' she added.

'Oh, he's all right as far as he goes. But it doesn't alter the fact that it's jolly unfair. Even Simon has dining-room supper and he's only twelve. You have to admit that there's not much justice there.'

'No, there isn't. Pass the soap.'

They were sitting in each end of the bath, not washing. Clary's plate lay on the mahogany shelf by the tooth mugs. Their backs were pink from the sun, with white marks from their bathing dresses. The soles of their feet were dark grey from not wearing sandals. Polly scrubbed her flannel with soap and began to wash a foot.

'We should stop washing as a protest,' said Clary.

'I'm only washing the bits that are dirty, only my feet, in fact. Mummy always inspects them.'

Clary was silent. Zoë wouldn't dream of bothering with her feet and Dad wouldn't notice. In some ways this was better, and in some ways worse. Polly looked up, and recognising Clary's silence, said quickly, 'It was a jolly good meeting. Christopher was super. Think of having all those butterflies. It

228

was a good idea of yours to make him Curator of the Natural History section.'

'And if Louise doesn't like it she can lump it.'

Without a word, Polly got out of the bath and wrapped herself in the threadbare bath towels that the Duchy felt were good enough for children.

'You haven't washed your other foot!'

'I don't want to stay in the bath with you. You're too horrible. First you're against everybody, then poor old Wills, and now Louise. You're getting like Richard III.'

'I'm not!' When Polly didn't reply, she said, 'I'm really not. Give me your other foot. I'll wash it for you.'

'How do I know you're not going to drag me off my balance? You're in a very treacherous state of mind. I don't trust you as a matter of fact.'

Polly was perfectly right, of course. She was horrible. Angry things just mounted up in her until some of them had to come out – an explosion of nastiness, and then she felt awful, like now, ashamed and confused to be so much worse a person than Polly, who never seemed to have bad feelings about anything and certainly not about people. 'I wouldn't drag you,' she muttered. Her eyes were full of scorching tears. A grey, horny foot was thrust over her left shoulder.

'OK,' Polly said. 'Thanks.'

Clary washed with tremendous care. 'I'm trying not to tickle,' she said humbly, when Polly wriggled.

She didn't want to be too nice, which would make Clary cry more, so she said, 'I know you are.'

'I bet Jesus tickled the disciples' feet when He washed them. There were so many of them, He would have got careless.'

'Bet they didn't dare laugh, though. Have you noticed how in books people do things with hair that you never could do?'

'Like what?'

'Well, like Mary Magdalene drying Jesus's feet with it, or heroines embroidering handkerchiefs. I bet when you ironed them the hair would just sizzle away. And Rapunzel, Rapunzel, let down your hair. You couldn't climb somebody's hair like a rope – it would be agony.'

'I suppose it's just that in books you can say what you like.'

'They ought to stick to real things,' Clary said, getting out of the bath. 'When I'm a writer, I shall. I shan't write any old nonsense that doesn't work.'

'You are so lucky having a career! Don't forget your plate.' Clary looked at the plate. One minute she was lucky, the next minute, the reverse.

'I was going to forget it,' she said sadly. 'You might have shut up about it.'

'Put it in,' advised Polly. 'Then take it out again, and I won't say anything. That'll be sort of true.'

Clary picked it up and put it in with an audible click. Then she took it out again. Then she looked at Polly. '*You* wouldn't do that,' she said. 'You'd stick to the truth.'

Their eyes met, and Polly said, 'Sorry! I suppose I would. But you don't have to wear it.'

'But if you had, you would.' She put the plate back in. 'I admire your character enormously,' she said even more sadly. The plate hurt immediately: it really spoilt meals. She picked up her towel and sneezed.

'You won't have to wear it for ever, and I think you're frightfully brave about it. You'll end up as beautiful as the day.'

'But not good, like all those princesses in the books. More likely to be a wicked ugly sister. Or cousin.'

'Tell you what. When they've started their dinner, let's take our supper to the orchard and have a midnight feast in the tree.'

'That's a brilliant idea! We'll have to wait till they've said good night to us. We'll have to pretend to eat the food and hide it in our beds, and *then* go out.'

They were friends again.

∞ ∞ ∞

Rupert fairly reeled out of his father's study, started to go upstairs to Zoë, and then changed his mind and went to the drawing room, which he knew would be empty since the Duchy never used it until after dinner. It was cool and full of the comfortingly familiar scent of sweet peas: the Duchy adored them, and there were always large bowls crammed with them about the house in the summer. The blinds were still drawn against the sun: the Duchy, who lamented the room not facing north, kept it well shrouded until all danger of sunlight had passed. He went to the window and released the blind, which flew up with a snap revealing a tumultuous orange and purple sunset and, as he·watched, a train, like a small black toy, puffed steadily from right to left in the distance. He badly wanted to talk to somebody, but not to Zoë since he could imagine exactly what she would say and it would not resolve his dilemma. 'The Brig has asked me to join the firm.' 'Oh, Rupe! What a marvellous idea!' 'He has only asked me to consider it. I haven't made up my mind.' 'Why ever not?' And so on. She would see it only in terms of a relief from financial anxieties. She would not for one moment consider what it would be like to stop being a painter of any kind, and become a businessman – something he would dislike and be no good at. On the other hand, it wasn't as though he was painting much now, anyway: in term time he was too fagged from teaching all day and the holidays were more or less spent with, or on, Zoë and the children. It was certainly true that their car was absolutely on its last legs and, due to Clary's extremely expensive dental treatment, he could see no way of getting a new one in the foreseeable future. And when Zoë could drive, she would want a car more than ever.

If he joined the firm, he wouldn't have to worry about things like getting a new car. He could paint in his holiday. No, he couldn't. He'd only get a fortnight a year, plus Christmas and Easter, and if he couldn't manage to paint in the long school holidays, he certainly wouldn't manage in one short one. Zoë would expect to be taken somewhere exotic – skiing or something like that. He thought fleetingly of the Sunday painters, and even more fleetingly of the lengths to which Gauguin had gone to be a painter. Perhaps I'm not a real painter, at all, he thought. It needs to be put first, and I never do that. Better to give it all up. He wished that Rachel was back from London. She would be the best person to talk to. Either of his brothers might have views either way about it that pre-empted them from giving him good advice. 'Don't expect you to make up your mind at once,' the Brig had said. 'Think about it. Serious decision. I needn't say how delighted I should be if you agree, though.' The poor old boy was having to give it up by degrees, although he'd fight his blindness all the way. He didn't want what he described as outsiders. But it was difficult to go into a job feeling that your greatest, if not only, asset was that your name was Cazalet. The drawing-room grandfather clock struck seven. He'd have to go up if he wanted a bath before changing.

He'd planned not to say anything to Zoë, who was lying on their bed reading yet another novel by Howard Spring, but when he went to kiss her forehead and greet her she simply said, 'Fine, thank you,' without taking her eyes from her book.

Some childish urge to startle her, get her attention, made him say, 'The Brig has asked me to join the firm.'

She dropped her book on her stomach. 'Oh, Rupe! What a marvellous idea!'

'I haven't made up my mind yet. There's plenty of time to think about it.'

'Why haven't you?'

'Made up my mind? Because it's a very serious decision and I'm not at all sure that I want to change my profession.'

'Why ever not?'

'Because it's something I would be doing all the time. For the rest of my life,' he began patiently, but she sat up, threw aside the eiderdown and ran to him, throwing her arms round his neck and saying, 'I know what it is! You're afraid you wouldn't be any good at it. You're so . . . ' she searched for what, to her, would be the right word, 'so awfully . . . *unassuming*. You'd be a marvellous businessman. Everybody loves you. You'd be wonderful at it!'

She had bathed and cooled after her bath, and her skin smelled of rose geranium. He realised now that her charms touched him, not with excitement but more with the poignancy of their fidelity. He kissed her with a tenderness she did not recognise and said, 'I'm off for a bath. One thing. This is a secret. I don't want to discuss this *en famille* tonight or at all. So will you keep mum?'

She nodded.

'Truly, Zoë? You promise?'

'I wouldn't dream of it,' she said in her haughty voice. It did not always suit her to be treated as a child.

As she made up her face and dressed for dinner, she

thought of all the things that would be better if Rupert stopped being a schoolmaster and became like his brothers. They could have a nicer house – she loathed Hammersmith – get a decent car, Clary could be sent to a good boarding school ('good' showed that she cared for Clary's welfare), they could go out in the evenings more, since Rupert would not be so tired. She would entertain for him – she would give wonderful dinners which would help him in his career, but most of all, relieved of the constant worry about money and not having enough of it, he would become the carefree, lighthearted Rupert she had married. Because somewhere she knew that their marriage was not exactly as it had been four years ago, although, heaven knows, it was not *she* who had changed: she had never, for a second, stopped taking trouble with her appearance which she could see – look at Sybil and Villy, and worst of all, Villy's pathetic sister – was what happened to most women, but in spite of everything she did about it she could sense fleetingly, and with a terror that congealed to resentment, that Rupert did not respond to her with the same unthinking passion that he once had. There had been times when she had felt that she was resistible, something she had thought she would never be. He was nicer to her in public, and less to her when they were alone. 'Don't be ridiculous, darling,' or 'Zoë, sometimes you are a silly ass!' he had used to say sometimes around the family table, and how hurt she had been! But their rows about that sort of thing had resolved themselves in bed – marvellously, wonderfully – and in the end it had always been she who had apologised for being silly, for not understanding what he had meant. She had always been prepared to admit her faults. But he never said those sorts of things now; it was ages since he had teased or snubbed her, and the sweetness of the inevitable reconciliation was also distant. Of course, one day she would be old, and then she supposed that things would be different, but that was ages away – she was twenty-three and women were supposed to become more attractive up to the age of thirty, at least, and she would probably last longer because she had always taken such trouble. She examined her face now with a stern, dispassionate care: she would be the first to find fault with it, but no fault could be found. All I want is for him to love me, she thought. I don't care about anything else. She was not aware that the secret lies are the ones that endure.

∞ ∞ ∞

After he got back from golf Hugh read to his father for an hour and then played some patient, very hot tennis with Simon. His serve was still very erratic, but his backhand was becoming more reliable. Sybil came and watched them for a bit, but then she went away to bath and feed Wills who was getting hungry and restive. Hugh missed her presence and the midges, clouds of them like animated haloes round their heads, were distracting. 'I think I'm going to call it a day, old boy,' he said after the second set. Simon agreed with the show of reluctance that was proper to his pride but, actually, in spite of an enormous tea, he was extremely hungry and supper, since he was having it in the dining room, wouldn't be for ages. He sloped off to the kitchen, to see what he could coax out of Mrs Cripps, who favoured him and admired his appetite. Hugh had left him to wind down the net and collect the balls and racquets and wandered towards the Duchy's rose garden, where he could see her in the distance wearing her hessian apron and carrying a trug, dead-heading her beloved roses. But I don't want to talk to her now, he thought, waved and turned right on the cinder path that led back to the house. Passing his father's study he could hear him talking – a pause, and then Rupert's voice. He climbed the steep back stairs and went to their bedroom, the room in which Wills had been born – in which the little unknown baby had died. There was a tidy dazzlingly white litter of baby things at one end: Sybil must be bathing him. Usually he loved to see him in his bath, but this evening he wanted to be alone.

He unlaced his tennis shoes and lay on the bed. The conversation at lunch with Edward was still knocking about in his mind. There *was* a danger of war: everything that Edward had said about it seemed reasonable and was, after all, as he knew perfectly well, what most people said, but it didn't convince him at all. Most people, of his generation at least, so much didn't want a war that they refused to think about it. And younger people couldn't be expected to know a great deal, since when the last war ever came up – at the club, or at City dinners – it was discussed in a manner both cheery and heroic: old songs, camaraderies, the war to end wars; there was this girl in a café at Ypres – The one with the little brown mole on her lip? Yes, that was the one! But no earthly idea of what it had been *like* was ever passed on. Even he, when he had his war nightmares – less often these days, but still occasionally recurring – never told Sybil what they were actually *about*. No, the long silence on the subject continued, and he, in his own way, was a party to it. But silence about that war was one thing, the general refusal to consider the facts of what was happening now was another. Germany had had conscription for several years, nearly four, and people didn't seem to think that there was anything odd about that. And Hitler: he was laughed at, called Schickelgruber, which they thought extremely funny, although it was his name – called a mere housepainter, which he had been, and written off as not only absurd but mad, which somehow enabled them to refuse to take him seriously at all. But it was clear that the Germans took him seriously all right. When Hitler had simply walked into Austria last spring, he had been almost glad because he thought that now, at last, other people would have to take notice of him. But it didn't seem to have made any difference at all. There was one bloke in politics who'd had a go at the Nazi regime, but that simply meant that he was kept out of the Cabinet. And Chamberlain, although of course he had a good political family background, did not strike him as a leader who would be much good at getting people's heads out of the sand.

On their drive back from Rye, he had made another attempt to get Edward to consider the matter – asked him what he thought was going to happen in Czechoslovakia where there was a German minority that looked like being the Nazis' next target. Edward had said that he knew nothing about Czecho-slovakia except that they were supposed to be good at making shoes and glass, and if the country contained a whole lot of Germans it was perfectly reasonable of them to want to ally themselves to the rest of their race, it really wasn't any-thing to do with Britain or France. When Hugh, who realised then, for the first time, the degree of his brother's ignorance in the matter, pointed out that Czechoslovakia was a democracy whose borders had been determined by England and France at the treaty of Versailles and that, therefore, it could reasonably be said to be something to do with them, Edward had replied almost irritably that Hugh obviously knew far more about it than he did, but that the main point was that nobody *wanted* another war, and it would be foolish to get involved with Hitler, (who seemed rather an hysterical chap), about, something that clearly had more to do with Germany than it did with Britain, and, anyway, they'd probably have a plebiscite as they had with the Saar, and the whole thing would straighten itself out. No point in getting jumpy, he had added, and had immediately started to talk about how they could deter the Old Man from buying the vast quantity of teak and iroko that seemed to be far in excess of the firm's requirements and was tying up far too much capital. 'There's another shipload lying in bond at East India now. All those logs are going to take a hell of a lot of space not to mention the West African mahogany at Liverpool. I can't think where we're going to put them all. Have a word with him, old boy. He won't take a blind bit of notice of me.'

As you won't of me, Hugh thought, but he did not say so.

He had shut his eyes and must have dozed off as, without his hearing them, he found Sybil sitting on the bed beside him with Wills, wrapped in a bath towel in her arms.

'One baby,' she said, setting him on the bed. Hugh sat up and took Wills in his arms. He smelled of Vinolia soap, and his hair, long and straggly at the back – like an unsuccessful composer, Rachel had said – was damp. He smiled at Hugh, and thrust his fingers with surprisingly sharp nails into Hugh's face.

'Just hold him while I get his night clothes.'

Hugh removed the hand. 'Steady on, old boy, that's my eye.' Wills looked at him reproachfully for a moment, and then his gaze wandered to the signet ring on his father's finger, which he grabbed and drew powerfully up to his mouth.

'Isn't he *clever*?' said Sybil returning with nappies.

Hugh looked at her with relief. 'Enormously,' he said.

'He's laughing at us,' Sybil told the baby as, having folded the Harrington square, she laid him back in the appropriate position. He lay watching both his parents with benevolent dignity while his loins were wrapped and pinned for the night.

'He hasn't a care in the world,' said Hugh.

'Oh, yes, he has! He lost his duck in the bath, and he simply loathes brains and Nanny makes him have them every week.'

'It doesn't seem very bad to me.'

'Other people's troubles never do,' Sybil replied, adding, 'I don't mean just *you*, darling, I mean anyone. Can you keep an eye on him while I get his bottle?'

'What's Nanny up to?'

'She's in Hastings with Ellen. It's their day off. They've gone to the *Fol-de-Rols* on the pier. Then they'll have a terribly rich tea with éclairs and meringues and Nanny will have a bilious attack tomorrow.'

'How on earth do you know that?'

'Because it happens every week. Nannies have to have their childish side or they would be no good at playing with children. She's a very good nanny in other ways.'

When she left, Wills frowned and began to get red in the face, so Hugh picked him up and showed him how the electric light switches worked, which cheered him at once. Hugh found himself wondering whether Wills would grow up to be a scientist. He might be anything, even a timber merchant, but the great thing was that Wills should be allowed to choose and not simply drift into the family business as he felt he had done. The war again. It seemed to him as though that war had been his youth; before it had been his childhood – life measured by wonderful holidays and terms at school that could be endured for the regular bouts of family life and, best of all, the reunions with Edward (they had been sent to different schools on some mysterious principle that he had never understood). He had done quite well and hated it; Edward had done badly and had not minded at all. And then the last term and not only the glorious summer stretching ahead, but the even more glorious prospect of going to Cambridge – all dashed in August.

He had joined the Coldstream Guards in September; Edward, wild to go with him, had tried to do the same but, at seventeen, they had told him he must wait a year. So he had gone off to the Machine Gun Corps and lied about his age and got in. In a few months they were soldiers in France taking their own horses from home. In those four years he had seen Edward only twice: once in a muddy lane near Amiens when their horses had neighed in greeting before they caught sight of each other; and once when he had been wounded, and somehow Edward had contrived to visit him in hospital before he was shipped back to England. Edward – a major at not quite twenty-one – had breezed into the ward, captivating the VADs and telling the gaunt battleaxe of a matron, 'Take extra care of him because he is my brother,' and she had smiled, looked twenty years younger, and said, 'Of course, Major Cazalet.' 'How did you get a pass?' he had asked. Edward winked. 'I didn't. I said, "*Pass*? I'm an E.D.W.A.R.D.!" And they said "Sorry, sir," and let me through.' And Hugh had found himself starting to laugh but, in fact, crying helplessly, and Edward sat on the bed and held his remaining hand, and then mopped him up with a silk handkerchief that smelled of home. 'Poor old boy! Did they get the shrapnel out of your head?' And he'd nodded, but of course they hadn't – some of it was too far in, they had told him after, he'd have to live with it. Funny thing was that what had *hurt* most at the time had been his two broken ribs – his stump, after they had amputated his hand, had been more an agony of the mind. It had hurt, of course, but they'd given him a lot of morphine then, and the worst thing had been when they dressed it. He couldn't bear them to touch it, or rather, the only way he could bear it was by never looking to see what they were doing. In between being dressed, it ached and twitched and itched and often felt as though his hand was still there. Well, none of that was much compared to some of the things he had seen. He looked now at the black silk stump with the small pad at the end and thought how incredibly lucky he had been.

When Edward had got up to leave he'd kissed him – something that they did not usually do – and said, 'You look after yourself, old chap.' 'And you,' he'd said, trying to sound casual. Edward had smiled, winked again and said, 'You bet.' He'd walked away down the ward without looking back. And he had lain there watching the doors at the end of the ward still swinging gently after Edward had passed through them and thought, It's a bloody awful world, and I'll never see him again. Then he'd realised that Edward's handkerchief was stuffed in his left hand.

They'd got him back to a hospital in England – some large

country house that had been turned into a convalescent home – and his ribs and the stump had healed and the Godawful headaches, the nightmares and sweats had abated somewhat and he was sent home, weak, irritable, depressed and feeling too tired and too old to care about anything much. He was twenty-two. Edward, of course, did come back, with nothing worse than rocky lungs, from living in trenches where the gas hung about for weeks, and frostbite that had caused him to lose a toe, but the funny thing was that *he* didn't seem changed at all, seemed to be just as he had been before they had both gone to France, was full of energy and japes, would stay up all night dancing, and go to work all day as fresh as a daisy. Girls fell for him easily – he was always having little gold pencils and bracelets engraved with Betty and Vivien and Norah, was always going off for weekends to play tennis or shoot or go to country dances, must have met more parents of girls he readily got engaged to than most and always came off with flying colours. He never mentioned the war: it was as though it had been like a particularly nasty boarding school where death and mutilation rather than mere bullying had been the norm, but now he was out the other side of it into eternal holidays. The only time Hugh remembered him as having been at all out of his depth was when he fell for a young married woman whose husband had been so badly shell-shocked he was a permanent invalid. He had been really smitten by her – Jennifer something she had been called – but then he had met Villy and that had, but not immediately, been that. But then *he* had met Sybil and fallen so much in love with her that he had ceased to notice anything else that was going on. Sybil! She had changed his life: meeting her had been the most incredibly—

'Sorry to have been so long. It had got much too hot and I had to cool it down.' She squirted the teat onto the back of her hand. 'You'd better give him to me or he'll get cross.' Hugh kissed the back of his baby's neck – his hair was drying into little tender curls – and then in the middle of handing him over, he kissed his wife on the mouth.

'Darling! What's all that about?' She took the protesting baby and settled herself in a chair.

'I was remembering when I first met you.'

'Oh! That!' She gave him a glance half appraising, half shy.

'The luckiest day in my life. Listen, in this heat, you don't want to come up to town – just for a night?'

'Of course I do!' She had been wondering whether she should get out of it. Not that she didn't want to see him, but she did hate leaving Wills, and London was so hot and smelly after the country.

'Sure? Because I'm perfectly happy on my own.'

'Sure.' She knew that he wasn't.

'I'll take you to see the Lunts. Or would you prefer the Emlyn Williams play?'

'I'm happy with either. Which would you like?'

'I don't mind in the least.' He would have preferred to dine quietly with her and not go anywhere. 'Oysters will have started. We can go to Bentley's first. We'll have a great night out.'

So far as the unselfishness game went, it was checkmate.

∞ ∞ ∞

Sid caught her 53 bus at the corner of Trafalgar Square and went upstairs to a seat right in the front. She paid for her fourpenny ticket before she went up; now, with any luck, she'd be left in peace. She settled herself, blew her nose, and tried to be what Rachel would call sensible. But what started happening at once, as it nearly always did at times like these, was resentment, bitter and continuous, and on a scale that she utterly concealed from her darling R. She could understand that the Brig was going blind, and that this was awful for him, but why did that make Rachel the person who had to look after him? He was married, wasn't he? What about the Duchy doing her share for a change? The idea seemed never to have occurred to any of them. The Duchy was perfectly capable of reading aloud to him, of taking dictation at a pinch, of helping him with his letters and conducting him about the place. Why should Rachel feel that her parents – both of them – depended upon her so entirely? Why did they not see that she was entitled to a life of her own? Rachel had even talked today of possibly having to give up her Babies' Hotel, as the Brig would require too much of her time for her to do her work there properly. And if she did give that up, bang would go the only valid excuse she ever had for getting away during these interminable holidays. It was the English Victorian concept of the unmarried daughter that did it. For a second, Sid contemplated the idea of Rachel having married someone, and therefore escaping this onerous fate but the thought of Rachel being touched by someone else – a man – was, in fact, worse. There might have been children: Rachel would *never* be free of them. But if the husband had died or went off with someone else, *she* could have helped Rachel with the children – they could have lived together. Oh, no, they couldn't: Evie loomed with her ill health, her dependence, her hopeless crushes on unsuitable people who were usually ignorant of Evie's feelings for them and couldn't be seen for dust if they were not. Evie had nobody in the world but her as she so often said. She never succeeded in sticking to any job for one reason or another; she was jealous of Sid's life wherever it did not touch her own. She had no money, and they staggered on together on Sid's salary from the school, her private teaching and the bits and bobs that Evie spasmodically contributed. They had been left the little house in Maida Vale by their mother and that was it. No, she was tied, too – tied, in real terms, more inextricably than Rachel. But she did not have Rachel's goodness: she deeply resented her imprisonment, was not even sure that if Rachel were free, she would not behave very badly to Evie – leave her the house and tell her to get on with it. But Rachel would never agree to that. The image of Rachel's face in the tea shop when she said, 'I'd rather be with you than with anybody in the world', recurred. It had moved her so much at the time that she had resorted to a kind of music-hall jauntiness, but now, on her own, that painful declaration dropped deeply into her heart – was balm indeed. 'She does love me – me, of all people – she has chosen to love *me*! What more can I ask than that?' Not a damn thing.

The feeling of richness, the fortune of being so loved saw her through the hot and dreary evening – the fish pie Evie had made that tasted of wet laundry, her persistent questioning about what she had done all day, and even, when Sid was making some decent coffee, her burrowing in Sid's handbag for cigarettes (she was always running out – too lazy to go and buy them for herself) and her finding the piece of walnut cake. 'What on *earth* have you got this in your handbag for? Oh – walnut cake!

241

I adore walnut cake did Rachel give it to you you don't mind if I have just a teeny piece sure I know it's bad for my ulcer but I do so want a little treat!' then eating it with her pale, sly, anxious eyes fixed on Sid's face for the slightest sign of rejection or injury. She gave neither: whenever she felt her pity or affection waning, she conjured back that unsteady, casual voice and was able to continue indifferently kind.

After supper they took the coffee tray up to the stuffy little sitting room, so full of the grand piano that there was barely any room for their two battered old arm chairs. It was so stuffy that Sid opened the french windows that looked onto the small back garden. It contained a huge lime tree and a small square of lawn that she had not mowed for weeks. Willowherb and Michaelmas daisies grew in the narrow beds against the black brick walls, and the gravel path that separated the beds from the lawn was full of dandelions and chickweed. It was not a garden they either used or enjoyed. The iron balustrade and steps that led down from the windows to the garden were rusty, the blistering paint needed burning off. If they were not invited to Home Place, Sid thought, she should really spend some of the holidays refurbishing things. She did not dare tell Evie of this infinitely more inviting possibility because her disappointment, and her ruminations about it if it did not come off, would be unbearable. And also, of course, Waldo might not go on tour. Jewish members of his orchestra were distinctly uneasy about going to some of the parts of Europe involved, and it looked likely that the tour would be curtailed, if not possibly cancelled. In which case, Evie would want to stay in London and she could not go. Sid turned back from the dusty warm air of the garden, to the dustier warmth of the room and asked if there was any news of the tour.

'He won't take me. I actually asked, this morning. I think it's his wife. She's terribly jealous, she's always coming into the room when he's dictating. Quite ridiculous!'

It was, actually, just that. But Sid reflected that the poor woman could hardly be expected to distinguish between one potential menace and another, since her husband was famous for his affairs – the sudden short ones, and the two mistresses he was known to keep, one of whom actually met him wherever he went abroad. Evie seemed to be the only person who did not know about the mistresses or, rather, who refused to believe what she called malicious gossip. What she really meant was that the wife, an ex-opera singer called Lottie, never gave it the chance to become *not* quite ridiculous. Waldo kissed any women who got near enough and so, of course, he had kissed Evie, who had been unable to resist telling Sid about it. This had been six months ago, and she now implied that the immense difficulties of the situation were all that stood between her and cosmic joy. (The difficulties included Waldo's heroic nature: immense, sombre Lottie was, according to Evie, the cross he had to bear.)

Evie was lying back in her chair, on the arm of which an open box of coffee creams was precariously perched, and every now and then, she stretched out a hand, felt for a chocolate, and popped it in her mouth. She was extremely fond of sweets and subject to frequent bilious attacks that, like her sallow and greasy complexion, were never attributed to this predilection. She was perfectly determined in this, as in her emotional life, never to learn from experience. She is a monster, thought Sid, but she thought it protectively. Since Evie's birth, when Sid was four, she had been conditioned to feeling that Evie was up against circumstances rather than her own nature – she had always been subject to ailments, and an early and bad attack of measles, acute appendicitis and perito-nitis had enfeebled her frame and strengthened her powers of manipulation to the point where she could be certain of special consideration for whatever she did or didn't do and resulting consequences kept her steadfast in her discontent.

She was yawning now – one yawn started before the first one had finished – and exclaiming, in that subdued foghorn voice common to yawners, that she was sure there was going to be a thunderstorm. 'You said you'd cut my hair,' she added. She passed a languid hand through her fringe. 'It's far too long, only I don't want it cut so much as you did last time.'

'Well, I'm not cutting it tonight. Anyway, I wish you'd go to a decent hairdresser: I can only do a pudding-basin job.'

'You know I hate doing that sort of thing by myself. And you won't let me go to yours.'

'Evie, for the hundredth time, I don't go to a ladies' hairdresser. The place I go to doesn't cut women's hair.'

'They cut yours.'

When Sid did not reply to this, she said, 'If you had it shingled, a women's hairdresser would do it.'

'I don't want it shingled. I simply like it very short. Shut up, Evie.'

Evie thrust out her lower lip in sulky silence, during which the distant rumble of thunder was distinct. Sid got up again and went to the window. 'Goodness, I wish it would rain. Clear the air a bit.'

As Sid knew she would, Evie went on sulking until Sid offered a game of bezique, which was grudgingly accepted. Three games, or the best of three, Sid thought, and then I can escape to bed and write to her.

'I couldn't cut your hair with all this thunder about,' she said. 'Don't you remember Mama used to wrap all the knives in her mackintosh? She thought the rubber would deflect the lightning?'

Evie smiled. 'She was terribly nervous. Ladders, and the new moon and black cats – poor little Mummy – she did have an awful life! I suppose we've inherited some of that. I have, anyway. I get terribly nervous about things. Like, you know, I thought you might not come back this evening. I thought Rachel might invite you down to Sussex, and you'd simply go.'

'Evie! When have I ever done anything like that?'

'Well, but you always might. And now, with Mummy gone, we've only got each other, after all. I'd never leave *you*, Sid. If I *do* marry anyone, I'd only do it if he said you could live with us.'

'Darling, we'll cross that bridge when we come to it.'

'I know *you* think we never will, but extraordinary things can happen you know. Fate can intervene . . . ' The game was abandoned as Evie embarked upon her hopes and fears and – Sid was afraid, her sheer imagination – about Waldo. Two hours later they went to their beds.

∞ ∞ ∞

When he had bathed and changed for dinner, Edward said he'd just nip out to the pub to get some cigarettes. Villy thought she had enough for both of them, but Edward said better be on the safe side. Really he wanted to ring Diana. He had to have a quick gin to get change for the machine that Mr Richardson had recently installed for the benefit of his customers. It was situated in a dark passage on the way to the gents' – not really very private, but better than nothing. Diana answered the phone just as he was beginning to think she must be out.

'It's me,' he said.

'Oh! Darling! Sorry to be so long, I was at the end of the garden.'

'Are you on your own?'

'For the moment. Are you?'

'I'm at the pub. In a passage,' he added in case she thought that the pub was private.

'Are you ringing up about tomorrow?'

'Yes. I shall be fairly late, I'm afraid. Probably about nine. What about the boys?'

'Ian and Fergus are still up north with their grandmother.'

'And Angus?'

'He's with them. Till the end of the week. There's just me and Jamie.'

'Hooray!'

'What?'

'Hooray. Good. You know what I mean.'

'I sort of think I do. I love you.'

'Entirely reciprocated. Must go now. Look after yourself.'

As he drove back down the hill to Mill Farm, he remembered that he hadn't bought any cigarettes; then he remembered that there were twenty Gold Flake in the front pocket of the car. He was in luck again! He wasn't doing any harm as long as she didn't know about it, but it would be devilish stupid to slip up on a little thing like that.

∞ ∞ ∞

They all had dinner – fourteen of them round the immense three-pedestal table extended to its uttermost and even then they were crammed round it. They ate four roast chickens, bread sauce, mashed potato and runner beans followed by plum tart and what the Duchy called Shape – blancmange. The grown-ups drank claret and the children water. They talked about what they had done that day; the beach party – Rupert was very funny about Neville and his jellyfish. *'Bexhill?'* said the Duchy, wiping her eyes (she always cried when she laughed). 'What on earth made him call it Bexhill?' Rupert, although he could think of little else, said nothing about the Brig's offer to him. Edward recounted Teddy's brilliant shot with the rabbit, and Teddy sat scarlet and smiling; naturally Edward said nothing about his telephone call. Hugh imitated his caddy imitating him playing golf with one hand; he said nothing about his political anxiety. Rachel described the nearly deaf, and, according to her, quite mad, President of the Babies' Hotel conducting the meeting without having the slightest idea which charity he was presiding over. 'He spent the first half-hour under the impression that it was the home for retired horses – it was only when he started on bran mashes and regular deworming that Matron realised that there was some mistake somewhere.' She said nothing about her day with Sid about whom, with effort that gave her a headache, she had not wept in the train. The Brig told two long stories – one about when he was in Burma and met an extremely interesting chap who turned out to have known someone he'd met in Western Australia (coincidence, with which his long life seemed to have been fraught, never failed to amaze and confound him), and another about the Suez canal, and when Edward said yes, they'd heard it, he simply said never mind, he'd tell them again and did. This took a very long time, and not everybody even pretended to listen to him.

Zoë and Angela eyed one another: Zoë instantly realised that Angela was interested in Rupert and scrutinised her more carefully therefore. One had to admit that she was very pretty – for those who liked blondes with rather pale blue eyes. She was tall and large-boned, like her mother, with a long, very rounded white neck, which poor old Jessica's certainly wasn't any more. She had the same cheekbones as Jessica, and the same sculptured mouth, only hers was painted a rather bright pink which was coming off as she ate her dinner. She was certainly fascinated by Rupert, who seemed, thank goodness, entirely unaware of it, but she met Zoë's eyes guilelessly. She's

246

only a schoolgirl, really, Zoë thought with a mixture of relief and contempt.

Angela, who had not seen Zoë for over two years, was confounded at how much the same she looked. She, Angela, had changed so much herself in that time that she assumed Zoë would have done so, but she showed no sign of ageing. She was just as glamorous and beautiful as ever, but from novels she had read, Angela knew that there was a very fair chance that she did not *understand* Rupert, in which case it would not matter what she looked like. The Brig finished his story; he did not mention his satisfaction in having built enough accommodation for his family, which, like the large number of hardwood logs he had bought for veneers, was just in case . . .

Christopher and Simon both spilled their water, and Simon some bread sauce, but nobody, Christopher noticed, was sarcastic about it. He met Simon's eye when the bread sauce happened and gave him a sympathetic wink. Instantly, Simon decided that Christopher was the best egg in the room. And when the end of the holidays was mentioned – barely three weeks away now and Simon felt terror and despair engulfing him – he again saw Christopher's face, noticing and minding. From that moment, Christopher became his hero. As he grinned and lied in response to Aunt Jessica's idiotic question about was he looking forward to his new school (*forward!*) Christopher winked – which was a jolly kind thing to do.

Villy, who carved the chickens beautifully, giving everybody the right bits, apportioning the four wishbones between Teddy, Louise, Nora and Simon, did not say very much. Her peaceful afternoon with Jessica had left her feeling oddly drained: the weight of what had not been said – on her part, at least – lay heavily inside her like indigestion. She sensed that Jessica envied her, and longed to be able to tell her that the bed of roses contained thorns. That her sister clearly had too much to do was not, Villy felt, entirely unfortunate. Jessica did not have time to wonder what she was for, to be bored, and ashamed of it, to long for some cataclysmic event that would provide the opportunity to *do* something and therefore *be* somebody. But besides these general feelings about her life there was one particular fact that she had fully intended to discuss with Jessica, and then all the afternoon baulked because she was afraid that Jessica would be unsympathetic, for different reasons from those that she might expect from Sybil, for instance, or from Rachel . . . Rachel! *She* thought that anyone having a baby was the most marvellous thing that could happen. For that was it. She had missed one period, was coming up to the second and felt fairly certain that she was pregnant and the idea appalled her. She was forty-two, after all; she didn't really want to start all over again, having what would amount to an only child – Lydia was seven. But what on earth did one *do* if one didn't want a baby? She knew, of course, that there *were* people who did that sort of thing, but how on earth did one find them? She had thought of Hermione as a possible source of information, but she did not at all want to confide in her. Also, of course, she hadn't *absolutely* made up her mind; she was clinging to the idea that she might easily be wrong. She decided to wait until she was due and if she missed again she would go to London and see Dr Ballater.

Nora, who was by nature greedy about food, decided to give up her second helping of plum tart for the glory of God. She did not decide this until she was half-way through her first delicious piece, then she could not help supposing that He would have been better pleased if she had not had any at all. 'Eschewed it, instead of chewed it,' she explained to Him (she was always trying to encourage His sense of humour). But surely He could see that until she knew how delicious it was, she wouldn't have been making a *witting* sacrifice. But really that didn't wash: food always was delicious at Home Place – it was like Sunday lunch at home every day. Mummy was a jolly good cook, of course: it was simply that she had less to cook *with*, and the other side of that was that opportunities for sacrifice were seldom come by. It was common sense to eat enough to keep alive, so she did. She felt that she was full of common sense, and longed to have more of the other kind, to be full of mystic certainties. She talked a good deal to God, but He hardly ever said anything back: she was beginning to be afraid that she bored Him, which would be pretty worrying, because as He was known not to mind what people looked like, it followed that He'd mind more than ever how they *were*. And boring was something Mummy has always told her one should never be. Christopher was eating her piece of tart, his third, but she knew how awfully hungry he got after he'd been sick, so she didn't grudge him. Angie had eaten her fruit and left the pastry. Well, if He really didn't mind what people looked like, God would have been bored with Angela. She looked across at Louise. They had spent a long fascinating afternoon in the hammocks together where a number of secrets had been exchanged, although there were still things that she had not yet confided, which was probably true of Louise also. In any case almost nothing that they had talked about was suitable for family public and they would be bound to shock their mothers, as, mad and extraordinary though it was, they still seemed to be widely regarded as the children.

By the time the plum tarts were entirely eaten, the younger members of the party longed to get down from the table: Simon and Christopher and Teddy because they couldn't see the point of sitting at a table when you'd eaten everything on it; Louise and Nora, because they longed to resume their private conversation; and Angela, because she wanted Rupert to see more of her than he could when she was sitting down. The women, too, were ready to leave, since the Brig had embarked upon his distressingly lovely Stilton – Christopher thought it was unexpectedly kind of him to let the maggots go on eating at the same time – and his views about Mr Chamberlain whom he felt was nothing like so suitable a prime minister as Mr Baldwin, who should never have been kicked upstairs as he put it. The Duchy surprisingly said that she had never liked Mr Baldwin, but she certainly did not think that Mr Chamberlain was an improvement. Whereupon Rupert said, 'Darling, you know you only *really* admire Toscanini and the great British public would never accept him for such a post, so you are doomed to disappointment,' and before she could retort that even she was not so idiotic as that, the thunder that had been rumbling distantly at intervals suddenly crashed over their heads. Sybil started up to see if it had woken Wills, and this was a general signal for the women and children to leave the Brig and his sons to their port.

In the hall, they could hear the rain drumming on the skylight and a few moments later Louise and Nora, rooting about for macs they could borrow to run home in the rain, were met by Clary and Polly, drenched in their nightgowns. 'Where *have* you been?' asked Louise, but she knew really.

Having a midnight feast somewhere or other, as she had done last year with Polly.

'Having a midnight feast,' said Polly. 'Where are they all? We've got to get upstairs without them seeing us.' She thought Louise sounded distressingly like them and easily might not help.

∞ ∞ ∞

The rain stopped some time in the early morning and the day began with white fog. It was decreed not a day for the beach. Clary tried to whip the others into a state of indignation about this, but although there was a general agreement that it was jolly unfair, nobody seemed to mind enough to do anything. 'Anyway, what could we do? We can't drive cars,' Polly pointed out. Aunt Rachel said that Mrs Cripps wanted a lot of blackberries for jelly, and whoever got the most would get a prize, so the seven older children set off with bowls and baskets. Bexhill had died in the night; Neville refused to believe Ellen, but Aunt Villy, when fetched to view the motionless white blob in the bath, said that she was afraid there was no doubt.

'He wouldn't have felt any pain, though, would he?' said Judy earnestly. 'Or *would* he?'

Villy quickly said that she was sure that he wouldn't.

'Then what *happened*?' Neville demanded. 'How did he simply stop being alive?'

'He just gave up the ghost,' Lydia said. 'Died. It happens to everything.' She looked rather frightened. 'It's a perfectly ordinary thing. Either you get murdered, or you simply die. You stop being around. You can't do anything any more. You're just like – breath.'

Those remarks were not reassuring anyone, Villy could see, so she suggested that they have a really good funeral. This seemed to cheer everybody up, and they spent the rest of the morning arranging it.

∞ ∞ ∞

Mrs Cripps sat in her kitchen dispensing rock cakes to Tonbridge who had dropped in for middle mornings – his

250

ulcer, enhanced by Mrs Tonbridge's furiously fried breakfast, could only be assuaged by cake and a sympathetic ear. Mrs Cripps passed no remarks about Mrs Tonbridge but received the oblique information given about her with impassive interest that none the less contrived to show which side she was on.

'It's the quiet, you see. It gets on her nerves.'

'I expect it would do.' She spread the *Sunday Express* on her spotless table. 'CRISIS OFF TILL A WEEK TOMORROW,' it said. 'NO SENSATIONS EXPECTED.' She tipped a heap of runner beans out of the trug onto the paper. 'Do you fancy another cup?'

'I wouldn't say no.'

She went to the range and topped up the brown pot from the large iron kettle that sat there. She had a fine bust, Tonbridge thought with self-pity. Mrs Tonbridge's bust had never been a salient feature.

'I took her for a drink up the pub the other night.'

'Oh, yes?'

'She said that was too quiet. Course, it's not the same as the pubs in town.'

'It wouldn't be.' Mrs Cripps had been to London once or twice, but she'd never been to a pub there, and with Gordon dead, there was nobody to take her to one at home. 'What a shame!' she added. She wasn't one to pass remarks about other people, but the unpassed remark hung heavy and gratifying in the air. Tonbridge took the last rock cake and watched Mrs Cripps stringing beans. Her sleeves were rolled up revealing muscular arms, as white as marble in striking contrast to her hands, which were not white at all.

'She could go on the bus to Hastings. Look at the shops and that.'

'She could.' He left that suggestion in the air; he had already thought of it and discarded the notion. What he was hoping was that she would find it so quiet she'd go off home, back to town, and leave him in peace. He belched softly, and Mrs Cripps's nose twitched, but she pretended not to have heard. She decided to change the subject to something that didn't matter.

'So what do you think is going on with Hitler and all that?' she asked.

'If you want my opinion, Mrs Cripps, I say that it's all the newspapers and the politicians. A storm in a tea-cup;

scare-mongering. There's no cause for alarm. If Hitler did get above himself, there's always the Maginot Line.'

'Well, that's something,' she agreed. She had no idea what he was talking about. A line? What sort of line? Where? For the life of her she couldn't see what a line had to do with anything. She fell back onto social law. 'If you ask me, Mr Tonbridge, I think Hitler should keep himself to himself.'

'He *should*, Mrs Cripps, but don't forget, he's a foreigner. Well,' he got to his feet, 'this won't clean Mr Edward's guns. That was very nice, I must say. A welcome change. Someone to talk to,' he added, to make sure she realised that she was being compared favourably to some he could mention.

Mrs Cripps bridled and a huge kirby-grip fell onto the kitchen table.

'Any time,' she said shoving it back.

∞ ∞ ∞

In the evening, a neighbour of Zoë's mother rang up to say that she had had a heart attack and there wasn't really anybody to cope. So the next day, Rupert drove her to the station. 'I'm sure I shan't have to stay,' she said, meaning that she desperately didn't want to.

'You stay as long as you need. If it's easier to look after her in our house, you could move her there.' Since Zoë had married her mother had moved into a tiny flat. 'Oh, no! I don't think she would like that.' The thought of having to deal with her mother *and* their empty house without Ellen to see to things appalled her. 'I'm sure Mummy would far rather be in her own home.'

'Well, give me a ring to tell me how things are going. Or I'll ring you.' He remembered his mother-in-law's terror of toll calls. He got her suitcase into the ticket office and bought her ticket for her. 'Got enough money, darling?'

'I think so.'

He gave her another five pounds to be on the safe side. Then he kissed her: on her high cork-wedged shoes she reached higher above his shoulder than usual. They had had a row in bed the previous night about whether he should go into the firm or not. When she had found him truly undecided, she had tried to bully him and, for once, he had lost his temper and she had sulked until he apologised and then she had cried until she had got him to make it up in the usual way, but it hadn't been as much fun as usual. Now, she said, 'I know you'll do whatever is right,' and watched his stern, worn expression relax to a smile. He kissed her again and she said, 'I know you'll make the right decision.' Luckily the train came in, and he did not have to reply.

But when she had gone and he had got back to the car trying to banish an awful relief, he felt more confused than ever about the whole thing.

∞ ∞ ∞

Sharing a room with Angela was driving Louise and Nora round the *bend*: she either behaved like a film star or a schoolmistress and really they didn't know which was worse, so they decided to emigrate. And the only place to go was one of the attics, which you reached by climbing a steep little ladder that was concealed by a cupboard door. They went up and found themselves in a long room with a steeply sloping roof so that they couldn't stand upright except in the middle. At each end was a small lead-paned window encrusted with dirty cobwebs. The place smelled faintly of apples and the floor was thick with dead bluebottles. Louise felt that it was not very promising, but Nora was delighted by it. 'We'll scrub it all out, and whitewash the ceiling and walls and it will be wonderful!' So they did, and it was. They wore their bathing suits for the whitewashing because it was fearfully hot up there until one of the Brig's men, who were always working for him on building schemes, came and made the windows open and shut. It was while they were whitewashing together that they had a conversation that actually, she felt, changed Louise's life. She had been holding forth about her career to Nora who was a very good listener, and seemed suitably impressed with Louise's current ambition to play Hamlet in London.

'Won't you have to go into a repertory company – you know in Liverpool or Birmingham, or somewhere?'

'Oh, I don't think so. I think that would be boring. No, I'll go to some drama school – the Central or RADA, and then

I'll get noticed when they do the end-of-term plays. That's my plan.'

'I'm sure you will. You're awfully good.' Louise had acted some bits of Shakespeare to her last year in the summer and her Ophelia had reduced Nora to tears. 'Why particularly Hamlet?' she asked after a silence. 'Why not Ophelia?'

'It's such a tiny part. But Hamlet's the best part in the world. So of *course* it's my ambition.'

'I see.' She said it quite respectfully, did not argue or snub like most people.

'Meanwhile, of course, instead of getting on with my career, I have to go on wasting time with Miss Milliment. And they won't even tell me *when* they'll let me go to drama school. It's all very well for the others. Polly just wants to have her own house and put everything she's collected into it, and Clary is going to be a writer, so it doesn't matter what she does. I've done that bit. Let's have a rest.'

They went and sat by the little window and shared a Crunchie. There was a peaceful silence.

'What are you going to do?' Louise asked idly: she did not expect a very interesting reply.

'You promise not to tell anyone?'

'Promise.'

'Well – I'm not *absolutely* sure – but I think I'm going to be a nun.'

'A *nun*?'

'Yes, but not immediately. Mummy is sending me to a sort of cooking finishing-school place next summer, so I'll do that first. I've got to because it's Aunt Lena who is paying for it, and she gets awfully cross if people don't do what she wants.'

'But cooking – and whatever else you do at those places! What use will that be if you're going to be a nun?'

'You can do anything for the glory of God,' Nora answered serenely. 'It doesn't actually matter a bit what it is. Why don't you come too?'

At first it seemed an idiotic idea, but as Nora pointed out, Louise couldn't be a world-famous actress if she went on being homesick and couldn't ever leave home. 'And if you come with me, we could share a room, and you wouldn't feel anything like so bad. And I bet they'd let you, because domestic science is considered to be good for girls.'

'I'll think about it.' She could feel her heart beginning to thud and the back of her neck getting cold, and resolved not to think about it then. She diverted Nora by asking her a lot of questions about what being a nun entailed.

∞ ∞ ∞

On Friday morning Raymond telephoned Jessica to say that Aunt Lena had a chill and he was unable to leave her. This news, when he heard it, caused Christopher such relief that he threw up in the drive at Home Place on his way to collect Simon. It was wonderful: it meant that with luck they would have collected enough stuff to be gone before his father arrived, much easier than going under his nose. For he and Simon had decided to run away: Simon because he couldn't face his new school, and Christopher because he could no longer bear life at home. They had spent four feverish days carting stuff to Christopher's secret place in the woods – a small tent, since Christopher had given up the idea of trying to build a waterproof house, and any stores or equipment they could find about the place. They took things on the basis that once they were gone, they wouldn't be costing anyone anything, so it was quite fair to collect what was needed, provided they could do so without being noticed. Mrs Cripps couldn't think where the saucepan she used only for boiling eggs had walked to, nor the smaller kettle that was only used as a back-up to the big one. Eileen was missing cutlery – plate, thank goodness, not the silver – and two large tins that were used for biscuits and cake disappeared from the pantry. She had also noticed that however often she filled the sugar basins they were empty the next morning. Christopher made enormous lists of what they needed, and they crossed them off when they got the things. The worst blow had been the camp beds, which the Duchy kept in the gun room and which, just as they had been about to take them, had gone to Mill Farm for the girls' blasted attic idea. They had found an old Lilo in the shed with deck-chairs, but it had holes and they had to spend a lot of time mending it. On the other hand, Simon had discovered a store cupboard in

255

the kitchen regions crammed with jams, tins of sardines and corned beef, and every night, when Teddy was asleep – and luckily he slept like a log – he crept down and filled his new school laundry bag with these things. He got awfully tired because he had to stay awake for ages after Teddy dropped off and be sure the grown-ups had all gone to their rooms as well. The list never seemed to get any shorter, because they kept thinking of things that were or might be essential: tin opener, torch batteries, a pail – Christopher proposed milking cows in the adjoining fields very early in the morning before they were herded to the farm which Simon thought was absolutely wizard of him.

This morning they were going to get potatoes out of the shed where Mr McAlpine stored them. They both had rucksacks – admirable for the purpose, but Christopher warned that they would have to make several trips. 'We'll need them until we learn to make bread.' Simon, trying to imagine life without bread, felt so hungry that they had to stop for a bit while he ate four apples. They planned to store Simon's bicycle at the far end of the wood by the road, so that he could use it to get emergency rations if they ran out. The worst problem was money. Christopher had two pounds three and six, Simon only five bob. Taking money was stealing and Christopher was dead against it: they would have to learn to live off the land, he said, but Simon felt uneasy at the prospect. You wouldn't get chocolate or fizzy lemonade off the land, but he knew that these were unworthy thoughts. 'You have to be prepared to give things up,' Christopher said, but he *wanted* to get away from his parents whereas Simon was rather dreading that he would never see his mother again, or Polly, or Dad – who, except for Wills, might easily be stricken with grief – or even Wills. 'Supposing we have to go to the dentist?' he asked.

'If you were on a desert island, there wouldn't be a dentist. We'll just have to pull the bad teeth out. Better take some string for that.' Simon thought of Mr York who only had three or four teeth – although they were extra long in his upper jaw – but then he was old; it would take them years to get like that.

'What if there's a war?' he said when they had crammed the potatoes into the now crowded tent.

'I shall become a conscientious objector.'

'Wouldn't you have to go to London to do that? I mean, how would people know, otherwise?'

'Oh, I expect you just have to send in your name somewhere. I shall cross that bridge when I come to it,' he added rather grandly. They had fallen into the relationship where he was the leader and knew everything, a role to which he was not accustomed, and he was enjoying it too much to want his authority eroded.

'Perhaps schools stop if there is a war?' Simon suggested as they trudged back.

'I doubt it. Do you want to go through the wood today, or shall I?'

'I will.'

In order to fox possible spies about their whereabouts, Christopher had decreed that they should return to the house separately and from different directions. So far as he could see, nobody seemed in the least bit interested, but Simon ran up the east side of the wood behind the house, sat on the stile that was its entrance there, and obediently counted to two hundred before he walked – slowly – through it. In the afternoon, he would have to play squash with Teddy who was beginning to notice that he wasn't available for bicycle rides. Teddy did not very much like Christopher, whom he described as a bit weird, he was the person Christopher said must certainly have no idea of their plan. Simon had explained to Christopher that he couldn't get out of playing squash and sometimes tennis, and Christopher said quite right, and spent those times making bows and arrows for them and reorganising the list. Actually, he enjoyed playing squash – which he would soon be giving up for ever – but today he felt that what he would really like would be to have two helpings of everything for lunch and then go to sleep.

∞ ∞ ∞

Every morning when she woke up, Angela stood by the window of the bedroom that she now, mercifully, had to herself. By leaning out, she could just see the blue smoke that came out of the kitchen chimney of Home Place three hundred yards up the hill – she had carefully paced the distance. Then she would pray – fervently – aloud, but under her breath, 'O God, don't let her come back today,' and so far God hadn't. Five days ago, she had been a completely different person; now she had utterly changed, and would never be the same again. Now, sometimes, when absence and longing were locked together, she could almost sense the nostalgia of the old feelings of boredom, the endless weeks and months – years, even – she had been through of waiting for something, or attending to stupid little details because she could find nothing worth being serious about. The old, recurrent daydream where Leslie Howard, Robert Taylor or Monsieur de Croix (the French family doctor in Toulouse) had knelt at her feet, or towered over her, their undying passion wrenched from them while she sat in various romantic dresses that she did not wear in ordinary life, gracefully accepting their homage, bestowing her hand (her *hand*, simply!) whereupon the dream dissolved with their speechless, reverent gratitude – *that* old dream withered to a ridiculous and embarrassing myth. She could remember all that, and remember, too, that then she had eaten and slept and gone through her days in the tedious serenity of ignorance. She could not regret that infantile past when she had not had the faintest idea of what life was about. But now its whole meaning was feverishly clear; she existed for every second of every day in a trembling, humble delirium that she contrived, almost with brilliance, utterly to conceal. Jessica had noticed that – thank goodness – her eldest daughter had seemed to have stopped sulking and, at Home Place, where Angela spent as much time as possible, the Duchy found her manners and general desire to please quite charming. The first day she had walked slowly up the hill to Home Farm she had hung about on the front lawn, just waiting to see what might happen. Teddy and Clary and Polly were playing the overtaking game on their bicycles round and round the house. The third time round, Clary fell off trying to overtake Teddy.

'Ouch! It's not fair!' she called after Teddy. 'You squeezed me against the porch!'

Angela looked at the large dirty graze that was beading with blood. 'We'd better go and find your father. You ought to wash it.'

'He's out. He's taken Zoë to the station 'cos her mother's ill.'

'Honestly, Clary, we'd better get some iodine. I'll do it for you.'

This was Polly, who had arrived on the scene. 'It's kind of you, but you wouldn't know where the things were,' she said to Angela, as she led Clary into the house.

So Angela was free to leave. She started walking down the hill, past Mill Farm towards Battle. She walked slowly, as she didn't want to get too hot and have a shiny nose. All the same, she was quite tired by the time Rupert's car slowed up and he hailed her.

'Where are you off to?'

'Just going for a walk.'

'Hop in. Have a drive instead.' He pushed open the door, and she stepped demurely in. It's easy! she thought that first morning.

They drove back up the hill in silence, but when they reached the gates of Home Place he said, 'I don't feel like going back to the house now. Why don't we go a bit further? But I'll let you out if you have better things to do.'

'I'll come with you,' she said, making it sound like a concession.

He seemed to take it as such, because he said, 'That's good of you. Actually, I've a problem and I could do with someone to talk to.'

This was so unexpected and so flattering to her that she could think of no answer mature and offhand enough. She gave him a sidelong glance: he was frowning lightly, eyes fixed on the road. He wore a dark blue flannel shirt open at the neck so that she could see his long bony throat. She wondered when he would start to tell her whatever it was, and what on earth it might be that he and Zoë—

'I'm taking you to see a cracking view,' he said.

'Oh, good,' she answered, and smoothed her apple-green voile over her knees.

When they got there, it was much what she had expected. She could never see the point of views: they simply seemed to mean an awful lot more of whatever you could see when there wasn't one, in this case miles of hop fields, and ordinary fields and woods and a few old farmhouses. He parked the car on the verge, and they walked to a gate that had a stile beside it. He invited her to sit on the stile, and he leant on the gate beside her and stared and stared. She watched him staring.

'Marvellous, isn't it?' he said at last.

'Yes, marvellous.'

'Want a cigarette?'

'Please.'

When he had lit them, he looked at her, and said, 'You're a very composed person, aren't you? Very restful to be with.'

'That depends,' she answered. She did not wish to be restful to be with; yet she longed for him to go on talking about her – to discover the fascinating person she was planning to be for him.

'The thing is, that my father wants me to chuck teaching art and go into the firm. And, of course, if I do that, it would be rather burning my boats from the painting point of view. On the other hand, the teaching seems to take up so much time and energy, that I don't get much painting done anyway so it seems a bit unfair, to everybody, not to opt for a much more comfortable life. What do you think?'

'Goodness!' she said at last, after trying to think about it and utterly failing. 'What does Zoë think?'

'Oh, *she's* all for it. Of course I can see her point of view. It's certainly not much fun for her being the poor relation, and she's never been particularly interested in painting. And then there are the children . . . ' His voice tailed off and he looked deeply uncertain.

'But what about you? I mean, what do *you* want?' Her self-possession had returned, and one thing was quite clear to her: she wasn't going to be on Zoë's side.

'That's it. I don't seem to want anything very much – or, at least, not *enough*. That's why I think I ought to—'

'Do what other people want?'

'I suppose so.'

'Then you'll never find out, will you? And, anyway, how do you know you could keep it up?'

'Wise girl! Of course, I don't.'

'Couldn't you stop teaching and simply be a painter?'

'No, not possibly. I've sold precisely four pictures in my life and three of those were to the family. I couldn't keep three people, not counting me, on that.'

'And you couldn't join the family firm and paint in your spare time?'

'No. You see, the trouble about being a Sunday painter is that Sundays are for the children – and Zoë, of course.'

'If I was Zoë,' she began carefully, 'I'd look after the children on Sundays. I'd want you to paint. If you love somebody, you want them to do what they want.' As she heard herself saying that, she felt that it was probably true.

But he simply threw away his cigarette stub and laughed. Then, when he saw those enormous blue eyes turning reproachful, he said, 'You're a perfect sweetie, and I'm sure you mean it, but it isn't as easy as that.'

'I never said it was *easy*,' she retorted; she did not like being called a sweetie.

But Rupert, in a situation more familiar to him than she could possibly know, felt he must make amends.

'I'm sorry. I really didn't mean to sound patronising. I think you are a wonderfully clear-headed person, wise beyond your years, and on top of that,' he touched her face lightly, 'you are remarkably beautiful. Will that do?' He looked searchingly at her with a small apologetic smile.

It was like a thunderbolt – she felt literally struck by love. Her heart jolted, and stopped, then made some wild, irregular rapid movements; she was breathless, dizzy, unable to see, and when his face became clear again, she felt a sense of unutterable weakness – as though her limbs were dissolving and she would fall from the stile and melt into the grass and never be able to stand at all again.

' . . . don't you think we should?'

'Yes. What?'

'Go back to lunch. You didn't hear me, did you? You were miles away.'

She got carefully, clumsily, off the stile and followed him to the car. Her face, where his fingers had touched it, burned.

Driving home, he remarked that it had been jolly nice of her to listen to his boring old problems and what about her? What was she planning to do? It was the opening that earlier she had craved, in order that she might fascinate and impress and entrap him. Now it was too late: she was unable to be anything but her new self, about which there seemed to be nothing she could, or ever would, dare to say.

∞ ∞ ∞

'Let me see . . . it's the fifteenth, you were due on the first?'

'On the second, actually. But, of course, I missed the one before. And honestly, Bob, I really don't feel that I *can*—'

'Now, now, we don't want to cross that bridge till we get to it. You pop behind the screen and divest yourself of your nether garments and we'll have a look at you. Mark you, it's probably too early to be sure.'

But I *am* sure, Villy thought, as she did as Dr Ballater had suggested. The family joke among the sisters-in-law that if they were in doubt about being pregnant a drive with Tonbridge would settle the matter, since he invariably drove them at twelve miles an hour approximately five weeks after conception, proved not to be a joke to her that morning. Tonbridge had driven her with such a lugubrious slowness that she had been afraid of missing the train. All the same, she lay down on the hard little high bed with feverish hope. And if the worst came to the worst, Bob was not only a very good GP, who had delivered both Louise and Lydia, but a *friend*: Edward and he played golf in the winter on Sundays, and they dined regularly in each other's houses. If anyone would help, surely he would?

'Well,' he said some uncomfortable minutes later, 'I cannot be *sure*, of course, but I think it's very likely you're right.'

Villy with a suddenness that confounded her, burst into tears. She had meant to be calm and rationally persuasive, now she found herself sobbing, ridiculously half-clothed with her bag and a handkerchief left on the chair by his desk. But he brought her the bag without being asked and told her to get dressed and they would have a chat. When she joined him, he had mysteriously produced cups of tea and gave her a cigarette.

'Now,' he said. 'Let us suppose that you *are* pregnant. Is it your age that's worrying you?'

'Well – yes, that among other things.'

'Because I'm not in the least worried about that. You're a

healthy woman and you've had three healthy children. It isn't as though you're starting at . . . forty, is it?'

'Forty-two. But it isn't just that, I *feel* too old to start all over again – besides it wouldn't be much fun for it, it would be like an only child.' She wanted to say, 'I simply don't want another baby at any price,' but he was a man as well as her doctor and would be most unlikely to understand. 'I'm sure Edward doesn't want any more children,' she added.

'Oh, I can't see Edward kicking up a fuss. He can afford it, which is the main thing. I take it you haven't talked to him, but I'll bet you he'll be pleased as punch when you do.' There was a short silence, while both of them separately wondered what on earth to say next.

'I suppose I couldn't be – starting on the change – could I?'

'No hot flushes? Night sweats?' She shook her head, blushing at the disgusting notions.

'Not feeling depressed?'

'Well, yes – I am about this, I really and truly don't feel *up* to another baby.'

'Well, we can't always choose these things. And I've known many women who thought they didn't want another and discovered how wrong they were when it arrived.'

'So you don't think that there is anything – at all – that I could do?'

'I do not,' he said sharply, 'and I hope I'm not reading your mind, my dear, but just in case I am let me tell you two things. I would do a great deal for you, but I would never even contemplate helping you get rid of a baby. I've had women in this room who would have given everything they possess to be in your position. And I'm also telling you not to try and find some other means. I've also had women in here wrecked by backstreet abortions. I want you to promise me to do nothing at all, to come back here in six weeks when we shall be able to confirm your condition or not as the case may be.' He leant over the desk and took one of her hands. 'Villy. I'll see you through this, I promise you. Now, will you promise me?'

So she had to, really.

Seeing her out and feeling the need to neutralise the slight feeling of tension, he asked her whether Edward was worried about the crisis and she told him that she didn't think so, 'Although I haven't seen him because I'm in Sussex with the children, and he couldn't come down last weekend.'

'Is that so? Well, you keep the children there – far the best place for them. Mary has my two in Scotland, and it has crossed my mind to leave them there for a few weeks, till we know where we stand.'

'Are you worried, then?'

'No, no. I'm sure our unflappable Prime Minister will sort things out. I have to admire him taking his first flight at sixty-nine. And I don't suppose he speaks a word of German. It's quite impressive. Look after yourself, my dear. And mind what I've said.'

Outside, she stood irresolute: she had told Jessica and her mother that she would be catching the four-twenty back to Battle, but she was a short walk from Lansdowne Road, and she felt a sudden craving for her own house, blessedly empty of relations, with the prospect of tea and a rest, and then, a quiet evening with Edward, to whom, she felt, she might even be able to talk about the whole thing. So she walked through the large Ladbroke Square, empty now of its perambulators and nannies and children for the summer, to Ladbroke Grove, where she had seen straw laid across the wide road because an old gentleman had been dying at the large house on the corner. She walked past Hugh and Sybil's house, shuttered and looking very closed up, although she knew Hugh used it in the week, and then turned right down Ladbroke Road. As the back of her home came into view, she experienced a surge of relief: the country was all very well, but really she adored London, and particularly this house. Edna would be there, if it was not her afternoon off, and she could have her tea and a bath. It had been an oppressive, sunless day, and she felt hot and sticky.

When she had let herself into the quiet house, she remembered that it was Wednesday and that therefore Edna would almost certainly be out. I'll have to make my own tea, she thought, and wondered if she'd be able to find everything. There were two stacks of letters on the hall table, but they all seemed to be for Edward: it was naughty of him to let them pile up like that. She decided to ring him up at once to tell him she was here, in case, on his own, he decided to play billiards at his club or something of the sort. The study, where the telephone was, was looking rather dusty and by the telephone there was a large ashtray, full of Edward's cigarette stubs, which looked as though it hadn't been emptied for days. She hoped the rest of the house hadn't become like that or she would have to sack Edna. When she got through to the office and asked for Edward there was a pause, and then Miss Seafang answered his telephone, and said that Mr Edward had left at lunch-time saying he would not be back. She was ever so sorry, but she did not know where he had gone. She would tell him in the morning that Mrs Edward had called and get him to call Mill Farm first thing. Then she rang off before Villy could tell her that she was in London. Not that it matters, she thought. I might as well be there as here. Baulked of the evening she had just started looking forward to, she felt thoroughly cross about everything. She wandered into the drawing room where the blinds were down. It was incredibly stuffy and smelled of smoke and some other stale scent that when she drew up a blind, and saw a vase of half-dead carnations, she assumed came from them. Really, Edna was *not* doing her job at all: she clearly needed Phyllis to keep her up to the mark. She decided against tea, and then thought she would have a rather large gin and tonic and drink it in the bath. Then she thought she would ring Edward's club, in case he was there. He wasn't. The nicest bath was in Edward's dressing room, which was in an awful mess. It had dawned on her that Edna must have left – possibly only that morning – or surely Edward would have told her, for even she would not have left damp bath towels all over the floor, the dressing-room bed unmade, and discarded shirts and pants and socks of Edward's everywhere. The whole thing was shocking. Poor Edward, coming home after a hard day's work to this! She would have to sack Edna supposing she materialised to be sacked, and send Phyllis up tomorrow to look after him. She picked up the towels and hung them on the towel-horse, but decided to leave the bed, as Edward would be sleeping in their bedroom. It seemed odd of him not to be sleeping there, anyway. She would have her bath and change, and then clear up his clothes.

After a good soak, and her drink, she felt much better. Of course, gin and hot baths were supposed to be one of

265

the good old-fashioned ways of bringing on a miscarriage, but she recognised that there was something half-hearted (or craven) about her attitude to that. Really, she simply wanted *not* to be pregnant: Dr Ballater had somehow made her feel uncomfortable about her wittingly achieving such a state. The thought of talking to Hermione about it now seemed insurmountably difficult. Hermione might easily recommend someone, but she would have no idea of how safe or discreet he might be. She wondered how many of the friends – well, people she and Edward dined, or went to the theatre or danced with – had ever been in this predicament? There must have been some, but the trouble was that it was a subject that absolutely none of them ever mentioned, let alone discussed. The assumption was that you had as many babies as you wanted and then used birth control and hoped for the best. She could think of several women who had had what were described as 'afterthoughts', and their friends always said how lovely, and how easy they would find it now they knew all the ropes.

If she had stuck to her career, things would have been different. She knew, when she had been in the company, that girls had become pregnant, but such was the spirit of dedication – she remembered bleeding feet, the performances when you danced in agonising pain from torn muscles, the lying on your bed between rehearsals because Diaghilev hadn't paid the company for the third week running and you were living on a pint of milk and two rolls a day – that a backstreet abortion would have been regarded as simply another hazard of the life. But when she married, she had left that society for one where women seemed not to be dedicated to anything but having children and dealing with the servants. Life was one great man trap, she thought, and sex, which obviously had to be pretty trapping for women to contemplate it at all considering what it actually came down to – hours and hours over the years of painful, unpleasant, and ultimately dull intimacies of an inexplicably unsatisfactory nature – was simply something that one exchanged for the comfort and security of being a couple and having in other ways a pleasant time . . . after all, look at the unmarried women she knew! She surely wouldn't want to join that patronised, commiserated-over band! Even if she had continued with her dancing she would be past it now, or past her best at any rate. She thought of Miss Milliment. No one could ever have wanted to marry Miss Milliment, who had lived out her life, ugly, alone, and extremely poor, and when the children stopped having lessons with her she would be even poorer. She must do something about Miss Milliment. She could have her stay in Sussex in the holidays, which might be difficult as Edward was not keen on her and she would have to dine with them, but really she deserved a holiday without any expense. She would talk to Sybil and see whether she would help. The last time she had talked to Edward he had pointed out that Miss Milliment was earning seven pounds ten a week, three times the amount of a bus conductor who probably had a family to keep. 'And she's a woman,' he had added, as though this made her a less expensive receptacle for shelter, food or clothing. 'I'll definitely do something,' she told herself; she felt fortunate, guilty and a little frightened, as excursions beyond her own discontent so often made her.

By now she had dressed in the cream foulard with a navy spot: a cool little frock with a short jacket to match – the sort of frock that, Hermione had pointed out, one could have any sort of evening in, had added some powder and a touch of dry rouge and a discreet lipstick, had put on her wrist-watch, changed bags. She did not feel like tidying Edward's clothes, and really longed for a second gin, but this was probably not wise. She filled her cigarette case and went downstairs. She would try Edward's club once more, and if he wasn't there, she would ring Hugh and see if he would take her out to dinner.

He wasn't at his club. Hugh, however, was back from the office – just about to have a bath, he said. Nothing wrong in the country, was it? She explained that she was in London.

'Edward seems to have disappeared,' she said. 'Miss Seafang said he left the office at lunch-time, and she had no idea where he went. He's not at his club. You don't happen to know, do you?'

There was a pause, and then Hugh said, 'No idea. Look. Why don't you have dinner with me? You will? Good. I'll be round to fetch you in an hour.'

She was putting the receiver back on its hook when she heard the front door opening and Edward's voice and then a woman laughing. Who on earth, she thought, as she went into the hall.

In the hall was Edward, and standing beside him was a tall, dark, rather glamorous-looking woman whom she had never seen in her life before. She was wearing a loose white coat slung over her shoulders, and as they saw her, they moved apart: Edward's right arm, that had been concealed by the coat, came into view as he said: 'Good Lord! Villy? I had no idea you were coming up!' he came forward and kissed her.

'I just came up for the day. Then I thought I might as well stay.'

'Splendid! Oh, this is Diana Mackintosh, I don't think you've met. Diana's husband had that marvellous shoot in Norfolk I told you about. We were having lunch and he's had to go off to Scotland, poor dear, so we saw him off and I brought Diana home for a drink.'

While he was saying this, a thought so horrible came into her mind that she was momentarily stunned, then instantly felt incredulous, ashamed that something so treacherous and unspeakable could ever even have occurred to her. As she led Mrs Mackintosh into the drawing room apologising for its state, pulling up the blinds, removing the dead carnations to a far corner, she tried resolutely to pretend to herself that she had never had such a thought. 'I think our wretched housemaid must have disappeared,' she finished.

'Oh, aren't they tiresome?' She had a charming smile, and a small streak of white hair that was dressed in fashionable horn-like curls round her head. She was about thirty-eight, Villy thought.

'Do you live in Norfolk, Mrs Mackintosh?'

'Oh, please call me Diana. No, in London, actually. Angus manages the shoot there for his elder brother. He's gone to Scotland to fetch the older children back for school.'

'How many do you have?' Information was soothing.

'Three. Ian is ten, Fergus is eight, and then there's Jamie, who is three months.' An afterthought, thought Villy. I wonder if she wanted him.

Edward was back with a tray of drinks. Diana said, 'I was telling your wife about Angus kindly fetching the children. They spent the summer with their grandmother in Easter Ross.'

'Lucky little beggars,' Edward said. 'Cocktail in order for everyone?'

'Just one. I mustn't stay, have to get back to Jamie.'

A three-month-old baby. I hope I look as good as that three months afterwards. Edward, shaking the cocktails, said, 'Yes, Angus gave me such a marvellous lunch, I felt the least I could do was take him to the station – Godawful places. Euston was like a Victorian beehive.'

'King's Cross,' Diana said, quite sharply, then, with her appealing smile, said more gently, 'It was King's Cross. Didn't you notice?'

'Edward doesn't know one railway station from another,' said Villy. 'He never goes on trains. Or buses,' she added.

'I drove one in the General Strike.'

'That could hardly provide you with a general knowledge of public transport. No, thanks, I don't smoke.' Edward had lit his and Villy's cigarettes, and noticing he hadn't offered Diana one, Villy had proffered her case. There was a short silence while they sipped their drinks, and Villy wondered why she was feeling *odd*, as she put it, again. Aloud, she said, 'Darling, has Edna abandoned you? The house is an awful mess.'

'Her mother's ill, so I let her go home to look after things. Forgot to tell you.'

'Oh. When will she be back?'

'Don't know. Didn't ask her, I'm afraid.'

There was another silence, then Edward, draining his glass, said, 'I wonder how old Chamberlain is getting on. I must say things have come to a pretty pass when a British prime minister has to travel all that way to persuade a foreign feller to be reasonable.'

'I quite agree,' Diana said. 'It really ought to be the other way round. Did you see that cartoon of a huge dove carrying an umbrella in its mouth? I mean, we shouldn't be *asking*, we should be telling Mr Hitler where he gets off.'

'That's perfectly true. But I expect "ask" is Foreign Office for "tell", don't you, Edward?'

'Well, it's all rather beyond me, but I expect you're right. But a very sensible bloke at the club said that the Czechs haven't got any choice, really, so I don't think we need worry unduly.'

The atmosphere had lightened. Diana now got to her feet, and said, 'I really must go. Thanks awfully for the drink.'

Edward said, 'Shall I run you home?'

'I wouldn't hear of it. I'll pick up a cab.'

Villy said, 'We could ring for one. The rank's just up the road.'

'No, truly, the walk would do me good.'

She had left her white coat in the hall. When Edward had put it over her shoulders – it was too hot to wear it, she said – she turned to Villy saying thank you so much it was lovely to meet you. She had a wonderful complexion and her fine eyes were the colour of dark lavender. A striking woman. 'Turn left and the rank's at the next crossroads,' Villy said.

'Thanks. Goodbye.'

'Goodbye,' said Edward and Villy almost in unison.

'She seemed charming. What's he like?'

'Angus? Oh, he's a good sort. Bit of an idler though. Darling, what brought you up? You never told me.'

'Oh, I wanted to do some shopping, and I popped in to see Bob Ballater.'

'Nothing wrong, I hope?'

'Just a woman's thing.'

'Well, now you're here where would you like to dine? The Hungaria?' He knew she loved the place and the music.

'That would be lovely. Oh! God, I nearly forgot! When I thought I'd lost you, I rang Hugh, and he said he'd take me out to dinner. He'll be round any minute.' Now she wouldn't be able to tell him at dinner.

Edward frowned. He had emptied the cocktail shaker and subsequently his glass. 'Damn! We can't put the old boy off.'

'Why would you want to?'

'Well, he's obsessed with what he persists in calling the crisis. Says we're prostrating ourselves, or prostituting ourselves, I forget which, anyway, he won't keep off the subject and you know how he can argue.'

'Well, we could go to Bentley's and then to a flick. He won't be able to talk through that.'

'Good idea! I'll nip up and have a bath.'

'Darling, I'll send Phyllis up tomorrow to look after you. Your dressing room's too ghastly for words.'

He made a face. 'Is it? Well, as you know, I'm always a bit slack about my housework. Make us all another drink. Hugh'll probably want whisky.' And he bounded upstairs.

They went to Bentley's, where Villy and Edward ate oysters and Hugh smoked salmon, and to Leicester Square to see *The Thirty-nine Steps* with Robert Donat, which they all enjoyed. The subject of the crisis was hardly touched upon; the Mackintoshes were mentioned, but Hugh did not know them. He was very sweet to Villy, she thought. He did not say very much to Edward. By the time they had dropped Hugh off and got home Edward pronounced that he was dog tired, asleep on his feet, and it was clearly too late to start up the pros and cons of adding to the family. So she did not tell him anything, but decided to wait until after her next visit to the doctor.

∞ ∞ ∞

The following weekend, secure in the knowledge that Waldo's tour was cancelled and that Evie would therefore be occupied, Sid accepted the Duchy's invitation to stay at Home Place. 'You don't mind sharing your room with her, darling, do you?' the Duchy had said to her daughter. The house was full to the brim as two of her unmarried sisters, deemed to be unable to cope with the Situation, as it was now called in the family, had been collected from Stanmore by Tonbridge, who, to his enormous satisfaction, had succeeded in ridding himself of Mrs Tonbridge on the same journey. He had pointed out that if she was wanting to get home, it would be nicer to go in the car from door to door, than by train and Underground to Kentish Town. 'And don't ever ask me to put up with anything like *that* again,' she had said when he deposited her. He wouldn't, not on his life he wouldn't. It was with a light heart that he collected the two old ladies from Cedar House, packed the boot with their buckram suitcases that had the battered initials of their father on them, and tucked them in. They wore jersey suits and carried holland bags filled with revolting embroidery and a Thermos leaking Bovril. They sat with the bear rug over their bony knees and he drove them sedately down to Sussex, with them making the quarter-hourly ritual remarks about how lovely the country was looking and asking after his wife and child to show that they were good with servants. He didn't mind any of it: a life both soothing and exciting with Mrs Cripps seemed now to be on the cards.

Sybil and Villy had an earnest but indeterminate discussion about whether, if the Situation got worse, the boys should go back to school or not. Sybil thought that Hugh might agree that they shouldn't; Villy knew that Edward would think that they should. They resolved to ring the school and see what the general form was.

Lady Rydal, who had now been ensconced for nearly a week at Mill Farm and sat sighing in the largest armchair all day doing nothing whatever, said that if there was another war, she felt that the best thing she could do was to put her head in a gas oven. 'There isn't any gas in this house, Grania,' Nora had said. 'But I suppose you could electrocute yourself, only I think that needs one to have more technical knowledge.' This caused Jessica and Villy to have to leave the room, they were laughing so much. 'Honestly,' Jessica said, 'if there was a war, Mummy would think it was entirely done to ruin her life. A sort of personal last straw.'

'There won't be, though, will there?' Villy began, but at that moment, Nora joined them. 'It's all right,' she said, 'you needn't be cross. I told her it would be best to pray for peace. She had to agree with that. God comes in very handy with old people.'

On the Saturday evening, Clary, who had been flushed and grumpy all day, was pronounced Coming Down with Something by Ellen, who had a scene with her about answering back. Her temperature was taken: it was 101., so she was put to bed and Dr Carr called. Simon went to the squash court by himself where he prayed aloud that she had measles, which, he felt, might get him out of everything. As Zoë was still away Clary had Rupert and Aunt Rachel, who made her some lemonade. Dr Carr said that whatever it was would doubtless develop the next day and she must stay in bed. 'Which I would be, anyway, as it's night time,' Clary said to Polly rather peevishly. 'He surely can't think I go to nightclubs.' But Polly, who was being kind and understanding, said he was just being on the safe side, 'which grown-ups usually are,' she added. 'I'll read to you, if you like,' she offered. It had crossed her mind that she might be a heavenly kind nurse when she grew up. But Clary said she would rather read to herself. When her father came to say good night to her, she told him that she thought he ought to stay being a painter and not go into the firm. Rupert, who had by now – apart from Angela – consulted Rachel, Sybil, Jessica and Villy (all for his going into the firm) and Louise and Nora (against), which had left him as ignorant of his own mind in the matter as he had been a week ago, said that her opinion was extremely helpful to him and he would think about it. 'Oh, Dad! I do love it when you talk to me as though I was a person!'

'Don't I always?'

She shook her head. 'Quite a lot of the time you treat me like a child. I do so *loathe* it. When I have children I shall treat them wonderfully – as though,' she searched for the most adult profession she could imagine, 'as though they were bank managers.'

'Would you, indeed! Well, they don't get treated so well. People either fawn on them saying things like, "Oh, Mr Pinstripe, *could* you let me have another three pounds?" Or they hate them and keep as far away as possible.'

'Really! Is that what you do? Both those things?'

'Both of them.'

'Poor old Dad. It must be awful getting old and not having enough money. If I were you, I'd look for a nice second-hand bath chair while you've got the time.'

'Right, I'll do that. Now I'm going to tuck you up.'

'Don't! I'm absolutely boiling. Dad! Tell Ellen I'm sorry. And could I have a drink of water? And could you ask Polly to come up? And, Dad, will you come and see me after you've had your dinner? To see if I'm all right because I might not be?'

'Yes,' he said, and went.

That night Sid sat on the side of Rachel's bed and held her in her arms. They had talked all day whenever they were alone: on the way back from the station, after luncheon, when they had gone for a long walk and found a rickety tent in the woods by a stream, which they did not explore as Rachel said it had an air of secrecy about it, that it should be left to itself. 'I expect it belongs to Teddy,' she said, 'he's a very camping sort of boy.' And then, after tea, they slipped away again, and sat in the field beyond the wood by the house. It was an overcast evening, and autumn was in the air. They talked about going to the Lake District together – at Easter, perhaps – and whether Sid would get a better-paid job if she taught part time at two

273

schools instead of one, and whether she should try and buy a little second-hand car. Rachel longed to give her this, but she wouldn't hear of it. I should just have done it, Rachel thought. And they talked about Mr Chamberlain's impending second visit – to Germany, this time – and whether appeasement was the best policy. Rachel thought that it must be, but Sid was concerned for the Czechs whom she thought were in line for a rotten deal. 'After all,' Rachel argued, 'there wouldn't *be* such a place if it hadn't been for the treaty of Versailles.'

But Sid had retorted: 'Exactly. Therefore, we are responsible for their sovereignty. Treaties can start wars just as easily as they stop them.' Then she smiled and said, 'I know you think it's my left-wing politics that is making me argue with you, but it isn't. A lot of people on your side think the same.'

'The awful thing is that whatever we think won't make the slightest difference. I find that very frightening.'

'If there was a war, you wouldn't stay in London, would you?'

'I expect so. There's Evie. What else could I do?'

'Oh, I don't know. But I *do* know that I couldn't bear you to be there and me stuck down here.'

'Which you would be?'

'I imagine so. Perhaps you and Evie could have the Ton-bridges' cottage. That would be an answer.'

'Evie would be impossible.' They were on to Evie again, and after the conversation had completed a circle they gave it up and strolled back to the house.

Dinner, and Sid had played bridge with Hugh and Sybil and Rupert while Rachel sewed and watched them. She loved to see Sid getting on with her family and every now and then their eyes met fleetingly, and both were nourished by the contact.

Now they were alone for the night, and there was a faint tension in the room. Rachel had wanted Sid to have her bed while she slept on the narrow little child's bed that had been set the other side of the room, but Sid would not let her. What Sid wanted, and in the end obtained, was several hours of lying beside her love, pretending that this was all she wanted, a torturing pleasure that she would not have missed for worlds, but the secret vistas that it opened up remained secret, and in the early hours of the morning, when Rachel was contentedly asleep, she crept to the narrow little bed and took imaginary recompense. Afterwards, when she had wanted to sleep, to sink into oblivion and wake to a new day, she could not. She lay thinking about Rachel, who had given her so much but could not give her everything; whose gentle, affectionate nature was enclosed by an impenetrable wall of innocence. She had once told Sid that she knew that she would never have children, since she could not endure what would have to happen first. 'The idea of it revolts me,' she had said beginning a painful blush. 'I suppose some women manage to shut it out – when it happens, you know – but I know that I couldn't. And the idea that – the man – actually likes it, simply makes me feel worse about them.' Somebody, whom she had thought she was fond of, had once kissed her. 'But it wasn't an ordinary kiss – it was disgusting.' She had tried to laugh then, and said, 'I'm just no good at bodies. I think my own is bad enough, and I don't want anything to do with other people's.' Sid had remained silent: the revelation then had been new to her, and Rachel had slipped her arm into Sid's, they were walking in Regent's Park, and said, 'That's why I so love being with you, Sid darling. We can be together and none of that ever comes into it.'

And it will always be like that, Sid now thought, and I could not even give her a child. *And* I love her and shall never want anyone more – or else. She wept before she slept.

∞ ∞ ∞

On Monday, Clary was covered with spots and was pronounced by Dr Carr to have chicken pox. When Louise heard this, she called a meeting to be held at the fallen-down tree in the wood behind Home Place. She, Nora, Teddy, Polly, Simon and Christopher were asked to come, and Neville and Lydia and Judy got to hear of it and went.

'We didn't ask you or you or you to the meeting,' Louise said, as these last three stood uncertainly on the outskirts.

'You said children's meeting, and we're children,' Lydia said.

'Anyway, we're here,' Neville said, 'so I would have thought that was that.'

'Oh, let them stay,' Nora said.

'Promise never to tell the grown-ups anything that is said by this tree on this Monday, 20 September 1938?'

'OK.'

'Don't say OK like that. Say, we solemnly promise.'

The girls repeated this, but Neville said, 'I laughingly promise. It's just the same,' he said when Lydia looked shocked.

'Right. Well, what we're here for is Clary's chicken pox. Hands up anybody who's had chicken pox.'

Nobody put up their hand.

'The thing is, if we organise it properly, we could all be in quarantine or having it for the rest of the term. Do you see?'

'Gosh, I do!' Teddy exclaimed. 'We couldn't go back to our schools.'

'Exactly. We'd *have* to stay here until the Christmas holidays, and then there'd be them.'

'How do we catch it?' Polly asked. 'I mean, how can we be sure?'

'You've probably got it already, as you're sharing a room with Clary. It's quite infectious, it's quite a long quarantine.'

'We all go and hug her!' Judy said. 'Would that do it?'

'No. We don't all go. If we did, we might all get it at once and that would be hopeless. Two of us go. And one of them had better be you, Polly, as you're the most likely next one.'

'Wait a minute,' Teddy said. 'Perhaps we don't *want* not to go back to school.' Much as he enjoyed the holidays, he was quite looking forward to getting back into the squash team as he'd practised so much.

'*I* don't want chicken pox,' Christopher said, 'and nor do you, Simon, do you?'

Simon blushed, and squashed a fir cone with his sandshoe. 'It depends . . . no – no, not really,' he added. He had decided, cravenly, he knew, to go and hug Clary on the quiet, every night, to be on the safe side.

'Does it *hurt*?' Lydia asked. 'I mean, could people die from it? Can grown-ups get it?'

'They *can*, but usually they've had it.'

'Anyway, people don't die of it, Lydia,' Louise said kindly, remembering Lydia's besetting anxiety.

The meeting ended with a list being arranged of the order in which they were to hang over Clary, and with instructions to do this as secretly as possible.

'*She*'ll have to know, so it can't be completely absolutely secret,' Neville pointed out.

'Of course she'll know. But she'll be on our side.'

∞ ∞ ∞

On Tuesday the Brig, having measured the squash court, went to London and bought twenty-four camp beds from the Army & Navy Stores, to be transported, immediately, in one of the firm's lorries to Sussex. He did not mention this to anyone.

∞ ∞ ∞

On Wednesday, Sybil and Villy woke up to the fact that Clary's chicken pox meant that all the children, excepting Christopher, were in quarantine. They rang up Teddy's and Simon's school to inform them of this. Villy thought it might be worth writing to Miss Milliment, who was not on the telephone, to see whether she could come down to Sussex and give lessons. The Duchy approved of the idea, although she said that Miss Milliment would have to be put in the Tonbridges' cottage. 'Tonbridge can sleep in the boot room quite well,' she added tranquilly. Rachel said how sweet the children all were to Clary, always going to see if she wanted anything – it really was rather touching. 'More a case of being rather catching,' Rupert said, coming in on the end of this. 'The little blighters are quite cunning.' Villy went back to Mill Farm and told Jessica about the Milliment plan. 'And Nora and Judy could join in,' she said.

'Oh, darling, you don't want us to stay, surely?' Jessica had spent the morning wondering what on earth she had better do. Raymond was still stuck with Aunt Lena, who now looked as though she was dying – extremely slowly and painlessly, as she had always lived. Taking the children back to Hendon and then coping with chicken pox and Angela's future seemed, after these halcyon weeks, a hideous prospect.

'Of course you must stay. At least until things settle down.'

'What about Mummy?'

'I suppose we'd better ask her what she wants.'

Lady Rydal said that it didn't matter in the least what she wanted and they must do with her as they would. Bryant, her cook, would have returned from her holiday, and Bluitt (her house-parlourmaid) would be back next week, so possibly it might be better if she stayed until they were both back as one on their own made heavy weather of looking after one poor old woman.

'That's it, then.' Villy made a face when she was alone with Jessica. 'Edward said he didn't think he could wear another weekend with her, but he'll just have to.'

'After all, he missed one by having to work,' Jessica pointed out.

'Yes, he did, didn't he? Any news of Raymond?'

'I think I'd better ring him tonight. Just to see how Aunt Lena is doing.'

∞ ∞ ∞

On Thursday, in London, Hugh was waiting for Edward who was late for lunch. As it was Edward's club, he had to wait for a drink, and wandered to the large round table that was strewn with newspapers and magazines. The *Daily Express* lay with headlines blaring: WILL CZECHS ACCEPT HITLER'S ULTIMATUM? WHAT HE ASKS: EVACUATION OF SUDETENLAND BY OCTOBER 1ST. He was bending over it to read more when Edward put a hand on his shoulder and said: 'Don't worry, old boy. It's all up to the Czechs now, isn't it? And they'll have to give way. They've got no choice. Two large pink gins, please, George. I'm going to give you a very good lunch.'

But at lunch they met somebody who knew somebody who had met Colonel Lindbergh at a party and he had told them a good deal of interesting and alarming stuff about the German Air Force, which was larger and better equipped than was commonly supposed. He also informed them that trenches were being dug in the parks, a fact that seemed to unnerve Edward far more than news about the Air Force. 'Perhaps in the end we shall have to take the buggers seriously,' he said. 'My God, this time I shall join the Navy.'

'The Navy can't do much against bombers,' Hugh said.

'We're wide open to a massive air attack. It won't be like the last war. They won't stop at bombing civilians.'

'Well, we'll keep our civilians in the country,' Edward said with the levity that Hugh recognised Edward employed when he was uneasy. For the rest of lunch, they talked about work and Rupert's indecision.

'I mean, if he *does* join us, he's going to have to make up his mind about things all the time, and his track record for that isn't extremely dynamic.'

Hugh said, 'Well, he'll have us to break him in.'

'I don't know whether he will.'

There was a brief silence while they both recognised that they were back on the brink. Then Hugh said, 'I think it would be sensible if we had a contingency plan.'

'About Rupe?'

'About everything.'

Edward looked at his brother, at his anxious, honest eyes, at the nervous tic starting now beneath his right cheekbone, at the black silk stump resting on the corner of the table and then back to his eyes again. Hugh's expression had not changed. He said, 'You think I'm a windy obstinate old bugger, but you know I'm right.'

∞ ∞ ∞

Zoë had got herself into a rather sticky position. The solution was perfectly simple and perfectly dull, and she regarded it as a last resort. Her mother's condition had improved enough for her to get up for part of the day, which meant that Zoë had to spend hours more time with her than she had had to do when Mrs Headford had been confined to her bed. It also meant that Dr Sherlock had far less reason for his visits, although he still made them. The first three days, when Mummy had really been quite ill, Zoë had made her lightly boiled eggs and frightfully thin bread and butter – even managed to stew some prunes – made her bed each day, and cleaned the bath – horrible old jobs that it made her tired even to contemplate each morning as she lay on the uncomfortable sofa in the sitting room. She only got out to change their library books; Ruby M. Ayres for her mother, who required something light, and whatever she could find for herself – Somerset Maugham and Margaret Irwin chiefly. She had been deeply bored, and the only highlights of the day had been Rupert's telephone call in the evening, a strict three minutes because the Duchy regarded the telephone, especially toll calls, as an indulgence, *and* the visit from Dr Sherlock. Dr Sherlock was a man of about forty, she thought, as his hair, which was thick and wavy, was brindled with grey. He was unusually tall with brown eyes and a soothing voice, and Zoë noticed that her mother made great efforts to be what she called tidy for his calls. The first time he had called, she had shown him into her mother's bedroom where she lay propped up in bed in her peach-coloured bedjacket edged with white swansdown, shut the door on them and quietly gone back to the crowded little sitting room to tidy it up. Her mother had moved to a smaller, cheaper flat after Zoë had married and as she had not brought herself to part with anything very much, the place was overflowing. There was nowhere for Zoë to put her clothes, or even the bedclothes she used for the sofa at night: she had to keep her make-up in the tiny little dark bathroom. Every flat surface was filled with photographs – mainly of Zoë at every stage of childhood and up to the present day. The walls, that were mostly a peachy pink – the colour her mother had learned from Miss Arden was the most becoming for women – were now discreetly dirty and toned in with the soupy net curtains that covered every window, subduing and suppressing all daylight. It was a fourth-floor flat in a mansion block; to go out you had to use an incredibly slow cage-like lift that was frequently stuck on another floor because the tenants had failed to close the stiff and ponderous gates. It was like a prison, Zoë thought, and just as she thought it, Dr Sherlock came into the room.

'Well, Mrs . . . '

'Cazalet.'

'Mrs Cazalet, your mother's making a good recovery. I've told her she must stay put for a few more days, at least. She should have light diet – chicken, fish that sort of thing . . . '

'I'm not much of a cook – you don't think she should be in hospital?'

'No, no. I'm sure she'd far rather be looked after by you.

You *can* stay a few days, can't you? She seemed rather anxious about that.'

'A few days. My husband's in the country – with the children.'

'Ah, I see. And you don't want to leave them for too long.'

'Well, it's my husband, really. He doesn't like to be left for too long.'

He gave her a small smile. 'I can imagine he wouldn't. Well, perhaps you could move your mother to the country in a few days.'

'Oh, no, I couldn't! We're staying with his parents, you see. The house is simply full of people.'

He had been writing something on his prescription pad, and now looked up at her. This time his admiration was unmistakable. He tore off the prescription and handed it to her.

'Well, whatever plans you make, don't let your mother be in doubt about them. The most important thing for her is that she should be free of anxiety. I'm prescribing a mild sedative that should help with that and also ensure that she gets a good night's sleep.'

'Will you be coming tomorrow?'

'Yes. By the way, do you have a bedpan?'

'I . . . I don't think so.' She had never seen one in her life.

'Well, get one from the chemist. I'd like your mother to be absolutely still for a day or two. Don't want her traipsing back and forth to the lavatory.' He was putting the pad of paper back into his bag and preparing to go. 'See you tomorrow, Mrs Cazalet. I'll let myself out.'

She heard him open the front door, close it, and then there was silence. She spent a ghastly day, buying food and getting the prescription and the bedpan, and then persuading her mother to use it, and *then* having to empty it, and clean it out and put it back in the peachy bedroom with a peachy towel covering it. A nice woman at the fishmonger in Earl's Court Road – she had to walk miles to find a fish shop – told her how to cook the fillets of plaice she bought. 'For an invalid, is it? Just put it between two plates, dear, over a saucepan of hot water.' That was fine, but she hadn't asked how long for and she burned her fingers on the top plate trying to see whether it was cooked or not. Quite soon the whole flat smelled of fish, and then her mother didn't seem to want it in the least. 'I thought you knew me and fish, Zoë,' she said. 'Never mind, I can make do with some bread and milk. And some grapes,' she called, after Zoë had gone out of the room with the tray. 'Did you get the grapes?'

'You didn't say you wanted any. I asked you if there was anything you wanted and you said nothing. I'll go this afternoon.'

'I don't want to be a trouble.'

But you are, she thought, scraping the fish off the plate and putting it into the rubbish bin. The bedpan business had made her feel totally unhungry. She went out again and bought grapes and a tin of turtle soup for her mother's supper. In the evening she had a good moan to Rupert about how awful everything was and how much she missed him. He was sweet about it all, said that he was sure she was being a wonderful nurse, and it couldn't be helped and he'd ring tomorrow.

After that, things changed rapidly. Dr Sherlock came in the morning and she'd made some coffee – about the only thing she was good at making – and offered him some after his visit to her mother. He agreed to a quick cup. Her mother was making excellent progress, he said, should be up for an hour or two quite soon, but he had told her to have an afternoon rest and to settle down early for the night. 'And what do you do with yourself once your mother is settled?'

Zoë shrugged. 'Nothing. My friends all seem to be away, and I don't care to go to a cinema by myself.' She had tried one or two old schoolfriends, but got no results. She looked down at the cup on her lap and then back at him with a small, appealing smile. 'Still, I really shouldn't complain.'

'That rarely prevents one from doing so, I find. Well, I can complain as well. My wife took the children to Hunstanton for what was supposed to be a fortnight, and now it's three weeks and no sign of them returning.'

'Poor you!' She proffered the coffee pot.

'Thanks, it was delicious but I've got some more calls before lunch.' He got to his feet. He really was amazingly tall. That afternoon, she went back to her own house and collected some more clothes.

By the end of the week, her mother was getting up for a part of each day, was able to bathe and use the lavatory. On Friday, he asked her if she would care to dine with him. 'If you have nothing better to do.' She had nothing better to do.

By tacit agreement, her mother was not actually informed of this arrangement. She told her mother that she was going to the cinema, and he said nothing. He took her to Prunier's, and, over their Pâté Traktir and Chablis, exchanged those elliptical, fascinating and often misleading pieces of information about themselves that pave the path to physical attraction. How long had she been married? Nearly four years. She must have been very, very young, then. Nineteen. A child. And the children? She was afraid she had none. Her husband had been married before; the children she had mentioned were by his former wife. She was very young to take on step-children. Yes, it was sometimes difficult. She was wearing a halter-necked dress that made her minute shrugs of semi-denial – about extreme youth, or the consequent difficulties – particularly attractive. She had wanted to go on the stage, she volunteered, but marriage had put an end to all that. He could quite see why she had wanted to go on the stage. They had reached the Sole Véronique by now and she asked him about himself. Nothing to tell; he was a GP with a fairly large practice, a house in Redcliffe Square, had been married for twelve years and had two children. His wife disliked London and with some money inherited from her father had bought a cottage in Norfolk from which she found it difficult to tear herself away. He was not too keen on the country himself – much preferred town. Oh, yes, so did she! This agreement, as they drank to it and looked at each other escalated to a delightful significance. 'How extraordinary,' he said with simulated lightness, 'that we should be so alike!' They had reached the coffee stage before a waiter came to say that there was a call for him. When he returned, he was awfully sorry, but they would have to go – he had a visit to make. No, no, finish your coffee. He called for the bill.

'It is a pity,' he said. 'I was hoping to take you on somewhere to dance.'

'Were you?' She could not entirely suppress her disappointment. 'How did they know you were at the restaurant?'

'I always leave a number with any serious case if I'm

going out. It's all part of the job. I don't have a partner.'

As he dropped her back at the mansion block, he said, 'Do you mind if I don't see you in?'

'Of course not. Thanks for the dinner. It was lovely to go out.'

'It was lovely to go out with you,' he returned. 'Perhaps we could go dancing on another occasion?'

'Perhaps we could.'

He watched while she ran lightly up the steps and opened the door to the block with her key. She turned and waved, and he blew her a kiss. It was the first time she had gone out to dinner alone with a man who was not Rupert, since her marriage, and she felt herself back on ground that was both familiar and exciting.

The next day she went home again to fetch an evening dress, and two evenings later, he took her to the Gargoyle. He was a divine dancer, the band played all her favourites and the head waiter greeted her by name. This time, no telephone call interrupted them: she wore her old white backless dress (after all, it would not seem old to him) and a green velvet ribbon round her throat with a diamanté buckle stitched onto it and her old, comfortable green shoes that were so good for dancing. Excitement and pleasure animated her beauty, making it at once more childlike and more mysterious, and he was entrapped. He told her she was a marvellous dancer and how lovely she was – at first, lightly; she received these tentative compliments politely, like a rich woman being given a bunch of daisies. But later in the evening, when they had drunk quite a lot and his admiration ascended from compliment to homage, 'I have never even *seen* anyone *half* so beautiful in my life,' her responses became more serious. Confident in the effect her appearance had made, she was able to indulge in flirtatious half-truths. 'I'm awfully *dull*, really. I've got rather a frivolous mind.'

'You're certainly not *dull*. Would you like some brandy?'

She shook her head. 'I am! And I don't know a thing about politics and I don't read serious books – or – ' she searched for more harmless shortcomings, 'or go to *meetings* about things or do charity work.' There was a pause, he could not take his eyes off her. 'And I don't know if you've noticed that there are a lot of pictures – drawings of women – on the walls in the bar here? Well, they are by someone quite famous called Matisse, but I can't see the point of them all.'

He said, 'I do adore your honesty.'

'Bet you'd get bored with it.'

She looked at his brandy, and he beckoned the waiter. 'You always change your mind about brandy, don't you?' This had happened the previous night; he was delighted in knowing something so well about her.

She looked at him with faint reproach. 'Not absolutely always. I never do anything *always*.'

'Of course you don't.'

'And I'm hopelessly undomesticated – can't cook to save my life – and to tell you the honest truth, I don't think I'm even maternal. Actually.'

But he was too far gone to recognise the honest truths.

And now – what was it? eight days later, she realised that the whole thing had gone far enough. He was madly in love with her. He had tried to get her to bed with him, but she had resisted what she found to be a surprisingly strong temptation. This had made her feel quite self-righteous in her telephone conversations with Rupert, which had become increasingly dishonest. Mummy was making progress, but slowly, she had been saying; she could not possibly leave her until she felt happy about her being well enough to live alone. With her mother, things were different. Her mother had looked up from her novel after Zoë had finished one of her guarded telephone conversations with Philip who rang at least three times a day, and said, 'You're going out with him, aren't you?'

'What on earth are you talking about?'

'With him. With Dr Sherlock. Does Rupert know?'

Ignoring this, she said, 'I've had dinner with him once or twice – yes. Why shouldn't I?'

'It can't be right, Zoë. You have such a nice marriage – and everything. But if Rupert knows, and doesn't mind, I suppose it's all right?'

Zoë still didn't reply to this tacit question, and her mother had not the courage to ask again.

Zoë told Rupert never to ring after seven in the evening, as it might wake her mother, and felt safe.

That evening, he took her, as he had promised, to see

285

Lupino Lane in *Me and My Girl*. She enjoyed it, and her enjoyment was heightened by the knowledge that through it he was watching her rather than the show. Afterwards, they went to the Savoy, had dinner and danced. She wore her strapless olive-green corded silk, her newest dress that she had bought because the colour matched her eyes and enhanced the white sheen of her shoulders. She had piled her hair on top of her head and fastened the green velvet ribbon with the diamanté buckle at the back (her jewellery was in Sussex, which she felt was a great pity). She knew that she looked her best, and was silently piqued because, so far, he had not told her so. However, everybody else seemed to notice her: the head waiter, the wine-waiter, even Carroll Gibbon playing the piano smiled at her, his spectacles glinting when they went onto the dance floor to dance.

'You're very silent,' she said, at last. 'Don't you like my dress? I put it on specially for you. Aren't I smart enough?'

'Not smart,' he replied. 'That's not how I would describe you at all.' She felt his hand press the small of her back. 'You're entirely irresistible. I want you more than anything in the world.'

'Oh, Philip!'

But not much later, when they had dined, and the lights were lower, he asked whether, if they were both free, she would marry him.

She stared at him, incredulous: he looked completely serious.

'But we *are* married!'

'In my case, only just. My wife has written saying that she thinks there may be a war, and she therefore won't be coming back to London. She's going to keep the children in the country. I think she would give me a divorce if I asked for it. It hasn't been a *marriage* for years, anyhow.'

'Poor you!'

He looked at her with a faintly sardonic smile. 'Don't be sorry for me. I've found consolation elsewhere from time to time that has seemed adequate – until now. I am a very good lover,' he added.

There was a short silence: she was embarrassed. She searched for something mature and dismissive to say.

'Of course, I'm awfully flattered, but, of course, it's out of the question. Rupert would never divorce me.'

'Would you want him to?'

Afterwards, she realised, that if only she had been truthful – said that she didn't *want* a divorce, that although he attracted her, she wasn't in love with him – things might, almost certainly *would*, have turned out very differently. But earlier she had made the mistake of implying that things were 'difficult' at home and had basked in his sympathetic attention. If she had not been such a fool, she would never have got herself into this mess. For mess it was. She realised uncomfortably that he was far more serious than she had meant him to be. His intensity frightened her, and she descended into fresh dishonesty. It would make him feel better, she thought, if she allowed him to think that she felt as he did, but was prevented by her principles from doing what, of course, they would both like. This seemed to make things easier between them, but when he was taking her home, he begged her to come back to his house with him; she refused and he pleaded with her; she refused and he kissed her, she wept and he became tender and contrite. By the time she got to bed on the sofa she was so exhausted that she couldn't sleep, felt guilty and irritable and thoroughly out of sorts and simply wanted to get out of it all.

The next morning, her mother, who had been worrying a great deal more than she had allowed Zoë to know, announced that she was going to convalesce with her old friend, Maud Witting, who lived on the Isle of Wight and was always asking her to stay. 'Then you can go back to Sussex, darling, where I know you'd rather be.'

Deeply relieved, Zoë behaved, as her mother said, 'angelically', packing her case, going out to buy her toiletries and the regulation box of Meltis Fruits that her mother always took when she stayed with this friend, and finally going in the cab with her to Waterloo and seeing her comfortably on the train. 'Give my love to Rupert. Have you told him you'll be home tonight?'

Zoë lied about this. She knew she had not been nearly nice enough to her mother and didn't want to worry her. But walking out of the station she felt a sense of freedom. Her mother was better and going to have a nice time instead of being cooped up in that dreary little flat, and she, Zoë, could now simply disappear so far as Philip was concerned, if she wanted to. As she had to clear out what had become a considerable wardrobe from her mother's flat and return it to Brook Green, she decided to spend one more night in London and tell Philip that she was leaving for Sussex the next day. She managed to announce this on the telephone to him (he no longer visited her mother who was deemed well enough not to need it). There was a silence the other end, and then he said, 'Perhaps you would rather forgo a farewell party?' And she found herself saying not at all, she would love to see him if he felt like it. She felt she had been honest, and quite cool: if he wanted to see her, it was up to him.

He fetched her at the usual time, they dined in Soho in a restaurant he had not taken her to before and everything *seemed* to be the same, but it wasn't. She realised quite early on that he made no remark about her appearance – usually a recurring topic – and after a while this began to worry her. She was wearing a dress that by now he knew quite well, and also she had slept badly the night before, and finally she said something about this, but he simply said she looked the same to him and went on talking about whatever it was, a host of impersonal things – whether television would ever catch on to the general public – had she ever seen any? No? Of course, if it ever got away it would finish off radio and, he supposed, the cinema. 'I would have liked to have been a film actress,' she said.

'Would you?' he returned. 'Well, I expect you have that ambition in common with every shopgirl in London.' She did not like being lumped with all of *them*, and sulked. It wasn't turning out at all the sort of last evening she had envisaged. Eventually, they went dancing, and he stopped talking, and things felt better. Just before they went home, he kissed her on the dance floor and she knew he still wanted her.

He said he would come up with her to see her safely into the flat, and she said, don't bother, she didn't want to wake her mother. 'Your mother?' Yes, she was afraid they must have woken her last night and she'd promised not to do it again. 'I promise that we shan't wake your mother,' he said, getting into the lift with her. 'I just want to come in for a cup of tea and a chat. After all, it is our last evening,' he added.

'It has been fun,' she said.

'Has it?'

She shut the front door with exaggerated quiet, and they stood in the dreary, narrow little hall. He took off her wrap and laid it on a chair.

'You don't really want tea, do you?'

'No,' he said, 'not in the least,' and took her in his arms and kissed her. Always before, this had been exciting, but it had been his desire that she enjoyed – her own feelings had remained secure and aloof. Now she felt herself responding, and began to feel nervous.

She made an attempt to disentangle herself, and when he stopped kissing her, she said, 'This isn't talking. I think you'd better go, Philip.'

He put his hands on top of her bare shoulders and in a neutral voice said, 'You feel it has all gone far enough?'

'Yes! Yes, I do!'

'You would not like us to do something we should both regret?'

'Of course not.' She tried to say it in an offhand manner, but the expression of admiring, tender attention in his eyes that she had become used to was not there, and when she looked at him, she could not tell what had replaced it. 'Anyway, I told you, we mustn't wake Mummy.' In the very short silence that followed, she had time to think that the flat was horribly quiet and that nobody would ever hear her if she screamed before she saw that he was very angry, and was smiling.

'Such a little cheat! Your mother rang me this morning for a prescription to be posted to her. You could have rejoined your husband today, couldn't you? But you couldn't resist one more evening of games! You're very beautiful, my dear. You are also the most egocentric little creature I've ever met in my life. You've always known your own strength, haven't you, but you know nothing about your own weakness: it's high time you learned that.' With one neat, sudden movement, he picked her up, carried her into the sitting room and dropped her onto the sofa.

There followed some hours she would remember for the rest of her life with a kind of double-edged shame. Shame of a conventional sort, that it should have happened at all, and shame of a more true and insidious kind: that her resistance had been token, that she should have become utterly immersed in what had nothing to do with love-making as she had hitherto known it. For he did not woo her with sweet words – made no attempt to sue for her love – said nothing at all. He simply set about unlocking her sensuality by touch, observing each effect. Years later, when she saw a French film about men breaking into a bank and one of them feeling for the right combination of the safe, she recognised that look of acute, impassive attention, and came, and blushed in the dark. Once he had discovered what roused her, he used it, so that she, who had always been the granter of favours, became the suppliant, leading her past initial protest to compliance, until she became eager, when he withheld himself until she was frantic, was to hear her voice pleading with him for the rest of her life. Hours later, when this process had recurred and been resolved several times, she must have fallen asleep, because she realised suddenly that she was alone, with a blanket over her, the lamp still burning on the rickety table in the corner of the room, subdued by the grey morning light.

At first she thought, He must still be here, but when she got up, with the blanket wrapped round her, she quickly found that he wasn't. Her body felt stiff and sore, and she had a crick in her neck from sleeping awkwardly on the sofa. Her clothes from last night lay scattered on the floor where he had thrown them. Knowing that he had gone was a kind of relief. While she was having a bath, the telephone rang. But he needn't think I'll answer it, she thought, picking at the crumbs of her old image, the haughty, adorable Zoë who could manipulate any man and remain perfectly cool. But when it stopped ringing, she wondered what on earth he would have said to her. She found it difficult to think – at all – about anything.

Much later, when she had dressed and made herself a cup of tea, the telephone rang again. She left it for two rings, and then picked it up. Let him speak: she would not say anything, as he had not, last night.

'Zoë? Darling, I know it's terribly early for you, but I felt I must ring . . . '

It was Rupert. Hugh had rung last night, he said: he and

290

Edward were worried the way things were going, and Hugh had said that London was not going to be a good place to be if things got sticky. He had tried to ring last night, but she must have been out. So, would she bring her mother if need be and catch a train this morning? There was one at ten twenty-five, he added.

Zoë heard herself explaining about her mother having gone, and saying that she had planned to return today, anyway. 'Did you ring earlier?' she asked.

'Good Lord, no. You know what you're like if you're woken by the telephone. I'll meet you at Battle, then. Goodbye, sweetie.'

She put the receiver back on its hook; she was trembling and her knees were giving way. She stumbled into the sitting room and collapsed on the little gilt chair by the lamp. It was too soon to hear Rupert. She was too raw, and confused – she needed time before she saw him again and now there wouldn't be any. As she began to cry, she started to try and construct a version of what had happened that seemed bearable. She had gone too far with this man and he had taken advantage of her – had raped her. But he hadn't raped her. It was not her fault that she was so desirable, he was far older, she had told him that she was married and would not ever leave her husband, so why had he not simply accepted that and gone away? But she had *tried* to attract him, had *wanted* him to be in love with her, she had not cared at all. 'Such a little cheat!'

He had fallen so much in love with her that he had had to make love to her, and she had felt that she owed him that, at least. But last night, she began to know, had had nothing to do with love. She had not graciously given herself to him: 'Oh, Philip – please – *please*!' He had seduced her, he was obviously very experienced – must have gone to bed with dozens of women. He had planned the whole thing from the start. If she *had* resisted him last night, he *would* probably have raped her. But if you went dancing every night with a man you knew was violently attracted to you, and then you invited him into what you knew was an empty flat, what could you expect? What was it he had said? Something about, 'You don't know your own weakness.' Now, it seemed, she knew nothing else, seemed entirely to be made up of it. It was weak to be reduced into some kind of – words failed her here – an animal? A tart? But they did it for money, didn't they? If it had been a question of money last night, it would have been she who would have paid . . . No reconstruction that she attempted felt true enough to be comfortable. She turned off the lamp and, wearily diminished, set about tidying her clothes from the floor, dressing and packing her case for the journey back to Sussex.

∞ ∞ ∞

On the same morning, Raymond rang Mill Farm at breakfast time to say that Aunt Lena had died. Nora realised that that was what must have happened because her mother was using her artificial voice. Nobody, Nora felt, could honestly be terribly sorry that Aunt Lena had died as she was frightfully old and never seemed to have enjoyed anything much, but she noticed that Aunt Villy caught her mother's voice and they both sounded exactly the same as they said how sad it was. The funeral was to be on Monday, Jessica said, and Raymond thought that Angela and Christopher should accompany her to Frensham. 'Oh, can't I go too?' Nora cried. 'I've never been to a funeral!'

'Yes, you have,' said Neville. 'Bexhill had his funeral last week. You were at it.'

'A little week,' said Louise dreamily, 'or 'ere those shoes were old, with which she followed that poor fish's body—'

'Be quiet, children! Or, if you've finished breakfast, go.'

Lydia got down at once. 'Where would you like us to go to, Mummy darling? I mean, really *best* like us to go?'

'To hell,' Neville said, 'or the lav, I should think.'

Judy, who was always a slow eater, stuffed her toast into her mouth and said, 'Is it difficult to bury fat people? Aunt Lena was simply gigantic,' she explained.

'Judy, would you kindly shut up and leave the room!'

'We've got to go as well,' Louise said to Nora, to pre-empt being sent.

Villy heaved a sigh of relief, and then realised that Angela was still with them.

'It's all right, Mummy, I must go or I'll be late for my

sitting.' Rupert was actually painting her portrait from ten until one o'clock every day, an enterprise that enabled her to spend hours alone with him without having to say anything. The portrait was nearly finished, but she lived in hopes that he might start another one.

'I sometimes wonder whether she has got a bit of a pash for Rupert,' Jessica said when her daughter had left the room.

'Oh, well, that doesn't matter. He's a perfectly safe person for her to have a pash about. I expect she's simply thrilled to have her portrait painted. Don't you remember how excited *you* were when Henry Ford painted you for a fairy story?'

'Yes, but I didn't care about *him* in the least. It was just my vanity.' She gave herself a little shake. 'Oh dear! Poor Raymond! He's having to make all the funeral arrangements, and he's awfully bad at that sort of thing.'

'I suppose you must go to it?'

'Of course I must. But I really don't want to take the children. Christopher will get dreadfully upset and then Raymond will be cross with him, and Angela will probably sulk and say she hasn't got the right clothes. Nor have I, come to that.'

'I've got a black and white dress you could borrow if it isn't too short on you. And if you leave the children here, it means you can come back sooner.'

Although she had not told Jessica about the possibility of her being pregnant, she knew that she would miss her sister when she went away: there was nobody else with whom she had the same intimacy. In fact, being with Jessica these weeks had made her realise how lonely she usually was.

∞ ∞ ∞

At eleven o'clock that morning, one of the Cazalet lorries lumbered up the drive and the driver got down from his cab and tapped on the kitchen window with a stubby pencil from behind his ear. Mrs Cripps, in the throes of making an Irish stew with seven pounds of scrag end of lamb, sent Dottie to find Mrs Cazalet Senior. But Dottie was no good at finding people. She disappeared at once, but did not return as she knew better than to face Mrs Cripps with failure. Time went by; the driver got back into his cab where he ate a bun, dripping with shredded coconut, drank a Thermos of tea and read the *Star*. Mrs Cripps forgot about the whole thing, until she wanted the trug of Victoria plums, and realised that Dottie hadn't brought them in from the back door where McAlpine would have deposited them. She screeched for Dottie and Eileen said she hadn't seen her for some time, and there were the plums – the sun had come round onto them and the wasps were everywhere.

'Eileen, you'd better go for Mrs Senior, although it will be one more for dinner by now, as I can see with half an eye.' So Eileen went and knocked on the door of the drawing room where the Duchy and Sid were playing.

'Most extraordinary,' the Duchy said to Rachel and Sid when she returned to the drawing room. 'The man has twenty-four camp beds which he says William told him to deliver. What can they be for?'

'Evacuation of some kind,' said Sid.

The Duchy looked relieved. 'Oh, I do hope it's only that! You remember that awful time when he met that cricket team on the train and invited them for the weekend, and there was nothing to give them but macaroni cheese? Who do you think he wants to evacuate? Oh dear! It might be the members from his club. They all expect such *rich* food.'

'Darling, I'm sure it won't be. You know he likes to be on the safe side. And if he buys things, he always gets them in dozens.' Rachel spoke soothingly, but felt a twinge of uneasiness.

'Where is he, anyway?'

'He's gone to Brede. There's supposed to be an old man there who's a frightfully good water diviner. He wants him to sink another well for the new cottages. He said he'd be back for lunch. We'll deal with the lorry man, darling, won't we Sid?'

'You bet.'

'Don't let her lift anything, will you, Sid? She's just got her back right again.'

'Righty-ho.'

∞ ∞ ∞

'That's it.'

'Have you finished it?'

'No – no. But I've got to go.' He was wiping his brush on a rag. 'Got to meet Zoë's train. Hey! I'll be late if I don't scoot. You couldn't clean my brushes, like a darling, could you?'

Of course she could.

'Bless your heart.'

And he was gone. A bombshell – out of the blue. He hadn't said a word about Zoë returning. 'Got to meet Zoë's train.' Perhaps he didn't *want* to meet her – simply had to because they were married. She got slowly to her feet. She got awfully stiff sitting with her head turned towards him, trembled sometimes with the effort of keeping still. But it was all worth it for the being alone, and for the breaks of ten minutes every hour when he gave her a cigarette and told her what a jolly good sitter she was. Would he stop – now that Zoë was back? At least, he would probably finish the picture after spending so much time on it. She went over to the easel to look at the portrait. He had painted her sitting in the large high-backed leather chair that lived at one end of the billiard room. The leather was a kind of greenish black, and he had made her sit at an angle in it but looking up at him, with her hands on her lap. In spite of her bringing a selection of her best clothes for him to choose from, he had discarded the lot and, in the end, put her into a very old silk shirt of his that was a kind of greenish white. It was far too big for her, but he had rolled up the sleeves and left two of the front buttons undone. She was divided between the intense pleasure of wearing something of his, and feeling that she looked awful in it. He had also stopped her curling her hair, tied it back with a dull green ribbon that unfortunately belonged to Zoë, and he had said that he preferred her without lipstick. She thought she looked drab and watery, he had even made her eyes look a kind of aquamarine colour. She didn't feel it was actually *like* her at all. He said she looked beautiful, and what more could she want? For it to go on for ever, she thought, and felt her eyes filling with tears. Sometimes she deliberately got her pose wrong so that he would come and move her head with his hands, but he had never touched her face again. She took the brushes out of the jam jar where he had stuck them and started to wipe them on the

295

turps-soaked rag. And it will only get worse, she thought. Not only will Zoë be here from lunch-time onwards, but we shall finish our visit and they will make me go back to London and leave him. I won't be able to bear that.

∞ ∞ ∞

When Polly woke on Friday morning she felt just the same as when she had gone to sleep the night before – just as awful and frightened and full of doom. It was like a nightmare, except that it wasn't confined to the night: that was the only time when she hadn't felt anything – hadn't even dreamed about it. It seemed extraordinary that out of the blue, when everything seemed quite normal and nice with only small things to worry about, like would she manage to get chicken pox at the right time and how could she explain to the Duchy that hot milk was like a sick-making poison and therefore couldn't do her good, that with no warning at all, the thing she had dreaded most in the world for years now should not only be probable but imminent. It had started after tea yesterday: she had gone to her favourite tree in the orchard beyond the kitchen garden – the tree that she and Louise used to share, only now Louise wasn't interested any more and she made Clary jolly well have her own tree – and settled on the best flat branch quite high up where she could sit with her back to the trunk and read and nobody could see her. She had taken her holiday task: Miss Milliment had let them choose from a list she had made and Polly had chosen *Cranford*, which she was finding rather boring. So when she heard voices approaching, her attention was easily diverted. As they came nearer, she could see that it was Aunt Rach and Sid. She was just about to call out to them when she realised that Aunt Rach was crying, which was very unusual for a grown-up. Then she realised that they were stopping under the tree, and it felt too late to say that she was there. They were talking about someone called Evie and how she was making a fuss about Sid being away, and Aunt Rach suddenly cried out, 'But if you go back to London, and there *is* a war, there'll be bombs – terrible air raids – someone said that they could flatten London in two or three raids – or they may use gas – I couldn't bear you to face all that without me!'

'My precious, you're making a whole lot of fearful suppositions. *If* there is a war—'

'You know if the Czechs don't accept Hitler's ultimatum there *will* be. You said that yourself.'

'Darling, they're digging air-raid shelters. It was in the news.'

'That won't help against gas. Hugh said that gas—'

'They're going to issue everybody with gas masks—'

'It's not any of that. If we *are* all going to be killed, I want to be with you. So I beg you to ask Evie to come down here, only you must do it *now*. The next thing will be a state of emergency, and they probably won't *let* people travel—'

'Probably not. There may well be an invasion—'

'Oh, don't! Surely not that! We are an island.'

'We're also, so far as I can make out, totally unprepared for war. And I find it hard to believe that Hitler doesn't know that. He's calling the tune, and making the terms.'

'Sid, don't go on! Stick to the point. Stick to getting Evie down.'

'The little parochial point—'

'It's all we can do, isn't it? And it may not be for long. It may be the end – of everything.'

There was a silence, and when Polly, trembling, leant down to look, she saw that kind Sid had her arms round Aunt Rach and was kissing her to make her feel better.

'Courage, my darling, we do have each other. All right, I'll ring Evie. If you are sure the Duchy wouldn't mind.'

'She won't in the least. She just doesn't want us to talk about it in front of the children. She doesn't want them frightened.'

They began to walk away, and were almost immediately out of sight.

Polly stayed quite still. Her heart was thudding so hard that she felt it was trying to get out of her body. When she did start to come down out of the tree, she miscalculated the well-known route and scraped her shin badly in preventing herself from falling. She wanted to spit on the blood, but her mouth had gone quite dry. Terrible pictures were surging across her mind: this orchard, the trees blackened stumps, the ground a sea of mud, at night you would hear poor wounded people moaning – only I wouldn't, she thought, I'd be dead by then from the bombs and gas. London might be more dangerous –

well, obviously it was or Aunt Rach wouldn't have been in such a state – but they could easily drop bombs by mistake in other places. But London – Dad – *Oscar!* – she would have to get Dad to bring Oscar down with him tomorrow evening – if there was a tomorrow evening. Oh, God, she should make them come down *now* – at *once!* She got to her feet and began mindlessly running towards the house.

She had tried to ring Dad at his office: he wasn't in, and she asked them to tell him to ring Miss Polly Cazalet back. She thought of telling Clary and asking her what she thought, but Clary's spots were itching and all she seemed to want was for people to play Pegotty with her and the situation was far too bad for playing games. Anyway, the children didn't know, it *hadn't* been talked about in front of them. It was the grown-ups she must test. The responses she got were neither helpful nor reassuring. She tried Mr York when he brought up the evening milk from the farm, and he said he'd never trusted Germans and he wasn't starting now – not at his time of life. She tried Mrs Cripps because she seemed to be reading a newspaper in her creaky basket chair, and she said that she thought wars were just a waste of everybody's time and she had better things to do. When pressed about whether the newspaper was saying things about war, she said she never believed a word she read in newspapers. Perhaps, Polly thought, war wasn't talked about in front of the servants: *'pas devant les domestiques'*, as Mummy and Aunt Villy sometimes said about things. So she tried her mother, who was sewing name-tapes into Simon's school clothes in the day nursery with Wills sitting in a pen who was dribbling a lot and frowning at two coloured bricks that he was grasping. Polly had got more skilfu t asking by now, so she started with why wasn't Mr Chamberlain going off to see Hitler again, and Mummy said that there were a lot of things to be sorted out. And if Hitler wanted a war very badly, he could just have one, couldn't he? Mummy said that it wasn't as simple as that – but Polly noticed that she was beginning to look rather trapped – and then said, almost thankfully what on earth had Polly done to her leg? Go and wash it in the bathroom and bring her the iodine and some Elastoplast. Extraordinary, to fuss about a detail like a leg when there might be a war any minute, Polly thought wearily, as she did as she was told. Then she thought that perhaps men, who after all made the wars and fought in them, didn't talk about it in front of the ladies. The only person left was the Brig. He was in his study, which, as usual, smelled of geraniums and cigar boxes and he was poring over a huge book on his desk with a magnifying glass.

'Ah,' he said, 'the very person I wanted. Which one of you is that?'

'Polly.'

'Polly. Right. Just read me what I wrote here about the export of teak logs from Burma between 1926 and 1932, would you?'

So, of course, she had to. Then he told her a long story about elephants in Burma, how they could judge precisely where to pick up a log with their trunks, which would not, she must understand, necessarily be in the middle at all, and how they would all stop work, drop their logs at the same moment in the afternoon, when they knew it was time for their bathe in the river. It was a much more interesting story than the ones about people he'd met in strange, or the same, places, but she was not in the mood for stories of any kind. When he stopped for a moment, and was clearly thinking of something else to tell her, she asked him quickly whether he thought there would be a war starting this weekend.

'What makes you ask that, my duck?' She saw he was trying to see her with his rather filmy blue eyes.

'I just – sort of feel – there might be.'

'Well, I'm damned!'

'Do you think so?' she persisted.

He went on trying to look at her; then he gave a very small nod. 'Between you and me,' he said.

'Dad's in London,' she said; her voice was trembly and she didn't want to cry. 'And Oscar.'

'Who the devil's Oscar? Damn silly name. Who's Oscar?'

'My cat. It isn't a silly name for a cat. He's named after a famous Irish playwright. I don't want him bombed to death. I want Dad to bring him down. I can have him here, can't I?'

He pulled a huge silk handkerchief out of his pocket and handed it to her. 'Here,' he said, 'you sound as though you need to blow your nose. Of course you can have your cat.'

'Could you make Dad come down today?'

'No need for that. There may be another meeting next week and, who knows, that might just do the trick. Who's been putting the wind up you like this, my duck?'

'No one really,' she lied. She had an instinct not to betray her aunt.

'Well, don't you worry your pretty little head any more.' He was fishing in yet another of his numerous pockets and produced a half-crown. 'Run along, my duck.'

As if half-a-crown would make her feel all right! Anyway, Dad had rung her up and he said he would bring Oscar. Today, Friday, the same great weight of doom lay on her heart, but at least, in ten hours at the most, Dad would come, and she could spend the morning arranging Oscar's food and make a bed for him to sleep in. She knew that he wouldn't sleep in it, but he would resent trouble not having been taken.

∞ ∞ ∞

Miss Milliment – with an excitement that made her *most* inefficient – was packing. On receipt of dear Viola's kind letter she had, as requested, gone to a public telephone box and rung Mill Farm. She hardly ever used the telephone and was terribly anxious about not hearing properly on it, but dear Viola was very clear: catch the four-twenty from Charing Cross to Battle on Friday afternoon and she would be met. Now, on Friday morning, she had her father's largest suitcase – unfortunately, the mildew seemed to have penetrated the lining – laid on her bed and was filling it with clothes. She did not possess summer clothes as such, simply wore less of whatever she had in winter. But not having to make this kind of choice did not prevent the utmost confusion. Pale grey and coffee-coloured lisle stockings resolutely unpaired, lay in surprising quantity on the only chair. She had no idea she had so many, and was also daunted by there being so few that matched. Pairs of enormous lock-knit bloomers were piled in one heap, and some short-sleeved woollen vests (they were uniformly pale grey) were put in another. Someone had told her years ago that when packing one should start from the skin and work outwards. But every now and then she forgot this in agonised contemplation of the choice between her bottle-green jersey ensemble or the heather-mixture tweed. There was also the problem of a cardigan – the steel grey one seemed infested with what looked like bits of dried porridge and the fawn one showed distinct signs of moth. Her best mustard and brown foulard she must certainly take for the evenings. Garters! She was always mislaying them, so better take all she could find. They did not really keep her stockings up, but they prevented them from entirely falling down. Her nightdresses – one really needed washing, but the other she had only used for a few days – were draped across the iron bedhead. There were also two Viyella shirts that had been made for her by the landlady's cousin; they were not a very good fit, but perfectly serviceable under a cardigan. Her sponge bag was rather a disgrace. Again, it had belonged to Father and she had the distinct impression that it was not waterproof; she decided to wrap her flannel and toothbrush in newspaper before putting them into it. She would not take many books as, doubtless, the Cazalet family would possess a delightful quantity and she was sure that they would let her borrow from them. Her other pair of shoes, brown lace-ups, needed soling, she could see a hole in one of them, and they had worn dreadfully thin. How on earth was she to get all this into one case? She began cramming things in, first laying the foulard over the bottom in hope that it would not then be utterly crushed, and then stuffing everything on top. It was soon overflowing, and she could not get it shut. She did not like to ask Mrs Timpson to come and help her as there had been a distinct atmosphere ever since she had announced that she was going away for a while. Mrs Timpson seemed to feel that she should have been given more notice, which was nonsense, really, since she would still be paying for the room. It became clear that the case would only be shut if she did not take her cardigan. Or she could wear it? But she did tend to *perspire* rather and she must, of course, travel in her better coat, which was quite thick. There was nothing for it: she would have to take two cases, and this, she feared, would mean a cab, which, from Stoke Newington to Charing Cross might easily come to two pounds. Or even more. Well, she had summoned up all her courage and cashed a cheque that morning for ten pounds. 'I am going on a journey,' she had explained to the cashier before he could say too much.

She was on her knees trying to pull the other case out from under her bed. It seemed intractably heavy, and she remembered that it was full of papers, photographs, and a few pieces of china that she had kept from home: a teapot with cowslips on it and a pair of fruit plates, with grapes and cherries in the centre and a dark blue and gold rim. All these things would have to go into the chest of drawers and this, she knew, meant that they were not safe from Mrs Timpson's prying eyes. Well, she would take Eustace's letters – they must remain private – and the rest would have to take pot luck. Going on a journey! How extremely fortunate she was! And the invitation had come at the end of a long summer when she had to admit that she had become a little tired of her own company. It was not so much the days when she was quite able to interest herself in galleries, but the evenings, when her eyes were tired and she could not always read as much as she would have liked. A little conversation would have been pleasant then, if there had been anybody to converse with.

To be going to the country! She did miss the country. They would be hay-making and, perhaps, in that part of the country, picking hops, and they were only nine miles from the sea! She had not seen the sea for years. However, she must not forget that she was going to work, to teach the girls; she had thought so much about them all the summer – so different, but each with qualities that she endeavoured to bring out, and little faults that she feared she was not strict enough to correct. Louise, for instance, her eldest pupil and now fifteen, needed to be made to work harder at the subjects she did not care for, but she was very clever at getting her own way, would prolong the discussions after their morning Shakespeare reading in order not to start upon her Latin or mathematics. In this last year, Miss Milliment had begun to feel that Louise was outgrowing the situation of being taught with Polly and Clary, neither of whom presented a challenge to her. Of course, they were two years younger which was a great deal at their age. Louise had become aloof and indolent, and Miss Milliment had noticed during her Friday luncheons that her relationship with her mother seemed a little strained. She was growing up, whereas Polly and Clary were still little girls. Polly caused her no anxiety. She seemed content to read

Shakespeare without wishing in the least to become an actress, to listen to Clary's compositions with wholehearted admiration and no desire to compete, to have no airs and graces about her appearance although she was a very attractive child with the promise of beauty. She was full of frankness and fervour; moral questions that Louise would evade neatly and with flashes of wit, and that would incense Clary to almost tearful diatribes, were chewed over by Polly with a kind of anxious honesty that Miss Milliment found most endearing.

But Clary – although she knew she should not feel this – was her favourite. Clary was not pretty like Polly, nor striking like Louise, Clary, with her sallow round face, her freckles, her fine straight mousy hair, her smile disfigured by the gap in her front teeth and the steel plate, with her bitten nails, her tendency to sulk, was in some ways a very ordinary, not very attractive little girl, but she *noticed* things, and it was the way in which she did this and how she wrote about them that Miss Milliment felt was not ordinary at all. Her composition, in the last year, had graduated from imitative accounts of the life of animals in anthropomorphic terms, to stories about people, which showed that she sensed, or perceived, or *knew* a remarkable amount about them for someone of thirteen. Miss Milliment encouraged her, always gave her homework where there was some scope for this gift, often made her read her pieces aloud, and was punctilious about the meaning of words when they were loosely or inaccurately employed. This had inspired Louise, who did not like to be outstripped, to write more herself, and she had written a three-act play – a domestic comedy that was both precocious and entertaining. Both those girls should go to university, Miss Milliment thought, but she thought it rather hopelessly, as the Cazalet family did not seem to take much interest in their daughters' education.

And here she was, mooning about on the floor with her knees getting stiff in front of this awfully full case. She would finish her packing, walk to a telephone box and ring up the nearest cab rank. Better get to the station, buy her ticket and then see if there was time for a cup of tea and a sausage roll – or something dashing of the kind.

Much later, as she was being driven to the station – she really could not remember when she had last taken a cab and

303

the extravagance in spite of its necessity was pricking her – she reflected with a sudden anxiety that since they would be keeping her she could not expect her full salary – they might, indeed, consider it fair to knock off as much as three pounds, but she would still have to pay the twenty-eight shillings rent for her room with Mrs Timpson, or she might find herself homeless. 'Now now, Eleanor, you must cross that bridge when you come to it,' she admonished herself. 'What is that small worry, compared to what poor Mr Chamberlain is having to face?' She read *The Times* every day, and there was no getting away from it: this splendid, secure country seemed once again to be nearing the brink of bloodshed and disaster.

∞ ∞ ∞

Edward was late getting to Mill Farm that evening. The traffic, he said, and he'd started too late. Actually, he was late because he'd collected Diana and Jamie and a good deal of luggage from her house in St John's Wood and driven them down to Wadhurst where Angus, in a telephone call from Scotland, had decreed she was to stay with his sister until things blew over, as he put it. This was a frightful blow to Diana: it would put Edward quite out of reach for an unknown amount of time, added to which she found her sister-in-law rather a strain, as she put it to Edward. When he asked her why, she said that Janet was very religious and held rather liberal political views.

'Good Lord! Does that mean I can't even ring you up?'

'I think it would be safer if I rang you – on Monday – at the office when she is out. She goes to meetings and things like that. We *must* be careful.' Being confronted by Villy at Lansdowne Road ten days before had given them both a fright; Edward had soon started saying what an incredibly lucky escape they had had, but Diana had taken it more seriously. Supposing Villy had turned up when she had stayed most of the night there? When they had been upstairs, in Edward's dressing room? She felt angry with him for exposing her to such a humiliating danger. Edward's response – that Villy had never done anything like that in her life before – had made things a little better, but not much. And the worst of it was that now she felt she could never go there again. She had asked

Edward if he thought that Villy suspected anything, and Edward had said, Good Lord, no, of course she hadn't: she wasn't that kind of person. I would be, Diana thought. If I was married to Edward I certainly would be. Although naturally she would not admit it to Edward, she had been fascinated to see Villy who had surprised her. She had expected a pretty, perhaps rather faded woman, and there was this small, neat, intellectually handsome creature; grey and white curly hair, striking dark, heavy eyebrows, aquiline nose and fastidious mouth – not at all an appearance that she had imagined. She seemed an odd person for Edward to have married: he was, after all, rather a catch. It must be wonderful for Villy never to have to worry about money: it seemed to Diana that her entire life was spent in keeping up a bewildering variety of appearances and, in between them, in making do. Angus, as a second son, was not due to inherit anything very much, although he had been left some money by a godfather which was probably the worst thing that could have happened to him since it enabled him to avoid any serious work. He had romantic (unrealistic) ideas about what was due to him. The honour of the family (his own comfort) ranked high, and often left Diana with humiliating economies. Another appearance that had to be kept up (to his parents) was the one that he worked extremely hard – and successfully – which entailed things like them meeting him from a first-class carriage at Inverness, his sending them unspeakably extravagant presents at Christmas, and – mercifully only once a year – giving them luncheon at the Ritz. Their friends were all richer than themselves, and for years now Diana had got her clothes second hand from an advertisement in the *Lady* from someone whose chief virtues were that she was exactly the same size and lived chiefly abroad. She sighed, and Edward put his hand on her knee. 'Cheer up, darling. It won't be for ever.'

If there was war, it might last for a very long time, she thought. She knew that if Edward was parted from her for months at a time, he would find someone else; somehow or other, she had got to prevent that. They were climbing the hill to Wadhurst: in a few minutes he would have deposited her and gone speeding off to his family – and Villy. Perhaps he sensed something of this: he slowed down, and said, 'What's up, darling?'

'Nothing. I just feel rather blue.'

'How about we stop at a pub for a quick drink?'

'It would be lovely, but there's Jamie.'

'I can bring it out to you.'

But as soon as they stopped, Jamie, who had been as good as gold in his basket in the back throughout the journey, woke and began to cry. She got him out of his basket and walked up and down with him. He was, she thought, exceptionally beautiful – unlike the other two, who had been fat and placid with reddish-blond hair, Jamie was dark and wiry with the most endearing beaky little nose that looked too grown-up for the rest of his face. I'm sure he *is* Edward's baby, she thought for the thousandth time. Sometimes when she looked at him she felt quite faint with love. He was wet – he never cried without good reason; she laid him on the back seat of the car and got some clean nappies out of his basket. As she unpinned him, he gave her a fleeting, conspiratorial smile so full of gaiety and trust that her eyes filled.

'Here you are, darling.'

'Hang on a sec.' A tear splashed onto Jamie's midriff and he blinked.

When she had finished changing him, and put him back into his basket, she turned to Edward to accept her glass, but he said, 'Let's get back into the car.'

When they were in, he put her drink in her hand and an arm round her. 'Poor darling, you are feeling rotten. Cheer up. It'll all be the same a hundred years hence.'

'I don't find *that* comforting at all. Who on earth ever thought of anything so silly?'

He shrugged. 'Don't know. Well, one thing. I love you – for what it's worth. I hate leaving you. Is that better?'

'Much better.' She took his proffered handkerchief and blew her nose.

'Your hankies smell so *nice!*'

'Lebanon cedar,' he said. 'Drink up, my sweetie, we ought to get going.'

When they had finished their drinks, he kissed her, and then took the glasses back into the pub.

'You must admit, Jamie's been angelic,' she said as they drove through the village.

'He's a splendid little bloke,' he answered absently. He often wondered whether it was his, but felt that to say so might be venturing onto dangerous ground. 'Now you'll have to direct me.'

So, by the time he'd dropped her, got all her stuff out of the car, exchanged a few breezy words with the sister-in-law (who thought him absolutely *charming*) and driven the further ten miles or so, it was after seven, but Villy seemed neither cross nor curious: she was far too concerned with how he would take the news that not only was Lady Rydal still there, but that Miss Milliment had joined them.

∞ ∞ ∞

When Christopher and Simon made their early visit to their camp they got a terrible shock. The front flaps of their tent were open. Simon was about to exclaim about this, but Christopher held up his hand and put a finger over his mouth. Together they crept silently nearer. One side of the tent was bulging and moved slightly. Someone was actually in there. Christopher dropped the stores he was carrying, and picked up a stick: it wasn't much good, but better than nothing. Simon copied him. Then Christopher called, 'Come out of there, whoever you are!'

There was a pause, and then Teddy crawled out of the tent. He was eating a packet of biscuits, but Simon could tell he looked dangerous.

'Well,' he said. 'I must say you're a secretive pair. How long has this been going on?' and Simon realised that he was very angry.

'Not long,' he said.

'You know I like camping. Why didn't you let me in on it? What's so special about it, anyway?'

'It was Christopher's idea,' Simon mumbled.

'Oh, was it? Well, a good many of your things are here as well. What's up?'

'It's a secret,' Christopher said. 'I didn't want anyone to know.'

'And I'm anyone, am I? You're just a guest,' he pointed out to Christopher. 'I should have thought you'd have the

307

common politeness to let other chaps in on your game. And as for *you*,' he turned to Simon, 'no wonder you've never had time to play squash, or help me practise my tennis – or even go for a decent bicycle ride. You're just a traitor.'

'I'm not a traitor!'

'That's what traitors always say. You've got enough food here to feed a cricket team. What's it all in aid of?'

'We were going to—' Simon began, but Christopher said, 'Shut up!'

There was a fiery silence. Then Teddy stood up and said, 'Are you going to tell me?'

'No.'

'Why not?'

'Because I simply don't want to. That's why.'

They stood glaring at each other. Then Teddy said, 'I see. You want war.'

Simon said, 'Christopher's a conscience objector. So he can't want war.'

'Shut up, Simon.' They were both against him now, Simon thought.

Christopher said, 'I don't want war. What is it you want?'

Teddy seemed slightly taken aback. 'A good deal. A lot. I'd have to think. Your biscuits have gone all soft, by the way. You should have put them in a tin.'

'We know, but we ran out of tins.'

'Simon, you take the things we've brought and stow them away in the tent. Teddy and I have got to talk.'

You could talk just as well if I was out of the tent, Simon thought. He was angry at being treated in such a junior way – told to shut up by both of them and ordered about by Christopher in front of Teddy. I'm nearly crying out of rage, he told himself. He certainly was nearly crying. 'I can hear everything you say in here, anyhow,' he called, but they did not reply.

What it amounted to was that Teddy realised full well that they'd been so secretive because they didn't want the grown-ups to know about the camp, and if he, Teddy, didn't get what he wanted, he would jolly well tell them. Christopher said that was dastardly, and Teddy said that Christopher had been dastardly to him and he was simply being dastardly back.

He still hadn't said what he wanted. Well, he wanted to be the leader of whatever it was. Christopher could be his main general, and Simon could be his infantry; this was in return for not letting him in on it in the first place, and what he most wanted was to know what they planned to *do*? Christopher immediately said, nothing.

'It can't be nothing. You wouldn't have lugged all this stuff here for nothing. And, anyway, if you want to know, that tent is really mine.'

'It isn't.' Simon, really shocked at Teddy's awful lie, came out of the tent. 'The Brig gave it to all of us. It's mine as much as it is yours.'

'It isn't at all Christopher's, though.'

'There isn't room in it for three.'

'That doesn't matter in the least. You can sleep outside. You're only the men, after all.'

'You're changing the whole game!'

'Ah! Am I? Well, what is it I'm changing it from?'

Christopher, who had gone very quiet, now said, 'You state what your terms are. Then I'll consider them and tell you tomorrow whether I can accept them or not. You'd better write them down.'

'You're not prepared to tell me what you were going to do now?'

'No. And if you tell anybody at all about this place, I won't ever tell you.'

Teddy looked at him. 'Do you want a fight?'

'Not particularly.'

'Not particularly. And what does that mean, may I ask? That you're afraid? I bet you are. You're not only a sneak, you're a coward.'

'I am *not*!'

Simon crawled out of the tent: they were glaring at each other. Teddy was bright red, and Christopher was white with rage. Then Teddy took out his penknife and opened the largest blade. Oh, God! Simon thought. He can't use a knife when Christopher hasn't got one. He can't be as horrible as that!

But what he did was walk over to the tent and stab the roof and then make a large gash in it. With an inarticulate cry of fury, Christopher went for him.

It was a pretty even fight, Simon thought. In spite of Christopher being a year older than Teddy, he was nothing like so sturdily built and, besides, Teddy was learning to box at school. But Christopher had longer arms, and he was wrestling, trying to catch Teddy off balance and throw him to the ground, so that whenever Teddy got near enough to punch, he was in danger of being grabbed and thrown. Fury made them both reckless, however, and two of Teddy's punches landed on Christopher's face. His nose started to bleed and one of his eyes began to look funny.

It ended because Christopher managed to grab Teddy's right shoulder; he gave it a heave and a twist and threw him so violently to the ground that Teddy was winded. He stood over his adversary panting for a second, then turned and went to the stream to wash his face. When Teddy could speak, he said, 'Right, I've told you my terms. I'm blasted well not writing them down. If you don't agree to them by eleven o'clock tomorrow morning, I declare war.' He got up, rubbing his right shoulder, and walked away. He did not look at Simon.

There was a silence. Simon picked up Teddy's knife and then went to look at the tent. The gash was not very big: they ought to be able to sew it up or put the ground-sheet inside the tent under it, so that rain, if there was any, didn't ruin the things inside. Then he went over to Christopher who was kneeling by the stream. He had taken off his shirt, and was mopping his face with it; he had a knobbly white back and didn't look at all like a person who would win a fight.

'You were jolly good,' he said. 'You won, really.'

Christopher stopped mopping his face and Simon saw that apart from his puffed-up eye and the red trickle that was starting again from his nose, he was crying. He squatted down beside him. The great thing when people cried was to cheer them up to stop them. 'It was frightful bad luck, him finding us,' he said. 'But he won't tell anyone, you bet. He wants to be in on it himself. And we can mend the tent.'

But Christopher, brushing his nose with his hand and looking at the smear on his knuckles, said, 'But I'm supposed to be against fighting. And I *started* it!' His good eye looked so desperate it was almost worse than his bad one.

'He started it, really. But at least we've got the terms to consider.'

'Yes. We *must* negotiate.'

Simon did not reply. He thought that negotiate would turn out to mean doing what Teddy wanted.

∞ ∞ ∞

They were eleven for dinner at Mill Farm, because Villy had invited Rupert and Zoë, feeling that poor Edward was otherwise going to be swamped by her female relations and Miss Milliment. She had also asked Teddy, as she thought it would be nice for Christopher, but Christopher had forgotten to give him the message until it was too late. Judy, Neville and Lydia were ostensibly in bed, but with Ellen comfortably in the kitchen helping Emily dish up; they were playing a rather quarrelsome game of hospital with Lydia as patient (chicken pox), Judy the nurse and Neville, only because he was the boy, being the doctor. Even so, eleven round the table in the long narrow room, made it difficult to hand the vegetables, as Phyllis – who had come down on the afternoon train – discovered.

Villy put her mother between herself and Jessica: Lady Rydal had behaved all day as though the death of Aunt Lena – whom she had never met – was a personal tragedy that made her coming down to dinner (appearing in public in deep black) a courageous concession that required constant sympathy and support. Jessica was very good about this, adopting the muted, slightly religious tone that was expected of her and that so infuriated her son and daughter for different reasons – Christopher because he loathed humbug, and Nora because it seemed sacrilegious to pretend anything about God. Villy had also contrived that Edward sat between Zoë and Angela, which she thought would mitigate against the elderly elements of the party, but Angela, who was wearing a shapeless pale grey dress and who had not bothered to make up her face, was quite silent, and looked so washed out that her mother remarked upon it. 'Darling, I do hope that you are not the next chicken pox victim.' But she said no, she merely had a splitting headache. Zoë, who usually flirted with Edward (in a perfectly acceptable way, of course), seemed rather off-colour, and Edward had to

311

resort to Christopher's black eye. 'I say, old boy, you've got a real stunner there? How did you get it?' And Christopher, for the fourteenth time, said that he had fallen out of a tree. Nora knew this was a lie, and wondered what *had* happened. Had a quarrel with someone, she thought. Chris had a temper although it never lasted for long. The most successful part of the party – unexpectedly to Villy – was Rupert and Miss Milliment, who talked with great admiration about French painting and from thence to painting of all kinds. Rupert, who had only met Miss Milliment once when Clary had started lessons with her, was enchanted by this surprising lady, dressed in colours that resembled a ripe banana, who adored so many of his favourite painters. But Louise, who sat opposite them, became obsessed by the mounting fragments of spinach and fish that were accumulating in the various folds between Miss Milliment's chins. She made discreet little wiping gestures, having tried to catch her governess's eye, which, of course, at that distance, was impossible. It was Nora who dived under the table, came up with Miss Milliment's napkin and presented it to her saying, 'I'd dropped my napkin and I seem to have found yours as well: one does so need them with the fish, don't you find?'

And Miss Milliment immediately took the hint and wiped a lot of her face and, after some thought, her tiny, steel-rimmed spectacles as well. 'Thank you, Nora,' she said.

And Louise, who felt furious that she had not thought of such a tactful and impressive ploy, immediately said, 'But you love Chinese painting as well, don't you, Miss Milliment? Do you remember the marvellous drawing of the three fishes in the exhibition you took us to?'

'Yes, indeed, Louise. That was one of your favourites, wasn't it? An exquisite pen drawing – so simple and perfect. Do you think', she continued, lowering her voice, 'that they will be removing some of the great works from our London galleries to a place of safety? I should be grateful to know that.'

'You mean, if there's a war?' said Rupert. 'I should think they could put a lot of stuff in their basements. Unless, of course, they turn them into air-raid shelters.'

Edward frowned at his brother. He felt it was not on to talk about the Situation in front of old ladies and children. 'It doesn't matter what you do as long as it doesn't frighten the horses,' he said – Cazalet expression for shut up.

But Louise, who did not know, chipped in at once, 'Mrs Patrick Campbell said that, but I think it was about something rather rude. Not war, anyway.'

'Who was Mrs Patrick Campbell?' asked Zoë, and Rupert glanced at her in surprise – not at her not knowing, but her admitting this in public.

'An actress, but years ago. You can tell that, because it was before motor cars.'

Plates were being cleared, and Phyllis brought two large summer puddings on a tray that was set before Villy.

'Hooray!' said Edward. 'My favourite pudding. You ought to put some raw steak on that eye of yours,' he added, reverting to Christopher who, Nora saw, turned faintly green at the suggestion.

'What a disgusting idea!' she exclaimed. 'Anyway, we've had fish, and I shouldn't think that would be much good.'

'I don't know,' said Louise pensively. 'Better than a slap in the eye with an old fish, I should think.'

'A thoroughly foolish remark,' said Miss Milliment, who had drunk a glass of wine and was feeling not at all herself, which meant better. 'Naturally anything would be nicer than that.'

'A slap in the eye with a wet jellyfish would be worse,' said Nora and started to giggle.

'What an absolutely beastly idea!' Angela turned to her grandmother for support, but Lady Rydal, whose double dangling row of rock-crystal beads swung perilously over the summer pudding, drew herself up and said, 'Angela darling, gairls do not use words like beastly or nasty. You should say horrid, if that is what you mean.'

'Have some cream,' Edward said, and winked at her, but she was so full of chagrin that she did not meet his eye.

∞ ∞ ∞

Polly and Clary were having an uneasy supper in their room. Clary was much better, although some spots still itched, but she was bored. She'd written five short stories that day – there were to be seven, each about a deadly sin – and now she was

313

bored because she was too tired to do anything interesting. Polly was making such an effort not to talk to Clary about the war that she couldn't think of anything else to say. Oscar dominated the room. In spite of an enormous supper of giblets and milk, he made it plain that their supper would probably have been much better for him. He felt the same about his bed, which Polly had lifted him into several times whereupon, refusing to sit let alone lie down in it, he had waited until she had stopped holding him before jumping out. He then sat washing his white-tipped paws occasionally passing his tongue, the colour of fresh pink ham, over the rich grey fur on his flanks – not that there was the slightest thing wrong with his appearance. When Polly said his name, he stopped and glared at her with his Siberian topaz eyes and jumped up onto Clary's bed where he settled cracklingly onto her exercise book.

'I don't mind,' said Clary. 'I like him, really.'

'But if he won't use his bed, do you think he'll use his lav?' She had made him a box, with newspaper and a pile of cinders from the greenhouse boiler, which lay in a discreet corner of the room. He hadn't taken to that, either.

'I'm sure he will. Cats are awfully clean.' There was a silence while they both watched Oscar gradually settle down to sleep. Polly found Clary looking at her with a kind of embarrassed appeal. She knows something, Polly thought. If she knows *any*thing, it would be fair to talk about it.

'Are we thinking about the same thing?' she said.

'Why should we be? What are you thinking about?'

'You first.'

'Well,' Clary began. She started to get pink. 'It's about lust, really. I sort of know what it is, but not entirely. I wouldn't bother with it at all, only that it's one of the deadly sins and I've done all the others except for gluttony and that's going to be about a pig who turns into a boy – or a boy who turns into a pig, I haven't decided yet. And that.'

'What?'

'What I just told you. Lust. What's your opinion of lust?'

'Well,' said Polly slowly. 'It makes me think of the Old Testament – and tigers. You know, a tiger lusting after his prey.'

'Really, Poll, I can't see that a tiger simply trying to get a

314

meal is a deadly sinner. It can't be that. What I mean is, how do you have it? What does it feel like? Writers have to know these things. I know what all the other ones feel like—'

'Bet you don't!'

'You bet wrong. I bet you know as well.' She searched in an exercise book for her list. 'Listen. Pride. When I wrote that story about Jesus being born from the innkeeper's point of view I thought it was the best story that had ever been written in the world. Gluttony. I took out all the violet and rose creams from the box of chocolates I gave Zoë for Christmas last year and put nasty old coconut crunches from an old box in before I gave it to her. Course I ate the creams. Envy. I envy you and Louise having mothers. Often. Nearly all the time. Avarice. I was too mean to buy a larger box of Glitterwax for Neville for his birthday. I kept the rest of the money to buy my cactus. Sloth—'

'OK,' said Polly. 'You needn't go on, I've done all that sort of thing myself.'

'But not lust?'

'Unless one can do it without knowing. And considering how easy it is to do the others, I suppose it's quite possible. It's funny, isn't it? You'd think deadly would mean more difficult.'

'No wonder there are murders and wars and things,' Clary said, 'with everyone sinning away like mad in ordinary life. I think lust's to do with bodies, and honestly I couldn't be less interested in those.'

'Except animals,' said Polly fondly stroking her love. 'Does war worry you?' she added as casually as possible.

'Is that why you got your dad to bring Oscar down?'

Polly stared at her cousin, confounded. 'Yes,' she said. 'I beseech you not to tell anyone, though.'

'Oh, well! If there *was* one we'd stay here for ever – long after chicken pox. It could be quite nice!'

'It couldn't! You don't understand! It will be ten times worse than the last war. You don't know about that. You don't know about poison gas and this time there will be far more bombs and everyone will live in trenches with barbed wire and rats – it won't be like it all happening in France somewhere, it will be everywhere – even here! It will go on until everyone's dead, I know it will!' She was crying – past caring whether she frightened Clary or not, almost *wanting* to frighten her so that some of her own anguish could be shared with someone, at least. But Clary did not seem frightened at all.

'You're imagining,' she said. 'I often do that.' She knelt up in bed and hugged Polly. 'You've got me,' she said 'and Oscar. There's not going to be a war. And even if there is, think of history. We always win.'

And although none of this should have been comforting, Polly felt, it actually was. She blew her nose, and it was agreed that she should look up lust in the Brig's dictionary and/or Miss Milliment could be consulted.

'She knows everything. She's bound to know all about lust,' Clary said. And Polly, as she took their supper tray down to Eileen, felt – compared to the last twenty-four hours – quite hopeful.

∞ ∞ ∞

After dinner, when the Duchy and Sid were still playing Brahms sonatas, Hugh gave a signal to his wife that meant he would like to retire with her. Outside the drawing room, he took her hand, and they went upstairs, first to the little dressing room where Wills lay in voluptuous sleep, his covers thrown off, one leg in the air. Sybil gently put it down and tucked him up. His eyelids fluttered and he sighed. She picked up the small golliwog that lay on the floor and put it beside him.

'Where did he get that?'

'Lydia gave it to him. It was hers. He's called Golly Amazement. It's his favourite thing.'

'A very good name for someone with that expression.'

'Brilliant, isn't it?' She turned off the light and they went next door. 'What is it, darling? Something's on your mind?'

'Yes,' he said. 'Edward would say I'm a scaremonger, but London is quite full of them at present. They're issuing everybody with gas masks. I'm going to take people tomorrow to get them.'

'Oh, darling! Where?'

'Battle probably. The Church Hall, the Brig thinks. He's going to find out in the morning. He agrees with me.'

'Will they have them for babies?' She began to look frightened. 'Because *I* won't if—'

'Of course they will.'

'He won't like it – terribly frightening for a baby.'

'It will be all right. But we must do all the other children first. I don't want them frightened. I think Polly is already.'

'Why?'

'She wouldn't have asked me to bring Oscar down if she wasn't. Has she said anything to you?'

'No. Hugh . . . ' she sat on the side of the bed. 'Oh, God! Hugh, do you really think—'

'I don't know, but I think we've got to consider that it might.'

'But nobody *wants* it! It's ridiculous! A nightmare! Why on earth should we go to war about Czechoslovakia?'

He tried to tell her why he thought they might have to, but he could see that the reasons were meaningless to her. Eventually, having gone through the motions of accepting his argument, she said, 'Well, if it does happen, what do you want me to do?'

'Stay here with the children. We'll have to see.'

'But what will you do? I can't let you stay in London all by yourself.'

'Darling, I don't know where I'll be.'

'What do you mean?'

'I might be wanted for something or other. Don't worry. It would probably be a desk job.' He looked down at his stump. 'The days of Nelson are over. Or, if Edward goes, I may have to help the Brig run the firm. Wood is going to be needed.'

'You talk as though you *know* it's going to happen!'

'For God's sake! You asked me what I'd do if it did. I'm trying to tell you.'

She looked so stricken that he went to her, and lifted her to her feet. 'I'm sorry, sweeting. I'm tired. Let's go to bed.'

When they lay together in the dark, holding hands as they often did, she said, 'At least Simon isn't old enough.'

And glad that she should end the day with this comfort, he said heartily, 'Nothing like!'

∞ ∞ ∞

317

' . . . she *is*!'

'Nonsense, darling, she simply had a headache.'

'It wasn't that. She's in love with you.'

'For God's sake! She's a sort of niece!'

'If you've been painting her all this time, you must have noticed!'

Rupert hooked his arm in hers. 'Well, I didn't. You always say that men don't notice things like that. I'm a man.'

They were walking up the hill back to Home Place. It was dark and overcast; a thin white mist veiled the ground of the large hop field that had once belonged to Mill Farm. After what felt to him like a companionable silence, he said, 'Anyway, she's a child. Only nineteen.'

'How old was I when you married me?'

He stopped. 'Oh, Zoë, my *dear*! All right. There is no earthly reason why I should not be in love with her. She is nineteen, very lovely to look at, and you have been absent far too long. But the fact is, I'm not. Anyway, how do I know what you've been up to in London?'

'I told you – I only saw a girl I was at school with.' She began to walk ahead of him up the drive.

Oh dear, she's going to be cross with me and sulk, he thought, and caught up with her. 'I was only teasing you,' he said. 'I know you've had a hard time with your mother. I really admire you for being so good and staying home so long. It must have been very dull. I'm glad you saw your friend.'

They had reached the little white gate that led onto the front lawn and main door. He pulled her towards him and saw that her eyes were glistening.

'Such a beautiful girl,' he began – but she stared at him as though for once she did not want to hear that.

'It's *all* I am,' she said. 'I'm *nothing* else!' and turned and ran ahead of him into the house.

As he shut the gate and followed her – slowly – he thought that she was desperately overtired with all her unaccustomed nursing. Then he remembered that she'd slept the whole afternoon. It must be the time of the month for her, he thought. But she'd had her period just before she went to London – which meant that it wasn't due for at least a week. It couldn't be that.

Then he wondered whether she was right about Angela; pretty dim of him not to have noticed if she was. But what could he have done about it if he had known? He hadn't led her on or anything like that. It was – if it was anything – just a phase in her life. Then he thought what cant that was. It was what older people always said about inconvenient feelings or behaviour of the young; as though *they* were not subject to phases – what a word for it, anyway! But she hadn't asked him anything about his decision as to going into the firm or not, which had been a relief because he still hadn't made up his mind and, if the Brig and Hugh were right, it would get made up. He'd be called up, or he might even get into one of the Services first.

By now he had reached the door of Clary's room, intending to look in on her to make sure she was all right before he went to bed. But a notice on her door said OSCAR IS HERE. PLEASE DO NOT OPEN THE DOOR AT NIGHT. Who the hell was Oscar? He didn't know. He listened for a moment, but there was no sound from within. The whole house was quiet. If he did go away, who would look after Clary? She would stay here, and she would have Miss Milliment, who, it had become clear to him after dinner, was very fond of Clary. He went to the bathroom, had a pee, and then leant out of the open window. The white mist lay over the kitchen garden, the air smelled faintly of cold woodsmoke; an owl hooted like a spectral foghorn once, a silence, and then twice more. If he was on his own, he would have gone to look at his picture to see if he had finished it, pretty sure he had but sometimes it was difficult to know when to stop. Isobel would have come and looked at it with me, he thought, and buried her again because thoughts of her always seemed to connect with a kind of disloyalty that he could not afford. It was only when approaching their bedroom door at last and assembling excuses for her if she was sulking, or provocatively chatting and dawdling in half her clothes, that he was suddenly struck by what she had said when he had started to tell her she was beautiful. 'I'm nothing else!' A fearful and costly truth – was it? But he could not bear it for her. A surge of protective love encrusted his honesty: if she said anything more about that, he would deny it.

In the room, which was almost dark with only his small

bedside lamp alight, she was in bed, so still and quiet that he thought she was asleep. When he got into bed and touched her shoulder, she turned and threw herself into his arms, without a word.

∞ ∞ ∞

On Saturday morning, the Duchy woke as usual when the early-morning sun streamed through her white muslin curtains and fell in a wide stripe across her narrow hard little white bed. The moment she was awake, she got up: lolling about in bed was a modern (soft) habit that she deplored, just as she considered early-morning tea unnecessary, even decadent. She put on her blue dressing gown and slippers and padded off to the bathroom where she had an uncomfortably tepid bath: hot water was another thing she was chary of, she considered it to be bad for the system and in any case spent only enough time in the bath to wash properly. Back in her room, she unwound the plait of hair that she had pinned up for her bath, and brushed it out for fifty strokes. Like her daughter, she favoured blue and her clothes, summer and winter, were much the same: a dark blue jersey skirt, a paler blue cotton or silk shirt, and a cardigan-like jacket. She wore pale grey stockings and shoes with two straps and low heels. Then she sat at her dressing-table – draped in white muslin, but with hardly anything upon it excepting her tortoiseshell brushes initialled in silver – a brush, a comb, a shoehorn and a buttonhook comprised the set – and put up her hair. She had a fine complexion, a broad brow, over which the hair was looped, and a heart-shaped face with no trace of a double chin. She had been a beauty, and at seventy-one was still an unusually good-looking woman, but seemed now, and in fact always had been, unconscious of her appearance, only looking in a glass to see whether her hair was neat. Her final touches were slipping on her gold wrist-watch, a wedding present from William, and tucking the tiny lace-trimmed handkerchief under the strap so that it concealed the small mulberry-coloured birthmark on her wrist. Then she took the mother-of-pearl and sapphire cross on its silver chain and hung it around her neck. She was ready for the day. During the half-hour of her ablutions and toilet her mind had been full of embryonic lists of things that must be done that morning. She stripped back her bed to air it – she came from the feather-bed era when the airing of beds was a serious matter – opened the windows wide so that the room should also be thoroughly aired and went down to the morning room where she breakfasted earlier than the rest of the family on Indian tea and toast, one slice spread with butter, the other with marmalade – to have put both on one slice was, in her opinion, an absurd waste. With her second cup of tea she took a used envelope from her desk, and began to write the lists under different headings. With fifteen in the house – not counting five indoor servants, who, of course, had to be counted where food was concerned – the housekeeping had become quite a large matter. She would go into Battle with Tonbridge directly she had seen Mrs Cripps and discussed the weekend menus. Hugh and Edward would be ferrying the family to and fro to collect their gas masks, but she realised now that the servants would also have to be taken to Battle by him, and when on earth could Mrs Cripps be spared for such an outing? After lunch, she decided.

Then there was Sid's sister to be collected from the station, some time in the morning. Sid and Rachel could be put to work. Either they could get the camp beds, now cluttering up the hall, into the squash court where at least they would be out of the way, or they could put the finishing touches to Tonbridge's ex-cottage that she had been making ready for the overflow. She had finished machining the curtains yesterday. But before deciding about this, she really must make sure that William had not actually invited twenty-four people to *sleep* in the camp beds; she so much hoped not, but on the other hand what on earth had possessed him to buy them if he hadn't? He did not seem to have considered bedding, pillows, blankets, and the like, but he was a man and that was to be expected. Buying bedding, however, would mean going to Hastings, and even if it was ordered, it would be unlikely to get delivered before next week. And next week, they might be at war. *Again!*

The Duchy was of a generation and sex whose opinions had never been sought for anything more serious than children's ailments or other housewifely preoccupations, but this was not to say that she did not have them: they were simply part of the vast portmanteau of subjects never mentioned, let alone discussed, by women, not, as in the case of their bodily functions, because it was not seemly, but because, in the case of politics and the general administration of the human race, it was useless. Women knew that men ran the world, had the power and, corrupted by it, fought on the slightest provocation for more, while injustice permeated *their* lives like words through a stick of seaside rock. Take her unmarried sisters, for instance, educated, as she had been, only to marry, but even that career, the only one regarded by men as suitable, meant their dependence upon some man who might choose them, and in the cases of poor Dolly and Flo, nobody ever had. And then, if you *did* marry, would any woman in her right mind *choose* to have her sons go to France as Edward and Hugh had done, last time? She had never expected either of them to come back – had lived in an agony of secret tension through those four and a half years, when, it seemed, everybody else's sons were killed or shattered. When she heard that Hugh had been wounded and was to be invalided home, she had locked herself where no one would find her in the spare room at Chester Terrace and cried with relief, with anguish for Edward still at the front, finally with rage at the horrible lunacy of it all – that she should be sobbing with relief because Hugh's health might merely be wrecked for life. This time, surely, Edward was too old to go, but they would take Rupert and, if it went on long enough, Teddy, the eldest grandson. And she had always been supposed to be so lucky because William had been fifty-four in 1914 – deemed, in spite of his efforts, too old. His sons had called him the Brigadier as a kind of teasing recompense.

Her tea was cold and she was not getting on with things. She began another list. The shortages of all kinds of things the last time flooded her mind. She felt that hoarding was improper; nevertheless a few dozen extra Kilner jars for bottling fruit, isinglass for preserving eggs, and salt for runner beans, of which they had a bumper crop this year, was not exactly hoarding. After a pause she added 'packet of sewing-machine needles' to the list. Enough of that. The house was full of sounds now, children's voices, the hall being laid for their breakfast, William's wireless in his study, he must be back from his early-morning ride, Wills crying upstairs and, outside, McAlpine mowing the tennis court. It seemed impossible that they were on the brink of another war. She rang the bell for Eileen to bring fresh tea for William and her sisters whom she could hear coming slowly down the back stairs bickering gently with each other – a habit that drove William mad with boredom. She picked up her lists, went to the window and gazed longingly at her new rockery where she could easily spend the morning if there was not so much else to do. Rachel and Sid were walking slowly down the path beside it; she resisted the impulse to join them, but they saw her and started for the house. Rachel knew that her father could not be left to breakfast alone with her aunts, and Sid was a dear and read *The Times* to him to damp down Dolly's and Flo's sometimes quite frighteningly general conversation. Sid *was* a dear and she enormously enjoyed playing with her; she had been told that the sister was a bit of a wet blanket, but this wasn't the time for picking and choosing guests. Rachel was walking as though her back hurt her – her slightly stooping, hesitant walk. It would not do at all for her to move the beds, but she could be useful in a dozen other ways, as indeed she always was. It was wonderful to have Rachel at home; of course she had not *wanted* to marry, was perfectly happy with her charity work and helping her father. She was completely free to do as she pleased, so there was no comparison with Dolly and Flo at all.

When Eileen arrived with fresh tea and toast, she realised that her sisters had mysteriously not appeared, which meant that they must have waylaid William in his study interrupting him from hearing the eight o'clock news. She went to the window and called to Rachel just as Dolly and Flo entered the room. Their progress, as always, was impeded by their gigantic work-bags filled with crochet and *petit point*, and their nearly as large battered handbags in which they kept their various patent medicines, scarves, spectacles, little white handker-chiefs reeking of lavender water and faded chiffon squares wrapped round a swansdown puff impregnated with peachy powder, frequently applied in Dolly's case although this turned her complexion, naturally that of a mildewed strawberry, into an almost spectral mauve. They had been listening to the news, they said, but there wasn't any really. 'But dear William had his wireless facing the wrong way, so it was rather difficult to hear,' Flo said. She was a little deaf and full of theories of this kind.

'Is the dining-room breakfast in?' the Duchy enquired of Eileen.

'Mrs Cripps is dishing up now, m'm.'

Rachel and Sid arrived, and Dolly instantly asked Rachel to be mother, an invitation that if he had been there would have irritated William beyond measure, the Duchy knew, both the manner of it, and that it should be made at all. Naturally, in the absence of his wife, his daughter would pour out. She left them to it, gathered up her lists and went in search of Mrs Cripps.

∞ ∞ ∞

When Hugh assembled the first batch of children for the collection of gas masks, Christopher and Teddy were nowhere to be found, but the car was full, anyway, with Sybil, Wills, Polly, Simon, Neville and Lydia. It was agreed with Edward, when Hugh collected the last two from Mill Farm, that he would bring another contingent consisting of Nora, Louise, Judy, Angela and the two missing boys. Villy said that she would take her mother, Jessica and Miss Milliment, Phyllis and Ellen with her when she went to collect the meat and other provisions. Hearing this, Edward felt he was getting off lightly.

Hugh patiently answered the barrage of questions when they were not scornfully answered for him by another child than the questioner.

'What do they smell like?'

'Silly. They won't smell of anything – just air.'

'How do you know? How would Polly know, Uncle Hugh?'

'I know because Dad was gassed in the war and I've read about it.'

'Did you have a gas mask, Uncle Hugh?'

'Yes.'

'How could you get gassed if you had one? They can't be much good.'

'Well, there was gas about for rather a long time. We had to take them off sometimes, to eat and so on.'

'We can't not *eat*!'

'Yes, we could. We could choose between getting thinner and thinner or being gassed. Which would you rather, Uncle Hugh?'

'Don't be so *stupid*, Neville.'

'The one thing I'm not is stupid. Only a very stupid person would think I was stupid. Only a very, *very* stupid—'

'That will do, Neville,' Sybil said firmly, and it did.

'In any case, you won't have to *wear* your masks, this is just a precaution.'

'What's a precaution?'

'It's being careful before you have to,' Neville said at once. 'I've never seen the point of it, myself,' he added rather grandly; the idea that he was stupid still rankled.

'You're very silent, Poll,' her father said, but precluded from any private confidence by all the others she just said, 'No, I'm not.'

In the back of the car she exchanged glances with Simon, also silent: he was worried about something. Once, years ago, she would have known what it was without his saying a word, but he had been away so much and for so long at boarding schools that she no longer knew and he would not now say a word.

Lydia and Neville were chattering on about poison gas – what it smelled like and whether you could see it, and her father said that one kind smelled of geraniums. 'That's lewisite,' she said quickly before she could stop herself.

In the front of the car, Hugh raised his eyebrows and glanced at Sybil. Then he said, 'I think that gas is most unlikely, you know, Polly. It wasn't very economic last time. Weather conditions have to be right and so on. And, of course, if we all have masks, it will be less worthwhile than ever.'

'What would be a good idea,' said Neville, 'would be if the Germans let down huge enormous fly papers about a quarter of a mile long, from their aeroplanes, and people would stick to them like bluebottles and they wouldn't be able to get off it – would just be stuck waving their arms and legs until they were dead. I think that's a *very* good idea,' he added, as though someone else had thought of it.

'If you don't shut up,' Simon said savagely, 'I'll knock your block off!'

And Neville, who wasn't absolutely sure what his block was, became completely silent. In the front, Hugh and Sybil tacitly conspired to take no notice, but Hugh wondered whether he was dreading his new school, and Sybil whether he was sickening for chicken pox. He was usually such a gentle, easy-going child, she thought, as she cradled the sleeping Wills in her arms and began to dread waking him with the prospect of a gas mask.

∞ ∞ ∞

Even after the fight, Teddy had remained so angry that he could hardly think about the whole business at all. The moment he tried, it was like opening the damper on a furnace: rage flared in him, he wanted to kill Christopher and he loathed Simon. He was used to being the leader of his enterprises and Simon, two years younger, had always been his faithful henchman, happy to do whatever Teddy thought up. Before, when Christopher had stayed in the summer, he'd had something wrong with him which meant that he couldn't play games (which he was no good at, anyway), or, as his mother had said, 'do too much', whatever the hell that meant. So he had read books, and Teddy and Simon had played some token uneasy games of cards with him and spent their days playing bicycle polo, going for long rides, going to the beach, tennis, squash and some of the family games that the girls still wanted to play and that they secretly still enjoyed although they professed to scorn them. But this time Simon had sneaked off with Christopher, lied to Teddy about why he couldn't do things with him, as Teddy could now see, and never even considered asking him to join in whatever it was. He had made efforts to find out from Simon what it was, but when Simon, nearly in tears, had persisted in saying that it was Christopher's secret and he *couldn't* tell, Teddy had sent him to Coventry, had refused to answer or speak to Simon at all. But the more Simon had refused to tell him, the more passionately curious he had become: it must be something quite large and serious for Simon to hold out. So he resolved to go back to the wood early in the morning to see what he could discover. He would be able to stiffen the terms when they had their meeting if he knew what he was making terms for. So he crept out of their room, leaving Simon asleep, coaxed one of the maids to give him thick marmalade sandwiches, and set off for the wood.

There had been a heavy dew and the long meadow was full of rabbits. He wished that he had brought his gun, but Dad had said no shooting when he was on his own. Then he remembered that he'd seen a bow and arrows in the tent – *his* tent, he thought defiantly and feeling angrier because deep down he knew this wasn't true, it *had* been given to all of them. Stupid, to give something that was only any good for two people to dozens of people. It had *become* his tent because only he and Simon had ever used it, and it was more his than Simon's because he was the eldest.

He found the bow and arrows. There didn't seem to be very many of them; Christopher must have made them because Simon wouldn't know how to do that sort of thing, and he had to admit that the arrows looked quite good, tipped with goose feathers neatly trimmed, and the points had been slightly charred and then sharpened. He decided to practise before he went after the rabbits, and that turned out to be a good idea as it was far harder to aim right than he had thought. The trouble was that he kept losing the arrows. To begin with, he didn't bother too much if he couldn't find one, but when he was down to the last two he hunted more seriously, but in the wood, with all the bracken and dead leaves and stuff growing, the arrows were hard to find. When he couldn't find even the last one, he went back to the glade and opened up the tent to see if there were more but he couldn't find any. So he rummaged for more food – the marmalade sandwiches seemed hours ago. He found some eggs and a frying pan, and decided to make a fire. There was a site where they had had fires. So he collected twigs, and he used some sheets from an exercise book in the tent for paper. In the middle of getting the fire going Christopher arrived, before he'd even had time to go through the tent properly. It was nothing like eleven o'clock, which was the time they were supposed to meet.

∞ ∞ ∞

Christopher had not been able to eat much dinner the previous night – apart from his head aching, two of his front teeth were wobbly and when he tried to bite anything they sort of waved about his mouth making him feel slightly sick. He excused himself immediately after the meal, and crept upstairs to his room. He'd gone in and flung himself on the bed before he realised that there was a hat on it, which by then he had crushed rather. He leapt up and tried to unsquash it but it didn't seem to want to, kept collapsing back into a squashed position. In the end he put it on a chair in a dark corner of the room where the owner might not notice it till morning, and went along the passage to the little box room where a bed had been made up for him. But then he couldn't sleep. Being a conscientious objector obviously involved never losing your temper, since the moment that happened he had simply gone for Teddy without thinking, which was awful. How could one guarantee never to lose one's temper? And what on earth was he going to do about Teddy? Tell him? But he sensed that Teddy would not be sympathetic to the idea of running away and, if he wasn't he would almost certainly tell people where they had gone. But now that Teddy knew their hideout, he'd tell them, anyway, wouldn't he? Could they move the camp? That seemed almost impossible: it had taken two weeks to assemble all the stuff there and it was the perfect site. It would be no good making one where the stream wasn't, which meant that even if he moved it would be easy for Teddy to track and find him. Him – what about Simon? From the moment of the chicken pox meeting, he had realised that Simon's heart was not a hundred per cent in their adventure. He hadn't wanted to go to school, but due to the chicken pox that was postponed and, then, if there was a war, Simon seemed to think that schools might stop and he'd never have to go to one. So although he had carried on as though they were both in it together, he'd started not counting Simon. He might find another stream in another wood . . . but he was running out of time, and really he knew that there wasn't such a place within striking distance.

He seemed to wrestle with these hopeless possibilities all night, but he must have slept because he came to with the early-morning sun and it was half past seven, much later than he usually woke, and when he went downstairs he could hear the servants having breakfast. He took a handful of Grape Nuts from the cereal packet and set off for the wood.

When he woke, he had suddenly felt that there *was* a solution – there must be. Peaceful people always won in the end: all they had to do was be appeasing and persuasive, to stick to their guns. What a funny way of saying it, he thought. Guns were the last thing he wanted to have anything to do with, and in any case he hadn't got any. It was Teddy who used a gun.

He would try and find out what Teddy really wanted, he thought, as he jogged up the road, or what he wanted *most*, and then, probably, there would be some way of giving it to him, and then everything would be all right. If it was the tent he wanted, and some of the stores, they could be divided up. If it was that he wanted Simon to camp with? Simon was much younger and really he was in no position to mind effectively what decisions were made about him – well, he could have Simon. If it was the territory that he was after they would have to come to an agreement somehow. If they drew up an agreement – a treaty – then Teddy would have to stick to it if he signed, as of course *he* would if he signed. He would apologise for the fight, losing his temper, and sit down in a really reasonable way to get a fair agreement.

What he had not bargained for was finding Teddy already on the site, not where they were supposed to meet, which had been arranged to be the kennels at eleven o'clock which it wasn't – anything like. When he discovered that Teddy had been using his bow and had lost all the arrows, he started to feel his terrible, unacceptable anger, but this time he swallowed it down and managed to make his apology for the fight, and said he would write down Teddy's terms for proper consideration. In the tent, he found that his precious exercise book with all the lists and things in it had had pages torn out so that some of the lists were missing. Another test. And, when putting up with even this maddening depredation – anyone could light a fire without paper if they knew how – he sat down to listen to Teddy, he discovered that Teddy's terms had mysteriously got much worse than they had been yesterday . . .

∞ ∞ ∞

Zoë woke when Eileen brought in their early-morning tea, but she kept her eyes half closed while Eileen placed the

329

tray carefully on the table beside her, drew the curtains and murmured that it was half past seven. Rupert, beside her, was deeply asleep. She sat up and poured out some tea for both of them. Moving hurt – she was still very sore, and when Rupert had made love to her last night it had been painful, but she knew that she had concealed that from him. If only it was a bit of pain that she had to contend with, she thought, that would be nothing, no less than I deserve. But it was much more than that: he had been so trusting, so tender and considerate of her pleasure, and all she had been able to respond with had been more lies. She had felt gratitude and pain and altogether unworthy. The gap between her body and her heart seemed an abyss and all she was conscious of wanting was confession – to tell him everything, to be punished and forgiven and be able to start afresh. But she couldn't tell him, she could never tell anyone: if she had simply been raped perhaps it would have been possible, but it had not been rape – at all – and she could neither lie about that nor tell him. That's my punishment, she thought. To have to go on lying for the rest of my life.

'Darling! You're looking very tragic! What is it?'

As she turned away to reach for his tea-cup she felt her eyes pricking.

'I wasn't nearly nice enough to Mummy,' she said, remembering that that was also true.

He took the cup from her. 'Bet you were, pet. It's worn you out. How would you like me to bring you a lovely tray in bed?'

She shook her head, wishing he would not keep being so kind to her.

'I thought you might like to come to Hastings with me this morning. I want some more paints, and I wouldn't mind a couple of brushes if I could find anything decent.' He knew how she loved little jaunts alone with him.

'I thought perhaps I ought to help the Duchy with all the things about furnishing the cottage. Rachel said there was an awful lot to get done by this evening.' The thought of the morning alone with him was too much for her.

'Darling, what could you do? You know you hate all that sort of thing. I'm sure she won't expect you to.'

'I don't suppose she would.' Nobody expected anything of her, she thought, forlornly.

'Well, you can decide after breakfast. I'm off to try my luck with the bathroom. Do you want one? A bath, I mean?'

'No. I had one last night.' The tops of her arms were bruised, and she did not want him to see. When he had gone, she got up and dressed quickly in an old pair of slacks and a shirt of Rupert's and tied her hair back with a bit of black ribbon. Then she simply sat at the dressing-table, thinking that this time yesterday she had been at her mother's flat packing, trying to think how to face Rupert. And now, twenty-four hours later, she was back to married life as though nothing had happened at all, sitting in this familiar room that, when she had first seen it, she thought old-fashioned and dull, but now the wallpaper of huge imaginary peacocks, the paisley cotton curtains, the thick, white lace runner on the dressing-table, the plain rose-wood furniture and the prints of the British Raj in India, the subdued Turkey carpet with the stained and waxed boards surrounding it, all seemed familiar, comforting – even luxurious, in comparison to the pinched gentility of her mother's flat. How she had always hated it and its predecessor where she had lived until she was married! But now it occurred to her that perhaps her mother didn't like it much either, that lack of money had prevented her from having what she might have liked, whatever that might be. And her chief reason for there not being enough money had been herself. Her mother had gone out to work in order to send her to a good school, had spent more money on Zoë's clothes and amusements than she had ever spent upon herself. I just took everything I could get, and then got the hell out, she thought. I've never been nice to her – never been grateful, and she realised with a shock of shame that as her mother had become older and more frail she had actually become afraid of her, and that she, Zoë, had known this and had not cared, had complacently, even, found it easier to ration her visits, her telephone calls, any kind of minimal attention. She must change – somehow. But how? She thought of how Rachel or Sybil or Villy and sometimes the Duchy would say of one of the children when they behaved badly, 'It's only a phase', but that was always about one thing, and they were children. She was twenty-three and it seemed that she needed to change everything.

Rupert, back from the bath, announced, 'I need another

shirt. This one's got three buttons off – I look like Seth in *Cold Comfort Farm.*'

'I'll sew them on for you.'

'It's all right, darling, Ellen will do it.'

'Do you think I can't even sew on a button?'

'Of course not. It's just that Ellen always does it, that's all.' He was tucking a different shirt into his trousers. 'You've always said how you loathed mending.'

'I can at least sew on a button,' she said, and burst into tears.

'Zoë! Darling, what is it?' He did not say 'now', but she sensed it from the tone of his voice.

'You think I'm perfectly useless! That I can't do anything!'

'Of course I don't.'

'When I said I wanted to help with the cottage this morning, you didn't want me to. And now I can't even sew a button on your shirt!'

'I thought you didn't want to do those things. Of course you can if you want to.'

But this did not suit her new resolution.

'I might want to do things whether I wanted to or not,' she said, aware, as she said it, that this did not sound how she meant it to.

'All right, darling, you do what you don't want to do if you like,' he said. 'You look very sweet and businesslike, I must say. Shall we go and have some breakfast?'

∞ ∞ ∞

'You look rather like a horse – but not very—'

'Like one of those horses that wear things on their faces with just their eyes and nose showing, you know in Crusades,' Nora added.

'The thing is, they're no good for breathing at *all*.' Neville was wheezing in his chair at the tea table: he had had asthma in the car after they had collected the gas masks.

'I simply adore mine! I look so different in it.' Lydia stroked the box hanging on the back of her chair.

'We all look different.'

'I don't think Miss Milliment would,' Lydia said pensively.

332

'I should think it would be very difficult for a German to tell whether she was in hers or not.'

'That will do, Lydia,' Ellen said, 'and hand the bread and butter to your cousin.'

'Mummy said if we wear them for five minutes every day, we'll soon get used to them.' Nora realised that Neville had been frightened, and was kindly trying to encourage him.

'I shall wear mine nearly all the time except for meals. It's true you can't eat in them. You couldn't kiss anyone either.'

'Drink your milk, Neville.'

He did, and then he said, 'I know a good thing. If the great aunts were kept in them, we'd never have to kiss them.'

'Oh, poor them!' said Judy in her most affected voice.

'It's all very well for you. They're not your great aunts. Guess what their poor old faces feel like!'

'Very old strawberries,' Neville said at once. 'All softy and bluey – with damp fur.'

'That's just one,' Lydia said. 'The other one is – is – like kissing a huge dog biscuit. All hard and leathery with holes.'

'That will do, Lydia,' Ellen said again.

'Why will it always do for me and not for Neville?'

'That will do from both of you.'

'Aunt Lena's face was like kissing blancmange,' Judy said, 'and Grania's—'

'Shut up,' Nora said sharply. 'Aunt Lena's dead. You shouldn't say anything at all about her.'

In the rather surprising silence that followed, she poured a cup of tea to take up to Louise, who was lying down with a headache.

∞ ∞ ∞

It was indeed oppressive, Miss Milliment thought, as she zigzagged lightly up the hill to Home Place after tea with Angela. After the collection of the gas masks, she made herself useful reading those portions of *The Times* to Lady Rydal that she wished to hear: the obituaries, the Court Circular, and some of the letters. She had expressed her desire to visit Clary to dear Viola and Jessica, and Angela had volunteered to conduct her up the hill. She was a very pretty girl, astonishingly like her mother had been at that age (Miss Milliment had taught Viola and Jessica until they were seventeen and eighteen respectively), but she seemed most withdrawn, whereas Jessica had always been such an outgoing girl full of good humour and spirits. She tried talking to Angela about France, but Angela did not seem to want to talk about that at all, and Miss Milliment, reflecting that, at her age, Angela had probably fallen in love with some young Frenchman from whom she was now parted, tactfully changed the subject.

'Your uncle was telling me that he has been painting you. Do you think that there is a chance that I might see it?'

And Angela, who had been striding ahead, stopped at once and turning round said eagerly, 'Oh! I wish you would! I went this morning to sit, but he said he thought it was finished. It doesn't look like that to me at all! I should be so glad of your opinion!'

So they went in at the front door, through a room where old Mrs Cazalet, in a hat, was machining curtains, into an enormous hall where supper was being laid for the children, down a passage, rather dark and she nearly tripped but that was because one of her shoelaces had come undone – they were not really long enough to tie double bows – through a baize door to a long dark room with a billiard table in it and a bow window at one end. And there was the picture. An interesting portrait, Miss Milliment thought. He seemed to have captured the paradoxical ardour and languor of a young girl – that air that was both expectant and passive, and she noticed that the mouth, often the Achilles heel if one could think of it like that for many painters, had been made far easier in this case because Angela had her mother's mouth, a pre-Raphaelite affair, full but finely chiselled, a clear case of nature imitating art, but here a cliché that did not require the artist's creative perception . . . fashionable portrait painters, of course, had always imposed features upon people: the rose-bud mouth of Lely, for example . . .

'You see what I mean? My skin looks all blotchy. He wanted my hair all straight like that,' she added.

'I don't think anyone but the painter can decide when he has finished,' Miss Milliment said. 'And there is a danger, I believe, of painters overpainting a portrait. I think it is most interesting, and you should feel honoured to have been the subject.'

'Oh, I *am*! I'm sure he's really a marvellous painter. But it takes years and years to be one, doesn't it? So he mightn't have—'

'Well, perhaps he will want to do another one.'

'Yes, I expect he will. Oh, Miss Milliment! Your shoelace is undone.'

And my stockings are coming down already, she thought, looking down at the fat wrinkles round her ankle.

'Would you like me to tie it for you?'

'Thank you, my dear. That would be most kind.'

Angela knelt and tied the lace, thinking, Poor old thing! I don't see how she can bend down to do it for herself.

And Miss Milliment, who every morning and evening had this struggle alone seated on the side of her bed with her foot on a chair, suddenly thought of something, 'I wonder', she said, 'if you could tell me? Dear Louise gave me a tin of something called talc powder for Christmas. I have brought it with me, as with the Situation one does not know when one will be returning home, but I am not very clear about its *use*?' Angela, on her feet again, looked mystified.

'I tried it on my face,' Miss Milliment persisted, 'but that did not seem to be quite right.'

'Oh.' She saw that Angela was amazed. 'It's not for the face at all, Miss Milliment, it's for your body. You know, after your bath.'

'For my body, after a bath,' Miss Milliment repeated steadily with less idea than ever what it could possibly be for. 'Thank you, Angela. Perhaps you would show me Clary's room?'

So Angela took her right to the door, and then wandered away – hoping she would find Rupert somewhere not with Zoë.

∞ ∞ ∞

Evie's train was late, which was a good thing as Tonbridge was also late fetching her. He had had a tiring day, taking servants to get their gas masks. Mrs Cripps had enjoyed sitting in front with him, but had deeply resented the girls in the back and snubbed them whenever they opened their mouths, but the instant, uneasy silence that ensued each time left her irritably aware of their attention to whatever she might say to Mr Tonbridge, now called Bert by her whenever they were alone. So she confined herself to incontrovertible remarks about the weather with which Tonbridge instantly agreed: it *was* very close, they were likely to have another storm before the day was out; it wasn't as though they needed rain although a good downpour might clear the air and send them hop-pickers back to London where they belonged.

Then he had another trip to Battle, and he had to go onto the platform to find Miss Evie Sidney as Miss Rachel hadn't come with him to fetch her. She had the heaviest luggage he had ever had to deal with, and she seemed very put out that they hadn't come to meet her. He gave the message sent: that Miss Rachel had hurt her back moving furniture, and that Miss Sidney was moving her things over to the cottage where they were to sleep as the house was so full. But even after the message he sensed that she was put out. Oh, well. His orders were to show her in to the front door of the house, and to take her luggage over to the cottage. Then he could go and have his tea.

∞ ∞ ∞

William had had a fruitful day. The pair of cottages that lay beside a cart track a hundred yards from the road between Mill Farm and his own house and had been empty for nearly a year now since the tenant, a Mrs Brown, had died, were for sale. It had taken some time to find their owner, who in the end had turned out to be York, the farmer, whose farm lay a quarter of a mile further down the track. Mr York never said anything at all unless urged, and had never mentioned his ownership, but William, who had first noticed the cottages on his morning rides, had discovered about it from his faithful builder, Sampson, who had agreed, with relish, that if the cottages remained empty much longer they wouldn't be no good to anybody. So William had gone to see York, who proved to be doing something very slowly in his cowshed.

When he saw old Mr Cazalet, York propped his pitchfork against the cowshed door and stood waiting to see what was up. When old Mr Cazalet said he'd come about the cottages, he said, 'Oh, yes?' and then led the way silently to his house. They went in through the back – the front door was never used except for funerals or weddings, the last time had been when his mother had died. He had not married himself, it was said, because his fiancée had stepped in his pond in her rubber boots and got drowned. A lady called Miss Boot housekept for him, but her appearance was not one to excite improper thoughts, and indeed the uttermost propriety prevailed. They went through the pantry, where Miss Boot was making butter (she was tall and unsmiling with a slight beard) and through his kitchen, which smelled of dinner cooking and freshly ironed shirts, along the flagged passages to the little parlour, shrouded in blinds, reeking of furniture polish and Flit to kill the blue-bottles that lay on the window-sills like huge overbaked currants from a cake. William was seated in the best chair, some blinds were drawn up revealing a small walnut upright piano with sheet music on its stand between the candlesticks, three other chairs, a fireplace with a small iron grate and a large print of 'The Last of England' framed above it.

The cottages. Ah! Well, he hadn't rightly thought what he might do with them. They'd come to him through his mother, and Mrs Brown had been a friend of hers and, of course, she'd had her share of troubles, fourteen children she'd had, or fifteen, she'd never been sure. And when she'd passed on, the children were grown, or they'd gone to live with their auntie in Hastings. This burst of loquacity seemed to exhaust him, and he sat reiterating his agreement with himself about these facts.

At this point, Miss Boot appeared with a tray on which there were two cups of strong Indian tea rendered almost peach coloured by creamy milk and a plate of ginger biscuits which she placed with care upon a rather unreliable little table between them. Then, darting one withering look at York's boots – not meant for the house, let alone the parlour – she went.

The cottages. Well, it depended what Mr Cazalet had in mind. William explained that he wanted to buy them and convert them into a house for some of his family. Ah. Mr York put four lumps of sugar into his tea. There was silence during which William became aware of the sibilant ticking of a small black clock on the mantelpiece. He waited until York had finished stirring his tea before he mentioned a price. There was another silence, while Mr York ruminated about five hundred pound – a sum larger than any he had ever had come to him. A new roof sprouted upon the cowshed, a piggery was built in the twinkling of an eye, a tarpaulin for his stack out the back, a new scythe, get a digger for his pond, his own bull to cover his cows and get the gates on the big field repaired so he could run to some sheep if he'd a mind to, build her out in the kitchen that little greenhouse she'd been nagging for . . .

'I expect you'd like to think it over.'

'I might. And I might not.'

'There was one other thing . . . '

He might have known there'd be a fly in the ointment. 'I know them roofs need a bit of seeing to.'

'It wasn't that. But I'd like a bit of land at the back. Beyond the garden hedge, that is.'

'Ah!' Buying property was one thing, he'd never been much of a one for property, but land was different. He didn't care to sell his land.

'I only want a small bit. An acre. Just to make a kitchen garden.'

'Ah, well, that's another matter. Land's another matter.' His mournful brown eyes regarded William ruminatively. 'That's good land up there.'

It wasn't. Or not in its present state – full of thistles and rabbit holes and clumps of brambles. But William knew better than to argue. He simply offered another fifty pounds, and although it was agreed that Mr York should think it over, they both knew that he already had.

'Right. Well, York – an answer tomorrow morning? I want to get on with it, you see. We may have another war on our hands.' York was irresistibly reminded of the nightmare years when, starting at eighteen, he'd spent four years in France when in his memory he had always been wet and nearly always been frightened, when he had seen things done to men that he wouldn't stand to see done to an animal, when the land had been nothing but rats and lice and mud and blood and all because of those German Huns. He said, 'You wouldn't catch me going out there again, not for all the tea in China.'

338

William got to his feet. 'This time they may come to us,' he said.

York darted a look at him to see if the old man was having him on, but he wasn't.

'If they come on my land, they'll get what for,' he said quietly. William looked at him, surprised: he meant it.

∞ ∞ ∞

'What we've got to do is *pray*,' Nora said, so vehemently that Louise was startled.

They were lying on their beds after supper; the curtains were open so that they could watch the hectic, streaky lightning and then count until the faint rumble of thunder could be heard.

'Do you honestly think it would do any good?'

'Of course, it always does. It doesn't always get you exactly what you are praying for, but it always does *good*.'

'Surely not wanting a war is a good thing to want? So, if prayers work, God ought to let there not be a war.'

Nora, to whom something of the kind had already uncomfortably occurred, said, 'Oh, well, there are degrees. We might get a less awful war by praying. Anyhow, I'm going to church tomorrow, and I really beg you to come, too.'

'OK. We are rather an ungodly family. Church only at Christmas and for christenings and so on.'

'Doesn't even the Duchy go?'

Louise shook her head. 'Only at Christmas. Her father was a scientist, you see. They don't believe in faith. We'll have to walk, no one will take us.'

'We could bike.'

'Yes. I warn you, if I do go to church before breakfast I tend to faint. Unless I eat something first.'

'You can't possibly do that. You can't take Communion if you do that. You have been confirmed, haven't you?'

'Of course. The Bishop of London – years ago. In the church here you get squares of bread, not wafers like in London.'

'I think that's better, it's supposed to be bread. How's your pain?'

'Better. Less like a flat iron trying to drop through my

339

stomach, anyway. Will you still go to that cooking school if there's a war?'

'I haven't the faintest. I should think it would be rather a trivial pursuit if there was.'

'Not as bad as acting,' Louise said sadly. She could see her career going up in smoke. In which case, did she need to get over being homesick? Yes, because she needed to get away for other reasons as well. She couldn't tell Nora about them. Nora set her alarm clock for half past six. The thunder had got very much nearer and kept them awake but they had agreed to like thunderstorms so they kept the curtains open.

∞ ∞ ∞

Simon had had an awful day. After Teddy refusing to speak to him he had looked for Christopher, but he didn't find him until nearly lunch-time, and then he was in a bad mood. He said that Teddy was worse about everything, but that he was trying to make things all right and where on earth had Simon *been* all morning? Actually, Simon had gone and lain in the hammock because he had a headache and he had gone to sleep, but when he woke up he felt awful. After lunch Christopher took him off to the dog kennels and told him the new terms. They seemed simply to leave him out of everything, Simon thought, to treat him as though he wasn't of any importance at all, after all the fetching and carrying and getting things he had done. He was being turned into a kind of feudal slave and Christopher didn't seem particularly grateful that he hadn't sneaked to Teddy at all. He ended up by having a quarrel with Christopher, who said he couldn't back out of it now, he would have to stay in and do as he was told. He hated both of them, and in the end he shouted his worst words at Christopher and then ran away and hid. This was easy because he knew good places far better than Christopher, who soon stopped looking for him. When he saw Christopher disappear towards the drive, he came out of the runner beans and there was Mr McAlpine in a furious temper all because he'd trampled on something or other getting hidden. He ran away from Mr McAlpine into the house, straight up the stairs meaning to go to his room. Then he thought it might have Teddy in it. So he went to his mother's bedroom,

340

usually empty in the afternoon, but she was there, lying on her bed and reading.

'Simon! You must knock when you go into people's rooms.'

'I forgot. Anyway, I didn't think you'd be here.'

'Why did you come in, then?'

'I just wanted—'

'Well, shut the door, darling.'

He shut it rather loudly by mistake. She sat up. 'Don't slam doors. You'll wake Wills.'

'Wills,' he muttered. He kicked the chair leg. She thought of nothing but Wills. From morning till night.

'Simon, what is it? What *is* it?' She swung her legs over the side of the bed. 'Come here. You look very hot.' She put her hand on his forehead and tears spurted out of his eyes. She put her arms round him and he snuggled up against her, feeling worse and better at the same time.

'I think you've got a temperature, my darling.' She kissed him and he clung to her like a little crab. 'There. I expect you're rather dreading your new school. That's what it is, isn't it? I know it's rather a frightening prospect. But you'll have Teddy there, you know. You won't be alone.'

'I *will*! Teddy has become my enemy! It will be worse with him!' He was sobbing now. 'Honestly – I've thought about it, and I really don't think I can stand it! I don't want to be away by myself. Couldn't I just go to day school like Christopher? I'd do anything you like if I don't have to go!'

'Oh, darling! *I* don't want you to go. I miss you all the time. Listen, my pet. I want you to lie on my bed while I take your temp. Then we'll talk more.'

But they didn't much because his temperature was 101. and when he said he couldn't sleep in the room with Teddy she put him to bed in their dressing room, and brought him a mug of hot milky tea and an aspirin, and went to ring up Dr Carr. When she came back, he was feverish and sleepy. 'Bet you won't send Wills to a boarding school,' he muttered. 'Anyway, I didn't sneak. He's got to admit I didn't,' and he drifted off.

She sat and watched him, full of sad, helpless thoughts. Why *should* he be sent away for so many years from his father and brother and sister and, above all, from her? Why had boys always been sent away? He had been at boarding school since he was nine, and he was only twelve now. Even the little medieval pages had been sent to another house with the lady of it to care for them. It wasn't as though Hugh had been happy at school: he had loathed every minute of it, he said, but he still had the apparently immutable view that his son must go through the same mill. That remark he had made about Wills struck at her heart. It was true that she had been indulging herself with this last baby, paying far more attention to him than she had ever done with the other two. True, also, that since Simon had gone to his prep school she had braced herself to the loss by trying to be calm and worldly about it, although the very first time when she had seen him off from Waterloo she had wept bitterly all the way home in the taxi. In some way she had known then that it was the very beginning of saying goodbye to him. Even her letters to him at school had been cool and cheery, and she had found them harder and harder to write – harder to know what he would want to hear and, because none of them ever really could say how much she missed him, putting in nothing that really mattered. His letters – the homesickness was palpable early on: 'Darling Mum, please take me home I am board, board, board. There is nothing whatever to do here' – had contracted to demands for various things, chiefly food: 'Please send me six more tubes of toothpaste. I had to eat mine!' Mysterious descriptions of masters: 'When Mr Attenborough eats toast and marmalade at breakfast, his head steams. We did not have Latin prep today because Mr Coleridge has gone off his head again he rode his bicycle into the swimming-pool: he was smoking and reading and got stung by a wasp but nobody believed him.' She had read the letters to Hugh, who had laughed and said he seemed to be settling down. Well, in a way, he had. But prep schools were not at all the same as public school, and now he had six years of that lying ahead. Poor lamb. At least he's too young for war, she thought for the hundredth time, and Polly is a girl, and Wills is a baby and Hugh can't really be in it. She put a glass of water by Simon's bed; then she bent and kissed him with almost guilty tenderness. He was asleep, and there was no one else to see.

∞ ∞ ∞

That night, which was very hot and still, the thunder rumbled intermittently until dawn when there was a heavy and refreshing shower of rain. Evie, in the cottage, dropped off at last, and Sid, whom she had kept awake with her fears, was able to creep back to the other little room, get into bed and at least have her thoughts to herself. There had been a muddle about moving Miss Milliment to the cottage, which it had been decreed she was to share with Evie, and Evie had refused to sleep there alone. She had been maddening about it, and Sid had decided that she would move heaven and earth – and Miss Milliment – the next day. Evie considered that it was a minor insult to have to sleep there. She was not in the least grateful for the hospitality afforded her, and she had brought with her all the most useless, heavy, and hideous pieces of silver that had belonged to her mother, as well as pretty nearly all the clothes she possessed. 'After all, we may be here for years,' she said. 'It's all very well for you, you don't mind wearing the same things day after day, but you know how I feel about looking nice.'

Sid had hated leaving Rachel, whose back was clearly very bad. When it had transpired that William had decided that if the worst came to the worst the Babies' Hotel must be evacuated and that the beds were for the nurses to occupy in the squash court, Rachel had insisted on helping cart them over there. The Duchy had mildly enquired where the babies were to sleep, and he had simply said that they were small and could be fitted in somewhere. The billiard table could be moved from the billiard room, he had added vaguely. Anyway, the camp beds had done for Rachel's back, and Sid hated to leave her alone. Well, hated not sharing a room with her. In the daytime, she realised despairingly, Evie would never leave them alone together if she could help it. How quickly one got used to things! A week ago, she would have been utterly overwhelmed at the prospect of spending one day and a night with Rachel; now she was grousing because she couldn't spend *all* the time with her. 'Be grateful for what you have,' she told herself, but, then, one of the things she had was Evie, whose presence had never promoted gratitude in anybody. 'Swings and roundabouts,' she

told herself bracingly; she was never sure which was supposed
to be which, but there were usually more of one than the other.

∞ ∞ ∞

Louise got up half an hour earlier than she needed to because
going to church made her review her character, and one thing
that wasn't very good about it was the way she had stopped
really talking to Polly. She knew – and probably no one else
did – how much the idea of war preyed on Polly's mind, but
she had not once given Poll the chance to talk about it. So she
decided that when she fetched the second bicycle, which was
at Home Place, she would go and see Polly and invite her to go
to church with her and Nora.

It was a beautiful morning with yellow sun and a milky blue
sky; the steep banks each side of the road refreshed by the heavy
rain, glittered with beaded cobwebs that were precariously
slung between little drenched ferns, and the air smelled of
mushrooms and moss. She met Mr York in the drive, carrying
his pails of steaming milk, and she said, 'Good morning, Mr
York.' He grinned, which showed his most frightening tooth,
and nodded at her. The front door of Home Place stood open,
and the maids were shaking dusters and there was a smell of
bacon frying and the distant, squeaky, irregular sound of the
carpet sweeper. She ran lightly up the stairs and along the
passage to Polly's and Clary's room. Clary was not awake but
Polly was sitting up in bed with Oscar coiled in a paroxysm of
sleep at her feet. She had been crying. She brushed her face
with the back of her hand, glanced warningly at Clary's bed,
and said, 'Simon has got chicken pox now.'

'You're not crying about that?'

'No.'

Louise went and sat on the bed, and Oscar raised his head,
instantly awake. She stroked his rich fur, and he stared at her
as though he'd never seen her before in his life.

'I've come to ask if you'd like to go to church with Nora
and me. To pray for peace. Nora says it's very important.'

'Louise, how can I? I've told you, I'm not at all sure
that I believe in God.'

'I'm not sure either, but I don't think that's the point. I

344

mean, if there is one, He ought to take notice, and if there isn't, it wouldn't make any difference.'

'I see what you mean. Oh, it's so *awful*! Why don't they have gas masks for animals? I tried to put Oscar in mine last night – you know, put a lot more of him in than just his head, and it still doesn't fit anywhere. And he simply hated it. I couldn't keep him in it.'

'You couldn't give him yours because if he needed it, you would, too.'

'Not more than him. Anyway, I'd decided to say I'd lost mine and get another. To tell a lie about it.' She looked at Oscar with tears of anguish. 'I'm responsible for him. He's my cat!'

She stretched out her hand to stroke his neck and he got up, stretched and then jumped heavily off the bed, making a weak, clockwork sound as he reached the floor.

'Look, Poll, you'd really better come. It's all you can do.'

'OK.'

She leapt out of bed and began putting on her clothes that lay on the chair beside it.

'You can't go in shorts!'

'Oh, no. I wasn't thinking.'

As soon as she was out of bed, Oscar got back into it, settling himself where she had been for some peace and quiet.

'You'll have to wear a hat.'

'Oh, blast! It's got all my shells in it.' Emptying them onto the dressing-table woke Clary, who, the moment she knew what they were doing, wanted to join them.

'You can't. You'll give everybody chicken pox.'

'I won't. They said I could get up today, anyway.'

'There isn't another bicycle.'

'I'll borrow Simon's.'

'You'll faint,' said Louise. 'You may have been up, but you haven't been out.'

But Clary was hunting for clothes. 'Although I have to point out', she remarked as she pulled a blue cotton dress stained with blackberry juice over her head, 'that I don't think prayer works unless you *believe*. However, anything's worth trying,' she added as she saw Louise and Polly's faces: Louise darting her a black look and Polly starting to agonise about her uncertainties.

'You haven't got a hat,' Louise said in a crushing voice.

Clary looked from Louise's white boater with a navy blue ribbon to Polly's straw with cornflowers and poppies round the crown: Zoë did not buy her hats and Ellen chose such awful ones that she lost them on purpose.

'I'll borrow Dad's outdoor painting beret from the hall,' she said.

∞ ∞ ∞

'Sixteen student nurses, plus Matron and Sister Hawkins, and thirty-five babies under five! How can they imagine that they can all be fitted in?'

Rachel sitting bolt upright on her air cushion, put down her tea-cup. 'Duchy, darling, couldn't you talk to him yourself?'

The argument about the proposed immigration of the Babies' Hotel had been raging all day, with Rachel, for whom mobility was agonising, being sent from one parent to another – they refused to treat with one another, William because he had said he hadn't time for women fussing over details, and the Duchy on the grounds that he didn't listen to a word she said.

'I've told you that he said that Sampson is building three Elsans at the side of the squash court.'

'I daresay he is, but there won't be enough water!'

'He says he's going to sink another well. He's out water divining now.'

The Duchy snorted. 'You remember how long the last one took? *Three months!*' She scraped some butter onto her toast. 'And how does he think this multitude is to be fed? Answer me that!'

Rachel was silent. When she had put the same question to her father earlier in the day, he had retorted that they had a perfectly good cook, and, anyway, it was well known that babies lived on milk, which York could produce – and if he couldn't, he, William, could provide him with another cow.

'Well,' said the Duchy – she was wearing her hat for tea, a sure sign of rage. 'If he thinks that Mrs Cripps can cook for an extra eighteen people – not counting the babies – he must be mad.'

'Darling, it *is* rather an emergency.'

'If Mrs Cripps gives notice, it will certainly be one.'

'On the other hand, it may all blow over. After all, the Prime Minister is back and nothing has happened so far, which augurs well, doesn't it?'

'I do not think that Mr Chamberlain is the kind of man who would discuss war on a Sunday,' said the Duchy. It was not clear whether this was an indictment or an accolade.

There was silence while Rachel thought how extraordinarily unreal the whole situation felt. Then, wondering why they were alone, she said, 'Where are the aunts?'

'Having tea with Villy and her mother. She's very good in that way, dear Villy.'

'Villy and Sybil offered to help with the cooking. So did Zoë.'

'My dear, none of them have cooked a meal in their lives. They've probably been taught to make a Victoria sponge at their schools, but that will hardly do, will it?'

And Rachel, who had also never cooked a meal in her life and had forgotten how to make a Victoria sponge, had to agree.

∞ ∞ ∞

Sybil was both surprised and touched at how nice the other children were to Simon. During the day, practically all of them visited him although he didn't seem particularly grateful, but he was feeling pretty rotten so she didn't blame him. She tucked him up after lunch for a good sleep and left a notice on his door telling them to keep out, but when she went up with his tea she found Lydia and Neville seated each side of him in bed.

'They brought me presents. I couldn't tell them to go away,' Simon said. He looked very flushed, she thought.

'Didn't you read the notice?' she said after she had dislodged them.

'No. I can only read when I'm trying. I don't read naturally,' Lydia replied, and Neville said that he only read things when he wanted to, 'Which is hardly ever,' he added.

'So if you read on a gate into a field "Poisonous Snakes Keep Out" you'd get bitten to death,' Simon said.

347

'No. I'd read the word Snakes and that would put me on my guard.'

'And, anyway,' Lydia finished loftily, 'a field is hardly the same as a room, is it? See you tomorrow, Simon. I expect you'll be all spotty by then.'

That evening, Dottie, who had been clumsier than usual and given to tears since breakfast as Eileen remarked, broke out in spots, which was the pox, Mrs Cripps said, or she was a Dutchman. She seemed to regard this as a personal affront, and was being very nasty indeed to poor Dottie, who had just broken a sauce-boat and stood dithering with the dustpan and brush faced with clearing up china and sauce at the same time. 'Well, don't just stand there – clear it up, girl! And then change your overall and go and apologise to Mrs Cazalet.' Rachel, alerted by Eileen, heard this as she entered the kitchen. 'And don't use the dustpan and brush! Get a floorcloth first! Oh – Miss Rachel! That's a piece of Mrs Cazalet's summer service gone! Not to mention the bread sauce, which I don't have the time to make more! And it looks as though she's come down with it! Dear knows how, as if we didn't have enough to worry about.'

Rachel looked from Mrs Cripps's luminescent face to her heaving bust, contained against the fragile breaker of her flowered overall, and mustered her uttermost charm.

'Oh dear! Perhaps one of you', she looked appealingly at the housemaids, who stood thankfully surveying the scene (they hadn't done it, and you wouldn't catch them kitchen-maiding for Mrs Cripps, not in a million years), 'would very kindly clear it up because really I think Dottie should go to bed.'

'That's one place for her,' Mrs Cripps agreed, 'but someone will have to be found, Miss Rachel. Hitler is one thing. But I can't run my kitchen without a maid – nobody could expect that of me.'

'Yes. Well, we'll discuss all that tomorrow, Mrs Cripps. I think Edie down at Mill Farm has a sister who might be able to come in. Come along, Dottie, I'm going to take you upstairs.'

Leaving Peggy and Bertha dealing with the mess, she led Dottie, who was now crying quite noisily, up to her sun-baked little attic.

While Dottie undressed, she went to fetch a thermometer. Walking hurt her, but almost everything did. She longed to be in bed herself without the tensions and argument that had so marked this day. She had hardly seen Sid at all, who had spent most of the afternoon appeasing Evie about being left in the cottage with Miss Milliment while she returned to Rachel's room in what Evie kept calling the big house. If things were normal, she would have gone to London to see Marly, her amazing back man who always seemed to get her right. The thought of not being able to do this – either tomorrow, or any other day, was quite frightening. But it was absurd of her to mind such a petty detail when they were very likely on the brink of war. And if the Babies' Hotel *was* evacuated, she must pull herself together and somehow organise catering and sanitary arrangements, although even the prospect of that was defeating. It might mean moving everybody out of Mill Farm and squashing nurses and babies in there somehow, and putting all the children in the squash court. It was useless to talk to either the Brig or the Duchy about this. Villy would be the most practical person, and, in any case, such a move would affect her family more than anyone else. But it wasn't only the children, of course. There was old Lady Rydal: the thought of her on a camp bed in the squash court made her want to laugh, but laughing hurt, too.

She returned to Dottie now lying on her back with the sheet up to her chin snuffling quietly. The room was stifling. It had the hot-water tank in it, which left very little room for the narrow iron bed, the hard chair and a small chest of drawers. The small window was tightly closed, and when she asked Dottie if she would like it open, Dottie said that it didn't – never. The tank was making quite loud, irregular rushing noises – it wasn't a very nice place to be ill, she thought. Dottie's temperature was nearly 102.. Rachel smiled reassuringly at her and said that she would get Peggy or Bertha to bring her a large jug of water and a couple of aspirin. 'You must drink as much as you can to help your temperature down. I'll get Dr Carr to come and see you tomorrow. And I'll see if someone can get your window opened for you. You see if you can have a nice sleep. You've been a very brave girl working all day when you must have been feeling awful.'

'I didn't never mean to break it.'

'What? No, of course you didn't. I'll tell Mrs Cazalet about it. Of course she'll understand you weren't feeling well.'

She left to go and find one of the maids to collect the aspirin from her. 'And she'd better have a chamber pot up there. Her temperature's quite high, and she should drink a lot. But I'm sure I can count on you to look after her, and to come to tell me if she wants anything. The doctor will come tomorrow.'

Bertha, who thought Miss Rachel was a very sweet lady, said she would see to everything. In any case, a visit from the doctor raised Dottie's status, even with Mrs Cripps, who instantly said she would put a nice junket to set that evening.

Rachel went to her room and lay down on her bed, and it hurt so much getting onto her back that she wondered how on earth she would ever get up again.

∞ ∞ ∞

After a silence, Hugh asked, 'How's Oscar?'

'He's all right.' She did not look at him, and they walked on for a bit in more silence. It was early evening, the sun had gone, but it was hot and the same grey stillness prevailed. 'Care for a stroll, Poll?' he'd said to her earlier, and she'd slipped from her chair with alacrity and said that she'd just see if Oscar was all right and she'd meet him on the front lawn. But when they met she had become uncommunicative; if he did not know her so well he would have thought she was sulking. He asked her where she would like to go, and she said she didn't mind, so they walked up through the little wood at the back of the house and out to the big meadow with the Spanish chestnuts, and she plodded along beside him almost as though he was not there.

'I'm tired,' he said when they reached the big trees. 'Let's sit down for a bit.'

They sat down with their backs against a tree and still she said nothing.

'What's worrying you?'

'Nothing.'

'I feel that something is.'

'Well, aren't you?'

'Yes. Extremely worried.'

'Oh, Dad! Me too. It's the war, isn't it? There's going to be another war.' The anguish in her voice pierced him. He put his arm round her; she was tense as stretched wire.

'We don't know yet. There may be. It depends—'

'On what?'

'Well, what Hitler said to Chamberlain this week. Whether an agreement could be reached that is reasonable. Whether the Czechs can agree.'

'They've got to!'

'How do you know so much about it, Poll?'

'I don't. I don't know whether they want to or not. I mean they've *got* to. To stop it. They ought to do anything in the world to stop it!'

'It's no longer up to them.'

'Who is it up to?'

'Us – and Hitler, of course.'

'Well, everybody says that Mr Chamberlain is all for appeasement. That means not having it.'

'Yes, but there's always a limit to how much you should appease anyone. Personally, I'm afraid I think we've reached that limit.'

'Personally,' she returned stiffly, 'I don't.'

He looked down at her in surprise, she kept starting and stopping a frown, in the way she always did when she was struggling to think something out, or when she was trying not to cry. He was not sure which it was. He put his hand over one of hers and held it; her fingers felt for his and held them hard, but there were no tears. She made one sigh – a very sad sound, he thought.

'What's on your mind, Poll?'

'I was wondering – what do you think it will be like? When it starts, I mean?' She turned to look up at him and, faced with the candour and intensity of her gaze, he faltered.

'I don't know. I expect there'll be an air raid. On London, probably.' He did think that. 'I don't think they'll use gas, Polly, in spite of our trip yesterday – that was just a sensible precaution.' He wasn't so sure of that. 'I don't think there'll be an invasion or anything like that,' and then he thought, what a stupid thing to say – he was far from sure of this, she

351

might not have thought of it, and he wanted to provide some reassurance.

But she had thought of it.

'They could put tanks into ships, couldn't they, and land them here? Tanks will go through anything.' She glanced at the wood behind them and instantly he saw, as he knew she did, a tank crashing and lumbering through the wall of trees – a terrible, animate monster.

'We have a navy, you know,' he said. 'It wouldn't be all that easy. But listen, Poll, we're making too many assumptions. There may not be a war. What we've been doing today is to make contingency plans, just in case there is. And I should really like to discuss them with you. I know you're brave and sensible and you might have some useful comments.'

She was both of those things, he reflected afterwards, remembering how she had turned his heart over as she tried to *look* them. When they had walked back to the house, she seemed a little – though not much – happier. But, good God! What a conversation to have with your thirteen-year-old daughter, he thought afterwards, when she had gone off to get Oscar's supper and he was alone. Rage and impotence had taken over: he would give his life for her – for any of them, come to that – but it was no longer such a simple equation. Civilians were going to be in this war, the innocent, the young, the weak, the old. He could not even protect her from her fear; her expression as she looked towards the wood recurred, and he heard and saw the tank again. They were only nine miles from the coast.

∞ ∞ ∞

'Sorry you've got chicken pox.'

'That's OK.' He looked at Christopher standing awkwardly in the doorway. Old feelings of allegiance and affection surged back: it was jolly decent of Christopher to come. 'What's happening with Teddy?' he asked. 'You can tell me – I hate him.'

'He wants to turn the place into a fort. Dig a trench all round it. He wants to play at some kind of silly war.'

'You won't let him, though?'

'I don't want him to, but I don't know how to stop him. He

352

says it's his territory, and I'm an invader. He wants to take all our stuff over – says a lot of it, like the tent, is his, anyway.'

'You can't play at war if you're a conscience objector.'

'Of course not! But it ruins all my plans. I seem to bring out the worst in him. After all, you can't run away now you're ill.'

'I know. But why do you want to tell him?'

'Well, he might shut up about it if I did. And he might see the point and join me instead of his stupid idea.'

'Couldn't you just wait a bit? He might get chicken pox. Or go to his beastly school.' Simon felt very proud and helpful with Christopher saying 'our stuff' and asking whether he'd mind about telling Teddy, and somehow being in bed and not able to do anything made it easier to think of advice. 'I didn't sneak, you know,' he added, wanting approval as well.

'Of course not, silly. Why would I be *asking* you about telling him if you had already?'

'Sorry. I didn't think.'

'That's OK. I expect you're feeling rotten.' Simon looked as rotten as he could. Christopher wandered to the bedside and ate a grape off the plate. 'He's *there* all the time,' he said miserably, 'eating the food and messing things up. And he's brought his gun as well.'

'He's not allowed his gun except with a grown-up. You could tell Uncle Edward.'

'I'm not going to sneak—' he stopped because Uncle Hugh came into the room. He had a little chess set with him.

'Thought you might like a game before supper,' he said. 'Hallo, Christopher. Hope I'm not interrupting anything?'

'Oh, no,' they both said and then Christopher added that he was just off, anyway.

When the board was set out and Simon had picked the white pawn from his father's proffered hand, he said, 'Dad! If there is a war, will I have to go to school?'

'I don't know, old man. Are you worried about that?'

'School?'

'War.'

'Oh, no,' Simon said cheerfully. 'I should think it would be rather exciting.' On the whole he was quite glad that his father didn't pursue the subject; he didn't want to know that he *would* have to, really, and, anyway, it was weeks before they'd either let or make him go.

∞ ∞ ∞

On Monday, Jessica left Mill Farm at nine o'clock to go to the funeral. Angela and Nora went with her; she had not been able to induce Christopher to join them, and Judy, she felt, was far too young. She wore Villy's black and white outfit with a black straw hat and rather becoming veil, which sat on the back seat beside Angela who, though very pale and silent, seemed acquiescent to anything and made no objection when Nora said it was her turn to sit in front. Nora wore her navy blue jacket and skirt and had stitched a black band to her sleeve. Angela had allowed Villy to dress her in a black linen dress and a fairly white mackintosh. Various gloves and bags of the appropriate hue had been donated by the family for the occasion.

'We'll expect you back for dinner,' Villy said, as she saw them off. 'Or ring if you can't,' she added. In spite of the fact that Jessica had said that nothing would induce her to stay the night, Villy knew that Raymond might well change her mind. 'Although we haven't taken any overnight things,' Jessica had said, 'so even he could hardly expect us to stay,' and she smiled her little secretive smile at her sister as much to say, 'This is how I manage him: I always agree with him, but then I place a little obstacle in his way and he has to give in.' 'He'll simply scold me for being impractical,' she said serenely. 'I'm terribly used to that.'

All the same, it was a very long drive – to Frensham and back in one day – especially in their old Vauxhall (she had refused to borrow Villy's car). Villy gave a final wave and went back to the house to start the 'nice quiet day' that Jessica had earlier envied her. The dining room was to be used for lessons and therefore breakfast must be cleared away as soon as possible, followed by the interminable task of getting her mother up and dressed, which involved a bath, which in turn meant clearing the passages of children, and maids, since Lady Rydal refused to be seen either going to or coming from either a bathroom or lavatory. The children had no school books, she realised, and added them to the list of things she intended fetching from Lansdowne Road the next day. She got Louise, who was sulking because she had wanted to go to the funeral. 'I've never been to one, it's terribly unfair. I've never been a bridesmaid, I've never been abroad, *and* I've never been to a funeral. Honestly, you don't let me have any experience of life at all.'

'I've told you a hundred times, you cannot go to the funeral of someone you've never met.'

'It's not my fault I never met her.'

'Go up to Home Place and ask the Duchy if you may have some blotting paper and a bottle of ink. And if she has any pads of paper or exercise books—'

'We won't need them – Clary always has dozens.'

'Well, ask her to bring them.' There was a muffled cry from above.

'I *must* go up. Chop chop, Louise,' and she hurried upstairs.

'Strewth! Why can't she use the telephone? Go here – do that – she thinks I'm some kind of slave. A slave child.'

All the way up the hill she was a slave girl: meek, beautiful, with a heavy anklet round her right leg that they used to chain her up at night. Her long black hair hung nearly to her waist: people were *ravaged* by her beauty, but her cruel master and mistress treated her worse than their pet elephant. By the time she found the Duchy she was so filled with pity for her meekness and beauty that she couldn't remember what she had come for. The Duchy was unable to find the Brig and ask him to ask Sampson to send someone to the house to get Dottie's window open.

'Where is he?'

The Duchy looked up from the immense pile of linen sheets that she was sorting for her sisters to mend. 'He's out, darling, or I'd find him myself. Probably at the back of the squash court. Or else at those cottages on the way to York's farm. Do hurry. Dottie has chicken pox and it is most unhealthy for her to be without fresh air.'

Louise tried the squash court first, and there he was with Christopher. They each held the ends of forked sticks and were walking slowly about over the patch of rough grass. As Louise drew near, Christopher gave a shout. 'Hey! Look! Watch!' He stepped back a pace, and then forward, and the stick seemed to try to escape from his hands.

Louise thought he might be pretending, but the Brig came over and said, 'Do it again, Christopher,' and he did, and this time she distinctly saw the stick kind of writhe by itself. 'Well. I'm damned!' said the Brig. He tried the same place himself, but nothing much seemed to happen. He took off his hat – a large grey trilby – and put it on Christopher's head. It was too big for him and came down over his eyes. The Brig turned him round, then gave him a little push, and said, 'Try again.' And Christopher, after a few wandering blind steps, found the same place, and this time the stick nearly leapt out of his hands. The Brig took off his hat, and clapped it on the back of his own head. He was smiling. 'Good boy,' he said, 'you've got the gift. We'll call the well after you.' And Christopher went bright red.

'Can I try?'

The Brig gave her his stick. 'You may. No. Hold the stick so. With your thumbs towards the centre.'

Louise tried, but nothing happened. So she gave her message, whereupon the Brig sent her off to the stables to tell Wren to ride down to Sampson's place to send someone up to the house. 'See if you can find any course of the water now,' he said to Christopher. 'Run along, there's a good girl.'

A good girl! She was knee deep in errands now, and she was far too old for this kind of thing. She went as slowly as possible to the stables to find Wren sharpening the points on his pitch fork with a large old file. It made a horrible noise that set her teeth on edge. She gave the message, but he simply went on filing. 'Did you hear, Mr Wren?'

He stopped filing. 'I heard.'

'Why are you doing that? You don't need extra sharp points for pitching the hay, do you?'

He shot her a look in which ferocity and cunning were horribly combined. 'That would be telling, miss, that would.'

She went away quickly. She didn't much like Wren. Since she had outgrown the pony, he had taken her out on the old grey which she could not control since his mouth was like iron – the Brig had ridden him for years in a double bridle with a heavy hand – but it had been clear that Wren did not think much of her horsemanship so the rides had been frightening and dull and she had soon given them up. In the drive, she saw Miss Milliment with Clary and Polly setting off for Mill Farm. She remembered that she hadn't actually asked the Duchy for paper, etc., and decided that she would now, and *that* would make her late. What she was really minding was that Nora wasn't going to be there. Lessons with Nora had seemed quite inviting, and now, because of the funeral, she would be the odd one out yet again. She walked very slowly indeed round the house by the tennis court to look for the Duchy.

∞ ∞ ∞

It was grey and hot again. Mrs Cripps scalded the milk to stop it turning, but the butter became oil if it was out of the larder for two minutes. Edie, from Mill Farm, had sent her younger (much younger) sister up to Home Place to help out, but Mrs Cripps did not know her well enough to bully her, and the kitchen, hot from the range, was airless since no refreshing breeze came through the small open casement windows; the atmosphere, generally, was thick. Emeline scraped seven pounds of new potatoes, washed up breakfast, scrubbed the larder floor, made up the range, strung and sliced four pounds of runner beans, washed up middle mornings, greased two cake tins, peeled, cored and sliced three pounds of Bramleys for the dining-room pies, laid the servants' lunch, washed it up, and then washed all the cooking utensils used for the dining-room lunch, answered only when spoken to, and then inaudibly – which, Phyllis thought, showed a proper respect, but she, Phyllis, could sense that the strain of not being herself was telling on Mrs Cripps, who was conducting everything with an air of artificial patience and good humour that was unlikely to last. She would much rather have been a short-handed martyr, bullying one of the housemaids, but there it was. Her bark, however, was far worse than her bite, at least where Dottie was concerned, as a stream of tempting little snacks was slapped onto a round, painted tray with two parrots on it, and lugged upstairs by one of the maids to her sick room. A custard tartlet, some toast and dripping, the junket set the previous night, a coddled egg and the end piece of a baked sultana roll each accompanied by a cup of deeply sugared tea found their way there at frequent intervals where they silted up, since poor Dottie felt too ill to fancy very much. Bertha, sent to tidy the room for the doctor's visit, offered to dispose of the food – there was nothing she liked more than eating and reading *True Romances* in bed. She also lent Dottie a nightgown as Dottie only possessed one and Bertha felt that the doctor should not see her in it as it was too small for her, altogether not quite nice. Dottie, who had never been visited by a doctor in her life, felt very important and rather scared. 'What will he do?' she asked, and Bertha, who had no experience of this kind, said only what he had to and she would be outside the door.

One of Mr Sampson's men arrived and opened the window, but the room being next to the roof, remained bakingly hot. 'Try not to perspire till after the doctor,' Bertha advised, but it was no good, she couldn't help it, and her eyes hurt when she moved them, and it seemed a pity, what with all this nice food she couldn't fancy, and staying in bed and not having to do anything, that she couldn't enjoy it more. But Bertha said if wishes were horses beggars would ride, and Dottie, who could not think what that meant, said she supposed so.

∞ ∞ ∞

Zoë spent the morning darning sheets with the great aunts.

'It is quite like the war already,' Flo placidly remarked, as she fitted a section of sheet over her toadstool.

'I don't remember us mending sheets in the last war,' Dolly said.

'That's because you haven't got a very good memory,' Flo returned. 'I distinctly remember that we were always mending sheets. Mending something, anyway.'

'Something!' Dolly sniffed.

They were seated at the gate-legged table in the breakfast room. Zoë had joined them because everybody else she had asked for something to do had looked vague and been unable to think of anything. The Duchy, however, had firmly set her to work. 'That would be most helpful of you, Zoë dear,' she had added, and Zoë had glowed, had even managed to ask the aunts to show her how to do it. They had not agreed about the method, of course: Aunt Dolly favoured patches, cut from hopelessly worn pillow cases; Flo insisted upon exquisitely fine darning over and round the tear. Zoë did whichever they told her and found that she was quite good at it. She had always liked fine sewing, which her mother had taught her. The aunts quarrelled gently all the morning, but Zoë did not listen much: she had new guilt to contend with, and felt so miserable that she was utterly enclosed with her circular and irresolute thoughts. She had used no birth control with Philip – had had no chance to – and the thought that he might have made her pregnant now haunted her. This was made worse by feeling that the only way she could make it up to Rupert would be to have the child she knew he had always wanted. The whole dilemma had broken upon her the first night that she had come home when she would ordinarily have taken her usual precautions. But as she reached for the little box that contained her cap, the previous night and the fact that she used nothing struck her. She was paralysed by fear and guilt: the thought of Philip's child revolted her, but on the other hand, if she was already pregnant, Rupert must think it his. So she had used nothing that night either. And now, she reflected drearily, having hedged her bets, as it were, she would never know, if she got pregnant, whose child it was until it was born – and possibly not then. 'Oh, why did I do it?' she kept reiterating. 'Why didn't I just wait until after my next period, and then have Rupert's baby?' Because she had been terribly afraid that she was pregnant already was the answer. But if she had been, she could perhaps have got rid of it, and then everything would be all right. But how? The thought of asking Sybil or Villy (which, she felt, *must* entail telling them what had happened) was simply terrifying. They had never liked her much; they would think she was beyond the pale if they knew about Philip. I could say to them – or one of them – that he did rape me, she thought. The worst of it was that every time she sought some way out it involved more lying.

'Of course, you would be too young, Zoë, to remember the zeppelins.'

'No, she wouldn't.'

'Flo, she must have been a child!'

'Children have very good memories. Far better than yours. When were you born, dear?'

'Nineteen fifteen.'

'There – you see?'

'In a minute you will be saying that it is as plain as the nose on your face, which, Father used to say you remember, was very plain indeed.'

Aunt Dolly's naturally mauve complexion deepened to dusky lavender and she clicked her teeth. Aunt Flo caught Zoë's eye and actually winked; this and the red bandeau that was somewhat askew round her hair made her look like some old pirate, Zoë thought, relieved at being able to think something else for a change. But the morning seemed interminable. At one point it occurred to her that Philip was somebody who could actually *do* something if she turned out to be pregnant, but even as the picture of his knowing, sardonic gaze filled her mind's eye so a small, warm anemone started to open inside her . . . She could never see him again in her life . . .

' . . . very *hot*, dear. Would you like another window open? Dolly can always put another rug over her knees. She's always cold, no circulation at all. And very naughty about leaving her combinations off at parties.'

Zoë, who knew nothing about combinations, smiled as she was expected to, but Aunt Dolly got really angry, levered herself to her feet, stalked stiffly to the window and flung it open. 'I sometimes wish,' she said, her tone implying that it was not much use her doing so, 'that you would refrain from discussing my underclothes in public. Occasionally.'

'I'm fully prepared to discuss anyone's underclothes – when the subject comes up. Combinations are a fact of life. Why pretend they don't exist? Dolly has a lot of what I can only call Victorian hypocrisy – whereas Kitty and I have always been free of it . . .'

Zoë, although she did not want any, was quite glad when it was lunch-time.

∞ ∞ ∞

Rupert spent most of the day taking Rachel to Tunbridge Wells, where Dr Carr had recommended what he described as a rather shady little man who was very good with backs. He went there himself, he added. Rachel was in such pain that for once she agreed to being such a trouble. Sid had been going to go with them, but Evie, who had decided that the best way of protesting about being put in the cottage was to be a nuisance in it, said she had a sick headache, and couldn't possibly expect the servants to carry her meals all that way. 'So, of course,' Sid said, trying to be cheery about it and failing, 'I'll have to stay, darling – much as I should love to come with you.'

'But I'm sure a child would take her meals over,' Rachel said, 'and, anyway, she won't want very much in that condition, will she?'

'I told you it would be awful if she came!'

'I know. But that really wasn't the point, was it? It isn't the moment for thinking of ourselves.'

When would it ever be? Sid grumbled to herself when she had seen Rachel lever herself painfully into Rupert's car and watched them set off. However, the Brig claimed her to trace a large drawing he had done for the conversion of two cottages he said he might be acquiring. 'Rachel was to have done it, and it won't wait.' So she spent most of the day in his study with greaseproof paper laid over the drawing. He was out all the morning but in the afternoon, she had to read *The Times* to him, breaking off to hear some of the remarkable coincidences that he had enjoyed in his life. She liked the old boy although she could see he was a bit of a tyrant.

Evie, who had eaten every scrap of a cooked breakfast, ate all of her substantial lunch, which Sid carried over for her, complained that Sid was avoiding her, and kept asking what everybody was doing. She asked twice about Rachel, as though she didn't believe in the Tunbridge Wells journey, and, fetching her lunch tray when this happened, Sid lost her temper. 'Get up if you want to know what people are doing. I *told* you this morning that Rachel has gone to have her back seen to. If you go on behaving like this, you'll have to go home.' Somehow, having her own day ruined by Evie made it quite easy to mean this. Evie started to cry, which Sid, who was soft-hearted, usually could not stand, but now she found herself quite unmoved. 'For God's sake, Evie! Don't cry and don't sulk. You're welcome to go home if you'd rather.'

Evie started to get out of bed. 'My place is at Waldo's side,' she said. 'If I can't be there, it doesn't matter where I am.'

∞ ∞ ∞

'She said she didn't mind *where* she was.' Villy was pouring her sister a whisky and soda. They had had a late supper, and the children had gone to bed.

'She told me she wished to go home. Thank you, darling. How welcome!'

'Everybody else wishes the same, but really I feel we ought to wait and see how things turn out.'

They were talking, as they often did, of their mother about whom they were always in complete agreement. Whereas neither of them liked either Edward's or Raymond's comments about her, they felt free, when they were alone, to discuss her impossible nature, signs of which, when they were *not* in agreement, each could see in the other.

Now Jessica shrugged, stretched out her long thin legs and kicked off her shoes. 'Goodness! I don't usually drink whisky, but after such a day . . . '

'How *was* it – really?' She had been treated to a highly coloured version of the funeral at supper, largely by Nora.

'And poor Aunt Lena was propped up in the dining room in her coffin. She looked like one of those huge, expensive dolls you see in Whiteley's at Christmas. Except she was paler, of course. The blood had left her cheeks, I suppose.' At this point Angela, with some inaudible expostulation, had left the room. Louise had been fascinated. 'She wasn't wearing a party dress, though, was she?'

'Of course not. A white nightie, with a thick frill round the neck.' And so on – until they'd been told to leave the table which they wanted to do, anyway.

'How was it? Pretty awful, really. All the blinds down in the house, which was stuffy beyond belief, and people stumbling over huge arm chairs in the gloom. And then it rained in the churchyard. There weren't very many people and of course I didn't know any of them except the vicar who made the most fulsome address. About her wonderful capacity for life – I suppose he simply meant living for so many years – you know, like people saying a view is marvellous if you can see far enough, however dull.'

'How was Raymond?'

'Very touching. He really minds: probably the only person who did.'

'The other nephew wasn't there?'

'Oh, no. Safely in Canada. Which brings me to the Will.'

Villy sat up. 'No! You mean it was read then and there just like a play?'

'In the drawing room after we got back from the churchyard. Of course, I sent the children out into the garden. She left thirty thousand pounds to the other nephew,' she paused, 'and the rest to Raymond. The house, its contents, and really rather a lot of money.'

'Oh, darling! How wonderful! Wasn't Raymond rather thrilled?'

'It was very hard to tell. He went rather red, coughed and looked straight ahead as though the whole thing had nothing to do with him. The only thing is, I do hope he won't want to live in the house.'

'It's quite a pretty house, isn't it?'

'Oh, the house is all right. But if we stayed there, it would be full of all her possessions and I know he wouldn't allow a single thing to be changed. All those ghastly pictures – four deep on every wall! And hideous, very old Victorian furniture everywhere.'

Villy had wanted to say, 'Anything would be better than your present house,' but felt this would be unkind. Instead she got up and went to the whisky bottle. 'I think this calls for another drink.'

'I shall be completely tipsy.'

'Doesn't matter. You can lie in in the morning. And I've had a pig of a day too as a matter of fact.'

Jessica looked up at her; she *did* look tired. 'Darling, what?'

'Oh—' this would be the moment, she thought, but I don't know what she'd think and I haven't decided myself, and *she* wouldn't know what to do. 'Oh! You know. Mama at her most tragic. Trying to fit in the new schoolroom with meals; the servants got cross because they couldn't lay the table exactly when they wanted to. And I had a bit of a *thing* with Edward on the telephone this evening. I do so absolutely loathe rows on the telephone. The other person isn't there, and they can ring off whenever they like—' she stopped, because

363

her voice was shaking. Jessica got up swiftly, and put an arm round her.

'Villy! What is it? Has Edward—' She stopped. She really could not make such an awful suggestion, must allow her sister to make her confidence herself.

But Villy, giving that small heroic smile that had always maddened her, simply said, 'Oh, it was nothing. Just that I told him I was coming up to town tomorrow to collect some things from Lansdowne Road, and he said he had to be away in the evening, so there's not much point in my staying up. I'm dead tired. And I'm sure you are, too. You must have driven well over a hundred miles. And I shall have to as well tomorrow.'

Jessica, as she let down her hair and plaited it for the night, reflected how Villy had always done that: had always seemed to ask for sympathy and then warded you off the moment you tried to give it. She thinks she is being brave, but really she diminishes one by making one feel unworthy to be told anything that matters. She has a lot of Mama in her, all that pride and sense of things being worse for her than anyone else.

But, in bed, she also thought that if Raymond had got someone else she would find it very difficult to admit this to Villy, and felt ashamed of her criticism. He never *would*, of course: he was impossibly devoted to her. She had made her bed and knew that she must lie in it but the thought occurred (and made her smile) as she began sinking into oblivion that now, at least, it would have linen sheets. Or silk, if I choose. And Angela could be presented as Raymond had always wanted. If there was a Season for her to be presented in. What *trivial* thoughts! The whisky, probably. But as she drifted off, Nora was getting a complete new wardrobe to go off to her finishing school, and Judy could have riding lessons and Christopher – what did he want? Christopher could have whatever he wanted . . .

Villy, who undressed very quickly feeling that all she wanted in the world was to be unconscious, out for the night, locked her door and then put her two sets of teeth into a tumbler with Steradent very close to her bed (sleeping without them was a luxury only possible when she was alone), turned out the light and was immediately, tensely, awake. Going over and over the telephone conversation and the way it had ended. 'Must go, darling, someone wants me. For God's sake, Villy, didn't you hear what I said?' Did he hear what *she* had said? Did anyone ever listen to her? Did anyone ever listen to anything? Or were they so wrapped up in themselves that they were only aware of what complimented themselves? That's not true of me. I listened to Jessica tonight, and I'm glad for her. To have all her pinching, and scraping and making do over in one fell swoop! What was it she had said when I nearly told her? 'Has Edward—' been drinking, I bet she was going to say. A truly Victorian question; she is rather like Mama in some ways. But, of course, I'd never tell her that. Edward always drinks, and it doesn't make the slightest difference to him: he can carry it, like his father. I must go to sleep, or I'll be hopeless tomorrow. She began going through the lists of things she wanted to collect from home. All the school books for Miss Milliment. More linen, bath towels, etc. Some of the children's winter clothes, any minute now it would start to get colder, and this was a cold house. The electric fire from the spare room and there were two paraffin stoves in the attic. She had considered a second visit to Bob Ballater, but disregarded the idea. There was no point: she was perfectly certain now and he had made it clear that he would not help her. Hermione . . . But if there *is* a war, it will all be so complicated, she thought. I may not be able to get to London, or have a good enough other reason for getting there. Trapped, that's what I am. By the world situation, other people's views and marriage. It wasn't as though she was one of those people who wanted sex all the time. I could easily have been a nun or married to one of those poor wretches who lost their balls in the last war. I wouldn't have minded at all. I could have adopted some of these pathetic babies that Rachel cares for, whose parents never wanted them. She put on the light, found the aspirin bottle and swallowed two without water. Her mouth suffused with a dry bitterness, but she knew they would get her to sleep.

∞ ∞ ∞

'I had to come now, because of lessons.'

'Oh, well. Get on with it.'

Polly knelt on the bed, put her arms round her brother and

planted several kisses on his spotty face. 'You'd better breathe on me a bit.'

Simon opened his mouth and blew steadily at her. 'It would probably be better if I licked your tongue.'

'Don't be utterly repellent.'

'Anyway, if there's going to be a war, we don't need chicken pox. We'd stay here.'

She did not reply. He scratched absently for a bit and then said, 'Teddy's done something simply foul and I don't like him any more.'

'Simon! What?'

'Oh. Gone and spoiled something Christopher and I were doing.'

'What?'

For a moment, Simon simply scratched while he wrestled with the desire to tell her. It wasn't sneaking, because she wasn't a grown-up; he was bored of bed and wanted to impress her. 'Promise not to tell – specially the grown-ups?'

'Of course. I've wondered what you were doing. Clary and I often saw you going off – with things. We couldn't imagine what you were playing.'

'We weren't *playing*. We've made a camp – in the woods. To run away.'

'To run away? What on earth for?'

'Christopher hates it at home. He's a conscious objector. He doesn't believe in war. But then Teddy found our camp and gashed our tent and Christopher and he had a fight, and now Teddy wants to be the leader, but he doesn't know about the running away part.'

'Simon, were you going to run away with him?' As Simon hesitated, she added, 'Because that would be wicked. I should think Mummy might easily die of grief.'

'I know. That's why I didn't want to, really. Anyway, I can't now. But it's different for Christopher. His father is awful to him, and I think his mother is a weak character because she can't stop the rows that go on. So Christopher thought it would be better if he went. It started as a sort of game, but then it got serious – the running away, I mean. I didn't tell Teddy although he threatened me with torture. See?'

'He'd get found though, wouldn't he? He'd need things

like Elastoplast and toothpaste – and people would notice him getting them.'

'We'd collected all that sort of thing. It was a proper camp, with stores and everything. And it's no good Christopher running away there now, because Teddy could find him.'

'Oh, well,' said Polly, relieved, 'then he'll have to give it up.'

'I wouldn't count on that. It'll probably mean he'll run away further, and then people really won't find him.'

'Oh.' She went quiet soon after that, telling him not to scratch.

∞ ∞ ∞

'Mum! What shall I wear? Do open the door, Mum.'

Villy came to with a start. She reached for her teeth. Usually she would have rinsed them under the tap – she loathed the taste of Steradent.

'What is it?'

'What shall I wear for London? For my treat?' he said patiently.

She had clean forgotten. It had been arranged weeks ago that he should go up for the day, have lunch with Edward at his club and go to a film in the afternoon. He was to have gone by train, but now, of course, she would take him with her in the car. Why hadn't Edward mentioned it on the telephone yesterday?

'Let's go and see what you've got,' she said.

His room seemed to be a shambles while at the same time having hardly anything in it. This was partly because the curtain rail had become detached at one side and lay askew across the window with the curtains in a heap on the floor.

'I pulled it just a bit and it just fell down,' he said when he saw her seeing this.

'You'd better wear your Sunday suit.'

'Oh, no, Mum – anything but that. I feel such a nit in it.'

'Well, what would you suggest?'

What he would have liked were some Harris tweed plus fours – like the ones Dad played golf in – and a canary yellow waistcoat like the Brig wore for riding and a grey top hat like Dad had for weddings. And lovely thick stockings and shoes the colour of toffee. Useless saying any of that to her. She was rotten with clothes. In the end, they settled to their mutual dissatisfaction upon his long grey trousers and a blazer with his Sunday suit shirt and a foulard tie that Aunt Zoë had given him for Christmas, the only thing he liked and that his mother thought was far too old for him.

'Where on earth are all your socks?'

'I've been using them for an experiment,' he said sulkily. He really didn't want to go into all that.

'Are you taking me to the station?' he asked when she had fetched a pair of Dad's socks.

'I'm taking you in the car. I'm going up to collect some things from the house.'

'Oh, good! Then you can have lunch, too, and go to the film.' His obvious pleasure at including her touched her. She wanted to hug him.

'I don't know that I'll have time for all that. We'll see.'

∞ ∞ ∞

Christopher was running with his sandshoes loosely tied together by the laces slung around his neck. He preferred to run barefoot – in fact, he considered shoes to be only emergency apparel, to be used if the ground was actually dangerous, with things like glass or nails. The odd thistle or stone made no impression on his horny feet, and the feel of the damp grass was so refreshing that he felt he could run for ever. But he was doing his usual trek to the wood, only this time with the wonderful knowledge that Teddy would not be there, would not suddenly appear and interrupt him, was safely out of the way for the whole day. He had decided to use this time to move; he could not go far, and it would be useless to take the tent, because he did not want Teddy to realise that he had moved so he would take only the barest necessities, leaving some of everything behind. Even so, there was a lot to shift, and he had to make a final decision about the new site. The obvious place was the other end of the wood, by the pond, until he had time to find a further place with water. The fact that he could find water with a hazel branch meant, of course, that he had a far greater choice, but on the other hand, finding water was one thing, digging for it another. But his water-divining powers both astounded and enchanted him: he had never even seen it being done, and all these years the gift had lain within him, untouched and unknown. What else might he be able to do? He wondered whether there was a book that listed magic powers so that he could test himself, but he hadn't time for that sort of thing now. The most difficult thing to move without Teddy noticing was going to be the groundsheet, but if he couldn't take the tent, he was really going to need it. He'd have to sleep wrapped up in it if it rained, which it kept looking as though it was going to do. Now it was grey and very still, with a whitish mist; the trees were going gold and yellow and caramel-coloured, the bryony berries were ripening from green to red, the rose-hips and hawthorns were already ripe, the sloes were black beneath their lavender bloom. It was a pity they were no good to eat, any of them, but there were still blackberries, and the Spanish chestnuts were thick with fruits whose rind was like small green hedgehogs – the nut was lovely to roast. As he approached the wood, he saw a heron coasting low over the marshy bank that ran along one side of it – frog hunting. If people had to spend all of every day getting enough food to eat like animals, they wouldn't have time to make aeroplanes or bombs. The simplicity and truth of this notion struck him so forcibly that he felt he ought to do something about it – like write a letter to *The Times* or the Prime Minister, who seemed rather a good egg and not at all keen on war. He had reached his camp now – the stream, the little island, the mossy bank looking quite like home – only it wasn't going to be, after all. He undid the flaps, crawled in, found a rather silent biscuit and his exercise book, and started making his essential list.

∞ ∞ ∞

' . . . and you have lunch at your club with Mr Teddy at one.'

'My God! So I have! I'd clean forgot. Thank you, Miss Seafang.' His smile contained the 'What should I do without you!' expression that never failed to warm her heart.

'Give me ten minutes and then I'll see Hoskins.'

'Very good, Mr Edward.'

God! I must be getting senile! Edward thought. Lunch with

Teddy meant that he couldn't go to the wharf afterwards, as Teddy would expect a matinée or a film, preferably followed by tea at Gunter's. And he had meant to go to the wharf early and then, since it was the right side of London, slip down to Wadhurst to take Diana out to dinner. He'd managed to fob Villy off, although it had clearly not been popular, but now he'd got himself into a real mess. He pushed his chair back from the desk and rested his feet upon it, a position in which he always thought better. 'At least I don't play the fiddle,' he said to himself, referring to an eccentric younger brother of the Brig's who had asked to join the firm and then spent his time in his office doing just that. When the Brig had pointed out that this was not conducive to business, he replied that his wife had not liked him doing it at home. He had become a sort of remittance man, living up north somewhere. This had been his office, and alongside the large, dull photographs of men in white overalls standing proud but puny beside enormous logs, there was still a foggy photograph that Edward was secretly fond of, of Szigeti standing with his violin.

Now, then. Supposing he took Teddy to the wharf? No good, he couldn't catch a train from there. Supposing he went to the wharf the moment he'd seen Hoskins? Better. Must ring Diana first.

That didn't go well. She said she had managed to get someone to look after the baby all day and was coming to town and could they have lunch? Well, could he meet her at her flat later, but not too late as she had to get back? Eventually, it was agreed that he'd get there around six, they would have an early dinner, and he would drive her down. He could go on to Mill Farm for the night and that would please Villy. He rang for Miss Seafang, who ushered in Hoskins.

∞ ∞ ∞

When Mr York brought the milk up to the house that morning, he also brought a letter. He hadn't written one since his mother had died – there'd been no call to – so, of course, when he got out his writing things, his pen nib was rusty and the ink in the bottle had dried to nothing. He'd had to lend some ink from Enid who was always writing – wrote one letter a week, a

terrible expense in stamps since she had to send them through
the post to Broadstairs, fifty-two pence a year that was, as he'd
more than once told her. Then he had to think what he wanted
to say, and it beat him how the paper got dirty while he was
thinking, but it did. Several sheets, it took. In the end, he'd
got the milk pencil, the one he used to count up the pints
they used up at the house, and wrote it out in that first.

Enid's ink turned out to be women's ink – violet-coloured
– so he made the letter as businesslike as he could to make
up for it.

'Dear Sir,' he wrote, avoiding the difficult and fancy name,
'With respect to the land at back of cottages. I could sell one
acre for sixty pounds. Sale of cottages as agreed. Total £560.
Yours truly, Albert York.'

He hadn't put a date. It was near as nothing 27th, which
he knew as Arthur was coming over to fetch the red calf
that day, so he put that at the end of the letter on the bottom
line of the paper. The envelopes had gummed themselves up.
He had to use the kettle on one of them, and they didn't
fit the paper so he folded it up quite small and dainty and
put it in. Then he had to think about addressing it, which
there was no call for if he was taking it up himself, so
he put Mr William on it. It was nearly ten when he'd
finished. Still ten pound was ten pound whichever way you
looked.

He paid a visit to the privy, out at the back door and
down a rank little bricked path. It smelled of hogweed and
urine and Jeyes' fluid, but at night there were no flies. When
he came out he sniffed the air: the wind had shifted to the
west and there would be rain. He'd best get Dick Cramp –
one of Edie Cramp's brothers – up to help get the last of the
hay off the south field in case a storm broke. Then he turned
out the big oil lamp in the kitchen and found his way to his
bedroom in the dark. Working Dick cost less than losing the
hay. Five hundred and sixty pound! He'd fooled the old man.
He'd have let the cottages go for much less, but if he didn't ask
more for the land the old man might know he'd been fooled.
He was a foreigner, after all, wasn't born in these parts, fair
game, but he wasn't close with his money – he would say that
for him.

So next morning, he took the letter, tucked in his waistcoat pocket, up to the house, and handed it over to Mrs Cripps, who gave it to Eileen to put on Mr Cazalet's plate at breakfast.

∞ ∞ ∞

Teddy sat bolt upright between his parents in the Visitors' Dining Room at the club with a beautiful menu that had the Yacht Club burgee embossed at the top. There was an agonising choice of all three courses: potted shrimps or smoked salmon to start with (and boring old soup – he couldn't imagine anyone wanting that), and then lamb cutlets, steak or game pie, and a choice of boring old vegetables, and then treacle sponge, blackberry and apple tart with cream, or an ice. In the end, he decided on potted shrimps and game pie because saying to other boys that the game pie at his father's club was not half bad, sounded more worldly than saying the same thing about cutlets or steak. He needn't mention treacle sponge which he simply loved – he could *invent* a pudding he had had (on the first night of term after lights out there was a prolonged discussion of the food consumed in the holidays ending invariably with ribald comment on the fare to come). It was a lovely lunch. For once his parents took more notice of him and didn't have long boring conversations about things he couldn't possibly be interested in, although he wouldn't have minded because the food was so good. The potted shrimps came encrusted in yellow butter with thin triangles of toast under a white napkin on a plate just for him. The game pie was a slice like a cake: crisp, shiny brown pastry on the outside, then about half an inch of white not-very-cooked pastry – absolutely delicious – *then* a layer of stiff pale brown jelly, and then wedges of pink gamy meat, very juicy and tasting as though it was nearly too old but not quite. He had two glasses of cider as well. The conversation, as usual with grown-ups, mostly consisted of them asking rather pointless questions. 'And what did you do with yourself all morning?' his father was now saying.

'Helped Mum cart things into the car. If a bomb drops actually on our house, would it be flattened?'

'I should think it might be, if it was a direct hit.'

'I got my collection of cigarette cards just in case,' he

said. 'But, I say, it's jolly exciting, isn't it? Mum and I saw them building air-raid shelters, and they were digging trenches in Hyde Park. They don't expect the war to be fought in the Park, do they? If you could join up, if you weren't so old, what service would you go into? I'd go into the Air Force. There's a wizard new aeroplane called a Spitfire that can go at two hundred miles an hour—' He stopped. 'It might have been four hundred – anyway, it's the fastest plane in the world. Would you join the Air Force, Dad, if you weren't too old?'

'I'd join the Navy. I'm not too old for that, old boy.'

'And I suppose Mum could be a nurse,' he said, anxious to include her (she'd been jolly decent not making a fuss about the socks).

'I might join the Wrens,' said Villy.

'What's that? Oh, thanks.' A waitress had brought him some more cream.

'It's the women's navy.'

'Oh. I think it would be better if you were a nurse,' he added kindly. 'I don't think women should go on ships, Dad, do you? I mean skirts in submarines would be idiotic—' He spread his hands out and knocked over his cider glass. 'Sorry!'

'That's all right.' A waitress came to mop up the cider, and seeing that Teddy was rather dashed, Edward went on, 'As a matter of fact, a bloke who works for us came in this morning to tell me he'd joined the Air Force. A very useful bloke – we shall miss him.'

'Still, it's what people ought to do, isn't it? Dad, if there is a war, do you think it will last long enough for me to fight in it?'

'Not a chance,' Edward said at once, and met Villy's eye.

'Can we have our coffee next door?' she asked. 'I'd rather like to smoke.'

'It's after two o'clock, you can here if you like. Or we'll go next door. Have you finished, Teddy?'

'It looks as though I have.' But as this did not procure a second helping of treacle sponge, he got up when they did and followed them back into the room where they had had drinks before lunch. As they walked through, a very old man with a purple face and white hair called to Edward, 'I see we're getting a broadcast from Chamberlain tonight. Put us in the picture – and high time, too. That your boy?'

Teddy was introduced and called him sir as he was so awfully old.

'And your lady wife. How do you do, my dear? Let me offer you some port. I owe that husband of yours some port – he trounced me at billiards last week.'

Mum didn't want port, but Dad had some and let him taste it. 'I had port,' he'd be able to say. 'It wasn't bad at all.'

They had rather grey coffee in little cups with yellow roses on them, and he began to want to go to the film, but suddenly Mum and Dad *did* start one of those talks that were all about plans that they didn't seem to agree about. It transpired that Mum couldn't go to *Scarface* after all, as she said she had a lot of things to do, and Dad had to work immediately it finished, so then they went on and on and on about how he was going to get back to Sussex. He could easily catch a train by himself but Mum said that if Dad drove him home, she could load the car up with a whole lot more things she wanted to take down to Sussex. Dad didn't seem to want to do that and in the end it was decided that he should take the Underground from Oxford Circus or somewhere like that to Holland Park and be with Mum by six o'clock, which meant there would hardly be time for tea. He pointed this out and all she said was, 'But you've just had the most enormous lunch!' as if that had anything to do with it. He left them at it while he went to the lavatory, and when he came back they weren't talking about anything else. When she went, Mum gave that cheery smile that didn't feel like a smile at all, and said, 'Have a good time,' and kissed him, which he'd been trying to train her for years not to do in front of strangers – there were several other lots of people in the room. When she had gone, he rubbed the place where there might have been lipstick, and Dad said, 'Right! I'm just going to do what nobody else can do for me, and I'll be with you,' and things felt much easier again.

∞ ∞ ∞

'It doesn't matter whether it's Sunday or not. We must go on praying.'

'But couldn't we just do it in our own room?'

Nora shook her head. 'I think it would count more if we had a service. Also, I think we should be as *many* as possible.'

'Neville and Lydia and Judy will be having lessons.'

'Yes, that can't be helped. But Polly would come. And Clary, and Christopher. And Teddy, I suppose.'

'He's in London.'

'Oh, so he is. Well, the maids.'

'The maids?'

'Everyone is the same in the sight of God,' Nora said severely.

'That must make things terribly boring for him.'

'Louise, if you are going to be flippant about something as serious as this, I shall never speak to you again!'

'I won't be. I have a great many sides to my nature – it goes with being a serious actress – and you can't expect them all to be acceptable.'

'If we had the service after tea, then the children could come. And Miss Milliment.'

'You'll be asking the grandmothers next. And Bully and Cracks.' These were the private names for the great aunts based upon their appearance – Dolly a bloodhound and Flo nutcrackers respectively.

'Why not? I think everybody should be given the chance. Also, the Duchy might let us have the drawing room, and then we could use the piano for hymns.'

They spent the whole afternoon arranging things, roping in Polly and Clary to help. The Duchy said that of course they could have the drawing room, but they would have to collect chairs from the dining room and put them back afterwards. Polly wrote beautiful cards to invite people and Clary delivered them. 'Does everybody include Mr Wren?' she asked rather fearfully. There were stories about Mr Wren going bright red in the face and shouting if disturbed in the afternoon when he usually had a rest in the hayloft. 'Leave it on top of the oats bin. He's bound to see that,' Louise advised.

'But I do not believe in God,' Evie said when Clary found her in the hammock.

'Oh, well. I don't think everybody who is coming does, but you believe in peace, don't you?' And as Evie looked uncertain of this, she added, 'Anyway, you don't like Hitler, do you? And he's the person who wants there to be a war.'

'No, I certainly don't like Hitler. All right, you win. I will come.'

Mrs Cripps said, well she never, and she couldn't leave her kitchen but thank you all the same, Clary reported. Aunt Jessica said she would bring Grania up in the car. Dad was giving Zoë a driving lesson but when she stopped in the drive he said yes, of course, they'd both come. Aunt Sybil said she'd love to, but she might have to bring William. The only people they couldn't find were Aunt Rachel and Sid, who had gone to St Leonards to the swimming-bath – a bit mean, Clary thought, not even asking a single child whether they wanted to go, which of course, they would have – and Christopher, whom nobody had seen all day. McAlpine, who was planting leeks, stopped planting them to take his card which he looked at for some time with no expression, so Clary told him what it said, and he shook his head and handed it back to her, but he was smiling, so he didn't mind being asked. On the whole, the idea seemed to be a success.

It rained a lot in the afternoon, which was awful for Christopher but good for the leeks. It spoiled the swim that the man in Tunbridge Wells had told Rachel would be good for her back, but it enabled Sid to spend a whole afternoon alone with her with no danger of Evie suddenly appearing. Sid drove Rupert's car and, with Rachel beside her, she could have driven to Land's End, as she said. 'You are so good at it,' Rachel said. 'I do wish you'd let me give you a car,' but she knew that Sid would not. 'I'll pick one up one day,' she would say, her pride making her sound as though she could have done so already but had simply not had the time. I should have just given it to her – not talked about it, Rachel thought again, watching Sid's earnest profile: the high, rather bulging forehead, her fine beaky nose (like a Red Indian, Sid had said when Rachel had first remarked upon it), the wide, narrow, well-delineated mouth, and her throat erect above her collar and tie. Sid drove carefully, trying not to jolt. There was a large open-air pool in St Leonards; Rachel did not want to stumble over cruel pebbles at Coodden. However, as they drove, the sky darkened from a cool soft grey to indigo and it suddenly poured. So in the end they went to *The Private Life of Henry VIII* and had tea in a tea shop – a lovely afternoon, Rachel had said, although she didn't think much of the film, except for Merle Oberon as Anne Boleyn at the beginning, but Sid thought that Charles Laughton was pretty good.

'Doesn't it feel very odd to you? Every day we seem to be creeping, slipping into this ghastly nightmare, but we all go on as though nothing much is happening?' She took the cigarette offered her and leant towards her for a light. 'I mean a tea shop! Here we sit with toast and Banbury cakes . . . '

'Well, darling, what *else* can we do? It isn't as though we any of us have the slightest power to do anything else.'

'Do you mean we've never had it? Or that we had some, and simply elected the wrong people?'

'I don't think we've particularly elected the wrong people. I think the general climate is bad: opinion, ignorance, prejudice, complacency . . . '

'Us, or the Germans, or both?'

'Oh, the Germans are in a different position. Things have been bad enough for them to want change at any price.'

'You think they want a war?'

'I think they *expect* it. I don't think people leave their country and everything they have for nothing.'

'What people?' said Rachel, startled.

'The Jews,' Sid said, watching her intently for the faintest sign of dismissal or contempt and willing there to be none.

'But they aren't, are they? I've never heard that!'

'They've been leaving since 1936 to come here, or to go to America.'

'Just because you happen to know one or two—'

'Oh, I agree, it's a very small number in comparison to how many are left. But it's a sign. If I had to worry about whether the balloon was going up, that's the factor I should have taken most notice of.'

'But, Sid darling, that's because you—' she searched for the best way of saying it, 'because you—'

'Because I'm half Jewish?' Sid finished. 'You're probably right. It may not be my pure intelligence, it may simply be fear.'

'Now I've lost you.'

'Oh, well, never mind.' She suddenly wished she had never started this; it felt a nervous, risky conversation that she might turn out not to be able to afford with this person she loved so much.

But Rachel leant forward, and took her hand. 'Sid! I don't understand, but I'm listening. I want to know what you – feel.'

Right, Sid thought, here goes. She took a deep breath.

'The Germans had just as bad a war as we did. But after it they were weakened, humiliated, prevented from being able to defend themselves and endured an economy which resulted in hysterical inflation. Then along comes somebody who says he can give them back their national pride and sense of identity. He's a leader, a power maniac as most leaders are, and he sets about constructing an autocracy. He rearms them, sets them to work, everything swings his way and his notions of what can be done enlarge. He is no longer just an inspired leader, he acquires absolute power, and the only way he can keep *that* is to make conquests, to bring home the bacon – Sudetenland, Austria. But another thing that tyrants usually need to keep their subjects united for them, is something for them to be against. And there's always a convenient minority contained within the general population, defined by their race or their creed, Slavs, Catholics, you know what I mean. This time, I think it is the Jews – two birds with one stone you might say. The climate is just right for that.'

'How do you mean, "just right"? How do you know what Germans feel about Jews?'

'I don't. But I know what people here feel about them, and this is a democracy without a power maniac in control. Anti-Semitism is rife here. It takes the form of jokes, patronage and exclusion and making exceptions to the rule. "I don't usually like Jews, but you are an exception." That's what prejudice is made of. Oh, yes, and then accusing us of persecution mania when we notice and are hurt. We are the ideal scapegoats.' She noticed that she had begun to say 'we' and felt better for it. 'The views of a mongrel,' she finished, 'often noted for their acumen rather than their appearance.'

Rachel looked at her without speaking. In the end it was

Sid who looked away, whereupon Rachel said, 'I do love you. So very much.'

Sid brushed her fingers across her face. 'I love you,' she said, 'among much else, for not arguing – protesting.'

'I can't. What you said is true. I can't.'

When they left the tea shop and were out in the street Rachel put her arms round Sid and held her for a long time. People looked at them curiously – one couple nearly bumped into them – but Rachel did not relinquish her hold.

∞ ∞ ∞

The Brig's wireless had been moved from his study to the drawing room in order that there should be room for those who were to hear the Prime Minister's broadcast. Opinion was divided about who they should be: the Duchy thought it might not be suitable for the children, Lady Rydal expressed the view that it might not be suitable for the girls. Neither grandmother considered it necessary for the servants to be present, but Rachel and Sid fetched the set that was at Mill Farm and connected it up in the servants' hall at Home Place. Tonbridge was deputed to operate it, and dinner was arranged to suit the time for the broadcast. The chairs from the service (which had gone very well, until Nora had suggested that everybody present should pledge to give something they cared for in return for peace) were left in place in order that everybody, or nearly everybody, should have a seat. The children, except for the four youngest and, of course, Simon, were eventually allowed and sat on the floor, having been told by their mothers that they must be absolutely quiet and not talk at all while Mr Chamberlain was speaking. Everybody was quiet. Rupert – as concerned as any of them, he thought, since he was the only person in the room likely to have to go off and fight – found himself, none the less, so fascinated by seeing them all so quiet and so still that he could not help going from face to face, and wishing that they would not think it flippant of him to draw the scene. But they would: art had a strictly regulated place in the Cazalet scheme of things.

He looked first at his mother: the Duchy sat absolutely

straight with her eyes fixed upon the radio as though Mr
Chamberlain was in the room and speaking to her personally.
'How horrible, fantastic, incredible it is that we should be digging trenches and trying on gas masks here because of a quarrel
in a far-away country between people of whom we know nothing.' He looked at his sister who was reclining on the sofa with
Sid sitting on the arm at her feet. They seemed not to be looking
at each other, but Sid suddenly handed an ash tray to Rachel to
stub out her cigarette. 'I would not hesitate to pay even a third
visit to Germany if I thought it would do any good.' He looked
at Polly and Clary, side by side on the floor, arms around their
knees: Polly was frowning and biting her bottom lip; Clary, his
own daughter, was watching her and as he looked, she rocked
her knees so that they touched Polly's. Polly looked up and a
tiny smile flitted across Clary's face inhabiting it with such
encouragement and love that he was struck by her beauty, felt
dazzled and shut his eyes. When he opened them again, she was
just his usual Clary staring at the floor. He'd missed the last bit
of the speech. 'I am myself a man of peace to the depths of my
soul. Armed conflict between nations is a nightmare to me . . . '
Lady Rydal, her aquiline nose thrown into sharp relief by the
lamp, lay cast upon the best armchair, her right elbow upon
its arm, her Elizabethan hand, studded with large and rather
dirty diamond rings, resting upon her pale cheek. She wore
an expression of tragedy that most people would be unable to
sustain, but while he watched it remained unchanged. Villy,
sitting on an uncomfortable dining-room chair beside her, had
by contrast simply a natural look of utter exhaustion. She was
like her mother only in the sense that a really bad portrait is
like its subject, he thought – 'life for people who believe in
liberty would not be worth having . . . ' (oh, so he does want
war, does he?) 'but war is a fearful thing and we must be very
clear, before we embark on it, that it is really the great issues
that are at stake.' He looked across the room: Angela was staring
at him. When she met his eye, she started to blush. Lord, he
thought. I wonder if Zoë was right after all! Zoë was sitting
on the window-sill behind Angela. He blew her a kiss and her
look of anxiety softened to unexpected gratitude – an expression
he had only ever seen on her face when he gave her a present.
He reached his father just as the broadcast came to an end.

'All children to kiss their grandfather good night,' he said, 'and tomorrow everybody can start digging an air-raid shelter – it clean slipped my memory, that, till that feller reminded me.'

∞ ∞ ∞

Edward and Diana listened to the broadcast in a pub. He had met her at her flat where, after a brief sojourn, they drank the bottle of champagne he had brought with him. Then she wanted to collect some things to take down with her, so that by the time they were ready to leave they were in a quandary about dinner. Edward was for having it in London first, but she was anxious about her baby and also felt that somehow they must hear the broadcast. They decided to try and find an hotel that would give them dinner on the way, but by the time they got to Sevenoaks the only place that served dinner had served it and not even Edward's charm could persuade them to serve any more. In the end, they found a pub outside Tonbridge whose landlord said they could let them have some ham sandwiches. The landlord provided them with a small private room off the saloon bar where there was a wireless. Somehow, the evening was not going well. Edward was feeling guilty at the way he had treated Villy and half his mind was bent upon the fact that he was going back to Mill Farm that night as a surprise. The impending broadcast also weighed on him, as he felt it might produce news of one kind or another. Diana, on the other hand, seemed *distrait*, and not entirely sensible of the trouble he was going to to see her. She was still put out that he had not been able to lunch with her and she was secretly worried that Angus would ring up from Scotland and feel it odd that she was not at home. She had invented a dentist to account for her trip to London, plus her need to get some winter clothes (the cottage was very damp and she felt cold there), but she was now going to be much later than these ploys allowed. She had not wanted to stop at all. 'It'll be in all the morning papers,' she said of the broadcast. 'You must have something to eat,' he had replied. It was odd: all through her pregnancy, which had started a few weeks after she had met him, he had been so incredibly kind, and generous and thoughtful. But this one evening, when she was feeling really het up about Jamie being without her for

381

so long and having to lie to her sister-in-law, he was steadfastly determined to make her even later.

She toyed with her sandwich, refused a second, and drank her gin and tonic rather quickly. Then she realised that she was irritating him, and she didn't at all want to do that so she asked for another drink. 'That's the ticket,' he said, and went to fetch it at once. She repaired her lipstick and powdered her nose. When he returned with the drinks she asked him what he would do if there was a war, and he said that he'd join any service that would take him. 'Then you would go away! I should never see you!'

But he said that she'd probably see more of him since he would not be living at home. 'My movements won't be known in the same way as they are now.'

I could go on being his mistress for years, she thought. That's what happens in wars and he might easily find someone younger. 'What I hate', she said, 'is all the lying and hiding we have to do. I do so believe in frankness about everything.'

'I know you do,' he said fondly. 'It's one of the things I love about you.' He took her hand and kissed it. She saw the ball bouncing back into her court, and all she could do was pick it up and put it in her pocket.

Then it was the broadcast. At the end of it, Edward put out his cigarette and said, 'Well, I'm damned if I know any more than I did before. What did you think?'

'It sounded to me as though he was just trying to break the worst to us gently.'

'By Jove! I think you're probably right. I suppose we'd better be going. Get you back to your offspring.'

They parted in the car, at the gate outside the cottage as she didn't want her sister-in-law to see him. They kissed, each feeling that the other required it to be passionate, but passion eluded them. This did not worry Edward in the least – after all, she was jolly passionate in bed, which is what counted – but it worried her, and she lay awake half the night afraid that she was losing him.

∞ ∞ ∞

'So, Dad, you do see, don't you, that I had to tell you.'

Rupert looked down at her as she squatted before the gushing, mossy little pipe. They were filling bottles with drinking water from the spring down the hill just before Mill Farm. Her arms were wet, she wore a torn cotton shirt and one sandshoe had a hole where her big toe was coming through. She never has any pretty clothes, he thought with a pang. 'Yes, of course I see,' he said.

'I mean, I can understand now why people write plays about loyalty and disloyalty. Polly told *me* because I'm her best best friend, she was so worried, and, of course, she told me not to tell anyone, but I think the situation is so serious that we have to ignore that. Don't we?'

'I think we do.' She handed him a full bottle and he gave her another empty one from the box.

'So, could you talk to Christopher, do you think? I mean, he's got a mother and she'd go bonkers if he went. Polly thinks absolutely bonkers.'

'I'll give the matter a great deal of thought and then I'll decide.'

'Do you think I have to tell Polly that I've told you?'

'Not yet,' he replied, seeing her anxious face and remembering last night during the broadcast.

'I mean, if she asks me of course I'll have to, but I am afraid of her anger and contempt. She is the most truthful person I know.'

'So are you.'

'Am I? Nothing like Polly, though. Don't you think she is the most awfully pretty person you've ever met? Except for Zoë, I suppose.'

This touched him so much that he had to laugh. 'So are you. I'm simply hemmed in by pretty people. Except I don't think you're pretty, Clary, I think you're beautiful.'

'Don't be idiotic, Dad! Beautiful!' He could see her savouring it. 'That's a loony idea!' She was blushing to the roots of her hair. '*Me* beautiful?' she said again trying to conceal her enchantment with scorn. 'I've never heard of anything so silly in all my life!'

∞ ∞ ∞

383

When the Brig had said that everybody was to start digging an air-raid shelter, he had meant it. He had chosen a site between the tennis court and the kitchen garden, organised pegs and ropes to mark out its dimensions, had ordered McAlpine to produce every digging utensil in his possession, and sent Clary and Polly to round up the others. Rupert, Sybil, Zoë and Sid also joined in. Only the Duchy, Rachel, to whom he wished to dictate letters (and whose back was in no condition for digging) and Evie, who said that she had a weak shoulder, were exempted. Evie had found a niche for herself in any case: she spent hours mending linen quite beautifully – far better than Zoë who seemed to have given up – with the great aunts whom she regaled with largely fictitious accounts of her life. The aunts thought her a most interesting artistic person, and everybody else was relieved to be free of her. It soon transpired, however, that only a limited number of people could dig at one time, so Rupert organised shifts. The two who were supposed to be having lessons with Miss Milliment were sent back to them. Billy was deputed to chop away the roots that were early encountered, but quite soon he chopped his hand so badly that he was sent to Rachel to have his wound washed and dressed – a long job since his skin was deeply ingrained with dirt (McAlpine was not interested in whether he ever washed or not, and he never did).

'Cheeky monkey!' was all McAlpine said when he saw Billy pouring with blood. He had dug for about an hour, accomplishing twice as much as the rest of them put together, and then said that he'd be off, he had work to do. He regarded the whole enterprise as a gentleman's jape.

Villy and Jessica also escaped digging duty – in the morning, at least, as there was an enormous shop to do in Battle for both houses. It was agreed that Jessica should get Lady Rydal up, and that Villy would go and collect the list from Home Place. This suited Villy, who was feeling sick in the mornings – the drive to London yesterday had been awful – and still felt tired from the exhausting day. She had realised at the lunch with Teddy that Edward really had not heard her announcement on the telephone of the impending baby – it seemed almost unbelievable but he really hadn't. Before that, she had had one of those mornings when she couldn't do efficiently what she planned, because the house was in such a mess – well, not mess, exactly, but with a lot of things needing to be done. She changed the sheets on their unmade bed, collected fourteen dirty shirts from the laundry basket in Edward's dressing room to take to Sussex to be washed. There was a letter from Edna saying she couldn't come back as her mother was still poorly and didn't like her to be so far away. Just as well, Villy thought. She would not have felt happy about leaving the poor girl alone in the house if there were going to be air raids. Or one air raid: it might not take more than one. She got Teddy to help her cart silver, all the school books and music into the hall. Then she had to change for the lunch to which she had gone full of resentment at the way in which (she thought) Edward had received her news. Then, discovering that he hadn't received it made her feel frustrated and angry at having been so angry because, of course, she couldn't tell him in front of Teddy, and because she couldn't tell him that, she found it difficult to say anything else. But Teddy seemed to enjoy himself and neither of them noticed anything.

Leaving them at the club, she drove slowly up from Knightsbridge to Hyde Park Corner, but just as she reached the small dark green hut where cabmen were reputed to gamble wildly when they went there for cups of tea and meals, she suddenly decided that she would go to Hermione's shop – just to see what she had got. After all, she might never get another chance and, due to the Situation, Hermione might even be having one of her tempting sales.

She wasn't but she was delighted to see Villy. 'What a *treat!*' she exclaimed in her seductive, drawling voice that made quite a lot of things she said sound amusing. 'Just back from the most boring lunch in the world with Reggie Davenport, looking forward to the most boring afternoon, and now you're here! What can I do for you, my darling?'

'I don't know. I've just come to browse and be cheered up.'

'You've come at the perfect time. I've got the most divine autumn clothes, and people don't seem to be coming back to town as they usually do. Skulking in the country because of Mr Schickelgruber.'

'Who?'

'Hitler, darling. That's what his real name is, and he used

to be a house painter. I mean one *can't* take him seriously, can one? He seems to me to be quite without charm.' She snapped her fingers and at once Miss MacDonald emerged from some recess in the shop. 'Look who we have here! What do you think would really tempt Mrs Cazalet?'

'I can only buy one thing, Hermione.'

'Of course, darling. You shall buy *half* a thing if you like.'

An hour and a half later, Villy emerged from the shop possessing the most nifty little black woollen dress, the collar and cuffs of which were embroidered in jet, with a huge belt and jet buckle, a tweed suit the colour of dark blue hyacinths – very classic and exquisitely cut – a very dark grey flannel coat trimmed with mock black astrakhan fur, 'It looks like a tent off, darling, but it does hang rather sweetly – try it,' and a long-sleeved crêpe dress, cowl-necked, that was the colour of blackberry fool, Villy had said, and was much applauded for the description. 'We must remember that, Miss MacDonald, mustn't we? So much better than plum.' She got into her car full of elation and guilt. She had spent nearly sixty guineas, but she adored everything that she had bought, and drove back to Lansdowne Road feeling slightly intoxicated. It wasn't until she got back that she realised the only garment she would be able to wear throughout the winter was the coat, which would continue to be concealing until the end. The idea that she had earlier entertained – of consulting Hermione about doctors – had simply never entered her head. Impossible, anyway, with Miss MacDonald there. And she could wear the other things after the baby. She hadn't bought a thing for months. That part of the day had been a pure pleasure, of a frivolous kind. Edward would not mind, he was always generous about her buying clothes, although she did wish he noticed them more. She reflected with some pleasure that she would be able to show them to Jessica, something she could never have done before, as Jessica would now be able to afford herself some decent clothes. And I didn't buy a single evening frock, she concluded, to add a touch of virtue to the proceedings.

But the rest of the day had been absolute hell. She had packed and packed and loaded the car herself since Teddy was late because Edward had left him in Leicester Square and he'd made a mess of changing trains. It began to rain heavily when they left, and Teddy told her every single thing that had happened to Paul Muni throughout the film which, apart from being very boring, rendered it incomprehensible. They did not get to Mill Farm until eight, and there had barely been time for dinner before the broadcast. After it she felt impelled to unpack the car and then just as she was going up to bed, Edward turned up out of the blue presenting himself as a wonderful surprise. The bloke he had had to see, have dinner with, turned out to live half-way between London and here, he said, so he thought she would like him to come on.

'Don't let's go to bed yet,' he said. 'I'm for a whisky and soda. What about you, darling?'

'No, thanks.' She walked back to the sofa and sat down. 'I think Teddy enjoyed himself.'

'Yes. He told me he had a lovely time.'

'Jessica still here?'

'Yes. She went to the funeral yesterday, Raymond's been left a lovely lot of money – and a house.'

'That's good news. As long as he doesn't blow it all.' There was a pause; then he said, 'At lunch today – I thought you were angry with me. You were, weren't you? What's it all about?' She could tell he was nervous, because he'd begun picking his fingers, scraping the side with his nail – they often looked quite painful. He was always terrified of scenes.

'I was – a bit – because I tried to tell you something on the telephone the day before, and you practically rang off on me, and then I realised that you hadn't heard what I said.'

He'd become very quiet. 'What was that?'

She took a deep breath. 'I told you that I was practically certain I was having another baby.'

He stared at her for a moment, astonishment and almost a kind of *relief*, she thought, in his face, which then lightened. He smiled, got up and gave her a hug. 'Good Lord! You told me that and I didn't hear it? There was a road drill in the street, and Miss Seafang was telling me I was wanted on the other line. I'm sorry, darling, you must have thought me the most awful brute!'

'You're pleased?'

'Of course I'm pleased,' he said heartily. 'Bit surprised, though. I thought, you know, you were taking precautions.'

387

'I was. This one slipped through the net.'

'Good Lord!' he said again, and drained his glass and stood up. 'Better go up, hadn't we? I mean, you must be dead beat.' He held out his hand and pulled her to her feet.

While they were undressing, she said, 'I do feel a trifle *old* to start all this baby business again.'

'Nonsense, darling. You're not old at all!' He kissed her fondly. 'What you need is beauty sleep. I shall have to leave early. Don't bother about me in the morning.'

Now, walking up the hill to Home Place and remembering all this, she thought that it had not occurred to him to ask whether *she* wanted another child. He'd simply assumed that she would. 'What's done is done,' she said to herself, 'and if there's a war, we may all be blown up, anyway.'

∞ ∞ ∞

It rained after lunch, which, Louise felt, would let them off their shift of digging. 'Let's wash our hair,' she said. She had read that yolk of egg was supposed to be very good and was eager to try it. Nora, who did not care in the least about her hair, said that it was rather a waste of eggs, but Louise said they would make meringues of the whites, and then it wouldn't be a waste at all. 'Because if we were just going to make meringues, the yolk would be wasted,' she said.

So then Louise washed them both: Nora's was very dirty and she used water that was too hot so the egg scrambled rather and in the end she had to use another shampoo as well. There was nowhere to dry it, as the drawing-room fire hadn't been lit yet; they lay on their beds with their bath towels and jerseys on so that they wouldn't catch cold.

'About the service,' Louise said. 'You know when you suggested that everybody should give something up in return for peace? Well, why do you think everybody didn't seem to want to do that?'

'I don't know. Mummy said afterwards that it was each person's own business, but I don't see how one can tell whether they're minding it. Anyway, she said it was bossy and interfering – two things which I often am.'

Louise looked at her with awe. Bossy and interfering weren't romantic faults, like having hot temper or being too frank (tact-less), and she knew she wouldn't dream of publicly admitting to them.

'Your hair's looking super now,' she said, 'all shining and nice.'

'Oh. Well, I don't really care about it much, because when I'm a nun, they'll cut it all off. You could give up vanity,' she added.

'Am I vain? I don't like my face much.' She spent hours in front of the mirror, changing her hair, trying make-up, making different faces to see which one looked best. Nora pointed some of this out and said she was pretty sure that it constituted vanity. 'But, of course,' she added, 'you don't necessarily have to give something up, you could do something instead.'

That was when Louise decided that an earlier decision, to get out of going to the finishing school with Nora because of the agony of homesickness that she knew would ensue, should be changed. If there was peace, she would go, if there was war she needn't. She told Nora that she had decided on something, but didn't want to say what it was.

'You needn't tell me,' Nora replied. 'Simply write it down on a piece of paper and put it in my pencil box. I've cleared it out for the purpose.'

'Have you done it, then?'

'Of course. And I've asked Polly and Clary. And Christopher, and even Angela. Not Teddy, though: he doesn't seem to mind if there is a war or not.'

'Simon?'

'Forgot him. Now, you do yours. Oh, I asked Miss Milliment. I really like her, and she said of course she would – no stu-pid grown-up shilly-shallying seeing-both-sides-of-the-question stuff for her.'

'What about the children?'

'Haven't had a chance to ask them yet. We will after tea.'

Neville and Lydia and Judy, all secretly impressed to be called to a meeting even if it turned out to contain only Nora and Louise, stood in a row before Nora who was seated at the dining-room table, pencil box at the ready, papers and pencils to hand.

'I haven't got anything to give up,' Neville said at once.

'Your train set,' Lydia said.

'I *need* that! You can't give up the things you need.'

'You don't need it,' Judy said. 'I don't have a train set and I get along perfectly well.'

Neville turned on her. 'You're only a girl,' he said witheringly. They were all silenced for a moment. Then Nora said, 'All right. If you don't want to give something up, you could do something instead. Some job – some work thing.'

'Help Tonbridge clean the cars,' Neville said. 'I'll do that.'

'You're always asking him if you can do that,' Lydia said reproachfully, 'and you know he doesn't want you. I'm afraid he hasn't got the point at all,' she said to the others.

'Never mind about Neville. What are you going to do?'

'I shall . . . ' she shut her eyes tightly and rocked back and forth on her feet. 'I shall . . . save up all my pocket money and give it to poor people. There!' She opened her eyes and looked round to gauge the effect. 'That's a good give-up, isn't it?'

'Very good,' Nora said. 'Here's your piece of paper. Only you must put how many weeks' pocket money on it that you're going to give up.'

'Oh, a year, at least,' said Lydia grandly. She was slightly drunk with her generosity. 'I think a year,' she said.

'How will you know a poor person to give it to?' Neville asked sulkily.

'Easy. I shall just go up to people and ask them if they're poor, and if they say yes, I shall give it to them.'

In the end, it was suggested to her that she could give it to the poor babies in Aunt Rach's home.

Judy, who was a bit of a copycat, Lydia thought, said she would do the same. They were sat down at the table to write, and Nora turned her attention to Neville.

'What I'll do,' he said at last, 'is I'll go up to the great aunts and I'll kiss them twice a day – once on each cheek twice. For all the time they stay here.'

It wasn't entirely satisfactory, but the older girls decided it was probably the best he could do.

∞ ∞ ∞

'A change is as good as a rest,' Miss Milliment reminded herself as she struggled to find her mac that hung with a great many others on pegs in the hall at Mill Farm. Dinner was over and it was her plan to slip quietly away, trot up the hill and have an early bed, because to tell the truth she was a little fagged, as her brother Jack used to say. But very lucky and grateful. Everything was different here, so naturally there were little problems, but none that time and practice could not erase. One of the worst was that she seemed always to have damp feet, which was entirely her own fault, not having bothered to get her shoes mended. I am as bad as Rosamond in *The Purple Jar*, she thought, although, in her case, it was not because she had spent the money on that eccentric luxury, it was simply that not one but both pairs of shoes were in a poor state. Perhaps, tomorrow, she might ask dear Viola if she could go into Battle where doubtless a pair of galoshes could be purchased.

Attired now for the journey, she lifted the large iron latch of the front door, but the rain seemed to have stopped, although it was still very wet underfoot. Carrying her umbrella, and the copy of *The Times* with which Lady Rydal had finished, she started to trot waveringly down the drive. It was a dark, still, starless night; every now and then a tree above her shivered and a shower of heavy raindrops descended. There were puddles as well, which, of course, she could not see. Dear Viola had offered to drive her home, but she had felt that this was an unnecessary imposition; she would soon have to get used to the way, which, was not far. The little talk, accompanied by a delicious glass of sherry, that she had had with Viola about her salary was over. She had been so utterly generous: had absolutely refused to let her pay anything at all for her keep, had realised that she already had one rent to pay, had also insisted that the charge of two pounds ten shillings per child per week should remain the same for the three younger children, who she knew were every bit as much trouble (perfectly true, but Miss Milliment had known many employers who would have refused to recognise this), and had also said that her travelling expenses would be included in the first month's cheque. So she would now be earning seventeen pounds ten a week, 'And therefore no excuse, Eleanor, for you not buying a new pair of shoes as well as galoshes.'

And, then, to be in the country again! She sniffed the delicious air that smelled of damp leaves: it did so remind her of home, of walking back in the dusk after she had decorated the church for special occasions like Harvest Festival – back to toast and dripping and reading to Papa, who liked his study to be rather dim because of his eyes, which always made reading to him a little difficult. Carlyle's *French Revolution* had been one of his favourites; it had been an old edition that she had picked up at the church sale, but the print had been shockingly small, and Papa had always said that young people did not require spectacles, which in her case, had not turned out to be true. One of the first things she had done after he died was to have her eyes tested, and the spectacles had made an amazing – she felt miraculous – difference: she could see all kinds of things that she had not noticed before. That was when she had started to look at pictures, because she could see them. How wonderful that had been! And how fortunate she was now! She loved teaching, was fond of her three girls, and was delighted to include dear Jessica's Nora as, clearly, Louise was very taken with her. And the three young ones: Neville constantly amused her, but naturally, he would be treated the same as the two girls – she would make no distinctions. It was pleasant to look forward to getting to her little bedroom in the cottage. The Brontës would be quite shocked at how much I am enjoying myself, she thought as she turned into the drive of Home Place. The Brontës came to mind because she had given *Villette* as one of their holiday tasks. Louise had already read it but Miss Milliment simply told her to read it again and also *The Professor* in order that she might compare the two. Polly did not read so much or so easily, but she had a good eye, and Clary – Clary was, she knew, the *one*. The stories that she had been given when she had visited Clary at the end of her chicken pox had really startled her. They had a dash, a drive, a precocity that was well beyond the usual twelve-year-old. Some of her subject-matter was undoubtedly beyond her, but Miss Milliment had been careful not to criticise that, had confined her remarks to grammar, punctuation and spelling, having first said how very much she enjoyed the stories. 'One must not interfere,' she told herself, having no intention of doing anything of the kind. The creative process, beyond her in all respects, was, none the less, something to reverence: many people had been spoiled by too much of the wrong kind of attention. It was a natural process for Clary, and natural it should remain. The lack of interest that the family displayed was probably a good thing.

The house now loomed before her, golden light in the square windows, distant sounds of the servants washing up as she passed the kitchen quarters. By the time she reached the cottage and was clambering up the steep stairs, the glass of sherry she had been given before dinner was starting to wear off, and as she thought of doing the crossword in bed – a real luxury – she realised that the paper would be full of the Situation, the real, terrible state of Europe that she had been frivolously ignoring all the way home. She had been so wrapped in the silver lining that she had forgotten the cloud. If there was a war . . . but there would be a war – if not now then sooner or later. She thought of the lovely Renoirs at the Rosenberg and Helft gallery that she had haunted all summer, and sent up a prayer that they would be moved in time.

∞ ∞ ∞

Hugh came into Edward's office just before lunch, which they were going to have together. Miss Seafang, who stood by the desk to receive back letters she had handed Edward to sign, smiled a discreet welcome.

'Won't be a minute, old boy. Have a seat.'

But Hugh, who had been sitting all the morning, continued to wander about the large room, panelled in koko wood, apparently studying the dull pictures. Miss Seafang watched him with solicitude. He looked dreadfully tired – more, even, than usual: he was what her mother called a natural worrier, and that took its toll. He brought out the maternal in her, quite unlike Mr Edward, who brought out something quite else. Her gaze returned to her boss. Today, he was dressed in a pinstripe suit of the palest grey with a white shirt that had the tiniest grey stripe in it, and a lemon corded-silk tie. In his jacket pocket there was a corner of foulard silk handkerchief of a lemon and grey and dark green design. His slightly curly hair was glistened with brilliantine, and a faint, definitely exciting scent of cigars and lavender water seemed to emanate from his slightest movement. His left hand lay on the desk, displaying his gold signet ring with the family crest upon it – rather worn, but definitely a rearing lion – and the gold links gleamed on the immaculate cuffs from which his hairy wrists emerged, the left banded by a suitably glamorous and masculine watch. With his right hand, he was signing the letters in his bold rather careless manner with his fountain pen. It seemed to be failing: he shook it twice, and then turned to her. 'Oh, Miss Seafang, it's done the dirty on me again!' Smiling slightly, she produced another pen from her cardigan pocket. Where would he be without her?

'If anyone calls, Mr Edward, what time shall I say you'll be back?'

'He won't be,' Hugh said. 'I'm taking him to the wharf.'

Edward looked at his brother and raised his eyebrows: Hugh gave him the obstinate, but at the same time sweet-tempered glare that was one of his most habitual expressions.

'High-handed old bastard,' he said. 'The wharf it is, Miss Seafang.'

Bracken drove them to Hugh's club, which was not so far from the river as Edward's. They stopped on the way to buy an *Evening Standard* whose banner headlines were about the Prime Minister's journey that morning.

'"Out of this nettle, danger, we pluck this flower, safety . . . ",' Edward read aloud. 'That sort of remark's more up your street than mine. What does the feller mean?'

Hugh shrugged. 'That he hasn't much hope, but he's going to try, I should think,' he said. 'This time Daladier and Mussolini are going to be there, so it sounds like we're approaching the crunch.'

'What's the point in having *them* there? If Hitler doesn't take any notice of our Prime Minister, why should he take any notice of them?'

'Well, I suppose neither of them wants a war – three against one, that sort of thing?'

Edward didn't reply. He was wondering why Hugh wanted them to go to the wharf, but business of this kind was not discussed in front of servants.

When they were seated in the cavernous dining room that dwarfed its occupants by its immense marble pillars and distantly lofty ceiling eating Dover sole with a glass of hock, and Hugh still hadn't mentioned the wharf, Edward said, 'Come on, old boy. Out with it. It's obviously something you think I shan't agree to.'

'Well, there are two things. Let's take the logs first.' And he launched into his scheme to get all of their most valuable logs into the river Lee to save them in case of air attack. 'If we leave them where they are, and most of them are lying hard against the saw mill, and we get incendiaries, the whole thing will go up. We may lose the mill anyway, but we can replace that. A lot of these logs can't be replaced.'

'But apart from being tidal the river's very narrow, and I can't see the powers that be allowing us to block it up.'

'We can apply for barges from the PLA in which to lodge the logs, but you know them, by the time we get them the whole thing may have happened. If we simply drop them in the river they'll be far keener on letting us have the barges to clear the blockage.'

'What about a crane? We'll certainly need that.'

'I've got one. Ordered it yesterday. It should be there this afternoon.'

'Have you talked about this with the Old Man?'

'No. I thought it would be better simply to do it and then tell him. But I think,' he added, 'that we should be there while they're doing it. Or they'll make a mess of it, or someone will come along and tell them they didn't ought to and they'll stop.'

'If we turn out to be wrong, we'll have gone to a hell of a lot of expense, not to mention putting the authorities' backs up, for nothing. I mean, if peace breaks out after all.' Edward stopped and then laughed. 'This is ridiculous! It ought to have been me who had this idea and you who are putting in the objections! What has come over us? I'm game. I think it's a damn good idea.'

∞ ∞ ∞

They went on to discuss other things. Hugh wanted to get another night watchman at the wharf: Bernie Holmes had been doing the job for over thirty years now, nobody knew how old he was, but too old, Hugh felt, to have the responsibility of the place in an air raid. Edward said they couldn't possibly sack him, and it was agreed to get in a younger man to keep him company. Then there was the question of fire drill, or simply air-raid drill, not only for the staff at the wharf but at the office as well. They thrashed that out while they were at the wharf and waiting while men shackled each end of each log with chains and fastened the steel cable between them, attached the crane's hook to the ring on the cable and began the slow process of yanking the log into the air above the river and letting it down onto the mud – the tide was at low ebb – where it settled with gaseous bubbles and a stench of rotten seaweed and diesel oil. It all took hours. They got sixteen logs into the river by five thirty when the crane driver indicated that he had had enough and, in any case, they had used up all their river frontage. Edward was for moving up river, never mind the ownership, but Hugh said that would only put them in the wrong when the PLA woke up to what they were doing. So they called it a day, went back to their homes for baths, and met again at Hugh's house where a very simple meal had been prepared for them by the house-parlourmaid. They listened to the nine o'clock news on the wireless, but there wasn't any really except that the meeting in Munich was still going on. Hugh rang Sybil to say that he would be down tomorrow evening whichever way it went, and Edward thought that perhaps he'd better do the same with Villy. 'All well?' they asked each other after each of these sallies. They decided to have one whisky and call it a day.

'Is Louise upset at the prospect of war?' Hugh asked casually.

'Do you know, old boy, I haven't the faintest idea. Doesn't seem to be. Why? Is Polly?'

'She is, rather.' Edward noticed that the tic at the side of Hugh's forehead had started up. He drained his glass. 'Listen, old boy. You've had a long day, and you worry too much. She's probably perfectly all right, really. You worry too much,' he repeated affectionately, clapped him on the shoulder to conceal deeper affection, and went.

Hugh, as he walked slowly up the stairs to bed, wondered what 'too much' was. Too much for him? Or too much for the Situation? He hadn't broached the second problem he'd mentioned at lunch, which was that Edward would suddenly go off into some service and leave him, Hugh, with the whole firm on his shoulders. Unless Rupert came in. But Rupert would most likely want to join up himself. He was beginning to get a bad head and took some dope so that he could get to sleep before it started hammering.

∞ ∞ ∞

On Friday morning, the Brig, who had recognised the day before that the air-raid shelter was not making practicable progress (some people engaged upon it had wooden spades), ordered Sampson to put two men on to it. 'I can't be on the Elsans and the shelter at the same time, Mr Cazalet, sir,' Sampson said, but it was a hopeless plea. 'Nonsense, Sampson, I'm sure you can organise it.'

That morning, one dozen Primus stoves were delivered from Battle by Till's. Tonbridge was told to move the cars out of the garage, which was likely to become a kitchen. Wren, from his stables, watched this with glee. 'First 'is 'ouse and now 'is place of work. 'E'll soon be off and good riddance.' He hated Tonbridge – always had.

That morning, in lessons, Miss Milliment made Polly trace out a map of Europe, printing the names of the countries in her best lettering. It was, of course, out of date already, since it did not take into account Hitler's most recent acquisitions, which she now marked in. She felt that it was important for the children to have some comprehension of what was going on and a clear understanding of the juxtaposition of the countries immediately involved.

Mrs Cripps spent the morning plucking and drawing two brace of pheasant for dinner; she also minced the remains of the sirloin of beef for cottage pie, made a Madeira cake, three dozen damson tartlets, two pints of egg custard, two rice puddings, two pints of bread sauce, a prune mould and two pints of batter for the kitchen lunch of Toad-in-the-Hole, two lemon meringue pies, and fifteen stuffed baked apples for the dining-room lunch. She also oversaw the cooking of mountainous quantities of vegetables – the potatoes for the cottage pie, the cabbage to go with the Toad, the carrots, french beans, spinach and a pair of grotesque marrows, grown to an outlandish size by McAlpine, who won first prize every year for his marrows. They were, as Rupert had once remarked to Rachel, the vegetable equivalent of the rudest seaside postcards – not an idea that would have occurred to Mrs Cripps.

Everybody, in fact, went about their usual business except for Rupert, who was becoming more and more aware that he did not really have any. He had mentioned to Zoë that he thought Clary needed some new clothes, with the unexpected result that she had gone into Battle with Jessica and Villy to buy some material to make her a frock. Just as he was thinking what a good thing this was, he remembered what Clary had told him yesterday about Christopher; he'd done nothing about it. He was in the billiard room, 'his studio', absently staring at the portrait of Angela and trying to see what he had left out, and he spent several minutes trying to decide whom he should talk to or inform about the boy. Christopher? But he hardly knew him, and if he made a mess of it, it might make things worse. In one sense, Jessica was the obvious person, but Clary's saying she would go absolutely bonkers made him think twice about that. Villy, then. She was in Battle. Rachel – of course: if he was in trouble, his sister was the first person he would go to. He went in search of her, but the Duchy said that Sid had taken her for her treatment in Tunbridge Wells. Then he thought – sisters. Of course – far best person to talk to would be Angela. She had been so sensible that day when he had talked about his career problems. She was older than Christopher, but not too old: he would be more likely to listen to her than to anyone else. She was nearly always somewhere about the place.

He found her reading in the hammock in the orchard. She wore a white skirt and the pale greenish shirt that he'd lent her to be painted in. She did not hear him coming: he was afraid he gave her quite a fright, since when he called her, she gave such a start that the book fell from her hands onto the grass.

'Sorry,' he said, picking it up. 'I really didn't mean to startle you.' He looked at the book. '*Sonnets from the Portuguese*. Oh! Elizabeth Barrett Browning. Are they good? Did she translate them?'

'No, she wrote them to Robert. That's what he called her, "my little Portuguese". I think it was because she had such black hair and dark brown eyes.'

There was a short silence – he was thinking that he should have painted her in the hammock – then she said, 'Is there any news?'

'Oh. None so far as I know. No, I came to find you because there's something I want to talk to you about. Shall we go for a walk?'

'Oh, yes! Let's.' She was out of the hammock in a trice, left the book behind her.

'Where would you like to go?'

'Oh – anywhere! Wherever you like.'

'Well, just somewhere where we won't be interrupted.'

'Oh, yes!' she said again.

'Right. Well, there's a nice huge old fallen tree just the other side of the wood behind the house,' he said. 'I used to take Clary there when she wanted to play what she called shipwrecks. Off we go.'

∞ ∞ ∞

Teddy was feeling very out of sorts. After that smashing day in London, there didn't seem enough to do in the country. What was really the matter was that he had nobody to do anything with: Simon was still scratching and rather peevish – anyway, he'd quarrelled with him, although if Simon had been about he could probably have made it up. He went to the camp in the morning. It looked just the same, but it felt somehow different: deserted, an unfriendly place to be by himself. There was no sign of Christopher. Then he thought of being a Roman emperor, and having Neville and Lydia and Judy as slaves. They seemed quite keen at first, but by the time he got them there he recognised that their attitude was distinctly unslavish.

'Why do we have to do what you want all the time?' Neville said.

'Yes – why?' echoed Judy.

He explained about being an emperor, whereupon Lydia instantly said she was a queen. They raided the stores without asking, and when he sent them to get firewood to build a fire they wandered away and did not come back for ages. He thought of building a dam in the stream and tried to get them to help him with that, but they soon got bored and started to

399

drift away. 'Hey!' he shouted as he saw Judy trotting off after the other two. 'Before you go!' Lydia and Neville stopped and turned round, just as they'd reached the hedge with hazelnuts in it. 'I forgot to explain. This is a secret place.'

'No, it isn't. We know about it,' Neville said at once.

'I mean, secret from anybody else.'

'So what?' Judy said in an assumed and most irritating voice.

'You have to promise – all of you – not to tell anyone else about it.'

'It's so boring', Lydia said, 'that I shouldn't think anyone would want to know.'

'Yes. It's already made,' Neville said. 'We like to make our own camps. We've made thousands of them. If you wanted us, you should have asked us at the beginning.'

There was nothing he could do with them. He tried threats but they didn't seem at all frightened. 'You can't stop our pocket money, or send us to bed early.'

'He's got a gun,' Lydia interrupted. 'He could shoot us.'

'Yes, and then people would find out and you would be hanged,' Judy said. 'And I shouldn't think anyone would mind, not even your mother, if you shot your own sister.'

'Don't be so stupid. Of course I wouldn't shoot you, Lyd – or anyone, come to that. Listen. I'll give you a cigarette card from my collection, one each, if you'll shut up.'

'One card!' Neville scoffed. 'You must think we're nitwits.'

In the end, he had to promise them a Snofrute each as well as two cards. They went off then.

'Only I think, Teddy, you should play with someone your own age,' was Lydia's parting shot. Dignity forbade his going with them. He stood with folded arms watching them trail across the meadow, chatting to one another, and when he turned and went back to the camp he felt lonelier than ever. It would have been much better if he and Christopher hadn't had a fight. There wasn't anyone of his age. Well, there would be at school. His second year there must be better than the first. He wouldn't be so baffled by all the rules which people didn't tell you till you'd broken them from not knowing; he wouldn't be so bullied. Awful memories engulfed him: being tied in the bath with the cold tap left on and the bath slowly filling up; being icy cold, and if they didn't come back to untie him knowing he would drown; being flicked with knotted wet bath towels – that had been the summer term when there was swimming; finding a turd inside the bottom of his bed; getting beaten – twice – the only thing, though, that had made the bullying less. One friend, another new boy, who was a marvellous bowler. None of this could be told. During the year he had come to see that stronger people bullied weaker people, had determined to become strong so that he could take it out on someone for a change. Squash, the game he was best at, had been no good: first-year boys were not allowed to play squash, but he would this year. All the summer he had been pretending to himself that he was looking forward to going back – but he wasn't, really. He was looking forward to being too old for school, and then, if there was still a war, he'd join up and be the best fighter pilot in the world. He was fourteen now so it wouldn't be for four years.

∞ ∞ ∞

'Couldn't we just quietly look and then fold the papers back again?'

'Louise! Of course not. It's a sacred trust.'

'All right. It was just an idea. How many have we got now?'

'You and me. The three children. Christopher and Angela.'

'How on earth did you get her to agree?'

'Never mind. Don't interrupt. Miss Milliment, Simon, Ellen – I tried the maids but they just said it was very nice but they couldn't think of anything, Aunt Sybil, Aunt Rach, Mummy, of course, and yours. Uncle Rupe. I tried Grania and she said she'd gladly give her life not to have a war but obviously that was no good.'

'Why not?'

'To begin with because she was so glad about it, and to go on with she's really too old to commit suicide. I had to tell her that – nicely, of course.'

∞ ∞ ∞

She managed to walk back to the house with him in an ordinary dignified manner, as though nothing had happened – or nothing very much – or as though, perhaps, even if it had, it was now resolved. In the drive she said she must go back to Mill Farm for lunch, and he said, of course. Then he stopped her walking, by putting an arm on her shoulder and said, 'Look. I *am* so sorry. I mean, to have been so thick – and not realised. You're such a good person. You'll find a marvellous chap.' There was a pause: her face felt as stiff and rigid as if she'd put a face mask on it. Then he said, 'And you won't forget about Christopher, will you?'

She had shaken her head, and then she had smiled, which felt the right dignified thing to do, and said, 'No, of course not,' and then turned away and started walking purposefully down the drive. She heard the click of the gate as he went into the garden before she had gone a few yards away from him but she didn't look back. She had walked down the drive and started to go down the hill, but she knew she couldn't go home to the farm yet. So she turned in to the left along the cart track that led to York's farm and when she came to a gate in the hedge at one side of it, she climbed over and ran a few yards along the stubble and flung herself on the ground. Sobs engulfed her in great racking wordless waves. Grief poured out of her as though she had never contained anything else. When these first paroxysms were exhausted and she was still, the words and thoughts began. What he had said, what she had said – and, more scaldingly shameful, *thought* as she got out of the hammock so many ages ago. 'There's something I want to talk to you about.' Why should she have assumed that the yearned-for moment had come? That he wanted to tell her how much he loved her? Now she could think of no reason why she should have thought that, and yet she *had* thought it. And then, later, but when she still had the chance to be secret, why had she not? Why had she seized his hand and pulled him to face her? 'I love you. I am completely in love with you,' she had said, and endured the memory of dawning comprehension, and – yes – horror on his face to be succeeded quickly by compassionate kindness that hurt almost as much. It was too late to stop then – it had all poured out. She had only told him because there might be a war, and he might get killed, and in any case would go away, and she would not see him. 'I couldn't bear not to tell you,' she had said, now unable to bear having told him. She was weeping now, as she had then, but now without his arms round her. For he had held her, tried to comfort her by telling her all the hopeless, despairing things that meant nothing. She would get over it, she was so young, she had her whole life before her (as if a whole life that contained so much pain could be comforting!). Everything he said merely belittled her, diminished everything that she felt. In trying to present her love to her as transient, he took away all that she had. 'I would never say that to *you!*' she had cried: it had silenced him. He had held her until her tears had ceased, had given her his handkerchief. Then he had said something about how much he liked and admired her – but she couldn't remember any of those words – had said that he was so much older, and, anyway, married, and she knew all that, and in the end he had said how sorry he was, and there was nothing that he could say and she realised that this was true. She had mopped up and blown her nose. 'Keep the handkerchief,' he had said. They had walked back without saying anything more at all. And then, in the drive, he had said, 'You won't forget about Christopher, will you?' How could he say that? But she had forgotten. She'd listened to all the stuff about Christopher in a daze of radiant anticipation of what was to come. Nothing is to come, she thought. Nothing ever is to come. She turned over onto her face again and her tears ran straight into the ground.

∞ ∞ ∞

When Polly and Clary got back to Home Place in time for lunch after lessons, they discovered the door of their room open and, of course, Oscar was nowhere to be seen.

'There's a notice on the door,' Polly said almost in tears. 'Surely anyone can read that!' After a frantic but thorough search of the room, they stood on the landing trying to think of what to do next.

'It must have been one of the maids,' Clary said.

'Yes, but where do you think he would have gone? He might be trying to find his way back to London – cats do.'

'I'll try the kitchen. He's very fond of food. You search all this floor.'

Clary sped downstairs, through the hall and the baize door

into the kitchen quarters, but she did not get a good reception there.

'No, Miss Clary, we've never gone and been in there,' the housemaids said, and Mrs Cripps, in the state of pent-up tension that always preceded the serving of a meal, actually shouted, 'Out with you now, miss. You know the rules. No children in the kitchen when I'm dishing up!'

'Can't I just look for him in here?'

'No, you can not. Anyway, he isn't here. How many times have I told you to put the vegetable dishes to warm on this rack, Emmeline? Now you'll have to pass them under the hot tap. Look at Flossy, miss. She wouldn't have another cat in her kitchen. Be off with you, now, there's a good girl.'

Clary looked at Flossy who lay on the window-sill as round and voluptuous as a fur hat, and Flossy, who always seemed to know when people looked at her, lifted her head; Clary retreated from her steady malevolent gaze.

'Any luck?' she called from the hall.

'No.' Polly's white face appeared over the banisters. 'Oh, who could have been so wicked as to leave the door open?'

Most of the grown-ups were in the Brig's study listening to the news, but she found her father and Zoë in the morning room. They were standing in front of the gate-legged table looking at some cloth that Zoë was unpacking and Dad had a drink in his hand.

'Oh, Clary! Come and look!' he said.

'Dad, I can't look at anything now. Some really awful *stupid* person has left the door to our room open, and Oscar has escaped and we can't find him.'

And Zoë stopped pulling the paper off the cloth, looked at Dad, and said, 'Oh, dear. I'm afraid that was me!'

'*You?*' Clary stared at her. All the feelings she had about Zoë that she never really said any more to anyone because they were so horrible suddenly came up like sick in her throat. 'You! It would be you! You stupid idiot! You've gone and lost Polly's cat! I hate you. You're the stupidest person I've ever met in my life!'

Before she could go on her father caught one of her arms and said, 'How dare you speak to Zoë like that? Apologise at once!'

'I will not!' She glared at him. He had never spoken to her like that before, and she felt a prickle of terror.

Zoë said, 'I'm really terribly sorry,' and Clary thought, No, you're not! You're just saying that to please Dad.

'Why did you go into my room, anyway?' she said.

'She went to get one of your dresses because she's bought some material to make you a new one,' Dad said, and hearing the affection in his voice that was certainly not for *her*, she said, 'Bet you were just doing that to please Dad. Weren't you?' and stared sullenly at her stepmother trying to keep angry at all costs.

But Zoë looked up from the table, straight into her face and simply said, 'Yes, you see I know how much he loves you, so – of course.'

It felt like the first true thing she had ever said, and it was too much. She was *used* to her resentment and jealousy – congealed this last year into an armed truce, she could not shed it at a word, and unable to respond she put her face in her hands and wept and her plate, that had got comfortably loose at last, fell out onto the table. Dad put his arms round her, and Zoë picked it up and gave it back to her saying, 'Won't it be lovely when you don't have to wear it?' and nobody laughed, which was the best thing.

Oscar was not found until nearly tea-time, although Polly went without lunch to search for him. When Clary joined her after lunch, she had searched the house, the stables – braving Mr Wren, who shouted but was too sleepy to stand upright. ('He fell down again as soon as he got up to shout at me,' Polly said), the cottage, all the squash court, all the outbuildings, including the horrible coke cellar by the greenhouse. She and Clary then tried the orchard, the wood behind the house and finally the drive.

'My throat's sore from calling,' Polly said.

'If he's gone onto the road he may have got tired and gone to sleep somewhere,' Clary replied. 'I *know* we are going to find him,' she said, really to cheer them both up but Polly believed her at once. At the end of the drive there was a large old oak, and as they approached it they heard his voice. He seemed to be quite a long way up the tree, as they could not see him at first, but each time they called, he answered.

'He *wants* to come down,' Polly said. Clary suggested getting some food for him because it was well known that cats could smell for miles. She went off to do this while Polly tried to climb the tree. But the lowest branch was too high. When Clary came back with a saucer of fish, she found her friend in tears.

'I don't think he *can* get down. He wants to, but he's frightened,' she said. They held up the fish and called. Oscar made slithery scratching noises as though he was trying to come down but there was no sign of him.

'What's up?'

They had not heard the bicycle. Teddy had decided to go for a ride by himself. When they told him, he said, 'I'll get him down for you.'

'Oh, Teddy, can you? Could you really?'

But even he could not reach the lowest branch. 'Tell you what, you hold my bicycle steady, 'cos if I stand on the bar I could reach the branch.' This worked. 'He's not very far up. I can see him,' Teddy said. 'The thing is, I can't climb down with him in my arms. Ouch!' he added. Then he said, 'One of you get a carrier bag or a basket or something with a long piece of rope.'

So off they went to get that, which took some time. The carrier bag was easy but the rope wasn't. In the end they found some in the potting shed. Polly went back to Teddy to explain why it was taking so long. Teddy was very nice about it and said he had a bar of motoring chocolate, and just as Polly was remembering that she hadn't had lunch he kindly dropped two squares down to her.

They tied one end of the rope to the handles of the carrier bag. Then Teddy had to come down to the lowest branch to get it. 'Put the rest of the rope inside the bag,' he said. 'No, don't. Try and throw the end of the rope up to me.' They tried and tried, and just as his patience was wearing thin by girls being so rotten at throwing things, Clary did a really good throw and he caught it. The rest would be easy, he thought. He tied the other end of the rope to a branch and then climbed up to Oscar's level, but he had reckoned without getting Oscar into the bag. Oscar yowled, and scratched him badly, but he managed to cram him in and started lowering the rope. And that was it.

'Oh, Teddy, you were marvellous!' Polly hugged him. 'We could never have got him without you.' Clary agreed. She was clutching the bag handles closely together, but even so Oscar managed to get his outraged head out.

'Shall I carry him back for you?' Teddy offered. He was glowing with being so useful and admired.

Clary was about to say he needn't and they would, but Polly said, 'Please do. I feel quite tired and he might escape again.'

Clary wheeled Teddy's bike and they all went back to the house and burst into the drawing room where nearly everybody seemed to be and Clary cried, 'We've found him! And Teddy was—' and broke off because everybody seemed to be *different*, all smiling and Christmassy and the Duchy said, 'Mr Chamberlain has come back, children,' and seeing Polly's face she added, 'Your father rang from London, Polly. He especially wanted you to know. It is going to be peace with honour.' And Clary saw Polly's face go china-white and her eyes look blind before she fainted.

∞ ∞ ∞

'What did I tell you, Mrs Cripps? There's many a slip between cup and lip.'

'It just shows you never can tell,' she agreed. She was rolling thin strips of bacon round blanched prunes for the angels on horseback after the pheasant. 'Would you fancy another drop scone, Mr Tonbridge?'

'I wouldn't say no. No – as I was saying, it's an ill wind . . . Well, at least, now we can all get back to normal.' Mrs Cripps, who had never departed from it, agreed. For him it meant getting those dratted Primuses out of his garage, for her, getting Dottie back downstairs when she had stopped scratching herself silly. That night was the first time he took her to the pub, which wasn't at all normal, and she had a very nice time.

∞ ∞ ∞

'We regard the agreement signed last night, and the Anglo-German Naval Agreement, as symbolic of the desire of our

407

two peoples never to go to war with one another again.' Hugh, sitting beside Edward in the car, was reading from the evening paper they had bought on their way to Sussex.

'Any more?'

'One more bit. "We are resolved that the method of consultation shall be the method adopted to deal with any other questions that may concern our two countries and we are determined to continue our efforts to remove possible sources of difference and thus to contribute to assure the peace of Europe."'

Edward grunted. Then he said, 'Marvellous old man, Chamberlain. I must say, I didn't really think he'd pull it off.'

'Still, it was appeasement, wasn't it? I don't quite see where the honour comes in – nor can the Czechs, I imagine.'

'Come on! You were the one who was so keen on there not being a war. There's no pleasing you, old boy. Light me a gasper, would you?'

Hugh lit the cigarette. When Edward took it he said, 'Well, at least it gives us time to rearm. Even with the most pessimistic view, you have to agree that.'

'If we do.'

'Oh, Lord, Hugh! Cheer up. Think of the merry old time we shall have getting those logs out of the river.'

'And smoothing down the PLA.' Hugh smiled. 'Very jolly.'

∞ ∞ ∞

'Do you think', Louise asked, as she and Nora shared a bath that evening, 'that everybody who put their promise in the box will stick to them?'

'Don't suppose we'll ever know.' Nora was absently rubbing her flannel up and down the same bit of arm. 'We could ask them, which might make them feel they had to, but we'll never *know*. It's a matter for each person's conscience. I shall do mine.'

'Shall we tell each other?' Louise was dying to know what Nora would do. What could be worse than planning to be a nun?

'OK. You go first.'

'No – you.'

'I promised that if there wasn't a war, I would be a nurse instead of being a nun.' She looked expectantly at Louise. 'You see, I don't want to be a nurse and I do frightfully want to be a nun.'

'I see.' She didn't really – they both seemed ghastly professions to her, but there you were.

'What about you?'

'I,' she said, trying to sound modest. 'I *swore* that, if there wasn't a war, I'd come to the boarding school with you.'

Nora snorted. 'I thought you were going to do that, anyway.'

'I wasn't. I get awfully homesick even if I stay a night away. So it may sound nothing to you but it's jolly serious for me.'

'I believe you.' Nora looked at her kindly. 'But you'll soon get over it.' A horrible grown-up remark which was most unlike her, Louise thought.

∞ ∞ ∞

Angela waited by the gate at the bottom of the drive to Mill Farm to catch Christopher alone. She had returned to the house soon after Edward had rung Villy with the news about which she felt nothing beyond a second's wan thankfulness that now he would not have to go and fight. She had gone up to her room and locked the door. But then she remembered Christopher, and had gone out again and waited. She saw him come running down the hill, when he reached her, he stopped and said, 'Hallo,' and was about to go again, but she said, 'Don't go. I've got something to say to you.' And she began, but before she had finished the bit about not being able to say how she knew, he interrupted her.

'Has there been any news about the war?'

'Oh, yes. There isn't going to be one.'

'Phew!' When he had let out the breath he said, 'You needn't go on. If there isn't a war, I can't run away. That was my promise. You know – for Nora's box.'

'Your promise?'

'Of course. It was my promise,' he said. 'Didn't you make one? I say, what's the matter? Ange!' For the tears that she thought had all been shed for a lifetime had begun again. He put his arm round her giving her little shakes that were supposed to be comforting.

'Ange! You poor old thing! Ange!' he kept saying.

'Oh, Chris. I'm so unhappy, you can't imagine! I can't tell you. I just am!' and she clung to him.

'I've never seen you like this,' he said, 'but it must be pretty terrible. Bad luck.' Visions of going back to the day school and Dad being sarcastic and having rows with Mum about him drearily ranged before him. 'At least there isn't a war. That would be the worst thing,' he said, as his new little camp by the pond receded to a mere holiday ploy. A thought occurred to him. 'Was your promise a hard one when it comes to the point?'

'Mine has come to nothing. There *is* no point,' she answered, and the weary pain in her voice went to his heart. He took her hand.

'We'll just have to be kind to each other,' he said and looking up at him, for he was taller than she, she saw tears in his eyes. It was the first, small comfort.

∞ ∞ ∞

'So now it's back to the basic decision,' Rupert said, as he and Zoë changed for dinner.

'Is that what's been on your mind? All day?'

'Well, not all.' He thought, as he had done frequently since the morning, of the difficult, embarrassing, worrying scene with that poor girl – feeling he hadn't handled it right, somehow, but quite unable to see what would have been right. But he didn't want to tell Zoë about that: it felt a kind of disloyalty to the poor girl – and, anyway, he was far from sure how Zoë would take it . . . Well, no need going into that . . .

'I'd do what you want.' She was kneeling in front of the wardrobe searching for a pair of shoes. She had said this before, but it sounded different now – as she had with Clary this morning. She was becoming someone to be reckoned with just as, in a way, he had stopped expecting or wanting to reckon with her.

'You said that,' he answered irritably and without thinking.

But when she got up, he saw that she looked not sulky at the reproof, but stricken, and felt ashamed.

'Sorry, darling.'

'That's all right.' She went to the dressing-table and started to comb her hair.

'Actually,' he said feeling his way, 'something did happen today that upset me. No, not Clary. Something else. But I don't really want to tell you about it. Is that OK?'

She looked at him in the mirror without saying a word.

'I mean,' he said, 'sometimes, even in a marriage, there can be things – quite harmless – to the marriage, I mean – that all the same don't need to be talked about. Do you agree?'

'You mean, that there can be secrets, but it's all right to have them?'

'Something of the sort.'

'Oh, yes!' she said. 'I'm so glad you think that. I'm sure you're right.' She got to her feet and picking up the pink woollen dress off the back of the chair slipped it over her head, and turned for him to do it up. 'The point isn't other people,' she said, 'it's us.' When he turned round for a kiss, she gave him one, very nicely, but there was nothing either sexual or childish about it, and he thought fleetingly that he used to be sick of the wanton child that once she had seemed composed of and now, perversely, he missed it.

'I want you to be all things to one man,' he said suddenly. Once she would have looked at him from below her lashes and said, 'Who?' and he would have said, 'Me', and swept her off to bed.

Now, looking sincerely concerned she said, 'But, Rupert, I'm not sure that I know how!'

'Never mind. I've just decided to be a businessman.'

And she answered almost primly, 'Your father will be very pleased.' She gave him a little push. 'Go and tell him!'

∞ ∞ ∞

William sat in his study with his evening whisky to hand. He was by himself, and for once quite glad of it. His door, as always, was open and he could hear the comforting sounds of the household going on: baths being run, doors slammed, children's voices, the chink of cutlery being carried on a tray to the dining room, the sound of violin and piano – Sid and Kitty, no doubt. He had listened to the six o'clock news with Rachel and Sid, then sent them away. He was very tired. The immense sense of relief that he had felt when Hugh had rung from London had been succeeded by doubts of a kind he did not want to communicate to the family. There was something about the whole business – one could almost call it a transaction – that he distrusted, although he couldn't say why. The Prime Minister's motives were impeccable, he was a sincere and decent man. But that in itself was no bloody good unless he was dealing with another sincere and decent man. At the worst some time had been bought. Softwoods would be needed on an unprecedented scale and hardwoods as well, if they started building ships, as they should. He'd turn Sampson off the shelter and sanitary arrangements and get him on to those cottages. York's letter had amused him. The old boy thought he'd fooled him into paying too much – that was why he'd had the cheek to ask him for another tenner for the land: he hadn't realised what they were worth to him, William, who would have paid another £250 for them if asked. Well, they were both satisfied. He knew he'd upset Kitty with his plans for the evacuees – not necessary now – but he'd make it up to her. He'd buy her a new gramophone one of those damn great machines with a horn for playing records and all the Beethoven Symphonies done by Toscanini – that would please her. And Rupert had popped in and said that he would join the firm. So why didn't he feel jollier? 'I don't like my sight failing,' he said to himself, reaching for the decanter and pouring more whisky. He'd got up some decent port this evening – Taylor '21. He hadn't got much of that left. Everything came to an end. Have to stop riding if his eyes got worse. He'd get used to it. He remembered the last time he'd spent a couple of hours with – what was her name – Millicent Greenway – no, Green*croft*, that was it, in her flat in Maida Vale. She had been a thoroughly good sort. 'Never mind,' she'd said that last time, 'it's just not one of your days.' He'd sent her a case of champagne as well as the usual twenty-five quid. He'd got used to there being no more of *that*. Kitty had never liked it, which was natural for a decently brought-up gal. He could go on going to the office,

412

even if they did stay in the country and get rid of Chester Terrace. He needn't give up *work* yet. And there wasn't going to be a war.

∞ ∞ ∞

'When my father comes to see me, would you mind if I see him alone?'

'Not at all,' Clary said. She felt quite awed by Polly, never having met anyone who had fainted and in any case Polly had a temperature and was thought to be starting chicken pox. So she went off to see Simon when Hugh arrived.

'What ho, my pet. I hear you're under the weather.' He came and sat on her bed. 'I've had chicken pox, so I'll kiss you,' he said. Her face felt very hot. Oscar lay beside her.

'Well, Poll, it's good news, isn't it?'

'Amazing,' she said. 'Do you know, Oscar got lost today? We found him up a tree and me and Clary held Teddy's bicycle . . . ' and then she went into the whole thing.

'Anyway, you got him back.' Hugh stroked Oscar's head and he sneezed.

'All's well now, then,' he said.

'Yes,' she said listlessly, 'in a way, of course, it is. In another way, of course, it isn't.'

'What isn't?'

'There was this box that Nora made us put promises in, you see, for if there wasn't a war and now there isn't so we have to do them. At least I feel I have to. That's what it is.'

'Do you want to tell me what you promised?'

'I *do*,' she said consideringly, 'but I don't want anyone else to know.'

'Right.'

He drew his fingers across his throat, and she said, 'Oh, Dad, don't be so old-fashioned!'

'I am so old,' he said. 'I can't help it.' They looked at each other and both burst out laughing, and that was more like Polly.

'Well, it started with us going to church and I said I didn't think I ought to go, because, Dad, you see, I'm not at all sure that I believe in God.' She looked at his black silk stump and

413

said, 'In fact, I don't. But Nora said that if we prayed for there not to be a war and there wasn't one that would show me. So when it got to be promises I thought I'll have to believe in God if there isn't a war, so I put that in the box.'

She seemed only to pause, so he said, 'And?'

'Well, I feel just the same. I don't feel the slightest belief. How can you make yourself believe in something? I mean pretending is useless, probably evil.'

'I agree pretending is useless.'

'Do you believe in God?'

'Er – you know, Poll, I'm not sure.'

'You must have thought about it,' she said severely, 'by your age.'

'Yes. Well, no, probably I don't.'

'I mean, supposing I start managing to believe and *then* we have a war.' That's it, he thought, she doesn't believe the news.

'Polly, there isn't going to be one. Peace has broken out.'

'I know that. But can you solemnly swear, Dad, that there never will be one?'

'No.'

'You see? Oh, I wish I'd given up sugar in my tea or something manageable like that!'

'Could you swap?'

'Dad! That would be cheating!'

'Well,' he said, 'I think if you say every night that you wish you believed in God, and there is one, he'll hear you.'

'I don't wish I believed.'

'Well, then, you could say you wish you *wanted* to believe. I don't see how you can do more.'

'And the rest of the time carry on as usual?'

'Yes.'

'OK,' she said. 'That's what ordinary life is, isn't it? Carrying on as usual.'

'Does that sound boring to you?'

'It sounds it, but when you're in it, it isn't.'

When he kissed her she said, 'Dad! Do you know what I love about you best? Your doubtfulness. All the things you don't know.' As he reached the door she called, 'It really makes me admire you.'

414

∞ ∞ ∞

Clary met Zoë and Rupert on their way downstairs and stopped and said, 'Oh, hallo, Zoë! You do look nice. Pink is a very good colour on you.' She was starting upon her promise from the box. How can I keep it up? she thought. Thinking of things to say like that every day. When she'd put the promise in the box, she'd thought she'd just have to invent things, but after Zoë had been truthful to her, she felt she ought to mean them – be truthful back. That meant going on and on and on about what Zoë looked like, because she had to admit that Zoë was extremely pretty and beautiful. On the other hand, she couldn't think of anything else about her. I'll just have to stick to her appearance, she thought.

∞ ∞ ∞

'I bet she knew there wasn't going to be a war.' Neville was very grumpy and felt Nora was to blame for the beastly prospect ahead of him.

'The thing is the aunts will go home, and then you'll be free. It's much worse for us.'

'Yes,' said Judy. 'It jolly well is.'

'Can you imagine having no pocket money at all for a year? Having to live on Christmas and birthday presents for twelve whole months?'

'Six for me, actually,' Judy said. 'I changed my mind just before I put the paper in the box.' Lydia looked at her with loathing, and she went pink.

'Really, it would have been much easier for us to have war,' Neville said. 'I wouldn't have minded one at all. Aeroplanes and tanks everywhere – well, I'm extremely fond of them.'

'That's stupid, Neville. You might have got killed.'

'I wouldn't. From the sky I would be just the tiniest speck to a German – they wouldn't even see me.'

There was a silence. Then he said, 'What we could do is just not do any of it. Pretend we thought it was a joke.'

'Oh, we couldn't!' both girls exclaimed, but he could see that they really didn't mean it.

'I shall, anyway,' he said. 'You can do as you like.'

∞ ∞ ∞

'Well, Miss Milliment, we could scarcely have foreseen such a happy outcome to the last terrible weeks.'

'No, indeed, Lady Rydal.' A little smile twitched her small mouth and disappeared into her chins. She had known Lady Rydal for many years, and happy outcomes were hardly her forte.

Villy came into the room. She was wearing the most attractive black frock. 'Oh dear! You haven't had your sherry!'

'I didn't want to cause Miss Milliment any trouble.' This was the most delicate way she could think of to imply to Viola that one did not give governesses drinks, even if she was, due to difficult circumstances, having them to dinner. Democracy, she felt, should never be allowed to get into the *wrong hands*. But Viola did not take the hint.

'I expect Miss Milliment has been dying for hers,' she said as she handed them both a glass.

'Hardly dying, Viola, but certainly looking forward.' Miss Milliment sipped her drink with a grateful smile.

Lady Rydal, baulked, eyed Miss Milliment's banana-coloured ensemble with distaste. It looked like the kind of thing one might get in a *shop*.

'Polly has gone down with chicken pox,' Villy said. 'I must say, I wish our brood here would get on with it.'

'Then you would have hardly anyone to teach, Miss Milliment,' Lady Rydal remarked. 'However,' she went on with what she felt was the uttermost kindness, 'I'm sure you must be longing to get back to your own nice cosy little home with all your own things round you. I know that I am.'

Everybody else came into the room – Edward had brought two bottles of champagne – and the celebration began, but at intervals during the rest of the evening, and during the long and – in spite of Lady Rydal – merry dinner, which seemed to her full of laughter and affection and fun, and, perhaps most of all, when she slipped away for the dark walk back to the cottage, Miss Milliment thought of her home. She thought of the dingy room that was without heating unless she spent a fortune on the gas meter; of the lumpy bed and hard thin blankets; the single ceiling light with a white china shade, not near enough to the bed for comfortable reading (in the winter one spent the evenings in bed as it was the easiest way to keep warm); the linoleum whose worn places she was in constant danger of tripping over; the coffee-coloured wallpaper with its frieze of oranges and pears. She thought of the window, hung with grey net curtains, through which there was nothing to be seen but the row of houses identical to the one she lived in: not a tree in sight, nothing to nourish the eye during those long evenings, when, after her solitary supper, she would have to spin out the hours, without company or distraction of any kind, until it was time to make her glass of hot water and retire for the night. All these things pressed sharply and uninvited into her mind, splintering the warmth, and celebration, company and comfort that surrounded her. Now, Eleanor, I won't have you down in the dumps. Think how fortunate you have been to enjoy this wonderful change; this beautiful place, the country, this kind family. It has been a real oasis— but she could not go on with that.

In the cottage, she found Evie, whose bedroom door was open and room littered with luggage and belongings.

'I am going home tomorrow,' she said. 'I made a telephone call to my gentleman friend and I am needed in London. I knew I would be. I knew there wouldn't be a war, but she never listens to me, my sister. She always has to be right.' She seemed exhilarated and full of animation.

Miss Milliment wished her a pleasant journey and went to her room. She stood by the open window for some time enjoying the soft, warm and damp air on her face. There was a smell of woodsmoke and the scent of pine from some of the trees in the wood at the back. The black dog still sat on her shoulder and she thought that perhaps this was because she had so much wanted to see the sea – nine miles away in the dark, and that would not happen now. That might be it. You cannot expect to have your own way in everything, Eleanor. Wonderful scent of pine! She had become aware of it only today, when, before dinner, she had fulfilled her promise made for Nora's box and had taken the packet of yellowing letters and put them in her father's old oiled silk tobacco pouch – together with the lock of red hair – and gone up to the wood with them, and scraped a little grave in the soft leafy mould and buried them. Thus,

417

when she died, there would be no prying, indifferent eyes to patronise his memory.

She had been meaning to do something of the kind for a very long time now, but it was not easy. She had so little to remember of him, and after all these years what memories that remained had become distant, faded fragments, small matters of mysteriously unrelated fact, only saved from crumbling to spectral fantasy by the few relics, now safely buried in the wood. Now that she could no longer read his letters she knew that the rest of him would slip away: already, she had noticed, invention had been taking the place of memory. She would say (to herself) things like, 'He must have,' instead of 'He did': She did not want to turn him into a bad biography.

She shut her eyes to recall him for the last time on the evening before he had left for South Africa, when he had taken her out in the garden seized her hand and recited to her the end of 'Dover Beach'.

> *Ah love let us be true*
> *To one another! for the world which seems*
> *To lie before us like a world of dreams,*
> *So various, so beautiful, so new . . .*

His quiet, high-pitched, rather pedantic voice (although he could not say his r's) came magically back . . . and then she could not remember how the poem went on, and as she groped towards the darkling plain, it diminished, and was silent.

That was all.